THE LOST DIARIES OF
ELIZABETH CADY STANTON

A Novel

Sarah Bates

Sarah Bates

Published by BookLocker.com, Inc., Bradenton, Florida, U.S.A.

Printed on acid-free paper.

The Lost Diaries of Elizabeth Cady Stanton is a work of historical fiction. Apart from the well-known actual people, events and locales that figure in the narrative, all names, characters, places and incidents are the products of the author's imagination or are used fictitiously. Any resemblance to current events or locales, or to living persons, is entirely coincidental.

BookLocker.com, Inc.
2016

First Edition

For Jim who believes in me.

Men are what their mothers make them.
Elizabeth Cady Stanton

1

February 1875
Massillon, Ohio

A chunk of wood in the potbellied stove splinters and pops, startling the white haired woman dozing by the fire. For a moment, Elizabeth Cady Stanton cannot recall her location. She shivers, uncomfortable in the strange opera house near the center of Massillon, Ohio. An ice storm pelts the windows of the red brick structure, glazing tree branches and snapping them off in the wind. As an enormous gust rattles the window of the room where she waits, Elizabeth pulls the wool blanket over her knees tighter.

A much younger woman hovers nearby. She rushes to poke at the stove embers stirring up a fury of sparks. "Oh dear," she says. "I must have arranged the fire too high."

Mrs. Stanton shakes her head and sighs. She is so dreadfully tired. She plucks at the stack of handwritten speech notes in her lap. They have grown worn and creased from years of use.

"The time, Amelia?"

"Five o'clock, Mrs. Stanton. You have one hour to rest."

Elizabeth settles into the lone wingback chair then frowns. Her long black taffeta dress has twisted around her. "Bothersome clothes!" She tugs at the garment's voluminous skirts and pokes at the bustle behind her back.

"Do you need something, Mrs. Stanton?" the young woman asks. "Can I help you in any way?"

The woman's gaze of pure adoration proves offputting.

"No, Amelia dear," she says summoning what little patience remains. "Wait, yes I do. A cup of very hot tea will go down nicely."

"I'll fetch it straight away," Amelia says. Her hand on the parlor room door, she looks back at Mrs. Stanton, appearing reluctant to leave her for even a moment.

Elizabeth adjusts her glasses to focus on her notes and noticing Amelia pause, waves her hands at her in dismissal. "Go, my girl," she says. "I will be perfectly fine while you are away, but desperate for that cup of tea."

Would this young woman ever leave her alone? She tries to concentrate on the address she will give for what seems like the hundredth time. Can she make it fresh–if not for them, for her? She tosses the notes aside and reaches for her diary. When she glances at the pages, the events of the last few months flash through her mind in confusion: incessant travel, lumpy mattresses in drafty rooms, greasy boiled beef. The lecture tour has taken its toll on her health.

Even at sixty years old, she rarely rests her body and her memory, overwhelmed by fatigue, occasionally fails. Yet she persists. State after state, she presses on. The notes flutter to the floor. She longs for the comfort of her husband and the cozy seclusion of her home in Seneca Falls. An enormous wave of sadness engulfs her as she imagines the commotion of family life and pictures her daughters struggling to put dinner on the table.

She cannot give in to this self-pity. This is the path she chose.

"I have returned," Amelia says. She sets a tray beside Elizabeth's chair then stands before her rigidly, her hands clasped tightly against the bosom of her gray dress.

"Oh dear girl, do not act so subservient. And no more dithering around me, either," Elizabeth says, immediately sorry for her cross remarks. She closes the diary over her hand marking its place.

"But I am so grateful Mrs. Stanton. I want to do a good job because you are my heroine. Do you not know that? Everything you say? Everything you stand for? I want to be strong–just like you." Moved to tears Amelia kneels, her head bowed.

Elizabeth reaches out to cup the younger woman's face in her hand. "My dear, pull yourself together and share the tea with me." She motions to a tufted hassock nearby. "Sit there and enjoy the few moments I have with you."

When Amelia lifts her eyes to Elizabeth, her expression pleading for understanding, she says, "I know everything about you. That's why I respect you so much."

Elizabeth contemplates young Amelia, taking in her wide blue eyes and the bloom on her cheeks and for a moment she decides to dismiss her. Changing her mind, she leans back against the chair cushions, firelight softening her still unlined face. She narrows her eyes and gazes into the stove's embers, recalling the life that has led her to this room. "My dear," she says, flipping the diary open to its first page, "You do not know the whole story."

2

March 1823
Johnstown, New York

"Elizabeth, whatever are you doing?" Her father's voice echoed off the mahogany paneled walls of his law library.

Startled at the distressed sound, Elizabeth dropped the scissors she gripped in her plump fists. They fell clattering to the tabletop where a heavy legal book lay open. She looked up at her father Judge Daniel Cady with a smile.

Her father loomed above her, his eyebrows drawn together over deep-set eyes. Military bearing and knowledge of the law made the judge a courtroom adversary to fear. He did not intimidate his confident eight-year-old daughter, however.

Kneeling on the leather seat of the chair at the table, Elizabeth studied his concerned expression. "Father, I have found a way to help Mrs. Campbell keep her farm." Her dark eyebrows arched, animating her face. "Look," she said, her voice rising. She tapped her finger on the paragraph from the book that she planned to remove.

Judge Cady peered at the parchment page and the law that allowed Flora Campbell's squandering husband to mortgage the farm and her inheritance. When Flora's husband died, Flora's mother-in-law decided to let the creditors take it all.

"I listened to Mrs. Campbell in your office last week," Elizabeth said. "She told me she would be on the street if creditors took the only home she and her family ever knew. You told her you could do nothing, so I vowed to find a solution."

She leaned forward and traced the sentences on the page with a finger. "You see, Father, if I just cut these words out of the law book, Mrs. Campbell and her children will be saved." She lifted her chin with a self-satisfied expression.

"It is not that easy, Lib."

"Why do you encourage me to visit your office if not to help? I do not understand everything, but when men treat their families with disrespect I know it is wrong. Why do laws protect men and do nothing to help women and children?"

"Lib, even if you cut up my books there are hundreds of others. Removing the words from the law books in my library does not change anything."

"Why?"

"Because all the law books have the same information. There are hundreds of copies just like this one. Until the laws change, if they do, I must uphold them."

"But Father," she said, her enthusiasm replaced by resentment, "this is unfair."

Elizabeth looked at her father for an answer. He smiled, his expression softening. But when he spoke, she knew he'd dismissed her.

"It is the law, Elizabeth. It has always been that way."

She closed the book with a bang and jumped down. "When I grow up," she said, "I am going to change these abominable laws!"

*

March 15, 1823

Dear Diary, I got in trouble trying to help Father. I wish I were older–or a boy, so people would listen to me. It would be different. Boys get so much praise. Like Eleazar. He is only seventeen. Father thinks my brother is smart and asks for his opinion on things. No one asks for mine. I am smart, too. I hate being a girl.

3

Spring 1825

Two years later, the spring bloomed full of uncertainty in Johnstown New York. The season was fine, though, with tall oaks and elms leafing out alongside the gray brick Cady home on the corner of West Main and North Market Streets. Cherry trees in the orchard behind the home released their perfume to the warming air as usual, and the clipped shrubs edging the garden paths had burst into bloom. While the Cady mansion at the center of Johnstown appeared to be its most imposing building and visitors on their way to their lodging at the Cayadutta Hotel next door remarked on the home's stately features, would it always be so? The Erie Canal had just opened, diverting stagecoach travelers from the roads that ran through Johnstown, and business was suffering. Worried over changes they could not fathom, shopkeepers, innkeepers and farmers began to stop by Judge Cady's law office for advice. Since the rooms were adjacent to his home and accessible from the street and from the Cady home vestibule, a flurry of worried callers continued to stream through the Cady front door.

Disregarding of the lovely spring weather and the comings and goings of townspeople, Elizabeth's tall self-reliant mother supervised the annual housecleaning in a commotion of dust and scrubbing. Margaret Cady reveled in her conservative family life, moderating her orders with a queenly elegance and a gentle sweet voice. Like Elizabeth's father, she had gained the respect and admiration of the servants as she administered the affairs of her family and household with a firm but fair hand. While Margaret tended to the housekeeping chores, the judge's brisk step on the wood floor and cheerful whistle echoed through the house.

Elizabeth eagerly anticipated these vigorous cleaning events with the household in turmoil, because her mother's customary strict domestic routine relaxed for a while. Though Elizabeth had her own task of sorting her winter clothes into piles for mending, the housecleaning gave her a chance for freedom and adventure.

At present she hid from the nurses, the three harried women who looked after her and her two younger sisters, Madge and Kate. They were smaller versions of Elizabeth, but with coppery rather than chestnut curls. The nurses were strict and disapproving of the three girls whose antics caused no end of grief.

Still in her nightdress, Elizabeth crawled onto the roof from her second floor nursery window. This perfect vantage point to spy on the gardeners overlooked the back garden as far as up to the woods behind their property.

The nurses would be angry if they found her, but she didn't care. The fine day abounded with adventure.

For a while she watched ebony-skinned Abraham and his husky grown son Peter break up the thawing garden soil. Their hoes lifted and tumbled damp black earth into soft mounds. After a bit, she crept a little farther out on the roof ledge to peer at the young groom Jacob, who was repairing worn rails in the stables near the street. Sunlight glinted on the hammer he swung, and his dark skin and tightly curled hair gleamed with sweat.

She stretched out on the cool slate roof tiles, crossed her arms under her head and looked up through the canopy of budding elms at the bright sky and clouds skittering overhead. A spring breeze fluttered the hem of her linen nightdress, baring her legs to the balmy sunlight.

She started to daydream when a low whistle interrupted her reverie. She raised her head to look about, scrambled to peer over the edge of the roof, and saw Abraham and Peter drop their hoes and beckon to Jacob. The three men ran across the meadow behind the garden to disappear into the dense thicket of woods. A few moments later, they returned, with Abraham struggling under the weight of a lumpy burlap bag slung over his shoulder. Elizabeth continued to watch them as they hurried along the path to enter their quarters. They emerged almost immediately to return to their work. Whatever could be in that bag?

"Lib! Can we come out?" Madge's high voice piped from behind her.

The sisters poked their heads through the open window with mischievous smiles.

She nodded, choosing play for the moment, postponing an investigation of the contents of the mysterious burlap bag.

Madge and Kate wriggled out, and in whispers the girls began to plan their day.

"Take us into the woods, Lib! I want to look for bird's nests."

"Oh, yes," said Kate. "There might be ripe blueberries, too." Elizabeth smiled at her youngest sister who was always hungry.

The girls dared Elizabeth, knowing they would never get permission to do that. She debated the risk. Perhaps no one would miss them with their nurses distracted by the cleaning whirlwind.

There might even be baby toads to play with. She liked to use her hand to make little curved homes for them in the soft earth.

"All right, we will go, but let us hurry. We must return before Mother and the nurses finish their tasks."

They slipped into their identical red dresses with the starched white collars that scratched their necks, then sneaked out the kitchen door and stole off through the back garden, past the stables, into the woods.

A worn path led to a narrow stream cutting through the back pasture beyond the woods. Elizabeth had been there once or twice with Eleazar, but never alone or with her sisters.

"I don't like the shadows," Kate said pointing toward the clutches of huge ferns that grew beneath the old trees. "There might be a rat." She hung back to grab Elizabeth's apron hem.

"The barn cats keep the rats away," Elizabeth said.

"I don't like it anyway." Kate's voice quavered.

"Don't be so scared," Madge said. "Here, take this stick and smack the ferns. Anything in there will run away."

Each armed with a broken tree branch the girls marched into the shadowy woods, poking at the shrubby plants that grew along the path.

When the path curved into a patch of sunlit meadow, Elizabeth whooped. "A fairy circle place," she said. "Let's pick white daisies and make crowns so we look like fairies."

When Kate's stubby fingers struggled with the pliant stems Elizabeth showed her how plaiting them kept the flowers connected. Once the daisy crowns were finished, Elizabeth grabbed her sisters by their hands and pulled them around in a circle until they were running, singing, "Ring-around-the-rosie, A pocket full of posies, Ashes! Ashes! We all fall down." Finally, out of breath, they flopped down on the grass and looked up through the trees.

A rustling noise came from the woods nearby.

"What's that?" Madge asked. She sat up and peered into the underbrush. Elizabeth jumped to her feet and poked her stick into the dense foliage where the sound appeared to be coming from. A big toad jumped high in the air.

Kate screamed and began to cry.

"Don't be afraid," Elizabeth said pulling her little sister close to her side. "Let us return home, and we can eat wild blueberries along the way."

With the sun at their backs, the three girls emerged with mud-caked clothes and torn stockings.

"Madge, you've got berry juice stains on your mouth. Spit on the corner of your apron tail and wipe your lips," Elizabeth said.

She had made sure they got back to the house before dinner, but until this moment she hadn't thought much about how they would appear to the nurses.

Kate's hair looked a fright, a tangle of bedraggled ribbons and fading flowers from the garland she wove in her curls.

"Do let me tidy your hair ribbons that have come undone. Nurse will surely notice," Elizabeth said to her.

"Stop pulling," Kate whined.

Once Elizabeth made sure her sisters' aprons were tied neatly she led them back home through the garden to the kitchen entrance. The sun had set leaving cool blue shadows stretching across the garden. As they approached the door, their dirty hands clutching wildflowers, a handkerchief full of berries, and a bundle of pussy willows, a disapproving alto voice boomed.

"Girls. Look at you!" said Polly, the oldest nurse who had been with them the longest.

The sisters exchanged frightened looks.

"Elizabeth, this is your doing. I know it."

Polly grabbed Elizabeth's shoulders with her gnarled hands and bent down to confront her with a scowl.

Elizabeth flinched.

The other two nurses stood beside Polly's substantial figure, bearing equally sour expressions.

Elizabeth knew she had led her sisters into the woods without permission. As the oldest of the three, she shouldered the guilt. It was not the first time she'd gone against her mother's wishes and the nurse's instructions. Every time she found something truly fun to do, it seemed wrong to her mother. The things that her mother deemed *right* weren't fun at all. If Elizabeth could find the answer to this puzzle, she might be able to stay out of trouble, but with Madge and Kate urging her on, she forgot about trying to solve it.

She stepped in front of her sisters to face the angry nurse, but didn't dare speak. Her mouth set, she looked down and steeled herself for the scolding.

"Miss Elizabeth. You have caused us no end of problems. We have all been frantic with worry."

Elizabeth stood impassive, her face a mask, looking past Polly's round red face and her quivering chins. She bit her upper lip.

"Your dear mother has been desperate for fear you were lost and I have suffered her anger." Polly's tirade continued. "Shame on you for provoking her." She shook her finger in Elizabeth's face, while Madge and Kate cowered in fear behind their sister. "In the house, all three of you and I do not want this to happen again," the nurse shouted, her outstretched arm trembling as she pointed to the door behind her.

Elizabeth, Madge and Kate silently filed past the stern figures, all the while staring at the floor. When they were safe and alone in the nursery they burst into wild giggles. The girls threw their souvenirs of the day on a table, tore off the scratchy collars they hated and tossed them into the air. They unbuttoned their muddy dresses and, whirling them around their heads, began to run around the room until they collapsed in a panting heap on the floor, gulping for breath.

That night while Elizabeth lay in bed looking up at slivers of moonlight crisscrossing the ceiling, she remembered Abraham and Peter's hurried trip into the woods. What could be in the mysterious burlap bag? Perhaps Abraham was still awake. She got out of bed to pad over to the window and look down onto their quarters, but the windows were dark. She'd investigate tomorrow first thing.

The next morning, when she sought out Abraham to ask about his trip into the woods and the bag she'd seen slung over his shoulder, his answer seemed reasonable.

"Just deer meat, Miss Elizabeth," Abraham told her. "A hunter friend passed by."

She noticed the momentary look of alarm on his face, but said nothing. He was up to something. Of that she was certain. But what?

*

June 10, 1825
  Dear Diary, I got in trouble again. Madge said she would take the blame, but she didn't.

Harriet is five years older than me and she should take care of us all, but she is too dainty, Father says. She isn't. She pretends. So it is my fault. Always. Bah. Just because I am older I get the blame every time. Polly is mean and always blames me for everything. She hates me and I hate her.

4

September 1825

A gleaming black town coach clattered up the cobblestone street and stopped in front of the Cady home. Elizabeth ran to the second floor sitting room window overlooking the street and looked down. An imposing man in a black suit stepped down. She could see the top of his tall beaver hat and the shock of silver hair that brushed his collar.

Her father stood on the walk outside the front door.

Elizabeth stared down at the stranger. Who could this be?

The man removed his hat and gloves and shook Judge Cady's hand vigorously. Her father's voice rang out.

"Mr. Vice President, you do me an honor. What can I do for you, sir?" her father greeted the visitor, and then ushered him into the house. Judge Cady's beaming face dramatically juxtaposed the visitor's dour appearance.

John Calhoun, in her house. What could he want with Father?

She hurried into the upstairs hall and leaned over the railing to watch.

"Look, Cady, I'll get right to the point. It's this abolition issue. You know I do not support it. Since you're a farmer like me, I reckon our thinking will be aligned. Without slaves to work our farms, the industry we envision for the Republic cannot grow." His voice rose. "I've come to talk to you about promoting my opinions to your colleagues." Judge Cady's eyebrows lifted and his expression grew serious. He gestured towards his office.

The two men entered, closing the door behind them.

What was 'abolition'? Elizabeth crept down the stairs to place her ear at a crack in the door of her father's office.

"Mr. Vice President, the Negro men in my employ are freed men. They have always been treated like trusted family members. I'm afraid you'll find no ally in me."

Elizabeth knew her father admired John Calhoun since he led the fight to declare war on England. Calhoun's involvement was a familiar topic among her father's law students.

She inched closer to the opening, trying to hear their conversation better.

Her father's voice continued and he moved into her line of sight, silhouetted against a tall window with its heavy draperies pulled to reveal a view of the street. He gestured for emphasis as he talked. He looked angry.

"I do agree with your efforts to nurture industry. Certainly I am aware that profits from farming are important with this Erie Canal depressing our local businesses, but not at the expense of people who live in wretched slavery. We must have more respect for human life."

Her father's outspoken remark caused Calhoun to flinch.

A few minutes later the door to her father's office opened and she heard his voice bid the visitor farewell. As the sound of the departing coach on the cobbles faded Elizabeth slipped away from her hiding place. Father made her proud, standing up to the Vice President like that. She would have done exactly the same. Maybe she should have?

*

September 6, 1825

Dear Diary, I pricked my finger on a needle when the Vice President of the entire United States banged on the door with his cane and I got blood on my dratted sampler. I will wash the needlework and hide it. If Mother sees what I did I will be in trouble. Again. I could tell her the Vice

President caused it. Except I spied on them. I am not supposed to do that. Mother says it is rude and sneaky. Father is never sneaky. I should try to be more like him instead of my usual self.

5

September 1825

That afternoon Elizabeth decided to talk to her father about John Calhoun's visit, but when she approached his office she found him deep in conversation with her Uncle John. Her father and John Jacob Astor were business colleagues and for years the relationship resulted in growth of the Cady fortunes in real estate. Astor always brought gifts for his nieces. Elizabeth loved him.

When she heard his hearty laugh she impulsively burst into her father's office.

"Why, Elizabeth," Astor cried. "Come here, child, let me see what I have for you today."

She ran into his open arms and could smell the bay rum cologne on his cheeks as he hugged her to his broad chest. A tall handsome man, with close-cropped white hair, his Spencer jacket with brass buttons reflected the latest fashion from England. A heavy gold pocket watch on a chain testified to his wealth. He was much more colorful than her father. Reaching into a narrow waistcoat pocket he produced a tissue paper-wrapped horehound lozenge and placed it in Elizabeth's outstretched hand.

She thanked him politely then turned to face her father to ask her question.

"Would you and Uncle John please explain to me about abolition and slaves?" She looked back and forth between the two men.

Elizabeth's father paused a moment. He appeared ill at ease. Then he asked where she had heard those words. When she replied she'd heard the law students arguing about them and that she'd also listened at his door earlier, his face reddened and he glanced at his brother-in-law.

"Calhoun visited me," he said to Astor.

Her uncle nodded. "I suspected as much."

Judge Cady turned his attention to Elizabeth. "Slaves are Negro people owned by large landowners. They live and work on the landowner's property. He cares for them like horses and other stock. Some people believe owning a person is wrong."

Uncle John added, "These people are called abolitionists. It is as simple as that."

"Abraham, Peter and Jacob are Negroes. Are they slaves?" Elizabeth spoke with genuine worry.

"No, they are freed men," her father said. He paused then glanced at Astor. "I suppose that makes me an abolitionist."

Elizabeth felt relieved. Owning another human being didn't seem right.

Astor broke into the conversation again and Elizabeth gave him her full attention.

"Most people in the North feel it is wrong to own other people. In the South, where some farmers operate large cotton and grain plantations, they believe that without the slaves to work their land, they would not be able to make a living. The slaves have little say in their lives."

"Why do they not just go away?"

"They cannot. The law does not allow it." Her father paused as if considering an important fact and then shook his head. "Oh, Daughter, how I wish you were a boy." He paused again. "Now, run along and find your sisters. I must conclude my business with your uncle before night falls."

Her father seemed embarrassed. If he didn't own slaves, why were her questions making him uncomfortable? Why did it matter that she was a girl and not a boy?

Annoyed at being dismissed, Elizabeth left the house to seek out the three Negro men who were so dear to her. She wanted to make sure they weren't slaves. If the law didn't protect them, then they were no different than the poor women who sought her father's advice about their legal rights. That possibility confused and frightened her.

She found Abraham and Peter helping Jacob toss fresh hay into the horse troughs in the barn and decided to take up the discussion with them. They looked up as she clambered up onto the top of a stable rail and hooked her feet beneath the top rung to face them.

"Abraham, were you and Peter ever slaves?"

Without stopping the rhythmic hoisting of hay into the stalls, Abraham replied.

"Yes, miss, we were, but your father, he freed us. Too late for Peter's ma'am though. She died of hard work a'fore we got here. That's why we made our way to New York and found your father. The judge took us in."

He paused to look at her, flexing his stooped sinewy frame, then wiped his forehead with a red handkerchief.

"I told him I'm good with plants and growing things. He took a look at poor little Peter and said we could stay on with him for as long as we liked. That's a'fore you is born."

He returned to his task and a shower of pale green hay drifted over a stall door.

Elizabeth stole a look at Peter and considered her own mother, who likely never worked as Peter's mother had. How must it feel to die of hard work? Peter seemed much older than nineteen. Tall like his father, his youthful angular body was still straight. Abraham kept him busy, yet he never failed to greet everyone with a broad smile and respectful 'hello.' Peter seemed to like it when she sought him out to relate her day's activities while he worked. Sometimes he asked questions about her lessons, expressing genuine interest. She considered him a friend and her personal audience of one.

"Same with me, Miss Elizabeth," Jacob added. "I kept movin'. Those slave owners? They be mean. I got a way with animals, especially horses. They like me."

No one knew much about Jacob, a gentle soul who spoke only when asked a direct question. That he volunteered this information was a surprise. Some of the servants believed mystical powers allowed him to speak to animals and they with him. Elizabeth believed that, too.

"Your pap, he knew that right away, so I been here taking care of them ever since. Your pap's a good man."

Jacob took up a curry brush and started stroking the amber coat of her father's horse.

"Yep, Junie here and I are now best friends, aren't we Junie?" He slipped a bit of brown sugar into the mare's mouth and the horse tossed her head and whinnied.

Elizabeth trudged back to the house deep in thought. Her father was a good and kindly man. Everyone respected him and sought his legal advice. Why then, could he not change these terrible laws?

It was a vexing thought, but it evaporated when she caught sight of Madge, Kate and their older brother Eleazar, whose thin arms and legs pumped wildly as the trio dashed about, brandishing sticks at a large rolling hoop crisscrossing the lawn. When Elizabeth joined the game, Eleazar fled for the leafy canopy of a tree, his breathing labored, his skin ashy. In the warm fading sunlight of the afternoon her thoughts of abolition, slaves and laws vanished as she contemplated the gravity of her brother's condition.

*

September 7, 1825

Dear Diary, I know now what 'abolition' means. When I ask a question Uncle John answers me straight away. He does not just say 'I wish you were a boy'. Being a girl is terrible. Eleazar is home from school but I think he is very ill. He will not say if it is true.

6

July 1826

Plans for the Cady annual Fourth of July celebration were underway but they didn't excite Elizabeth. Her older sisters Tryphena and Harriet would help her mother, so she worried about Eleazar, home from college for the summer. He'd been ill for some time and July's soaring temperatures and windless days were taking their toll on his health.

To comfort him, she stole into his room one morning with a glass of cold milk and a slice of bread covered in spicy apple butter and set it on his nightstand.

"Good morning, my little Puss," Eleazar whispered with a wan smile and weak hug. A film of sweat glistened on his skin. With his hair damp and plastered against his narrow skull, Elizabeth thought he never had looked so sick and she tried to cheer him. It took all of his strength to rise each morning to splash water on his clammy face, only to then fall back upon the coverlet, his chest heaving from the effort.

"It is a good morning, indeed, my dear handsome brother. I've come to fetch you for a walk." She kept her tone light, hoping he would swing his legs over the side of the bed and rise. He didn't stir.

She tried again.

"Mother has sent in fresh bread and milk for you. I tasted it first," she teased and gestured toward the tray by his bedside. He looked at it then turned away to face the windows, his drawn face unreadable.

"Here, I'll open the draperies for you." She tugged the heavy damask fabric aside flooding the room with light. "The sun is up. Look how beautiful it is," she said, skipping in a little pool of sunlight reflected on the floor.

Her brother remained quiet save for his labored breathing, the ominous gurgle alarming.

"Please get up. The day is fine and you cannot lie abed and miss it," she said.

As a rule, Elizabeth cherished these early morning wake-up rituals. Eleazar seldom came home and she looked forward to spending time with him. They would talk awhile, her probing for details about college life and him embellishing the details with colorful anecdotes. This morning their conversation dwindled. Though he planned to make an appearance at the celebration to acknowledge his role in the family, she doubted it would happen.

"Close the draperies, little Puss. I need to sleep a bit more." He spoke from the depths of his pillows, the food ignored.

Elizabeth sat by his bed holding his hand until he fell asleep again.

When she left her brother's room she refused her nurse's order to put on her hated red flannel dress. Her mother thought it practical for the three youngest sisters to dress alike every day regardless of the temperature. Their aprons kept them clean, but the girls rebelled.

"It is too hot," she told Polly before she ran barefoot along the upstairs corridor wearing her white muslin chemise to look for Madge and Kate. She could hear them singing in the nursery.

Seated in tiny chairs beside the piano, her sisters sang as their tutor Maria Yost accompanied them, mouthing the lyrics under her breath.

"Mistress Mary, quite contrary, how does your garden grow? With silver bells, and cockle shells, and so my garden grows." Their voices piped in unison.

Elizabeth remembered learning the nursery song, too. She laughed and clapped her hands as they finished.

Both girls jumped up to join her in the doorway. In the shortest of white shifts, their feet bare, the three sisters looked like ghostly apparitions in contrast to Miss Yost's gray dress with its stiff white collar.

"Lib, Lib," they clamored, pulling at her hands, "did you come to play?" Elizabeth looked at Miss Yost for approval.

"Go ahead with your sister, girls, it is too hot to continue today."

The three sisters dashed from the warm nursery into the hallway.

"Come with me," Elizabeth said heading for the root cellar where sweets for the celebration were stored. Cool and smelling delicious, the cellar had sturdy brick walls and a stone floor never permeated by the heat.

Sunlight streamed into the room from a row of small windows set at ground level. Cakes and pies for the party lay on long wooden tables along with wheels of cheese, loaves of bread and bushels of peaches, plums, and melons.

Large slabs of brown sugar, used by their cook Mrs. Brewster to sweeten pastries, were also kept in the cellar. The children knew how to nibble a bit of the molasses- flavored sweet and then rewrap it carefully to avoid detection. They headed to the shelf bearing the sugar first. Sitting cross-legged on the cool stone floor, they were soon lost in savoring its taste.

They all heard the rustling sound coming from the dark recesses of the cellar at the same time.

"What is that?" Madge said. Kate's eyes widened. She froze with a brown sugar morsel halfway to her mouth.

"There it is again, like something moving in the shadows."

"It is a rat," Kate cried. "A big, horrid rat!"

"Shhh," Elizabeth said, standing up. "I will go look, you two stay here." She tiptoed slowly into the back of the cellar peering into its depths. When her eyes adjusted to the dim light, she made out the shapes of barrels filled with nuts and grain and white linen bags stuffed with fabric for sewing. She strained to hear the whispers of her sisters and barely noticed when something moved against the leg of her pantalettes. A muffled noise by her feet stopped her. Expecting to see the yellow cat that kept the rats away she looked intently in the direction of the sound. A large bundle of rags appeared to shudder and change shape before her eyes, and she found herself gazing into the dark face and frightened brown eyes of a boy. She gasped.

"Don' hurt me, Miss," the boy said, his hands up protecting his face.

In an instant, Elizabeth felt very brave.

"Get up," she said, standing as tall as she could. "Let me see who you are."

The boy was tall and thin, no longer a bundle of rags. A patched blue shirt and threadbare gray coat hung from his bony frame. Loose-fitting trousers were held closed with a frayed rope. He stood trembling before her, head down and shoeless, clutching a misshapen hat.

"Who are you?" Elizabeth said. An unexpected stranger a foot taller than her hiding in the cellar; this was exciting.

The boy raised his head to look at her.

This boy will not hurt me; his eyes are gentle, Elizabeth thought.

Madge and Kate inched forward from the safety of the cellar shelves to stand beside their sister and stare at the mysterious visitor.

"I asked who are you?" She shook the ragged sleeve of his jacket.

"Jermain, Miss. I am Jermain Loguen." His voice faltered. Please don' tell no one I is here, Miss. Mr. Abraham said the judge would let me stay, till tis safe to go on." A burlap bag lay on the floor by the boy's feet.

Abraham hid this boy here.

"What 'judge'?" Elizabeth stuck out her chin and squinted her eyes at the frightened boy.

"Mr. Abraham said the boss of this here house."

"The judge is our father," Elizabeth said, gesturing at her sisters. "Where did you come from"?

"Tennessee. A Master there owned me. He beat my father until he died. I saw it happen. My mother? She die a long time ago. I got scared the same thing would happen to me. I just up and left. I been travelin' ever since. Folks been hidin' me. Givin' me a place to sleep and food so's I do not die."

"You are a slave," Elizabeth said. One not much older than she.

"No, Miss. Folks say here in the North, everyone is free. I'm a freed man now." Jermain said with defiance, his brown eyes wide, and his voice no longer weak as he announced his situation.

"You are safe here, too," Elizabeth said, reaching for his hand to reassure him. "My father does not believe in slaves. If he knows you are here, he must have a plan to find a safe home for you."

Madge and Kate stood wide-eyed, looking back and forth between their sister and the tall Negro boy.

Madge tugged at Elizabeth's dress. "Come on," she said, "We must tell Father who we found in the cellar."

Elizabeth nodded. Startled by the creaking sound of the cellar door opening, she gestured to Jermain to get back down on the floor.

"Who is back there?" Mrs. Brewster lumbered down the stairs holding a tray of warm berry pies.

Elizabeth and her sisters emerged from the shadows of the cellar and started for the door.

"You girls," she exclaimed. "Keep out of the brown sugar and the hickory nuts. I have found the shells on the floor. How do you expect me to keep up with the baking?" Mrs. Brewster sounded exasperated, but not angry, as the three girls sped past her up the stairs.

Fourth of July party plans forgotten, Elizabeth and her sisters hurried to their father's office and burst through the door.

*

July 3, 1826

Dear Diary, we found a Negro boy. Hiding. He said Abraham knows him. At first I was afraid, then I wasn't. Madge said to tell Father and I said all right. He probably will not believe me because I am a girl. It makes me cross. I could tell Eleazar but I will not. He is too ill. I have no one to talk to. I wish I were a boy.

7

July 1826

"Father, we found a..." Elizabeth's voice trailed off. No one there. Her father's absence surprised her; usually he was deep in study, his leather-bound law books piled around him with heaps of records neatly sorted. More unexpected, the confusing disarray on his desk suggested he left his work in a hurry. She must seek him out and confront him with the discovery in the cellar. Her sisters were becoming frightened.

Kate's bottom lip began to quiver and Madge's frown of concern threatened to turn into bad humor.

"Go find nurse Polly and ask for your dinner," Elizabeth said. "When I have all of this sorted out, I will tell you what Father is going to do."

Her sisters kissed her then dashed away to the familiar comfort of their nursery. They seemed grateful.

Elizabeth spied her mother at her desk with a pile of notepaper and a bottle of ink in front of her. She liked writing individual menus for the party guests. When Elizabeth asked about the whereabouts of her father, Margaret Cady calmly told her an emergency meeting had called him away to confer with his nephew Gerrit Smith. They were meeting at the Montgomery County Courthouse.

"Why do you ask, my dear?" Her mother looked up from her writing.

"I wanted permission to borrow a book." She dared not tell her mother the secret, for Mother believed such things were for men to manage, not women. Especially not girls. Besides, what if her mother and father never talk about slaves?

"Oh," her mother replied. Margaret Cady returned to her writing, commenting that borrowing a book would not bother her father at all. Then she added, "Get dressed dear. Even in the heat, you must not run about the house dressed in your underclothes."

Elizabeth hurried to her room to put on the despised dress. Not to please her mother, but to set out to find her father. She crept down the back stairs into the garden. She knew she must hurry, but decided to take Peter with her. The courthouse stood only a block away on the corner of Main and William Streets and could be reached in minutes, but an eleven-year-old girl alone on the street would not go unnoticed. Some busybody might alert her mother.

She found Peter finished with his chores for the day and resting alone in the shade of a cherry tree, his straw hat pulled low over his eyes.

"Peter," she said, tapping him on the shoulder. "Are you awake?"

The man pushed the brim of his hat up to look up at her.

"I am now, Miss Elizabeth. Ya'll need something?"

"I have to deliver a message to my father at the courthouse and I want you to accompany me."

It may have seemed an odd request, Elizabeth knew, but she liked his company and felt safe with him. Especially important when she made up her mind to do something like leaving the house without permission.

"Well, I 'spect I'd better do that." Peter said. He stood and stretched, making sure to tuck in his shirt and straighten his hat.

"Come along then," Elizabeth said, motioning him to follow her. She looked up at the windows to make sure no one saw them and started walking up West Main Street.

As they approached the entrance, Elizabeth saw her Cousin Gerrit's shiny green gig tied up at the side of the building beneath a large elm tree. His horse munched a bit of hay left for her. Her cousin took good care of his animals, Elizabeth reckoned. And everyone else too. His generosity extended to anyone in need of money and even better, he was a man to honor and love.

"Wait for me outside," Elizabeth told Peter. She tugged at the handle of the heavy courthouse door and slipped inside. Sunlight streamed through the windows of the empty cavernous courtroom, yet muffled voices seemed to be emanating from beneath the floor. Taking care to be very quiet, she pushed open a door beside the bench where the judge presided. A flight of wooden stairs descended into the black depths of a long bricked hallway leading to the basement. She made her way along the darkened corridor over the cobbled floor, feeling her way against the cool brick walls to steady herself. The sounds grew louder and she detected the sharp tone of her father's voice raised in heated conversation. She tiptoed closer and, drawing back into the shadows, peeked around the brick archway leading into a small room with its door ajar.

The narrow opening revealed her father standing with his hands outstretched on a table. The light from windows set at ground level illuminated the faces of three seated men. A candle on the table flickered, its yellow flame reflected in silver tankards. Her father, Cousin Gerrit, and two other men she didn't recognize were engrossed in debate, their words rising and falling with emotion.

"No, by God, I will not have it," her father said, his voice angry. "The slaves sold on the steps of this courthouse in 1813 brought disgrace to Johnstown."

Elizabeth's father seemed to grow before her eyes. She never heard him raise his voice in this manner and felt both afraid and proud of his convictions.

"Never will I own slaves. In fact, there have never been slaves in my home."

Cousin Gerrit rose to stand by her father. "I applaud you, Uncle. Abolishing slavery is a true gesture of kindness and commitment. You say you are not an abolitionist but your heart gives you away."

Cousin Gerrit threw an arm around her father's shoulders and the two stood together looking at their colleagues for affirmation. "So we are in agreement, then? No one must know we are helping slaves escape." Gerrit directed his remarks to her father, but the other two men nodded, raising their tankards in consent.

Smoke from the guttering candle drifted into Elizabeth's hiding place and she sneezed.

"Who's there? Show yourself!" Judge Cady walked to the door and yanked it open.

Elizabeth stepped back.

"What are you doing here?" Her father pulled her into the room and closed the door. "Were you listening?"

She looked up at him, then at Cousin Gerrit and the other two men. She recognized former Congressman Enos T. Throop, now a judge, but not the other man. This meeting must have great importance. Emboldened by what she heard she spoke up.

"Father, I have discovered something of great mystery in the house. I must know at once what you would have me do about it. It is a most urgent matter." She looked up at her father awaiting his response.

Judge Cady knelt down on the floor and reached for her hands. He pulled her toward him, his face directly level with hers.

"Tell me, child," he said, leaning forward.

She held her hand to her lips and placed her face near her father's ear to whisper her discovery. She stepped back looking at her father for his reaction.

Judge Cady rose to his feet and placed his hands on his daughter's shoulders. He turned her towards the door and said, "Go home, child. I will be there straight away."

"But Father–," she turned to look at him.

"Go home, Elizabeth," her father repeated.

Outside, Peter hunkered down in the shade of a tree, dozing.

Elizabeth ran to him, angry that her Father dismissed her.

"Come on Peter, we must go home at once. If I were a boy, Father would care, he truly would," she muttered, and then stomped off, Peter in tow. *Go home, Elizabeth?* Indeed she would.

*

July 3, 1826

Dear Diary, Father and Cousin Gerrit are doing something secretive. I think it is abolition. If Eleazar instead of me had told Father what I discovered, he would have listened. Father says he wants me to learn and be like a boy, but he will not treat me like he means it. I cannot help being a girl but I am not like Mother and my sisters. I hate sewing, cleaning, even cookery except for eating. What is wrong with me? I wish I were a boy to please Father.

8

July 1826

As they approached the back garden gate they encountered a dour Polly standing in their way, her arms folded in front of her apron. Damp strings of brown hair escaped from her disheveled mobcap.

"Miss Elizabeth. You vex me child, with your wanderings. Madge and Kate have been waiting for you in the nursery and it caused me great distress when you were not to be found." Polly's look of exasperation, an attempt to wither Elizabeth, failed.

"Peter chaperoned me and I felt perfectly safe. I just visited Father." She kept her tone even.

"That's all well and good, but no one knew where you were. I'm afraid I have to report this escapade to your mother." A look of satisfaction drew Polly's mouth into a smirk.

"Up to your room at once to prepare for supper, my girl. Your mother and sisters will be at table shortly and your father is joining them there. I shall accompany you to make sure there is no dawdling." She grasped Elizabeth's shoulder and shoved her through the open door.

Recoiling from Polly's clutch, Elizabeth wrenched free and then turned to face Peter who stood waiting behind her.

"Thank you for going with me, Peter. I am ever so grateful." Elizabeth smiled and winked as she dipped into a tiny curtsy.

"Abraham is looking for you, too, Peter," Polly continued, brusque but level. The nurse shooed him with a flick of her hand as Elizabeth brushed by and ran up the stairs to her room.

What of the boy in the cellar? She must make certain someone looked after him. If her father wouldn't help, she would take care of him herself. But when? The day's events pushed and shoved each other out of order in her mind as she prepared with haste to join her family.

She splashed water on her face, ran a comb through her tangled curls, and retied her apron. Then she hurried to the dining room to rush into her chair scant moments before her father took his place at the head of the table with Eleazar at his left. Margaret Cady looked up from the far end of the table where she sat beside Tryphena and Harriet. As the youngest children, Elizabeth, Madge and Kate sat at their mother's left. When Elizabeth seated herself her mother spoke.

"All members of this family are to be at table promptly at five o'clock. I shall not like to remind you again, children. Elizabeth?" Margaret Cady said, then pulled her napkin from its ring and unfolded it onto her lap.

All eyes turned to Elizabeth. Her mother didn't ask about her unplanned visit to the courthouse. Yet. Perhaps Polly merely jested and her mother didn't know.

The maids began to serve the evening meal starting with a cold soup of peas and mint.

"How are you doing today, son?" her father asked. Though the topic of Eleazar's health came up often lately, her brother ignored the questions, changing the subject to discuss the party menu in detail.

"Will there be fried chicken?" he asked his mother.

"I want watermelon," Kate said. "And pie."

"Strawberries and cream," Elizabeth added. Her favorites.

"I am expecting a guest," Tryphena said.

"That is lovely, dear. Everyone is welcome," Elizabeth's mother said.

"I read that the British ship the Beagle, carrying that Darwin fellow, has set sail to survey South America," said the judge. "What do you make of that?"

"Darwin is cataloging new species of animals and plants, Father," Elizabeth said.

"Not you, Lib, I was asking your brother."

Eleazar looked up. "Not much, Father. Elizabeth is probably right. She follows that sort of news, I don't."

"I see. Thought you'd be the expert. Sailing and all that is sort of a young man's pastime."

"Not me. Doesn't interest me a bit," Eleazar said, turning back to spooning soup into his mouth.

"It's not just sailing," Elizabeth said. "It's scientific discovery."

"Oh," her father commented. If Eleazar had been interested, Father would have had much more to say. Considering her circumstances, it was best just to stay quiet.

The routine chatter amongst her sisters and brother deflected the family's attention away from Elizabeth's tardiness. Perhaps no one knew she had been gone after all.

When Mrs. Brewster brought in a poached fish and platter of boiled new potatoes with sweet butter and parsley, Judge Cady cleared his throat and his words drew attention to Elizabeth.

"Lib, is there something you wanted to discuss with me? Bring it up to the family, child, this is a better time than earlier today."

She looked at her father, his expression questioning, as though he gave no thought to the words she had whispered in his ear.

Madge and Kate sat motionless, looking back and forth between Elizabeth and their father. Tryphena, Harriet and Eleazar stopped eating to stare with curiosity.

"Father, it's a private matter. I wish to speak to you alone, please," she pleaded.

"Nonsense, this family has no secrets from each other. Out with it girl. Let's hear the urgent problem that caused you to interrupt my meeting at the courthouse today." Margaret Cady glanced up from cutting a dainty bit of fish to look down the table at Elizabeth.

"You left the house? Alone? Child, it is not safe or proper for a young lady to walk un-chaperoned on the street.

Running off whenever you please without approval? You disgrace me," her mother said, shaking her head.

Polly didn't tell after all, Elizabeth realized.

Judge Cady turned to his wife, "My dear, do not fear for her safety. She used good judgment to take Peter with her and returned home without incident, did she not?"

Her mother shook her head, seeming appeased.

"Answer your father, Elizabeth. We would all like to know what matter prompted you to defy propriety and take leave of the house without asking permission." Her mother's reproachful gaze fixed on Elizabeth's face.

"Mother, Father, please do not persist, I cannot speak of this here. Father, this is for your ears only." Should she implicate Madge and Kate? Would they get in trouble? What if Mother didn't share Father's beliefs?

Did Tryphena and Harriet and Eleazar know too?

"No, Daughter, tell us now," he said.

As all eyes once again turned on her, she stared directly at her father and blurted out the secret she told him in the courthouse.

Her older sisters and brother gasped and the little sisters watched their father with wide eyes, appearing afraid of being implicated in some terrible misdeed.

Judge Cady gazed at his daughter, seeming thoughtful, and then turned back to his meal.

His attitude abruptly changed as he replied, "There is nothing in the cellar save barrels for the larder and bundles wrapped for storing. You are mistaken, Elizabeth. It must have been an illusion or one of the new maids rummaging about." He picked up his knife and fork, not looking up.

The three sisters stared at their father, expressions of disbelief on their faces.

Elizabeth persevered, angry now, leaning forward to get his attention.

"I insist there is a slave boy there. Pray let me show you, I am certain he is still hiding amongst the recesses of the cellar and must be sorely in need of food and drink." Her chair teetered as she started to rise, assuming her father would recognize the urgency of her information.

"After supper, Daughter, then you may show me. But I insist, there is no one there. There would never be a slave in the Cady house."

His dismissive tone warned her back into her chair. There would be no more discussion of the subject as Judge Cady resumed eating and conversation turned to preparations for the Fourth of July party.

The food no longer interested her. She prodded the fish with her fork as she waited for her father, deploring time that crawled so slowly.

The scraping of heavy wooden chair legs on the polished dining room floor announced the end of their meal as her father wiped his mouth with his napkin and rose from his seat. Immediately the Cady entourage stood in respect.

"Come Elizabeth, let's investigate the contents of the cellar. I'll show you that your imagination has bested you."

Madge and Kate started to join their sister and father, but were warned off by their mother.

"No, little ones, it is time for bed for you. Elizabeth will report on her findings shortly. Do not be disappointed, I am sure she will give you a full account." Her mother smiled fondly at the little girls. She seemed pleased with the return to the satisfactory routine she strived to maintain.

Judge Cady led the way into the hall and through the kitchen. At the cellar door he picked up a lighted candle from a nearby shelf. The flickering glow illuminated father and daughter, distorting shadows on the wall as they made their way down the stairs into the now black depths of the cellar storeroom.

The low ceilinged main room with its shelves of sugar and herbs smelled sweetly of damp and cinnamon, but the odor didn't appeal to Elizabeth as it had earlier in the day. The windows at ground level that overlooking the garden only emitted fading light at this hour.

Elizabeth led her father into the storage area where she had discovered Jermain hidden among bundles of cloth that were piled against the wall. Certainly he would still be hiding.

"Jermain, come out," she called. "It is safe. My father, the judge, is here with me." Her voice sounded loud in the enclosed room, but no response occurred. "Please show yourself," she tried again. "You have no need to worry. My father is a kind man as you were told. We are here to rescue you."

Still no answer.

Judge Cady reached for his daughter's hand and gently turned her toward him. "You see, my daughter, there is no one here."

Elizabeth released his hand and ran into the darkest area of the cellar, calling out the boy's name. Gone. Surely her father knew she would not have invented the boy's name. Her spirits plummeted. Why didn't her father believe her?

"Come, Father, let's go back up the stairs. I fear I am wrong and you are right," she said, not wishing to press the matter further.

Her father would not believe her because she was only a girl, she was certain of that. If she were Eleazar? Her father likely would have reasoned man-to-man that the mysterious visitor left on his own devices.

Tired from the day's exciting events and overcome with sadness that once again her father did not hold her in esteem equal to her brother, she left him at the top of the stairs for the comfort of her bedroom.

The heavy door closed behind her, its latch falling into place with a familiar click. The waning hours of the summer evening bathed the room in lavender colored light, tinting the folds of the dove gray draperies pulled back from each side of the window. A fresh nightdress laid spread out on the coverlet folded on the foot of her bed. Her brushes, comb, and pins were neatly in place on the dressing case in front of the window. Favorite dollies occupied the two chairs that flanked it. Tonight she took no notice of their worn, happy faces. A pitcher of warm water, towels, and soap awaited her bath. By her bed, a carved wooden stand held a glass of milk, a lighted candle and her bookmarked edition of *Emma*. Even though she'd read the book before, she loved the story so it became a favorite bedtime indulgence.

She placed her shoes inside the wardrobe, took off her dress and apron and hung them up. She felt cooler and scampered across the room to wash quickly and pull her nightdress over her head.

By the time she sipped the last of her milk, wrote in her diary, and snuffed out the candle, night had completely darkened her room. Where was the Negro boy she wondered? Was he really gone?

*

July 3, 1826

Dear Diary, If my brother went to the courthouse he would be praised or even ignored for what he did. I should have asked him to go with me, but he is still too ill. Father made me say what we found in the cellar and he said it is impossible. He must think me a liar. I am not a liar.

9

July 1826

A clap of thunder woke Elizabeth from a restless sleep. She sat upright, pulled her damp nightdress from her sticky body and held her hands over her ears as yet another booming thunder roll rattled the windows. By midnight the heat lifted, but stale air still filled her warm bedchamber.

Outside, a yellow glow flickered and brightened the night. She padded over to the window, her bare feet cool on the polished floor. She pulled the heavy draperies back and flung the shutters open. A sulfurous glow came from the southwest near Montgomery and Perry Streets. Another thunderous boom accompanied by a shower of glittering fire burst in the sky from the same direction.

It was not thunder, but the start of the Fourth of July celebration. What a wonderful day this would be!

The glow, she reckoned, came from the Fort Johnstown jail where an enormous bonfire illuminated the firing cannons that ushered in the momentous event. Soon the ringing of bells would add to the clamor, and throughout the town popping firecrackers and exploding torpedoes would remind residents of their freedom from the British.

As a very young girl, the noise scared her. She feared then that the British would return. Each year local storytellers embellished the legends of the British offenses and the tales became more colorful. She need not fear King George III, but every time she visited Sir William Johnson's mansion at the end of Hall Avenue she ran her hand over the saber marks left by British loyalists marking the balustrades. Johnstown would have burned if defeat of the British had not occurred in 1776.

Today would be filled with excitement, edgy fear, and noise, as soldiers and citizens gathered to parade through the town. Later they would rally at the courthouse to listen to orators and to a passionate reading of the Declaration of Independence. Like her home, houses up and down the streets of Johnstown were hung with red, white and blue bunting and American flags. They fluttered in the warm July morning. Throughout the day, families would gather to sing songs of their devoted hatred of anything British and feast on the bounty of each other's kitchens.

Elizabeth dressed to join her family in the dining room for breakfast. In honor of the celebration and the summer weather, her mother allowed Elizabeth and her little sisters to dress in new Empire dresses of robin's egg blue cotton. Sheer white cotton aprons pulled up in the front, formed panniers that covered the dresses. The effect was quite elegant. Elizabeth pirouetted to admire her image in the looking glass front of her wardrobe then dashed down the stairs.

The house buzzed with activity. Her father rose early to take his coffee in his study to review the address he prepared to deliver during the ceremonies. Her mother busied herself overseeing last-minute preparations for the party to be held in their back garden after the speeches. Tryphena and Harriet had finished their tasks for the day hours earlier and were resting in their rooms.

A pitcher of cold milk, a platter of fried eggs and bacon and toast spread with butter were still set out when she entered the dining room. Eleazar sat reading the newspaper, frowning and mumbling to himself. A cup of coffee grew cold at his elbow. Madge and Kate dipped bits of toast into their eggs then stuffed them in their mouths, licking butter from their fingers as no one reminded them to use their napkins.

Elizabeth ran to Eleazar and threw her arms around his neck. "Oh, I am so glad to see you looking rested. Will you come with us today?"

"Perhaps," he said. He paused to smile at her then turned another page to read.

"Your presence will make our father happy. It distresses him to know you are ill and he cannot help." She hoped her handsome brother would gain strength from her encouragement.

"It depends on how I feel," Eleazar said, glancing up again.

"I know having you by his side today will add strength and conviction to his words."

Eleazar finally pulled her to him in an affectionate embrace and gazed into her face before he responded.

"My dearest Puss," he said. "I know you believe Father counts on me alone, but you are stronger and will serve him well as a clever and reasonable daughter."

Elizabeth sank into the dining room chair beside him as he continued, surprised at the seriousness of his tone.

"You are most like father," he said, "mirroring his convictions and intelligence. Tryphena and Harriet model mother's disposition and the personalities of our younger sisters is yet unknown."

"But Eleazar, you do not understand–".

He cut her off. "You, dearest, will fulfill his dreams when I cannot." Her brother's grave voice continued, his eyes burning with an unfathomable light. "I owe him so much, my life..." His voice trailed off as his expression softened. After a moment, as if his thoughts focused on some distant scene, he continued. "My health is too poor. Although I try to achieve his expectations, I fear they are unattainable for me."

The resignation in his voice alarmed Elizabeth. She reached for his hand to squeeze it then paused to consider the significance of his remarks before replying. "But he will never accept me instead of you. He has told me so. He is desolate that I am a girl. It is you who will brighten his future, not I."

"You must forget his words. He does not mean it." Her brother cupped her face in his hands and stared into her eyes. "I believe in you. Do not disappoint me by becoming less than you can be. You are a bright child full of promise and curiosity."

She felt heartened by Eleazar's passionate words. Should she confide in her brother about the mysterious events of the previous night? Before she could tell him, the door flew open and her mother appeared. For now the story would remain a secret.

"Come, children, let's hurry. We shall all walk to the courthouse together. Your father is waiting with Peter, Abraham and Jacob. Up from your chairs, come along." Fussing over Eleazar, her mother handed him his top hat and then tied Madge and Kate's bonnet ribbons under their chins. Their bright curls bounced as they skipped out the door.

Elizabeth tied her own bonnet at a jaunty angle beneath her ear. She felt quite sophisticated and grown up for all of her eleven years. Late again, she ran to join the family for the walk up Main Street to the celebration.

When they reached the assembled townspeople at the courthouse a tall, handsome young man stepped away from the crowd. The cut of his jacket emphasized his broad shoulders. Edward Bayard, Tryphena's betrothed, grasped his fiancé's hand and briefly held it to his lips.

His cordial greeting of each family member, even a vigorous turn shaking hands with Abraham, Peter and Jacob endeared him to Elizabeth. When he reached her, he took both of her hands in his and looked into her face.

"How pretty you are today," he said. "You are growing more comely with each passing week. I suspect one day soon, your beauty will compete with that of my darling Tryphena."

Elizabeth gazed up into his smiling face and felt the heat of a blush redden her skin. She turned away when a swell of lightheaded confusion threatened to disarm her.

Peter approached a moment later with Madge and Kate trailing behind him. He tapped her on the shoulder.

"Miss Elizabeth, your mother has given me permission to escort you girls around the courthouse lawn to watch the activities," he said with a bright smile. "She asks that I protect you from any frightening noises or discomfort." He looked quite resplendent in the blue suit with gilt buttons he reserved for church services.

Elizabeth turned her attention to Peter and her sisters, grateful for the interruption as Edward returned to Tryphena's side and they disappeared into the crowd.

Seeming eager to leave the staid company of their older family members, the three girls pulled Peter along in search of adventure. They pushed through the crowd of exuberant townspeople, drawn to a noisy cheering crowd gathered at one corner of the courthouse grounds. The sounds of hurrahs and shouts grew louder near a group of men strung out around a patch of dirt roughly scribed with a stick into a diamond shape.

"It is the new game," Peter said with excitement as he drew closer to where the girls could watch undeterred.

Small white muslin pillows were placed along the rough lines at each diamond point. A man stood beside each one watching two men poised at the uppermost point of the diamond. Three additional fellows were in the field beyond, behind the scribed lines. One faced the others grasping a long wooden stick holding it back over his shoulder. Another stood in the center of the diamond, a leather ball cupped in his palm.

The fellow with the ball reared back then hurled it forward. The ball flew at a tremendous speed and met the stick with a loud crack as the man holding it hit the ball with a mighty swing. The ball flew above the upstretched hands of the men on the diamond line and over the heads of the crowd standing far behind them. A cheer rose as the fellow with the stick threw it to the ground and ran from pillow to pillow around the diamond, kicking up dust until he regained his original position, gasping for breath from the effort. A group of men, his friends perhaps, surged around him jumping and shouting, clapping him on the back and hugging him.

Peter's eyes were shining and he cheered as loud as the others, raising his hands in the air with a great shout.

What a wonderful game, Elizabeth thought. More vigorous than croquet and certainly more exciting than that detestable British cricket.

"Perhaps they will let us play this wonderful new game, Peter. Go and ask someone," Elizabeth said, so intrigued by the fun they were having, she didn't notice girls and Negroes weren't playing.

"No, Miss Elizabeth, let's just watch for now. Perhaps we will play this game some other time, but not today." Peter looked up to see Margaret Cady beckoning to him. He gathered the girls to his side and they walked back to the company of the family.

"Help me up, little Puss," Eleazar called to her, his hand outstretched. He sat cross-legged on a blanket beneath a tree leaning against their picnic basket. Elizabeth gripped her brother's fingers and pulled him to his feet, almost toppling backward in the process.

They walked behind the rest of the family, dawdling and stopping now and then while she regaled him with details of the game. Encouraged by his smile, her words flew with excitement.

"You should have seen it too," she said.

"Perhaps next time," Eleazar said.

By the time the family returned home, Mrs. Brewster and the kitchen helpers had loaded the tables with sliced ham and cold roast beef, salads of potato, beetroot, and tomatoes, jewel-like jelly molds ringed with strawberries and grapes, breads, fresh butter–enough for the family and the invited guests. Beneath a canopy erected in the back garden, chairs were arranged in intimate groupings to invite conversation. The children's hoops leaned against the trunk of the huge Elm tree that shaded the remainder of the garden. For this special day, Abraham had pulled pots of scarlet wallflowers, white candytuft and dark blue lobelia into the shade to enhance their colors. Paper lanterns hung from tree limbs, awaiting nightfall to illuminate the party by candlelight. The moment Elizabeth's mother walked into the garden, she took command of the serving staff, and reminded the family to be on their best behavior. Elizabeth and Madge were charged with shepherding the littlest children and making sure even the shyest one participated in the games. Elizabeth gathered the children for a game of Whoop, soon dispatching the one who must hide by whispering the location of the secret hiding places in the Cady garden. Laughter reached a crescendo by dusk, while the women gossiped and the men sat off to the side smoking cigars.

Once the last bits of ham and beaten biscuits had been eaten, and Mrs. Brewster's berry pies and tarts had disappeared, Elizabeth climbed the stairs to her room, tired but happy. Eleazar had found enough strength to withstand the entire day. For that Elizabeth was grateful. She settled into her bed recalling the conversation she shared with her brother, the exciting game she witnessed, Peter's regal appearance as he guarded her and her sisters, and the charming face of her soon to be brother-in-law. What a fine day indeed. She felt herself drifting off to sleep when she heard the door to her room creak as someone entered. She opened her eyes to see her father approach with a lighted candle in hand to stand beside her bed.

She sat up, pulled her bed sheet up to her chin and stared at him, wide-eyed.

"Father, what is wrong? Has Eleazar taken more seriously ill?"

He shook his head, his expression grave.

"My dear, you were not mistaken about the young lad in the cellar. I told Abraham to hide him there for safekeeping. Cousin Gerrit and I are two of many who have pledged to help slaves who seek us for assistance. That fellow is one."

"You did believe me," she said. Her heart swelled with relief.

He nodded. "The boy has been moved again. To a safe place where he can live as a freed man. Do not worry about him, and do not speak of this to anyone, not even Eleazar. He already knows. I regret I could not tell you in the cellar. I believed someone might be listening. I merely insisted you speak up with the family and serving people present so I could deflect curiosity. No one must know, so do not mention this to anyone, do you understand?"

Although her father told her to keep the confidence, he need not have worried. Her convictions were just like his, even if he didn't think she was as good as a boy. Perhaps she would find a way to show him.

*

July 4, 1826

Dear Diary, Edward Bayard met us at the celebration. When he smiles and looks at me his eyes twinkle and I feel warm. I guess I am glad because I will see him often. Well, surprisingly, Father did believe me about Jermain and told me so. But it's a secret. I feel better because he trusts me. And, Father is an abolitionist. That is a secret, too. I may not be a boy, but I can keep secrets.

10

October 1827

"Time for school, Miss." Polly's voice broke in waking Elizabeth. A heap of logs that crackled and spit in the fireplace warmed her room. The weather had turned very cold. Autumn leaves in hues of gold, red and maroon that painted the trees surrounding Johnstown a month earlier were now piling up against the hedges, leaving the trees barren. The gray sky predicted snowfall before day's end. On the cobblestone streets, farm wagons hurried to their deliveries creating an incessant rattle of wooden wheels.

Elizabeth snuggled deeper into her featherbed beneath the tangle of soft linen sheets and down stuffed coverlet, her thoughts drifting back over the past year.

A month after the discovery of the runaway slave hiding in the cellar, Eleazar came home from college for the last time. Instead of a happy homecoming, the event turned somber, infusing family events with sadness. Six months later, when he was twenty years old, the prolonged illness that weakened his body claimed his life. The man who should have become the family leader of the next generation, now lay buried beside his two brothers in the Colonial Cemetery family plot, the third headstone inscribed with the name of a Cady son. Her father seemed to feel it most and despaired. Unable to comfort him, his wife and daughters moved as quiet shadows, coming and going, maintaining household duties, pausing to straighten the white mourning cloths draped on windows, pictures and mirrors. Days turned into weeks, until at last Elizabeth could stand the sadness no longer.

She sought out her father and found him seated in his office, his chair turned toward the window. He sat very still, his eyes fixed on some image beyond the windowpane. Scattered books and a sheaf of briefs he abandoned when Eleazar died lay open on his desk. A shaft of wintery light illuminated a film of dust on their pages.

Elizabeth climbed into her father's lap and placed her head against his chest. She could hear the steady beating of his heart through the soft fabric of his waistcoat. Judge Cady wrapped his arms around her and held her tightly and they sat in silence, undisturbed, as the sun moved across the sky. Contentment settled over her, like a warm blanket against a cold day. She felt so at home near her father, certain her presence would help heal his broken heart. Perhaps she would be the one to bring him back to the family again, brightening his spirits once more.

Twilight crept into the recesses of the room before Judge Cady broke the quiet with a deep shuddering melancholy sigh. "Oh, my daughter, how I wish you were a boy."

There it was again, Elizabeth thought, her belief that she had in some way helped him. Still the wretched sadness in his voice failed to anger her. Love for her father swelled, and somehow hoping once again she could take the hurt away, she threw her arms around his neck and said, "Father, I will try to be like my brother." How she would do this was uncertain.

*

October 10, 1827

Dear Diary, another day of school. Having lessons at home is cozy because Mrs. Brewster makes me hot milk when I ask. No one seems interested in Thanksgiving or Christmas. Madge and Kate ask whether Father Christmas will come and I tell them 'yes', but I do not know for sure. With Eleazar dead, I feel completely alone. Father has changed. I remind him of Eleazar, he says, but I don't know how. We are not alike. Mother is still grieving. I think we all are. I must prove that I am all that Eleazar believed I could be. I need a plan. Now I must work on my lessons for tomorrow. I have a new Mr. Webster's Spelling Book and I am a better speller than anyone else in this family. Except Father.

11

October 1828

In the months that followed, the Cady household slowly began its ascent into normalcy. Trips to the burial ground with its two tall poplar trees flanking the family plot grew fewer. The period of mourning came to its gradual end. Conversations became happier, social calls were once again noted on the calendar, and Elizabeth and her sisters returned to play. But that winter, though she joined Madge and Kate on their jaunts through the snowdrifts, helping build snow forts and figures, and sliding down the ice-covered woodpiles banked against the barn, Elizabeth began laying plans to replace her brother in her father's eyes.

With a boy's education and excellence at a boy's skills, she would receive the same respect and esteem, she reasoned. If they were equal in these two ways—why then, they would be equal in all things. Of course. The power and influence automatically conferred to boys would be hers.

By spring, with her plan firm, she took the first step. It meant resisting her mother's attempts at homemaking lessons and foregoing idle pastimes with her sisters. Instead, concentrating on her education and learning to ride a horse like Eleazar became her goal. By following the path he took she could duplicate his skills. So simple.

When her brother turned thirteen, he studied Greek with Reverend Simon Hosack, the pastor of their church. Deemed the local expert on the subject, he only taught boys. Elizabeth found him working in his garden one chilly spring morning.

The old cleric grunted with effort each time his booted foot drove the shovel into the thawing soil. He grumbled as he worked, stopping to swipe a gloved hand under his red nose. "Heavenly Father forgive me," he said aloud, looking skyward. "Why send me the urge to garden when you've not asked the earth to accept my shovel?" When he looked up again, Elizabeth waved from the garden path.

"Does the cold bother you, child?" he asked, his words exploding in bursts of frosty mist.

She stamped her feet and pushed her hands deep into the pockets of her wool coat. She shook her head. "Not so much, Reverend Hosack."

"Well then, I am happy to see you," he said. "Have you come to help me sow my spring vegetables?"

"No, Reverend. I am here to ask if you will teach me Greek as you did Eleazar." She held her breath.

"My-oh-my," he said, covering his surprise by throwing down the shovel. "I believe we need to warm up and discuss this," he said. "Come along." With a swing of his arm he waved her to follow behind him and hurried into his library.

Reverend Hosack tossed a log into the fireplace, poked the ashes, and with great vigor pumped the hand bellows to blow still-glowing embers into a crackling fire. He removed the patched linen smock protecting his suit and wiped his hands on a handkerchief then gestured to Elizabeth to sit opposite on a settee facing the fireplace.

The cleric settled into a worn leather chair and arranged a knitted blanket over his knees. "Elizabeth, my dear, what is your age?"

"I am twelve." She fidgeted. She rose to her feet and began to pace the room. "Reverend, which do you like best, boys or girls?" She awaited his response.

"Why, girls, to be sure. I wouldn't trade girls for all the boys in Christendom." He sat back, resting his chin on the fingertips of his clasped hands

"My father," she said, "prefers boys and I intend to be as like a boy as possible." She stopped in front of him, hands on her hips, her voice rising with emotion. "I aim to study Greek and ride horseback."

"Then I shall be delighted to teach you the language of the ancient Greeks. Willing students are my greatest reward." He leaned forward to take her cold hands in his and studied her serious expression. "My dear, I know your father well. I do not believe what you say is necessarily true. He's always been a fair and open-minded man."

"He is respected for those traits," she said, "but you do not know him as I do. Will you help me prove my worth to him?" The reverend did not know how her father had deferred to Eleazar on all things, giving him unquestioned access to schooling, money and asking his opinion on everything. As if they were equals.

Reverend Hosack sighed. "Then come, child, let us begin now," he said, gathering up his beloved Greek dictionary. He placed it and a slate before her on a table and began to lecture.

The Greek lessons continued throughout the spring and summer. Elizabeth told her parents she visited the reverend for *religious training*. They were satisfied with that explanation and seemed pleased that she spent time with a man they respected and revered. Each Sunday morning after services her parents would nod knowingly at Reverend Hosack. After they passed by his genial person, Elizabeth was sure the wink exchanged between her and the good man went unnoticed.

Gentle Jacob who kept the horses did not bend to her will so easily. He knew she loved the animals. Their soft whinnying at morning and nightfall, gleaming coats, and slender legs were beautiful to her. She longed to ride even before this. Nevertheless, he balked.

"You too small and them skirts will get in the way," he said. When she persisted, he argued that the horses were too large.

"No they are not," Elizabeth said. "How about Jenny? That horse is just my size."

"Miss Elizabeth, you wearing me down," Jacob said shaking his head. "You get your momma's okay first, all right?"

"No Cady girl before you has wished to ride," her mother complained. "What will people think? Riding is dangerous too. You could be injured if you fall."

"I am sure I can do it. And, I promise to be careful. Please Mother, say I may do this?"

Still reluctant, her mother only gave permission when Peter agreed to accompany Elizabeth. He assured her Jacob would be a patient and safe teacher.

Elizabeth struggled to sleep the night before her instruction began and hurried through breakfast to run to the stables. While Jacob held the horses' halter, Peter hoisted her high atop Jenny's saddle. Ever modest, he looked away when she hooked her right leg around the saddle horn then fit the stirrup to her left foot. She surveyed the two men, the barns, the fences and the outbuildings from her elevated position. Before Jacob could react, she pulled on the reins and dug her heel into Jenny's glossy side then cantered off into their pasture bouncing on the saddle. In an instant Jacob took flight and ran ahead of the horse grabbing its bridle to stop it. His boots slid on the tall grasses and nettles that parted in the horse's wake and clung to his breeches.

His placid dark face reddened in anger.

"Miss Elizabeth, I won't teach you to ride if you aren't careful," he said, barely able to breathe from the effort. "You will become a fit rider, but not like this."

"But how will I learn if I do not ride?"

The expression on his good and earnest face embarrassed her. She felt instant regret for her haste.

"You will learn. It takes patience and practice," Jacob said. He turned the horse around, keeping his hand on the bridle as Jenny ambled back to the stable yard. "You do not do me justice and I fear your father and mother will reproach me."

"Dear Jacob, please forgive me," she said to placate him. "I am so anxious to learn to gain my father's approval that I did not think." The excitement of the ride stayed with her, however. "Your admonishment is well taken. Riding Jenny is a pleasure and I will not do so again without your instruction." She leaned down and rested her face against the horse's rough flaxen mane, taking in the sweet barn odor of her and feeling the warmth of her skin. Impulsively she placed her arms around the horse's neck and hugged her. "Good Jenny," she said. "Thank you for not pitching me off."

Elizabeth passed her twelfth year, mastering Greek and learning to ride like a boy believing it would render her equal to her brother. But as she gained knowledge and discovered the power derived from assertiveness, nagging reminders of her feminine role constantly beset her.

"May I please see the progress on your sampler," her mother asked one morning.

Elizabeth held it out hoping her mother would not remember how it looked last week.

Margaret Cady inspected the cloth stretched within its frame. "My dear, you have not made one stitch since I saw this last," she said, looking up at Elizabeth with reproach.

"Yes, Mother, I did. See, right there." She pointed to a row of knotted roses, each a bit different than the other.

Her mother inspected the ugly uneven stitches then shook her head and handed the frame back. "Why are you not like Tryphena and Harriet? They know they must achieve excellence in needlecraft. It is an important skill to make a good marriage. I have reminded you of that over and over."

"I know, Mother." Elizabeth squirmed, not wanting to meet her mother's eyes. "It just does not interest me. I will try though, I promise." Perhaps her admiration for her mother's impressive abilities would inspire her.

She really tried. She wanted to please her mother and her older sisters, too. Why didn't she care for domestic learning? Surely she would need to cook and know how to run a household. If she were to list her favorite pastimes it would not include needlework, nor cooking or caring for her clothes or a home. She pushed this perplexing dilemma to the back of her mind. Forced to sit ladylike with Tryphena and Harriet after supper to hone her skills at needlework, she would fidget and then finally toss her sampler frame aside to seek out her father's office and his vast library shelves. In that office one day, she learned the profound difference between a woman's destiny in her world and a man's.

Several of her father's law students had gathered with him to debate current legal rulings and were in heated conversation when she entered the library unnoticed to take a seat near the door and listen.

"Hah, they are but slaves." A red faced young man named Arthur, whose waistcoat barely covered his middle, punched the air with his fist. "These laws govern a woman's role in society. She is subservient to us men and always will be. Just like the slaves in the South." His voice grew louder.

Judge Cady looked at him sharply.

Elizabeth wanted to barge into their conversation and chastise the loud-mouthed law student. She fought to keep quiet.

"Sit down, Arthur," her father said. "We know your views will never change, but I tell you, someday soon man's dominance over woman will be altered. Mark my words," he said, his tone steady and firm.

Arthur's mouth gaped.

"Your closed mind disappoints me, Arthur. You and my late son Eleazar were great friends and I hoped as you studied here his memory and potential would live on, perhaps in you."

Elizabeth gasped. The scene unfolding in the library now gained greater meaning. Surely her father didn't plan to bring Arthur into the family? Not with views like his. Not when she stood ready to take her brother's place.

The other four students stared at both men: one, their respected teacher to whom they were indebted, and the other, a canny hot head with a weakness for ale and spirits, but capable of convincing rhetoric.

Edward Bayard, Tryphena's fiancé, jumped to his feet. Spots of color rose on his high cheekbones and amber flames from the fireplace reflected in his deep-set brown eyes. "Look, chaps," he turned to focus on Arthur, but directed his comments to the others as well. "I agree that a man's dominant role is clearly stated in the law. But I concur with Judge Cady that the role will someday change. My own fiancé is a woman of tremendous strength and intelligence whom I turn to for advice and counsel. I would not think of her as any other than my equal. The law states that I need not defer to her wishes, but in truth, I do." He looked around at his fellow law students and then turned to Judge Cady. "You sir, I respectfully suggest are correct in your predictions. Although today no woman is perceived to be equal to a man by law or tradition, this too will change."

"It will not happen, Bayard, mark my words," Arthur said, his tone snide and condescending.

In the depths of her hiding place, Elizabeth frowned. How could her father have ever held Arthur in such high esteem? That lout could never take her brother's place. In Edward however, an ally existed. His beliefs aligned with hers. If he supported her, perhaps her father would admit she could replace Eleazar after all.

That afternoon, she rummaged in her bureau for the jacket Eleazar favored. She'd hidden it beneath a petticoat. She pressed the wool to her nose. The faint odor of the pomade he used on his hair lingered. She shrugged into the jacket and made her way to the family cemetery walking as fast as she could. Twilight had closed in by the time she knelt and brushed the snow from the marble that marked her brother's grave. "Dearest Eleazar, if I follow your path I can be strong and brave as you said I could be. Father will see that I can take your place. If anyone can do it shall be me, I promise. I miss you so and will love you forever." She wiped her eyes on the hem of her skirt. The crunch of footsteps on the frozen path nearby startled her. She whirled around and slipped on the ice.

"I did not mean to frighten you," Edward said reaching to grasp her arm to steady her. "When I saw you leave the house without proper clothing, I took Tryphena's wool shawl and followed you."

"I am fine," Elizabeth said, but indeed she was not. Her feet were so cold. The warmth of Edward's hand made her heart beat faster and she felt light-headed. "Thank you," she said as he slipped the shawl around her shoulders.

"It is growing dark, the family will be worried. Shall we return?" Edward asked.

She nodded, keeping her gaze averted as she followed him home. To prove her vow to Eleazar, she must excel beyond her father's dreams for him. Her plan would work. For tomorrow morning, just before her thirteenth birthday, she would take step two, and begin her lessons at Johnstown Academy. As they walked she thought about the lovely sensation of Edward's warm hand on her arm and the concern in his soft brown eyes.

*

October 12, 1828

Dear Diary, I started my plan. I must lie to my parents though. I do not care. If they find out I will make up a story. The other part is more exciting. Riding horses is splendid. Jacob became very cross and said I could have fallen off Jenny. Good gracious, I will not fall off of anything. Mother wants me to be more like Tryphena and Harriet, but I do not want to sew and tidy up all the time. I also do not want to learn how to cook things. I keep thinking my mind will change on that, but it does not. When I grow up Mrs. Brewster will work for me and do all those things I do not like.

12

November 1828

Dispirited and still visibly despondent over the death of Eleazar, her father plunged into his demanding career, setting aside his role as head of the family. Elizabeth's mother, who normally occupied herself with keeping house and caring for her family, had grown distant since her son's death. Now reluctant to consider even the smallest confrontation, she seemed contented to keep her fingers busy with needlework, depending on Tryphena to assume the role of mistress of the house. It didn't seem the same with Tryphena at the helm, yet the managing of the household continued.

Soon after Eleazar died, Tryphena and Edward were married. The subdued celebration of the grand event seemed fitting since they were still in mourning, yet the family welcomed Tryphena's new husband whose presence restored gaiety to their lives. Once he became a member of the family, he introduced the sisters to history and poetry, political economy, music, dancing and games. In particular, he observed Elizabeth's tenacity for learning and praised her mastery of Greek. One morning, after he overheard her arguing loudly with her parents and their raised voices, he hesitated a moment then knocked.

"Yes, Edward?" Judge Cady asked when he opened the door.

"Please excuse the intrusion, but I feel I must speak up on Elizabeth's behalf."

She stood by the window, near tears, her arms crossed against her chest.

Her mother appeared tired and gaunt. She twisted a handkerchief in her lap.

Judge Cady sat back in his chair his shoulders slumped.

"Ah, her champion," he said.

"I am that indeed, sir, as I am to Madge and Kate as well. I have the good fortune to converse with your daughters as their teacher and find them exceptional young women. Eager students, I must add. Particularly Elizabeth," he said.

"So she says," her mother said in a soft voice. "She wants to attend Johnstown Academy."

"And, we've said 'no'. What good will it do? It's a waste of time," Judge Cady said.

Elizabeth's mother turned to her husband. "You have done nothing but encourage the child," she said, her expression reproachful. "If she had but learned the duties of a housewife at the outset instead of lingering in your office listening to all those raucous debates we would not have this problem."

Judge Cady leaned forward, his head in his hands. "Yes, yes, I know it is all my fault."

"Sir, it is no one's fault. She is a clever girl and learns quickly," Edward said. "Moreover, she has insatiable curiosity about a wealth of topics. This should be nurtured. And you have done that." He glanced at Mrs. Cady. "Begging your pardon, Ma'am, you have set such a fine example for the comportment of a woman that Elizabeth seeks to emulate your grasp of facts and figures. She believes the only way to hone that skill is to continue her education. Surely you do not intend to squelch that?"

Elizabeth's mother managed a gentle laugh. "Edward Bayard, you are a gifted orator. I can see why your colleagues listen to you."

Judge Cady reached for his wife's hand. "So, my dear, you side with Edward despite your concern she will never be expert in the needlepoint you envision?" He smiled.

She nodded. "In time she will learn what she must. It is inevitable. She favors your skill with words and while I would like her to yearn for a more benign existence, I fear my wishes are in vain."

Judge Cady threw up his hands in surrender. "All right, she can go." He turned to his wife and drew her from her chair to look into her eyes. "An educated woman is both refined and clever," he said, "like you, dearest. Whomever Elizabeth marries, she will make him a wonderful wife and be a model to her children, as you are to ours."

Elizabeth could barely contain herself. It was all she could do to keep from jumping up and down. "Thank you Father.

And Mother, I vow you will not be disappointed." She turned to Edward. "You, dear friend, are my mentor and teacher. I am grateful."

Judge Cady had agreed to Elizabeth's pleas to attend Johnstown Academy because she'd receive the solid moral training she would need for her future role as wife and mother. Elizabeth knew that. Although he encouraged his headstrong daughter to pursue knowledge and rhetorical skills to placate her, she suspected her father believed this type of education would serve of no value beyond the home.

A light snow began to fall as Elizabeth stepped onto the stone porch in front of her home. Abraham had swept the walks earlier, but the flakes were coming down steadily and once again, a white carpet covered the ground. The snow blanketed the barren shrubs and piled onto leafless tree limbs. She flipped her knitted shawl up over the wide brimmed felt hat tied under her chin and pulled it tight around her shoulders. She turned left on West Main Street, and with a determined pace began walking toward South William Street and the Johnstown Academy. Her leather boots crunched on the frozen walkway. She kept to the inside of the walk to avoid the horse-drawn carts piled with stinking animal skins. At this time of the morning they crowded the street on their way to the tannery at the outskirts of town. Despite her efforts, the horses' hooves and the wheels on the carts churned up mud that flew onto her skirt. Even at this hour, bitterly cold and confronting the Erie Canal, Johnstown bustled with the business of an expanding city.

Elizabeth felt quite brave setting out afoot, her bearing straight and her chin lifted as she walked. Though a short distance from her home, keeping pace but out of sight behind her, Peter followed her to the academy building. The snow stopped falling by the time she neared the entrance to the two-story wood frame structure. She tilted her head back to look up at its plain wooden facade broken only by a modest portico over the front door, and caught sight of Peter who paused on the cobblestone street a short distance away. Snow lay mounded on the brim of his hat.

Elizabeth retraced her steps to stop in front of her dignified chaperone and stamped her foot in anger.

"How dare you follow me?"

Peter pulled the collar of his wool coat up around his neck and looked down at her face that was puckered in indignation.

"Miss Elizabeth, Mr. Edward insisted I accompany you to school. I have done just that and will return to fetch you at day's end." He shifted his weight, shuffling his feet to keep them warm.

"Humph! I need no watchful nurse. If I were a boy, you would not be standing here. I can make my way home alone."

She turned on her heel and with skirts flying hurried into the building.

Peter smiled benignly at her stubborn self-reliance and returned home as Edward had instructed.

Other students had emerged from the now swirling snowfall to converge on the entrance to the academy, the boys' trouser legs flashing as they playfully ran and kicked at each other. While they had seemed to ignore the petite-skirted figure coming toward them from the direction of the Cady home, a few turned to point at her. Elizabeth speculated that they were surprised since girls were rare at school. For them, she reckoned, she would be another source of amusement to tease as she tried to perfect her music and dreaded sewing skills.

As it turned out, she was the only girl studying mathematics, Greek and Latin. The classes were more than Elizabeth expected, though in some ways much less.

"Miss Cady, I see your hand raised there in the back of the room. Are you prepared to recite the Nines? If you have studied that multiplication table as assigned, please come to the front of the room and face the class."

"I am, sir," Elizabeth replied. She rose and felt a spitball hit the back of her neck. When she ignored it, someone giggled.

"I saw that, Mr. Barnaskey. Five minutes," the teacher said, pointing at a chair pushed into a corner of the room. The boy slumped into the seat, his expression belligerent.

"Turn your back to the room Mr. Barnaskey, I do not want to see your face."

The classroom fell silent as Elizabeth began. "Nine times zero is zero, nine times one is nine, nine times two is eighteen..." she only stopped when the teacher held up his hand.

"Thank you, Miss Cady. With that knowledge of multiplication you will make a fine keeper of the household ledgers."

Someone snickered.

When she slid into the chair at her desk, the boy behind her tapped her shoulder and handed her a note.

She unfolded the paper to see a scrawled comment. *"Good for you. Do not let Barnaskey annoy you. He acts like that to everyone who does better than him."* The note bore no signature so she glanced around the classroom to see if someone would acknowledge it. All she saw were the boys' heads down engrossed in their classwork. She had a friend, albeit a reluctant one. The thought of this made her happy.

The few girls at the academy clustered in a little group midday to read aloud from Jane Austen's *Emma* and *Persuasion*. When Elizabeth joined them, they listened enrapt as she read with dramatic emphasis. They told her no one enjoyed the colorful stories so much as when she read the passages in class. And, when the students began their reading of Mary Wollstonecraft Shelley's frightening new book, *Frankenstein*, they shivered with delight when the teacher chose her to read.

Because of her reading skill, the girls accepted her but couldn't understand why she wanted to pursue classes reserved for boys like science and nature study, and history, which she particularly liked.

"Why do that?" one asked. "After all, you will marry soon and need know no more than how to keep a clean and beautiful home and raise your children."

Your husband will take care of the books and his employment will supply the family's finances, other girls assured her.

She knew better. She had seen firsthand the results of this foolish thinking; women who sought her father's help with divorce citing husbands who squandered the family money leaving them abandoned and destitute, proved it.

"I do not want to blindly follow a man's wishes. That would make me a slave to him. I have my own opinions," she responded to a girl's question one day. "If I am educated as a boy and know what they know, I will have the same respect and esteem as a man."

The girl looked uncomfortable, then laughed and ran off, to no surprise. Elizabeth wished all girls thought like she did.

The boys who treated her as an equal at play still refused to accept her knowledge in the classroom. She ignored the slight. She refused to stay quiet during class discussions, much to the amusement of the teacher and frustration of the boys. She studied the Greek and Latin assignments until her recitations were nearly flawless. When called upon to display a complicated arithmetic formula on her slate, her response showed preparation. The boys' taunts hinting that she cheated on exams angered her, but she refused to respond. Finally, the few girls there formed groups that did not include her, chatting about boys and clothes and parties. Elizabeth covered her hurt and loneliness with indifference. She refused to change just to gain friends.

As the days turned into months, her trek to and from school, accompanied by Peter, became commonplace. Carrying books belted by a sturdy leather strap, she welcomed his helping hand and his ready ear as she recounted the events of the day as they trudged home. She would practice Latin recitation aloud, and he would repeat the words after her. Peter learned quickly, and one day Elizabeth ventured to ask him why he did not go to school, too.

"Miss Elizabeth, Negro people cannot go to school. I have been learning though. Ever since my pap brought me here as a boy, Reverend Hosack has been teaching me to read and write. And do sums. I read the Bible every night and I have some books, too."

"That is quite wonderful. The reverend is a good and thorough teacher," she said, looking up at Peter with a big smile.

"I'm grateful to him. What he teaches me is just fine."

"Even so, you're a man. You should be able to go to school just like my brother did. What difference does it make that you are a Negro and he was not? Peter, it isn't fair." Her eyes widened as she looked up at her chaperone's face.

"You can go to school, Miss Elizabeth, and you're learning fine things. And I am very lucky to learn from you, too."

They continued walking in silence for a while before she spoke again.

"Some day I am going to change the laws so that you and I can both go to school as long as we want and nobody can tell us different."

*

November 5, 1828

Dear Diary, snow is falling. Again. My plan is working fine. Father is still not quite the same as before Eleazar died and Mother has turned over running our home to Tryphena. I love my sister but she is more strict than Mother. Edward understands me like Eleazar did. I so appreciate his regard. Tryphena thinks I should be more like Mother, just without the housework or the needlework frame. The girls at school are silly. I much prefer the boys, but they do not accept me. So what. I am smarter than them anyway.

13

December 1829

By her last term at Johnstown Academy, fifteen years old and maturing into a confidant woman, Elizabeth Cady easily captivated the attention of any young man who looked her way or engaged her in conversation. Her curvaceous figure, impish smile and beguiling conversational gambits snared them. No longer obliged to dress like her little sisters, she developed a taste for fine clothes. Twice a year she joined her mother and older sisters in choosing from catalogs offering the latest fashions crafted in Paris and London. Each morning she carefully prepared for her day by arranging her glossy brown hair in the most popular coiffure, then fastening on a necklace and perfect brooch to match her gown. She checked the affect in her looking glass religiously.

She relished the bustle and excitement of activity, now an ever-present force in the Cady household. Especially since her mother would soon deliver another child into the family.

When the baby came into the world, its cries muted and its body weak, the midwife shook her head. Though her elated father named the baby boy Eleazar, it did not live long and joined its brothers in the cemetery. Her mother retired to her room exhausted, in seclusion. When that happened, Judge Cady called the rest of the family into the parlor.

"Children," he said, clapping his hands for attention. "I plead for your cooperation with this yet another upheaval in our family. Until your mother returns to us healthy again, I ask that you support Tryphena and Edward as they manage the day-to-day needs of our family." His voice cracked. "We all grieve the death of your infant brother, but your mother mourns his loss more deeply than any of us."

Elizabeth felt immediate remorse. How selfish she was. This child would have been the son her father wished for. Now, he was gone too. It is the right of women to choose their fates, and yet she discounted her own mother's quiet life of womanhood. God forgive her.

With Tryphena and Edward shouldering new responsibilities and Daniel Eaton, a law student in her father's practice, courting Harriet, Elizabeth was free to indulge her inquisitive nature. After Tryphena reviewed her dreaded needlework she would often challenge her father's law students to debate. The young men respected her father and thus tolerated her intrusions. They grew accustomed to her outspoken remarks but still fell into her verbal traps. The plight of Negroes and the demeaning laws undermining a woman's role in the country were her two favorite topics. The abolition movement, now openly discussed at parties and gatherings of friends, intrigued Elizabeth. She would listen thoughtfully to the discussions and form her own opinions, not yet willing to speak with abandon.

In November, Elizabeth had received a letter from the young Negro man she found hiding in the cellar five years ago.

"Who is Jermain Loguen?" her mother had asked. She handed the letter to Elizabeth, looking puzzled. "I don't believe I know that name."

"A friend from school," Elizabeth had replied. She took the letter to a window and unfolded it.

20 November 1829

Miss Cady,

Please express my gratitude to your father for his efforts on my behalf. I will never forget his kindness or yours.

I traveled far after leaving the warmth of your home and am now in Syracuse. I am an African Methodist Episcopal Zion minister and soon plan to marry.

Your friend, Jermain Loguen

There was no return address on the single sheet of paper. Finding him was an incident still too dangerous to discuss with anyone but her father, and Judge Cady never spoke of it again. Elizabeth refolded the letter and tucked it into her diary.

The sad dilemmas recounted by the women who sought her father's legal advice continued to touch her heart. Each wretched story she heard called attention to the heartless laws that did nothing to protect women. Those issues consistently provoked heated conversations between Elizabeth and any of the law students wishing to take on the daughter of their teacher and mentor.

One student, Henry Bayard, Edward's younger brother, loved to bait Elizabeth with an absurd remark then draw her into a debate which, as an older and more educated person, he would easily win. Although he was the most argumentative of the students, Henry also proved to be the most fair. He would intervene on her behalf if another student, such as Arthur, ignored the tenets of law when debating with Elizabeth. Unmerciful in his good-natured teasing, Henry used humor to distract her when he believed she appeared ready to substantiate her position, especially when his response would demonstrate his mastery of argument. Sometimes she knew to expect his onslaughts, other times he surprised her.

On Christmas Eve 1829, snow fell steadily all night throughout the Mohawk Valley. It blanketed Johnstown, cosseted as it was at the foot of the Adirondack Mountains. Dawn revealed a gray sky and a quiet shimmering white landscape. The incessant rumbling of coaches and wagons delivering holiday packages, smoked turkeys, geese and puddings past the Cady doorstep the previous week had ceased, giving way to holiday enjoyment.

Inside Elizabeth's home, the chaotic scene in the kitchen disrupted the quiet morning. Mrs. Brewster and her kitchen helpers bustled about pulling hot mince tarts out of the oven, chopping fruit for apple brown betty, and showering fried doughnuts with sugar. Green tomato and peach preserves, and catsup that tasted like summer, were brought up from the cellar to serve with smoked ham and boiled potatoes. Near a large platter of fried eggs stood a silver charger bearing a wedge of cheddar cheese. Warm buckwheat pancakes and maple syrup sat beside a steaming pitcher of hot chocolate. The hearty wintry cooking aromas of the breakfast drew the ravenous family to the large dining room table to devour the food in a noisy celebration of holiday expectation and good humor. Judge Cady's law students who had no families nearby joined them for the feast before resuming their work in the judge's office.

In mid-afternoon Madge and Kate returned to their rooms to read or play with new toys, Judge and Mrs. Cady excused themselves to nap, and Harriet and her fiancé, bundled up with mufflers, braved the icy streets for a walk. Edward, Tryphena, and Elizabeth, cozy and comfortable in front of the blazing fireplace, sat in contented silence.

Tryphena worked at her embroidery. Edward leafed through a book of Keats poetry he received from Elizabeth. They shared an interest in the poet's writing.

Elizabeth took the glowing coral necklace and bracelets Edward had picked out for her to the window to examine. They were the color of her cheeks, he said, when she opened the velvet box containing the finest gift she had ever received. On impulse she fastened the necklace, pulled her hand through the circlet of bracelets, and ran off to show her gift to the students. All but Henry turned back to their work after acknowledging her presence.

"Do you not have some new dollies to dress or a book to read?" Henry said, rising to his feet, barely visible behind a stack of books.

"Your teasing will not spoil this morning for me." She pirouetted in front of him, bracelets clicking on her outstretched arms.

Henry took the chance to tease her once again by bringing up the very vexing subject he knew would turn her smile to a frown. "Those trinkets could be mine, you know, if you should become my wife. I could lock them up and you could never use them without my permission. I could even sell them and use the money to buy cigars, and your lovely jewelry would go up in smoke." He laughed along with the other students who stopped their work to listen.

"That may be so for now, Henry, but not for long. When I am older, I am going to Albany to talk to the legislators about that nonsense. They will listen because I am right."

At that moment Edward slipped into the room.

Elizabeth stood toe-to-toe with Henry. "Dissolute husbands throw their wives' dowries into the wind without consideration for their families. Taxes are collected to create colleges that prohibit women from attending." She paused to catch her breath. "Men seek the counsel of their wives in private, but in public treat them as slaves, refusing them a vote on the country's behalf. When the law is changed–" Elizabeth poked her finger into his broad chest as her voice rose forcing him backward. Henry retreated and stumbled, and at that point, Edward laughed.

The two turned in the direction of the sound; Elizabeth stopping mid-sentence.

She faltered and dropped her hand to her side, the argument forgotten as she struggled to recover her composure. She had made points Henry could not dispute. Her arguments about abolition were sound, and the idea that women would someday have a say in their own futures was an opinion for which she would not be discouraged. For the first time, she believed she won an argument with him.

Edward approached his brother and slapped him on the back. "Brother, you have done well arguing the law with my sister-in-law. You are becoming a fine lawyer especially when holding your position against a fifteen-year-old girl. Judge Cady would be proud."

The broad smile on Edward's face took the sting out of his jesting words, but they hit home nonetheless. Henry took a step forward, as if to resume the argument, then winked at Elizabeth and turned back to his books.

For Elizabeth, Edward's comment created a different impact. Was he defending or mocking her? The uncertainty made her uncomfortable. She had grown increasingly fond of Edward in the months following his move into the house. Her parents welcomed his attentiveness to her welfare and that of her sisters, but Elizabeth began to suspect his main concern lay hidden. Often, she would catch him looking at her in a bemused way, causing her to turn away from him, her cheeks hot. His attentiveness became a disquieting aspect of this attraction—one that both excited and alarmed her.

*

December 27, 1829

Dear Diary, a lot of things have changed. When I return to the academy in January, it will be for the last time. In September I hope to attend Union, the same college as Eleazar went to. I know I am smart enough. I have asked Father and he said he will talk to me about it later. I think that is a good omen. I got in an argument with Henry Bayard. He is cunning and goads me. I showed him by tripping him up through his own argument. He is 22 and I am 15. Ha! Edward heard us and I became embarrassed. He did not laugh at me though and took my side. He is so charming and fine. My sister is lucky to be his wife.

14

January 1830

The routine of daily classwork became familiar as Elizabeth anticipated graduation from the academy in the spring. The studying that earned her a position at the head of the class required a daunting schedule, so for this last year she pushed all other interests out of her mind. No longer a familiar figure in her father's law library nor available to accompany her little sisters on their adventures, she concentrated all of her efforts on school.

Her desire to excel beyond her father's expectations influenced everything she did and she made progress. Still, she realized she needed one single achievement to prove she was equal to her brother.

When the Johnstown Academy language instructor announced the competition for two highly prized awards for excellence in Greek, the boys in her class crowded around the information posted on a wall in the library. Jostling and teasing each other as they intently read the rules, they ignored her as she studied the text from the back of the group.

That's it, Elizabeth thought after analyzing the importance of the prize. If I can win one of those prizes, Father will see that I am just as good as Eleazar.

Her enormous determination kept her focused. She often visited Reverend Hosack after his tutelage ended, and she knew he would be the one to help her win this coveted prize. She turned away from the knot of boys clustered around the contest posting to see Walter Barnaskey eyeing her.

"Lib, my pretty little classmate, what are you doing here? Planning the party to celebrate my win of the top Greek prize?" Walter's laugh echoed in the hallway. "Everyone will surely want to pat me on the back and present their regards. Do you not agree?" A hard edge in his voice belied his absolute intent to triumph.

Elizabeth looked at the boy thinking carefully about her reply. She didn't much like his behavior in school, as he reminded her of the loutish Arthur who studied with her father. With black hair sticking out at all angles and a complexion mostly red from bluster and outdoor games, Walter often bullied weaker students into submission to make sure he stayed at the top of the class.

"We shall see who has the party, for I am entering the contest, too," Elizabeth said, smiling at him in the sweetest way possible. She didn't expect an explicit challenge and continued to smile as an expression of disbelief knotted his brow.

"You do not fool me. No girl has ever tried for the Greek prizes and it's impossible that she would win if she did. My pretty Elizabeth, do not vex yourself with this notion. Demur gracefully and I will forget this silly nonsense."

Walter stood back, arms crossed over his chest with an expression of derision.

"We shall see," Elizabeth said then turned and walked away as the sounds of the boys' laughter and scornful taunts followed her down the hall and out the door. Winning the competition motivated her, but her goal was to prove her worth to her father. Achieving that would be her reward.

Reverend Hosack welcomed her return to his study with delight. However, in the three years following their initial lessons, the cleric had become ill. Confined to his home now, having Elizabeth by his side sharing his passion for Greek once again as they studied brightened his days and his outlook.

"I have copies of old exam papers from previous competitions," he told her and bent to drag a wooden box from under his desk. "Help me child," he asked, gesturing for her to lift the box onto the desktop. He pulled a key from the pocket of his frock coat and fit it into the lock. When the lid sprang open, Elizabeth looked inside to discover Johnstown Academy exam tests as recent as the previous year.

She pulled the yellowing sheaves of exam papers from the box and spread them on the desk. "Oh my, here is one with my beloved brother's name," she said.

"I expect the test will be similar," Reverend Hosack said. "So, we can use your brother's exams and the newest copies to review until I am sure you are ready."

She nodded, never taking her eyes from her brother's handwriting.

"Ádikon tò lúein toùs phílous ekousíōs," she read aloud, her expression growing puzzled. "Reverend Hosack, I think my brother made a mistake here."

"Let's see," he said peering close to the exam paper, eyes wide through the lens of his magnifying glass.

Before he could speak Elizabeth said, "It should read, ádikon tò lupeîn toùs phílous ekousíōs. *It is unjust to harm one's friends willfully,* a quote from Menander. The verb *lúein* means *to free*, not *to harm*, which is *lupeîn*. My brother made an error," she continued, "and on such a well-known phrase, too." Elizabeth smiled. Her father thought Eleazar was so smart. He was wrong. She snatched the exam from the cleric's hands, confused by the surge of betrayal she felt. She looked away from him, tears filling her eyes.

"Perfectly understandable, Elizabeth," Reverend Hosack said, handing her a clean white handkerchief.

"Thank you sir," she said, her voice soft. "It's just...I miss him. He would want the best for me, and yet I compete with him...my dead brother. How evil am I?"

"It is a natural reaction. Evil has nothing to do with it. You demonstrate a competitive urge, as do all who wish to succeed. Do not be dismayed. Shall we continue?"

When she nodded and blew her nose, Reverend Hosack adjusted his glasses and cleared his throat.

"You may be asked to translate that phrase on the exam," he said. "It's to your credit you noticed, my dear. Remember that."

"The exam is in two weeks, so I will come here every day after school for an hour, on Saturday after breakfast and on Sunday after church. Will that be all right with you?"

"It will indeed, child. I look forward to your company. I plan to be as hard on you as I believe your academy instructor will be." Reverend Hosack sounded gruff but his eyes twinkled.

The next day she all but ran to Reverend Hosack's home, arriving out of breath ready to begin reviewing her knowledge of Greek. A fire burned in the grate and a pot of hot chocolate stood at the ready. His beloved worn Greek texts were piled beside his chair.

The reverend picked up Elizabeth's copy of Buttmann's *Greek Grammar for the use of schools* and began to thumb through the pages. Stopping on one page and raising an eyebrow he said, "Recite for me the paradigm of the second nominal declension, using the word *lógos*."

Elizabeth's confidence rose as she fell into the steady rhythm of the recitation: "*lógos, lógou, lógōi, lógon, lóge, lógoi, lógōn, lógois, lógous, lógoi.*"

"Is that all?" inquired the reverend.

"Yes. That paradigm is easy."

"Wrong."

"What did I miss?" Elizabeth said, caught off guard.

"The dual. You recited only the singular and plural forms. But you are likely to meet dual forms in Homer in the exam, do you not think?" The cleric's firm tone challenged her. "The form is *lógō* in the nominative, accusative, and vocative dual; *lógoin* in the genitive and dative. Now recite."

Elizabeth set to reciting the paradigm, this time making sure to quote the dual forms before passing to the plural.

"Very well," the reverend said. "Now let me hear you recite the forms of the perfect subjunctive active of the verb *lúein.*"

She closed her eyes, searching her memory for the paradigm: "*lelúkō, lelúkēis, lelúkēi...*" passing from the singular of the first, second, and third persons to the plural. Then with a sudden outburst, "Oh, and the dual forms are all the same: *lelúkēton.*" With that last form she fell silent, venturing the slightest smile.

"Have you anything to add?"

"In addition to the dual?"

"That certainly cannot be all. What about the periphrastic forms? Based on the perfect active participle?"

"I'm afraid I haven't come across those forms," Elizabeth said.

"Well then, now we know where our studies shall begin."

She sighed. "You are right, sir," she said. "If I am not letter perfect, then I should not expect a reward." She picked up the grammar book and began to read, desperately trying to stuff as much information into her head as possible. Her eyesight had begun to glaze over by the time Reverend Hosack knocked the fireplace shovel against the grate signaling the time for her departure. She rushed home arriving just in time to hang her shawl on a hook and slip into her chair at the dinner table. When her mother looked up with a questioning expression, Elizabeth merely smiled, and unfolded her napkin on her lap.

*

May 14, 1830

Dear Diary, None of the boys think I can win a Greek prize, but I do. They make such fun of me, but I care less. The other girls do not even try. They are pretty and some of them are very nice, but none are interested in competing for anything besides housewifely tasks. That nasty Walter Barnaskey thinks he can win everything just because he is a boy. I challenged him and he laughed. I fear I will not learn all the conjugations and paradigms, but I must. Studying is very difficult. At least it is not needlework.

When she burst through Reverend Hosack's door after the awards were announced to say she took the second prize, he beamed, overcome with happiness. "Oh, my dear student, I am so deeply proud of you," he said, his eyes tearing up with delight.

"I missed first prize by two points. A boy I hardly know won. At least it wasn't Walter Barnaskey, who immediately argued that someone must have cheated. What nonsense."

After she'd discussed the exam with the patient cleric, Elizabeth ran home to tell her father. She rushed into his office breathless and placed the prize, a new Greek Testament, squarely on his desk.

"Father, I won second prize!" She stood beside him gazing at him with expectation. Now he must tell her she is equal to Eleazar.

Judge Cady took the book in his hands, thumbed the pages idly, and then handed it back to her. "Did you have difficulty with the examination, my dear? And your teachers, were they thorough?" He seemed more interested in the process than her prize. "How did they conduct the competition? Were there spectators?"

She answered his questions expecting that his next words would confirm her accomplishment; that she excelled as well as a son would have.

Judge Cady kissed her on the forehead, sighed then said, "Ah, the prize should have gone to a boy."

Stunned, she had no response. What else could she do to gain her father's favor? Would she always be relegated to less than her brother, or for that matter, any man?

He turned back to his work.

She left with her beautiful face set, fighting back tears. Clutching the prized Greek Testament in her arms Elizabeth ran into the back garden to collapse onto a bench weeping.

Edward discovered her there.

Her brother-in-law took his new role as master of the house seriously. Overseeing the care of the horses and other livestock, the orchards and gardens as well as the upkeep of the carriages and coaches now fell to him. By relieving his father-in-law of these tasks he repaid him for the legal education he obtained under his guidance. He welcomed the opportunity to fulfill his obligations. Edward had spent the morning riding the perimeter of the Cady property, checking fence rails and walls for repairs. His wife's demands for routine household timeliness made him attentive to her schedules. He now returned for supper, dusty and warm after stabling his horse.

He strode along the back garden path with the sound of gravel crunching under his boots and Mourning doves calling to each other in the balmy early evening. When he passed the herb garden he paused to follow a path in the direction of a muffled noise.

"Are you all right?" he asked Elizabeth, rushing to kneel on the path before her. She raised her tear-stained face, her mouth quivering.

"Oh, Edward. It is for nothing. I have studied so hard, and father does not care." Her eyes were rimmed with red and she clutched a balled up lace handkerchief in her hand. When she tried to rise to greet him, the Testament fell from her grasp onto the gravel path. Dismissing it, she sank back onto the bench.

Edward picked up the book and placed it beside her. He seemed unable to take his eyes from her distraught face and took her hands in his and pulled her to her feet.

She looked up at him, hoping for solace and reassurance, her cheeks and mouth flushed from crying. He seemed to fumble for the perfect sentiment needed to console her.

"Ah, Lib," he said his voice almost a whisper, "your achievements are glorious. They belong to you. No one else matters. Your father is pleased, but he grieves still for Eleazar." He pulled her closer to his chest, his face inches from hers. Edward spoke with such conviction that Elizabeth could hear only his words. The sounds of fluttering leaves, bird song and bees buzzing among the flowers grew faint. Edward's voice sounded like soothing music and she could feel the sadness and disappointment of the day fall away like a heavy cloak. His warm, brown eyes looked deep into hers and she became conscious of his slender fingers wrapped around her hands, holding them close to the lapels of the long gabardine coat he wore to ride. The setting sun glinted off his sandy blond hair, turning it gold and illuminating the dust of the day on his broad shoulders. Elizabeth felt her knees begin to wobble and her face redden as with embarrassment. She tried to speak, but words failed.

Edward said something she did not hear. When he gently brushed her brow with his lips and dropped her hands to step back and retrieve the forgotten Greek Testament from the bench, his grave expression surprised her. His hands shook as he handed her the book.

"Tryphena will be calling us to supper soon, Lib. Let's not anger her by arriving late." Edward turned toward the house and began walking.

Confused and uncertain about what had just occurred, Elizabeth slowly followed him.

*

June 3, 1830

Dear Diary, Bah! I won second prize. Reverend Hosack wept. Father didn't care. I do not know how to please him. I am smart and curious, but he does not value that because I am a girl. Only Edward understands me.

15

October 1830

When Elizabeth's male classmates at Johnstown started planning the next step in their education–leaving home to attend Union College–she planned, too. The opportunity to study where Eleazar and Edward had, beyond the confines of Johnstown tutors and schools, became an exhilarating prospect.

Judge Cady's matter-of-fact response had dashed her hopes. "No women allowed Lib. That's the rule," he said. "Union College is an all male school. Besides what more do you need to learn? Stay here and copy papers for my clerks and attend circuit court with me. That should keep you busy. There are the balls and dinners, too. You'll be attending many now that you will be courted. And of course you can learn how to keep house and make puddings."

"I cannot believe this. You have always encouraged my learning," she said. "If I were a boy, as you so often remind me, there would be no question. Why is it different for a girl?

Why, Father?" Mortified and angry that the dreadful rules again excluded her she found herself nearly speechless.

"I have no say over this, Daughter."

"I imagine there will be no Negro people at Union College either. Male or female." She felt the stirrings of anger and frustration, now becoming familiar. "This is unfair. I have studied well, reached the top of my class at the academy, and for what?" Elizabeth continued, ignoring the expression of warning on her father's face. "To copy papers? Make puddings? I think not. And I'm not interested in being courted, either." Her face clouded in indignation.

"Elizabeth," her father finally said, rising to his feet, "you forget yourself."

She fled from her father's office, fighting back tears, embarrassed that the law students heard her outburst—something else to tease her about. She ran down the hallway and collided with Edward at the bottom of the stairs.

"What's this? Oh, do not cry. Whatever is the matter?" He started to embrace her shuddering body, but stopped to hold her at arms length.

Sniffling, she wiped her eyes with a handkerchief, and looked up at him. "It is no different than before, Edward," she cried. "I cannot continue my education. Union College forbids girls. Even if those were the rules, he could ask them to make a change. He is important. They would listen to him." She began to calm down, but the sadness of her poignant resignation seemed to touch Edward.

"Perhaps there is something I can do. If you will let me try?"

She didn't believe his attempts to convince her father would change his mind. Maybe her father could ask Union College to make an exception. He has influence, so perhaps Edward's arguments would be more convincing. "Please help," she said. "I welcome any agreement with my father to let me continue my education. He believes further schooling for girls is pointless and I know it is not. I must go on." On impulse, she fervently grasped his hands between hers and touched his fingertips to her lips.

Edward recoiled at the gesture and stepped back, his face reddening. Within seconds he composed himself. "I will speak to him tonight," he assured her, and appearing shaken by his unexpected response to her innocent kiss, left her there.

After supper that night, Judge Cady called his children into the library. After kissing each of his five daughters, he stood before them with Edward by his side.

"Children, Elizabeth will be leaving us next month to attend Troy Female Seminary."

Elizabeth gasped and clapped a hand over her mouth then rushed to throw her arms around him. She had been so focused on following in her brother's footsteps she had not considered the legendary all-women college at all. Her heart thudded with excitement. "Oh, Father, thank you so very much. You will not regret this decision," she said.

Harriet, Madge and Kate ran to their sister and embraced her.

"How wonderful for you," Harriet exclaimed, grasping her sister's hands tightly in her own. For her, betrothal to Daniel Eaton meant marriage in the spring. She expressed no interest in education beyond her books of poetry and household ledgers.

"But what will we do without you?" Madge said, her voice breaking. "Who will lead us on adventures?"

"I do not want you to go," shouted Kate. "No, no, no! Mrs. Yost will make us practice our letters all the time now and without you here to distract her, I shall cry constantly." And as predicted, tears welled up in her eyes and began to slide down her cheeks.

Elizabeth placed her arms around her younger sisters, holding them close. "Please do not be sad. I will be home often. I will write you wonderful long letters filled with amazing stories for you to share, and I promise to reserve all of next summer for our usual exploits."

Her sisters seemed somewhat appeased and, as Elizabeth watched, Madge stepped into the role of big sister, soothing Kate as *she* once had.

After the commotion subsided, Elizabeth sought her father. She found him in the library seated in a wing chair staring out the window, an open book on his lap. A fire blazed in the brick fireplace, warming and lighting the room with a golden glow. She approached the chair to sit at his feet on a low hassock and lean her face against his knee. For a while the total quiet, save for the snapping of burning logs, served her well. When she broke the silence, she did so with passion. "I do thank you for allowing me to continue my studies. I want more than anything to make you happy and know how difficult this decision must be." She paused and then plunged on, expressing the words hiding in her heart for so long. "Girls should go to school too, and Negro people as well," she said. "Our bodies are different, but our brains are alike. I will make you proud, father, I will, I will." Near tears, she looked up into her father's face hoping for a flicker of approval.

"I know you are trying to take Eleazar's place. You cannot. You will never be a boy. Laws exist that will not let you gain esteem equal to a man no matter how much you strive." To soften the content of his words, he reached down and stroked her hair. "Nowhere are women's roles defined differently. This is not like the abolition of slavery that has support in many quarters. You think I can help change these laws, but I do not have that power. When I tell you I wish you had been born a boy, it is not because I don't think you are clever or intelligent, it is just that I know the barriers you face and that I cannot tear them down for you," her father's voice broke. Elizabeth reached for his hand to squeeze it. "But Father, you are powerful and respected."

"My wonderful and persistent daughter. Protest the laws to change them. That is something you can do. When you are older, many changes will have occurred. History provides that insight. Go to Albany and speak to the legislature. But for now, you can thank Edward again for pleading your case. He is your champion, not me. Make him proud and I will be pleased he convinced me to change my mind." Judge Cady kissed her on the top of her head, patted her shoulder, and turned back to his book.

For the first time, Elizabeth recognized the limits of her father's powerful influence. He didn't wish for another son, but for her to be treated equally. Why had he not told her sooner? Perhaps his lawyer's demeanor prevented him? That was it, she decided.

*

November 1, 1830

Dear Diary, I have been too busy to write lately. I thought I would be at Union College by now, but no. I do not think that is the least bit fair. Once again dear Edward pled my case so I am moving on. I am so indebted to him I can barely look at his handsome face for crying in gratitude.

16

November 1830

"This is Miss Elizabeth Cady, ladies. She has just joined us from Johnstown. Please make her welcome," said Mrs. Emma Willard, founder of Troy Female Seminary. She personally escorted Elizabeth to her first class. Entering at mid-term did not often happen, she told her. Elizabeth said that her parents were reluctant to send her until she had exhausted the pastimes available to her at home.

"I'm glad to have my mind busy with something important again," she said.

When she and Mrs. Willard entered the class in progress, the girls were reading their Latin textbooks to themselves.

In unison, the girls looked up, smiled, and replied,

"Welcome, Elizabeth."

She smiled and nodded before sliding into an empty chair behind a desk at the back of the room. She removed her Latin book from its leather strap and placed it before her then looked around at her fellow students.

Almost alike in their unfashionable ugly dresses made from gingham, calico print, or crepe without lace or jewelry, the girls' clothes followed the prescribed uniform directed by the school catalog. In her own blue gingham gown her mother's seamstress had labored over, complaining about the lack of trimming or ruffles, Elizabeth felt at home at once. Apart from this introduction, her inauspicious arrival midterm went unremarked. Few accommodations remained in the residence hall when she arrived with her trunks, which Peter dragged up the stairs.

"Where you want these, Miss Elizabeth?" he asked.

She stood in the doorway surveying the six by nine foot room void of decoration and shook her head.

She shook her head. "Not much space, I'd say." Like the dresses, the intent of the plain walls intended to foster uniformity and permitted unfettered concentration on study. A narrow wooden frame bed covered by a well-washed gray quilt dominated one long wall. Above it, a framed print of the Troy Female Seminary Rules reminded the resident of proper conduct. The opposite wall held a shallow bureau for clothes, a tiny writing desk with drawers, a chair, shelves for books, and a peg lamp filled with oil.

"Push the two big trunks back into the hallway, Peter. You will have to take them back with you. Leave the smaller red leather one in the middle of the room. That's all I need. Someone here will store it for me after I unpack." The window across the room from the door looked out over the street and the broad green of Congress Park. Elizabeth pushed the sash up and poked her head out to take a deep breath then slammed it shut.

"Oh, my goodness, it is growing cold." She shivered and rubbed her hands to warm them.

Beneath the window stood a small table with a looking glass along with a chamber set for washing up and late night emergencies. There was no place to store additional clothing. No sooner did she dispatch Peter downstairs with the two trunks filled with party dresses and extra clothing she would not need, a knock at the door interrupted her unpacking.

"Halloo!" trilled a petite dark-haired girl, rushing into the room in a swish of skirts. "I'm Amy Lee! Oh, your room is just like mine. They are just the dreariest of places. I've added some color. Makes it feel more like home. I brought too many clothes too, and sent some back," she said. "I saw your driver taking your trunks back down the hallway."

She paused, out of breath.

"I'm Elizabe–"

Before she could say her name the vivacious visitor continued. "I know who you are, and who your daddy is, and where you come from, and all of that. You are Elizabeth Cady, and you took the second place Greek Prize at Johnstown. Why, we all know who you are." Her bright eyes quickly took in everything in the room as she sat down with a bounce on the bed and smoothed her skirt across her knees. She looked up at Elizabeth who stood gaping at her.

"Well, hello, Amy Lee. I'm pleased to make your acquaintance. I cannot say I know anything about you, or the other girls for that matter." Flustered, she realized her comment was unnecessary. Clearly everyone knew she arrived midterm. Before she could think of anything else to say, the girl slid off the bed to peer out the window and continued chirping in her high, bird voice.

"Do you not just hate the dresses? They are dreadful and we all look alike." At this she bent to inspect her face in the looking glass. "Do you know there are boys nearby? Yes, at Rensselaer. And they are so charming and clever, and rich," she said with emphasis. She paused to catch her breath then continued. "I'm not here to learn anything, just to find a husband." Her words continued at a dizzying pace. "Since we have social gatherings with the boys from Rensselaer and Union College, my parents insisted this would be the best way to meet them before my coming out party." Amy Lee sat down on the bed again and began to tap her feet on the floor. "Why did you come mid-term?"

"I just turned sixteen," Elizabeth replied.

"Oh. Are you coming out? I do not know if they do that in Johnstown. We do in Albany." She jumped up to lift one of Elizabeth's combs to inspect its silver handle. She replaced it and kept talking. "I'm related to Governor Throop and he is so impor–"

The girl's shrill tone grated. Not wanting to seem inhospitable Elizabeth broke into Amy Lee's nonstop commentary. "Forgive me, I am so tired, and tomorrow is my first full day of classes. Please excuse me while I finish unpacking and get some rest." She placed her arm around her visitor's shoulders and guided her to the door.

"Oh, well. I'll see you tomorrow at breakfast in the dining hall. If I get there first I will save you a chair by mine. Ta, ta."

Amy Lee scampered off as quickly as she arrived, leaving Elizabeth feeling she'd been caught up in a whirlwind. "Good gracious," she said aloud. "I do not know if I can abide this all girl school if the other students are like her." Oh my, what if they are?

*

November 20, 1830

Dear Diary, I am at a college where no boys are allowed. Hah. We call it 'Emma Willard' after the lovely woman who decided girls should have an opportunity to learn to do more than be a housewife. No dreaded needlework here. Oh joy! Not even much work tidying my clothes. I have so few to keep up. I miss my family, especially Madge and Kate. I did not expect to be so lonely. My room is dreadfully bleak with not much to break its dreary existence. It is as sad and gray as I am.

"Heads out!" a girl shouted. At the familiar cry, windows flew open and the sound of rustling petticoats and soft-soled shoes echoed like a rushing wind in the residence hall of the Seminary.

Elizabeth looked out her window at the street below.

"What's going on?" she asked of a passing girl, expecting to see a giraffe or some other wonder from Barnum's museum.

"It's boys! Do you see them down there?" The girl pointed at a group of young men from nearby Rensselaer Polytechnic Institute gathered to raucously serenade anyone who would pay them attention.

To no one's surprise the residence hall matron scurried outside to shoo the Rensselaer students away.

"Oh, is that all? I've seen boys all my life," Elizabeth said.

An all girls' school didn't present the challenges she had experienced at Johnstown Academy. There were strict rules at Troy Female Seminary forbidding contact with unrelated males. However, despite her distain for the novelty of serenading male students, she missed the company of boys, if for no other reason than the conversation gambits. Casual discussions with her classmates never extended far beyond fashions and who had the most social invitations. To make up for it, by spring when she finished the term, she'd found a way around the rule and through planned social engagements with Rensselaer students acquired quite a number of new "brothers" and "cousins". Soon letters and an occasional social call from her former classmates at Johnstown also brightened her day. At first they were polite. Letters from those boys however, began to take on an intimate nature that she did not encourage. "If you cannot contain your information to news of the school and Johnstown," she wrote to some in an attempt to rebuff them, "I thank you to cease your correspondence." She suspected they were only writing to seek favor with her because of her father. When she told them courtship held no interest for her right now, the letters stopped.

*

November 27, 1830

Dear Diary, I think it might have been easier if I had come at the beginning of the school year instead of mid-term. These girls are very different–so taken with the boys from the engineering school nearby. Apparently the boys tease the girls and they tease back. That is not for me. That is just not what I do. Most of the girls come here to meet husbands. Most? I am not sure how this works.

17

January 1831

Soon the uncertainty of living in an environment without her family became commonplace and Elizabeth settled into a routine. It neither pleased nor vexed her, but it certainly did not become a lifestyle she would choose. Now so busy with classes in algebra, Greek and music, she ignored her correspondence and realized she had forgotten to write to her family for two weeks. She now sat at her desk staring out at the snow-covered landscape, a sheet of paper before her. The black and spindly trees against the white snowdrifts merging with a lowering gray sky created a melancholy mood she could not dispel. Ah, for the comforts of home. She blew on her fingertips to warm her hands then dipped her pen in the inkwell.

"January 15, 1831

My Dearest Tryphena, please forgive the tardiness of this letter. I am becoming accustomed to the early hours and boarding schedule. We rise at half past five and retire at ten, but I fear I still do not feel rested and am constantly hungry. The food is dreadful and without imagination. It's corned beef, and liver–you know how I detest that-and bread pudding with little sugar."

What else to write about? She needed very little more than food. She particularly missed sweets, candy being rare.

"Please do ask Mrs. Brewster to bake a pie in a square tin, put it in the bottom of a box, then fill it up with sweets and some apples, for we never get any. We cannot buy them for we are marked down if we go to a grocery shop. Send my red wool cape and hat with the fur trim. Just those things, for I have no room for more dresses, and send the food. My classes are going well. Greek and algebra are quite easy for me and I am enjoying the music instruction that for now requires me to learn dancing steps and singing. Another girl accompanies me on the guitar. The cold and drafty rooms have brought on sickness among many of the girls. Sore throats being their greatest discomfort. I hope I shall not be sick, as it means a visit from old Dr. Willard who obliges us to take medicine. I am keeping warm though, eating porridge for breakfast and venturing out with other girls for brisk walks at six in the evening when it is not snowing, so do not worry about me. Please give my regards to father and mother, and kiss Madge and Kate for me.

Your devoted sister, Elizabeth"

There, that should do it. She folded the crisp writing paper, wrote the address on the front, sealed the flap with wax and her brass initial stamp and took the letter down to the headmistress for mailing. Her stomach rumbled. Tea would be served in an hour, so with her Greek course work due tomorrow far from complete, she opened the textbook, pulled her wool shawl closer and began to read. Her sister might wonder why she did not ask after Edward, but she dared not. Instead she contented herself to recall the warmth of his touch that day in the garden.

*

January 15, 1831

Dear Diary, after Christmas I am falling back into a familiar routine. I do not like the food here. I eat it, but it is not like the food at home. I miss Mrs. Brewster's cooking and Mother's pies. I wonder how Edward is and if he misses our talks. One thing I did not tell you is that no Negro girl students are here. I heard about a girls' school for Negroes, but do not know where it is. None of the girls want to talk about that. Even when we read history and discuss what we learned, the girls do not seem interested. They ask no questions as I do. I think my teachers may be annoyed at me for that. My classmates do not seem to care that laws prevent women from holding property or even for keeping their dowries if they divorce. It is foolish of them I think, for these girls seek husbands. I must close now as I have studying to do for a morning class.

18

February 1831

Elizabeth's attitude about study marked her as a loner. Being younger than most of the other students also set her apart. Deep into the doldrums of late winter, with the scratching of her pen the only sound in the room, she finished an English composition then took it to the window to read aloud in the afternoon's fading light. The assignment was to describe her room. She thought it ridiculous.

"*Dull, dull gray, like the gloom of a cold winter day,*" Oh that rhymes," she muttered, then crossed out *day* and changed it to "*night blankets the bed with its linens and wool.* "Not again." She crossed out *blanket* and continued reading, "*and quilt adding lumps like piles of dirty snow. To lie abed staring at the rules adds somber depression to the area,*" she continued. "*I fear my dresses, my shoes, my skin and hair will grow as gray as this room and reflect an image of an old woman in my looking glass.*" She continued in this vein then paused to nibble on the end of her pen, overwhelmed by the sadness that filled her composition.

"Good gracious," she cried in disgust then crumpled the paper and began to write again, this time with humor and droll sarcasm. She spread the pages across her desk to dry when a knock at the door then a girl's voice called from the hallway.

"Can I come in, Lizzy?" Winnie Devereux said.

Elizabeth flung the door open. "I'm just finished with my composition," she said, gathering up the sheets of paper into a stack.

"May I read it?" Winnie asked.

Elizabeth handed her the composition then sat down on the edge of her bed to watch her classmate's reaction. A popular girl like Winnie never visited her. When Winnie began to laugh so hard she wiped her eyes on her apron, Elizabeth knew she'd succeeded. Perhaps Winnie might be a new friend.

"Oh! Lizzy this is so fine. Please do switch compositions with me, will you?" Winnie said. "I do not have a lovely way with words as you do."

"Switch?"

"Why, yes. I will turn in your paper you turn in mine. It is done all the time between us girls."

No one ever complimented Elizabeth on her writing. So, flattered by the enthusiastic praise, she agreed.

"Here is my essay," Winnie said, drawing it from her composition book. "Thank you ever so much," she said as she replaced it with Elizabeth's pages and started for the door.

"Can you stay and chat awhile?" Elizabeth asked.

Winnie looked back. "Perhaps another time," she said.

When Elizabeth read her classmate's composition she realized her mistake. The text was error-free, but lacked imagination. Nothing even close to what she had written.

The day after the essays were turned in, the girls filed into the classroom in a noisy din of laughter. They took their seats and looked at the teacher for instruction.

"Young ladies I have selected a few of the compositions to be read aloud. First, Miss Devereaux."

Winnie's eyes sparkled as she took center stage at the front of the room. Soon the entire class reeled with laughter and clapped with enthusiasm when she finished.

Winnie returned to her desk and leaned across the aisle from Elizabeth to pat her hand and wink. Elizabeth smiled politely.

"Miss Cady? Please let us hear what you wrote," the teacher said.

No sooner had she begun reading the composition from her book, with its dull and boring language, than another of the students fled from the room and returned with her own composition book. The girl flipped the cover open and laid it in front of the teacher, tapping her finger on it with an angry expression on her face.

"Miss Cady, please come to my desk at once," the teacher said.

The woman turned the composition book around for Elizabeth to see then asked, "Please explain how your composition found itself in this book." Both the teacher and the student looked at Elizabeth with contempt.

"I, I have no explanation," she said.

When the teacher shook her head in disgust, Elizabeth ran from the classroom, too distraught for tears. Once she reached the safety of her own room, she closed the door and flung herself on her bed. *It was not Winnie's composition after all. She stole it from someone else and said she wrote it, all while lying to me. This is horrible, egregious behavior. She is not the friend I thought she could be. Will I be sent home in shame?*

To her surprise a knock on her door announced Winnie who rushed in, her expression apologetic.

Instinctively Elizabeth drew back. What new trick could she expect?

"You were so brave not to betray me," Winnie said. "I could not endure the questioning. I am not as clever as you Lizzy. Promise you will not tell Mrs. Willard for she will surely expel me," Winnie continued, throwing her arms around Elizabeth in a passionate embrace. Her tearful voice melted Elizabeth's heart.

The next day the English composition teacher asked Elizabeth to stay after class. "Miss Cady, I am determined to sort out how it is you turned in a fellow student's composition as your own."

"Yes, Ma'am." Elizabeth's hands began to perspire. She searched her apron pockets for a handkerchief but found none.

The teacher placed two compositions on the desk then turned them so Elizabeth could read the names at the top.

"You see that each has a different author's name?" The teacher tapped her finger on Elizabeth's name at the top of the paper. "Yet the handwriting is identical. How did this happen?"

"We agreed to exchange."

"So whose composition did Miss Devereaux read?"

"Mine," Elizabeth said.

"Do you have it?"

"Yes Ma'am." Elizabeth pulled her original composition from her writing portfolio.

The English teacher glanced at the proffered composition then nodded. "Did you know she copied the one you read from another student?"

"No." Elizabeth's heart began to flutter, as a captured bird's seeking to fly.

"Would you have remained silent?"

"Yes, Ma'am." Elizabeth wiped her hands on her apron, grateful for the rough cotton against her damp skin.

"Did Miss Devereaux request that you do so?" the teacher asked, puzzled.

"Yes, Ma'am" Elizabeth said, her eyes downcast. Winnie's pleading expression mocked her confession.

The teacher rose from her chair and placed her palms on the desk. She leaned forward. "Look at me," she said.

Elizabeth complied, only to hear the teacher say, "I am both ashamed of you and disappointed in you. Complicity in such a deceitful act betrays my assessment of your character." She closed both composition books and handed Elizabeth hers with a dismissive gesture. "Leave," she said.

When Winnie finally stood before the entire student body to confess her deceit, not only did she suffer, but Elizabeth did as well. She felt remorse, not for herself but for Winnie. Worse, failing to live up to the expectations of a favorite teacher left her grieving. She learned a hard lesson about false friends. Having never experienced boundless appreciation for her achievements in a home where flattery is discouraged, Elizabeth learned that this was her weakness.

*

February 21, 1831
Dear Diary, I am in so much trouble I fear I may be expelled. I cannot forgive myself for this error in judgment. If Mrs. Willard reports me to Father I shall surely be sent home. I deserve it too. I am so sorry for what I did. I hope my other instructors know I do not regularly cheat. I love Emma Willard and the courses here. I cannot go home. Oh my, what have I done?

Distrusting of her schoolmates now, she'd grown to believe they were not who they appeared to be. Among strangers instead of her unconditionally loving sisters and her elegant, truthful mother, Elizabeth became lonelier. She took the classes designed to make sure the girls received a customary education for women, but she detected underlying forces throughout suggesting a more assertive role and celebration of power and intelligence. Being encouraged to speak freely by the instructors and to argue points of view was invigorating. Some of the girls spoke in such quiet plaintive voices they were urged to speak louder while making their points. As a result the ensuing debates became vigorous and exciting. So far, Reverend Hosack, Edward and, of course, Mrs. Willard cheered intellectual development, but was argument for her, too? She lived for the classroom give and take of ideas and controversy, so she decided to ignore the pettiness and gossiping of her classmates and concentrate on her schoolwork. She'd already studied arithmetic, geometry, chemistry, botany and algebra, and Greek at which she excelled, so she focused on logic, criticism and writing. With these courses her ability to debate became sharply honed. Without boys in the classes, however, discussions often took a different tack. Not always pleasant either. Sometimes there were tears. She learned to be ruthless in debate, but not mean-spirited.

"Please, Lizzy, do tell us about your beau at home," Amy Lee asked one day on their way to the dining room. She'd linked her arm through Elizabeth's and leaned in close. "Is he handsome? Rich? Very accomplished? Does he want lots of children? I do think those traits are important, do you not?"

At that, Winnie, who trailed behind them, ran forward as if to listen.

"I'm not interested in beaus right now. I do think intelligence is more important than any of those attributes, though," Elizabeth said.

"You are such a dear friend," Amy Lee said. "I can always depend on you for clever and thoughtful answers to my questions."

The girls surrounding Winnie laughed, one trying to talk over the other.

"Young ladies, we all have the right to our opinions and must respect each other. Is that clear?" said the teacher accompanying them.

"Yes Miss," Amy Lee said, her face turning bright red.

Outside the dining room Winnie added what Elizabeth believed to be an attempt at her own clever response. "Elizabeth holds herself in such high regard, I doubt she even knows what a boy is for anyway."

The voices of her classmates once again rang with laughter, making Elizabeth long for the honest opinions of the young men who clerked for her father. Girls and boys should go to school together. If that were allowed, silly conversations like the one that just transpired would not occur, she believed.

Amy Lee pushed through the crowd of girls filing into the dining room to put her arm around Elizabeth's waist and pull her away. "Lizzy, do not let mean old Winnie vex you. She's just jealous that's all." Her guileless smile warmed Elizabeth. She and Amy Lee had become fast friends in the weeks following that first visit. The girl's sunny disposition dispelled any gloomy thoughts Elizabeth might have; she now welcomed Amy Lee's presence any time at all.

Still thirsty for new challenges, Elizabeth enrolled in French classes, music and dancing. Once her classmates learned she could both play the guitar and sing, her position in their company became more favorable. Still, she worried over every compliment's true meaning.

*

April 5, 1831

Dear Diary, a big box of sweets and apples came today from home. Two pair of wool stockings! Both grey. Horrible. Elderberries to brew in wine for a cough if I get one. Mrs. Willard does not permit wine! I tossed them onto the ground during a walk. Maybe an elderberry bush will grow there. I did not get sent home, but most of the girls avoid me. Perhaps they believe I am untrustworthy. I care not what they think. I am smarter than most of them anyway.

19

May 1831

"Have you seen this, Lizzy?" Amy Lee cried, rushing into Elizabeth's room to fling up the window sash.

Horses hooves clattering over the cobbles outside made such a racket that Elizabeth closed her book, joining her friend at the open window to peer at the sight below. The roadway, slick with rain, reflected a bright spectacle. A red wagon draped in a wide yellow banner proclaiming the *Great Troy Revival of 1831* slowly made its way past the seminary. A tall man dressed in black with a shock of wild hair stood uneasily in the bed of the wagon, his legs spread wide against the lurching of the horses' gait. He shouted and gestured in sweeping arcs of his arms. Two women sitting behind the horses and two others in the back of the wagon threw armloads of printed-paper into the air. Crowds of Troy Seminary girls and boys from Rensselaer surged onto the sidewalks to grab the papers as they fluttered to the ground.

"Can you understand what he's saying?" Amy Lee asked, as the wagon grew nearer. "I hear the word, 'God', and 'the devil', but it does not make sense."

"I'll find out," Elizabeth said, gathering up her skirts and dashing for the door. Moments later she appeared on the street, grabbed one of the sheets of paper and turned to look up and wave it at Amy Lee.

She raced back up the stairs to collapse on her bed panting and wiping at her face with a handkerchief.

Amy Lee snatched the paper from her hand and began to read.

"Oh, my, it's a meeting about God." Amy Lee said. Her eyes opened wide. "Listen! *Sunday, Noon, May 10 Come hear the Reverend Charles G. Finney*–that must be the one in the wagon–*and save your soul. The Rev. Dr. Beaman's Church grounds. Everyone welcome. God knows the devil tempts many!* Look Lizzy, there's a big tent, too." Amy Lee thrust the announcement at her, pointing at the illustration of a circus tent with streams of people lined up to enter.

The door slammed open and two other girls who lived on her floor crowded into the cramped room with a rustle of petticoats. Camille and Mavis were twins but with opposite personalities: Camille was flirtatious and outgoing and Mavis, shy and reserved. Both girls possessed such developed intellect Elizabeth found herself drawn to them. She loved studying with them, and lively discussions about logic and criticism that bored most of the other girls didn't faze the twins. Their room adjoined hers and Elizabeth found if she stood on the bureau in her room, the girls could talk to each other through a pipe in the wall. Breaking the rule that conversations must cease after nine o'clock at night, they continued talking often well after everyone else fell asleep.

"Let's all go together," Camille said, shaking the piece of paper for the others to see. Her brown eyes sparkled beneath a fringe of brown hair that covered her brow.

"I'd like that, too," Mavis said. "I'm interested in what he has to say. We're Baptist, but that does not mean we cannot hear other opinions. Right, Sister?" She glanced at Camille, lifting a slender hand to smooth back a strand of hair dislodged from a hairpin holding her chignon.

"What a fine outing it will be," Amy Lee said. "It's so dreary here," she added then glanced at Elizabeth, who had looked into Finney's piercing blue eyes when he passed by. He seemed to gaze directly into her soul.

Excited but also a little frightened, Elizabeth nodded. Since she had enrolled at Emma Willard her attendance at Sunday religious services had been desultory. Each girl was given her own choice of churches, but Elizabeth usually chose to sleep in or read. Traipsing to church with her family had been mandatory, so she relished the absence of commitment. She had always thought, privately, that one's own intelligent and kind behavior was more important. This exciting prospect was different than church however. What could it hurt? "Let's go. Tomorrow, I'll ask matron if we can use a wagon. Reverend Beaman's church isn't far, but the ground is too wet and muddy to walk," she said. "It's such a bother to dry one's shoes."

Soon the entire seminary buzzed with the news and not one but three wagons were being readied for the Sunday trip.

That night, Elizabeth laid in bed listening to the rain pelt her window. What would her parents make of her decision to attend a revival meeting? They were Presbyterian, accustomed to worshiping quietly with a certain comfortable routine. She smiled in the dark as she recalled going to the Episcopal Church service with Peter and choosing to sit in the Negro pew with everyone staring at her. Her parents had hated it when she did that.

"It is not seemly," her mother had said, but did not forbid her from doing it.

"God does not care where I sit," she had replied.

"Do not be impudent, Elizabeth."

Religion meant little to her, so why this curiosity about a revival meeting whose subject would surely be religion? Escape from boredom? Perhaps it was Finney's hypnotic expression?

The preparations for the event swept up all the girls and few could concentrate on their studies. Even though brief respites from daily routine were usually marked by mild acceptance, anticipation raised Elizabeth's level of excitement. The night before the revival meeting, tangled in her blanket and quilt, she barely slept and woke tired and cranky.

*

May 2, 1831

Dear Diary, A traveling reverend named Finney has come to Troy. I do not think he is of the Calvinistic belief for his exhortations are dramatic and bombastic. Mother would not like me to attend but she will not know because I will not tell her. The less she knows, the better. It all seems very exciting and everyone wants to go. I shall be right up front.

20

May 1831

"You know they say he saw Jesus," Camille whispered in Elizabeth's ear. She and Mavis sat with Elizabeth wedged like bookends on the rear seat of the wagon as it swayed over the wet street. The makeshift canopy erected over the wagon bed to keep the students dry did nothing to stop muddy water from splashing onto their dresses. To avoid the mess, the three girls jammed together in the center of the seat, their skirts tucked under their legs.

Elizabeth turned to her friend with an expression of disbelief.

"No, it's true. In Rochester. Can you believe that?"

Mavis leaned close to add her comments. "He used to make a lot of money as a lawyer, but when *it* happened he just stopped to preach."

"Oh girls, look. Boys," Amy Lee cried from her perch near the wagon driver. She stood up to wave at the noisy group of Rensselaer students standing in the far wagon behind them and yelling and laughing to get the girls attention.

Elizabeth stood up and turned toward them, grabbing Camille's shoulder to brace herself. With the boys' damp hair blowing in disarray and floppy bow ties askew, they looked less like serious engineering students and more like children off on a holiday. "Let us see whose wagon gets there first," she called out.

"What?" a deep voice shouted from the Rensselaer wagon. "You want the drivers to race the teams?"

"Yes." Elizabeth answered as loud as she could.

"Lizzy, what are you doing?" Mavis said, tugging at Elizabeth's sleeve and pulling her off balance to collapse in a heap of skirts and petticoats.

"No racing, Miss," the driver said turning around to frown at Elizabeth.

"Oh, good gracious," she said, laughing so hard tears sprang to her eyes.

By the time the wagons reached Dr. Beaman's church, all the chairs up front in the tent were filled save a few on the farthest ends of the aisles.

Elizabeth and her friends jumped down and, ignoring the muddy ground, ran to the empty seats to settle in just as a drumbeat rolled across the assembled crowd. The man Elizabeth had seen earlier stepped up onto a makeshift stage erected at the tent entrance. He held the hands of the women who had thrown the papers from the wagon.

"Halleluiah," he said, raising his arms outstretched toward the ceiling, taking the clasped hands of the women with him.

"Halleluiah," the women shouted in unison.

A roar began to emerge from the people crammed into the temporary seating and standing in the wagons drawn up in the back. Horses whinnied and stamped the ground. The voices of men quieting the animals and the flapping of canvas loosened by a sudden burst of wind and rain added to the noise.

Charles Grandison Finney stepped forward, then raised his hands alone in prayer and closed his eyes. The four women scurried off the stage.

"God bless you all this amazing day of His grace," Finney said, his rich baritone swelling to the walls of the tent and beyond where the last Amen seemed to echo. His gaze swept the room. Was he looking at her? Elizabeth remembered his penetrating blue eyes that day in the street. She swore she could feel her blood run faster. Her hands trembled.

Mavis looked her way and reached out to take her hand in her own. "What's wrong, Lizzy?" she said with concern.

Elizabeth shook off her friend's grip and leaned forward to concentrate on the man's words as he paced back and forth on the stage, sometimes directing his voice to the sky, sometimes turning to crouch and whisper at the people sitting in the front row. Sometimes looking directly at her. A gasp from those who sat in the front row rippled through the crowd and a woman fainted. As Finney spoke, Elizabeth pictured his vivid description of writhing sinners impaled on pitchforks, mouths agape as they stared into a pit of flames. She shut her eyes to rid them of the images, but they were still there. Could she be one of those sinners? Yes, indeed. All that she'd ever done to disobey her parents, to tease her sisters, to taunt the boys who thought her stupid—were sins. Surely they were. And she'd been jealous, too. She envied her poor dead brother for his place in her father's heart. Why did she not accept herself as she'd been born? Why did she believe her role, as a woman as defined by others, was so onerous? A depraved sinner she was, and God hates sin. Finney explained how sinners would go to Hell and perish there, consumed by a river of flames. He exhorted his audience to repent. Elizabeth's heartbeat quickened. Tears filled her eyes and she fumbled in a pocket for a handkerchief. "He's talking about me, Mavis. Me," she said, her voice choked.

"But Lizzy, you are so nice. That is not you."

Elizabeth turned to her and said, "You do not know me. I am a sinner."

On the trip back to the seminary, she sat in stunned silence, hugging her wool shawl around her as if to hide the evils she knew were so obvious to others. The wagons rumbled down the darkened street with the students subdued and quiet. Little conversation transpired, and the recollection of Finney's sermon lingered in her memory, bleak and frightening.

The next morning, she sat at the breakfast table absently dipping her spoon in and out of the porridge she'd let grow cold. Sleep eluded her all night. The result was lavender half moons under her eyes.

Beside her, Amy Lee chattered without stopping, punctuating her conversation about the revival meeting with high-pitched laughter and amusing the other girls at the table.

"Amy Lee, may I get in a word, please? I thought Reverend Finney was quite dramatic," Winnie said. "Like an actor."

"You had your eye on one of the boys from Rensselaer," Mavis said. "I am surprised the Reverend made an impression on you at all."

"Do not judge me, Mavis. I listened to Finney, but I am a Catholic, and nothing shakes my belief. Especially not that man who merely shouted to frighten people."

Camille reached for her sister's hand. "Can we just agree the revival meeting meant different things to each of us?" she asked.

"Only she seemed hypnotized by his sermon," Winnie said, pointing at Elizabeth who sat at the end of the breakfast table.

"Not hypnotized," Elizabeth murmured. "I believe him." Disgusted and feeling weak, she pushed her cereal bowl away and left the dining hall. So troubled by the vivid images stored in her head she scarcely listened to the instructors in her classes that day. Later, pleading a headache, she ran to her room, closed the door and flopped on the bed. She ignored the call for dinner and pretended not to hear a gentle knock later that evening when Camille and Mavis called to her from the hallway. Even when Mavis climbed up onto the bureau in her room to get her attention through the pipe in the wall, she ignored her. Again she slept fitfully, waking often to hope the moonlight streaming through her window didn't bring demonic spirits into her room. What was wrong with her?

*

May 4, 1831

Dear Diary, I must write my thoughts while they are still whirling in my head. The Reverend Finney captivated my mind and soul. He singled me out for scorn and contempt. His gaze withered my strength and it was as if I lost power over myself. Every word he said was directed to me as an arrow pierces the heart of a rabbit. His words are not for me my friends said, but they are wrong. I know it. I am prideful and arrogant. I have sinned and seek absolution for my evil ways. Peaceful sleep evades me. My dreams are fitful and rife with images of demons and dark looming objects shrieking in the night. I try to eat but food is tasteless and my stomach aches.

21

May 1831

Elizabeth couldn't shake the bleak mood that seemed to hold her in its clutches. No matter how hard she tried, Finney's terrifying words describing the lost souls who'd died without Jesus grew louder each time she recalled them. Yet by Sunday, the opportunity to listen once again to the excitement of his powerful oratory drew her like a magnet. She resisted, promising herself she would not go, not listen again to his warnings about the evil she knew with certainty lurked within her. Yet, at the last moment, she grabbed her bonnet and raced down the stairs to squeeze into the last wagon headed for the revival. Now so confused about the fight of good versus evil within her, she listened enrapt, certain he singled her out for his message of salvation. Perhaps if she were more pious, her father would recognize her strength and intelligence. Would he accept her then? Could a strong belief in God be the difference between how men and women were treated?

Within a week, Finney's evangelical revivals were so popular he arranged to conduct daily prayer meetings at Troy Seminary after the evening meal. Nothing had united the girls like this so far, Mrs. Willard had told them. She was delighted when he said he would come to the school. Now with the revival preacher steps from her room, nothing restrained her from filing into the dining hall with the other girls. In fact, schoolwork sessions diminished into a series of brief lectures so the girls could attend the revival meetings.

No matter how illogical the preacher's commentary, its fiery purpose captivated Elizabeth until she succumbed to his artful pleas. Finally, feeling desperate and limp, she ignored her courses, consumed little food and withdrew from the day-to-day gossip of her friendships with Mavis and Camille. Even Amy Lee's giddy chatter couldn't cheer her. The twins pounded on Elizabeth's door demanding to come in one day after a Finney prayer meeting. They found her curled up on the bed, her open Bible beneath her cheek.

"Lizzy, we are worried about you. This has gone on too long," Camille said as sternly as she could. Their strict Baptist upbringing embraced revival meetings, but even they never heard anyone as convincing as Finney. The two sisters no longer attended the meetings, but fear for Elizabeth's welfare brought them to her door.

The circles beneath Elizabeth's blue eyes were now nearly purple. "You do not understand," she said. She pulled her disheveled hair away from her collar. The pins that kept her curls in place lay strewn on the bare floor. A pair of soiled stockings hung draped over the chair by her desk and a half-eaten shriveled bit of bread lay on the windowsill.

Mavis bustled around the room righting its contents after throwing open the window to let in the warm afternoon breeze. She hummed to herself as she worked.

"Do not do that," Elizabeth said, struggling to rise from her bed.

"You must not go back to that man," Camille said with a note of finality in her voice. "We will not let you, right Sister?"

Mavis nodded.

"I *am* going back. Tomorrow," Elizabeth said. "The Reverend said repent and I will become an angel."

"That is nonsense," Mavis said. "No one is an angel. Not till you are dead, that is."

"Well, I am going nevertheless."

"Then we will go with you," Camille said.

The next day, Elizabeth rushed into the dining hall to get a front seat with Camille and Mavis trailing behind her.

By the time the revival preacher reached the midpoint of his sermon and began to stride back and forth in front of the girls and their teachers, shaking his long black hair about his head with each gesture, drops of spit flew from his mouth.

"Ye shall repent, or forever be sentenced to eternal damnation. The Devil's disciples are waiting to usher you into a Hell so hot, so full of burning embers ye shall never escape. Do you see them now?" He stopped to point into the crowd and at that moment Elizabeth rose to her feet expecting to see the wretched people.

Mavis pulled her down into her chair. "Lizzy, it is all right, do not fret so."

"I must find out how to repent," she said, brushing her friend's hand from her arm. Her heart pounded and when Finney stopped to take a breath, winding up his message, she dashed to the sidelines of the stage.

She waited while the man ended his sermon and left his pulpit to shake hands with the crowd as it emptied from the dining hall. While Camille and Mavis hovered in the background, Elizabeth approached Finney.

"Sir, I am profoundly changed by your messages," she started. "And wish to repent, but I do not know how or what that means."

Finney stared down at her, his blue eyes narrowed. When he clapped a hand on her shoulder she trembled.

"Repent of your sins and believe in Jesus Christ child, that's all there is to it," he said.

"But I have done that and I'm still besieged with dreams of evil and terrible images."

"Believe in Jesus and He will bring happiness to you," Finney said, turning to gather up his Bible and his sermon notes.

"When does it happen?" She asked of his retreating back.

"Believe, my girl," Finney called as he closed the dining hall door behind him.

Despite Finney's words, nothing helped. She renounced sin for Jesus, yet she felt no better. If she was a sinner, how could she live up to her brother's memory, let alone replace him in her father's regard? She couldn't sleep, for closing her eyes meant the terrible dreams returned. Food lost its taste. Though she tried to eat, her dresses were becoming loose. She'd fallen so far behind in her class assignments she feared she'd be expelled. She tried to overcome this new obsession but for the next several weeks despair continued to plague her.

*

May 8, 1831

Dear Diary, My thoughts are so confused I do not know where to turn or which way to go. As iron shavings are unable to withstand the draw of a powerful magnet I cannot stay away from Reverend Finney. My school, once a haven, now holds little solace. He is here. I cannot turn away for he fascinates me. My course work is abysmal. I have lost weight and feel so ill.

"We will not allow it," Camille said. She and Mavis had knocked on Elizabeth's door early Sunday morning and now stood blocking passage from the room.

She stared at her friends, hollow-eyed. She sat on her unmade bed, fumbling to pull on her boots.

"You don't understand, if I don't attend the sermon and learn what I must do to repent, I will die," she said.

"Oh, pish, posh, that is nonsense," Mavis said. "You need fresh air, exercise and some food. Even the dreadful porridge will make you feel better." She sat on the bed beside Elizabeth and put her arm around her shoulders. "Why, you are growing so boney, I fear you will need lots of porridge to make up for it."

Elizabeth made a face. "Porridge is terrible," she said, her voice small and weak.

Camille laughed. "That it is, but porridge is what you need right now. Smothered in top cream too, with lots of sugar."

Her friend's suggestion sounded appealing, and she looked at the two dear sisters there to help her and smiled. "I will eat, if you go with me," she said.

Mavis snatched a shawl from the bureau and draped it around Elizabeth. "Come along," she said, reaching for her hand.

The three girls sat alone in the dining hall, the twins sipping tea with milk, watching Elizabeth eat. When she scraped the bottom of the bowl of its cream, they clapped their hands.

"Now, don't you feel better?" Camille asked.

She nodded. A loud noise erupted from the large room housing Reverend Finney, his acolytes, and the few girls still attending his sermons. Since Mrs. Willard welcomed Finney, townspeople flocked to the school to hear him speak also. Students were no longer alone filling the seats, but as his fame spread, the dining hall was packed with new followers driving from miles around to see and listen to the man. Mr. and Mrs. Willard had become infatuated with Finney and the acclaim Troy Seminary gained from his presence. The sound of applause rang through the rooms where the girls boarded.

Mavis looked up, alarmed, and shot a glance at her sister. "He is just finishing," she said. "We don't want to get drawn into the departing crowd."

"Come along Elizabeth, we are taking you for a long walk in the spring sunshine," Camille said. "It is time you gained your strength back and returned to us."

As the three girls left the dining hall and hurried out into the fresh air, Finney's speech concluded and Elizabeth looked back at the people streaming from the doors of the dining hall. At once she felt the fear rise again, and grabbed both girls' hands and held them fast. Her step quickened. "Thank you for rescuing me," she said. "I won't attend another meeting, I promise you." She looked back on the days prior to falling under Finney's spell and realized how vulnerable she had been. The weight of the essay disaster and her early loneliness certainly contributed, she now knew. She had expected a nurturing environment, safe and filled with new learning experiences. She had expected friends, too, but discovered some were false. Three true friends had emerged at last and with their strength she grew stronger too. What could Finney do to her when she surrounded herself with loving friends who only wanted the best for her? Nothing, she decided.

In a month the semester term came to its end. The dreams were still with her, but were not as frequent. Still, when they did occur, she would wake in terror, her nightdress clinging to her body. Elizabeth's depressed state of mind was unbeknownst to her family, but when her father sent Peter to bring her home for summer she hugged him with such emotion, a dam broke in her heart.

22

June 1831

When their carriage rolled up to the front of the Cady home, Elizabeth's younger sisters rushed through the door to wrap their arms around her.

"We have missed you so," Madge said.

"Yes, and Madge has tried to take your place, but it has not worked," said Kate.

"Please tell us all about school. We want to hear everything," Madge said as the girls helped Peter drag Elizabeth's trunk and parcels into the house.

Judge Cady walked into the hallway from his office to embrace her. "My darling, Lib. I have missed you too. And I have missed all the debates most of all," he said, his eyes twinkling with what Elizabeth believed to be tears. Perhaps her father had changed his mind about her not being a boy. Her heart leapt.

"I have missed you too," she said, her face against the twill jacket he wore. "No one at Emma Willard challenges me like you and your protégés," she said. She took a deep breath, drawing in the familiar scents of her home. "It is so wonderful to be here with my family."

"Lib, please come talk to us," Madge said.

"Kate. Madge. Leave your sister be for now. Find out when supper will be served and come tell me," he said.

"Where is Mother?" Elizabeth asked.

"She's resting upstairs. Go to her," her father said.

She kissed her sisters then ran up the stairs to her mother's room and knocked.

"Mother?"

"Is it you, Tryphena?"

"No, Mother, Elizabeth. May I come in?"

"Yes, child," her mother said in a faint voice.

Her mother's physical condition alarmed her. She was lying in bed, pale and thin, though with the warm smile Elizabeth recognized.

"Sit on the bed, dear," she said, patting the coverlet draped over her. "Tell me about school."

She began to entertain her mother with tales of her exploits with her friends. Amy Lee's gaiety and the twins' easy charm made her mother smile even broader. When Elizabeth ventured to tell her about the incident with Winnie, she expected reproach, but her mother only sighed. What happened to the stern queenly woman who ran the household?

From downstairs Elizabeth heard a familiar bell ring.

"It's suppertime, Mother. Let me help you with your shawl," Elizabeth said, rising to scoop up the length of blue cotton folded nearby.

When Elizabeth approached, her mother narrowed her eyes. "Lib, you are not looking well. Your dress is hanging loose about your shoulders," she said. "What is it about Emma Willard you have not told me? Are you studying too hard? Is the food not to your liking?"

Startled by her mother's questions, the shawl slipped from her hand. She knelt to retrieve it before she spoke. She could not burden her mother with the effect of Reverend Finney's sermons.

"It is merely exercise, Mother, a daily routine enforced in the spring. I admit I have not been eating as much, for the coursework is exhausting, but ease your mind. I am fine." She turned away from her mother's penetrating gaze as she replied. "Now, will you join us downstairs?"

"No, dear, Tryphena will bring my tray. I take my meals here now. Just until I regain my strength," her mother said with strained conviction.

Tryphena had written to say their mother was with child again, but Elizabeth had calmly accepted the information. Her mother had had several pregnancies, all easy. She ignored the fact that her mother was no longer a young woman, however. Being away for so many weeks opened Elizabeth's eyes to the perils a woman faces when bearing children. That her mother no longer could summon the energy to keep up with her home, its grounds, and their busy family life, should have been easy to understand; but she had been selfish. She vowed to be more attentive. Mother bore eleven babies, but only six lived. Sometimes she thought about her brothers and sisters buried before her birth. Would her life be different, she wondered? She desperately wanted to discuss the details of her encounters with the Reverend Finney, but decided that it was best to not to add to her mother's burden.

That night snuggled deep into her bedcovers, she felt safe and tried to sleep. She'd pulled tight the heavy draperies at her windows, but slivers of light from the full moon crisscrossed her rug and furniture turning them into unrecognizable shapes.

Pounding footsteps on the stairs outside her room made her jump and her eyes flew open. She sat up in bed and peered into the gloom to see a writhing ghost-like shape before recognizing it as the petticoat she had hastily tossed across a chair.

"Oh, good gracious," she said and flopped back on her pillow. Yet every time she closed her eyes that night, images of the poor lost creatures described by Finney destined for God's wrath crept into her mind.

Late morning sunshine replaced the cold slices of the moonlight by the time Elizabeth woke the next day. And only then because Madge and Kate were bouncing on the bed beside her, tugging at her nightdress.

"Wake up, wake up, wake up," their voices chorused, growing louder with each bounce.

Elizabeth covered her mouth with her blankets to hide her smile, then sat up abruptly and slid out of bed to chase her sisters around the room, all the while shrieking with laughter.

When they collapsed on the bed, hiccupping and panting, Elizabeth felt truly happy for the first time in weeks. All thoughts of her school courses and her obsession with Finney's horrible warnings about evil seemed unimportant.

*

June 10, 1831

Dear Diary, oh it is so lovely to be home where everyone loves me. Their affection swaddles me like a silken coverlet. I keep my mind occupied so as to reduce the memories of Reverend Finney's vivid rhetoric. I am not always successful. Worse, I cannot control it.

That afternoon Elizabeth noticed a stack of books on a hall table outside her father's office. Their spines were pristine. She picked up the one on top and lifted it to her nose to smell the fresh ink.

"I see you've found my books," a familiar voice said behind her. Elizabeth whirled around, almost dropping the heavy volume and hastily returning it to the table.

"Edward! You surprised me," she said, feeling a heated flush climb her cheeks. "What are these? New law books for father's students?"

"No, the subject is a new scientific discovery called phrenology."

"*The Constitution of Man*," she read out loud from one of the book covers. "It sounds like a law book."

"Yes, I know, but it discusses an amazing theory about the skull and parts of the brain," Edward said. "Maybe it is too difficult for you to understand," he added.

She frowned. "Brother-in-law, you merely said that to challenge me. Give me that book, and by tomorrow, I will have questions for you that we can discuss."

Edward handed her the book. She clutched it in her arms and then turned to leave him standing in the hallway.

"Good gracious, Edward, I am no longer a child. What do you take me for?" she said over her shoulder.

"A very smart young lady," he called out toward her retreating back.

She strode into the parlor, settled into her father's wing chair, and then opened the book on her lap.

A series of drawings caught her eye. One particular sketch, titled *Location of the Organs*, showed the front, back, and side of a human head with the areas from above the nose to the nape of the neck partitioned off and numbered. Some were defined with letters. Each corresponded to a list below the drawings.

"Hmmm, *Number 24 Individuality*," she said aloud then flipped the book to its *Introduction* and began to read.

Elizabeth was so absorbed in the explanation of phrenology; Tryphena caught her with her fingers tangled in her hair. Elizabeth jumped up to hug her sister.

"Whatever are you doing?" Tryphena said, gesturing at her sister's disheveled appearance.

Elizabeth grabbed the book. "Look Fini," she said, pointing to a page with a drawing, "It says the hard bumps on a person's skull can be used to determine personality. I have *Individuality* right here." Elizabeth pointed to her forehead then grabbed her sister's hand, placed it there and pushed. "Feel it. Does that not seem larger than the area on either side?"

Tryphena's hand felt cool on Elizabeth's brow, and when Elizabeth felt the pressure of her older sister's gentle touch and watched a smile play about her lips, she blushed.

"You mock me," she said.

"No, Lib, Edward has spoken to me of the same theory. It is just your enthusiasm that makes me smile. You are so like Father in that regard."

"The book says if a person feels a larger bump on his skull it means that person—oh, look," Elizabeth pointed to an area directly above the ear of the drawing. "This is *Destructiveness*. I'll bet a girl at school named Winnie has big bumps right there."

"Who is Winnie?" Tryphena asked.

"Not a friend. In fact, she never will be one to me either."

"I thought you made lots of friends at Emma Willard."

Should she tell Tryphena about Winnie? What happened?

"I hoped to make many good friends. But it turns out only three girls proved to be real friends. Winnie was and still is, a false friend. I have no use for her," Elizabeth said.

"I trust your judgment," Tryphena said. "Being away at school is something I never experienced. But your demeanor has changed. You are more mature in your assessments. I can see it," she added. "Whatever happened between the two of you is yours to tuck away. I will not pry."

"Thank you," Elizabeth said. She took a deep breath and realized she had been holding it, dreading her sister's interrogation.

Tryphena gestured toward the book on Elizabeth's lap.

"Edward does not quite believe in this new science," she said. "Perhaps you should discuss it with him, and Father too. I would do this before you talk about it with anyone else. It's so new, you know."

Elizabeth looked up at her older sister and smiled.

"You have such a clear head, Fini, I wish I were not so taken with these new ideas." She sighed and closed the book with a slam. "I will discuss it as you suggest."

Tryphena looked out the window. "Oh my, dusk comes too soon this time of year. I must hurry and see to Mrs. Brewster's dinner preparations."

When she turned to leave, Elizabeth caught her hand.

"Tryphena, I am so glad you are here to step in when Mother cannot manage. You are a Godsend to her and to all of us."

Her sister hugged her and whispered, "Thank you, dear," then hurried down the hallway toward the kitchen.

That evening Elizabeth's father pulled out his chair at the head of the table, signaling for the family to sit down.

When Mrs. Brewster started delivering the plates of soup to the table, Elizabeth wrinkled her nose.

"Is there something you want to say, Lib?" her father asked.

"Everything tastes so much better here at home, but I cannot abide asparagus soup," she said. "It bothers me later."

Madge giggled.

"That's enough, girls," Judge Cady said. "Eat your soup or do not, Elizabeth. Just keep your hands still till the plates are removed."

From the other end of the table, she heard Edward stifle a chuckle and she felt her cheeks flame.

"Lib hasn't been sleeping well since she returned home from school, Father. Maybe that is why the soup bothers her," Kate said.

"That is not why," Elizabeth said. "It's the dreams."

Judge Cady looked up in alarm.

"What is that?"

"Reverend Finney."

"You attended his revival meetings?"

"He came to Emma Willard to conduct them."

"Come see me after supper, Lib, and we will talk."

When the soup plates were cleared, the dining room doors swung open again. Mrs. Brewster brought in a large tray of salmon in caper sauce and baskets of rolls that she placed at each end of the table.

The family ate in silence except for the sounds of knives and forks clinking against china.

At the recollection of Reverend Finney, sadness engulfed Elizabeth and did not lift until a dessert of strawberries and cream were served.

"Oh, I do love strawberries, do you not, Lib?" Kate said, clapping her hands.

Judge Cady looked down the table at his youngest daughter and smiled. "Manners, Catherine."

Kate rolled her eyes and stuck out her bottom lip.

"I do," Elizabeth responded. She was grateful for the distraction of her younger sister's question. "Remember when we were very young, we would sneak off into the garden and choose the ripest ones before Mrs. Brewster found them?"

"We are too old to do that now," Madge said.

"We will never be too old to find those choice berries ahead of her," Elizabeth said.

Tryphena cleared her throat signaling that Judge Cady had finished eating.

"Madge, Kate, upstairs with you two," she said. "We have an hour or more of light before bedtime, so let us go upstairs and work on our samplers."

"Elizabeth, you come with me," her father said. "Let us find out what those dreams are all about."

Settled in Judge Cady's study, with its smells of leather bookbinding and cigar smoke, Elizabeth sat in the worn chair facing her father. He pulled up a hassock close by and leaned forward, taking her hands in his.

"All right, what's bothering you about the Reverend Finney?" he asked. "His evangelical exploits are well known and reported in the daily papers. I have been reading about his tent shows."

"It is not him, exactly, but the images his sermons evoke. The devils. The sinners writhing in eternal flames. Every time I close my eyes to sleep, I see them. They frighten me." Even as she spoke, a sensation of unease began to stir deep within her and she fought back tears. "I stopped going to his meetings because of these fears. I just could not listen any longer." She fumbled in her apron pocket for a handkerchief, but took the linen square her father pressed into her hand instead.

"I knew of his clever rhetoric but not that it would produce such frightening results," her father said. His grip on her hands tightened.

Elizabeth's eyes filled with tears. "I should have told you. But at the time, going to hear him with my friends seemed so exciting and marvelous. And so grown up, too. Then his words drew me in. The experience overwhelmed me." Just thinking about it triggered awful memories. She paused to wipe her eyes.

"I am glad you told me now. I have read lurid accounts of experiences occurring during his sermons. I can see how you– or anyone for that matter–could be influenced. You poor child." Her father pulled her to her feet and enfolded her in his arms, patting her gently on the back.

When her tears subsided, she pulled away and blotted her face with her father's handkerchief. "What shall I do?"

"It's not what you will do, but what I will do. You need a change. Spring is a lovely time of year at the Falls of Niagara. Pack your valise. Peter will drive us and we'll take Edward and Tryphena with us too. I'll tell them to prepare for the trip."

"What about Mother, and Madge and Kate? Are they to accompany us as well?"

"Your mother is not well enough to travel yet, and your sisters must continue their lessons. They will all be in the able care of Mrs. Brewster and the household staff."

"Thank you, then. It's a splendid idea," Elizabeth said. The very thought of a trip like this brightened her spirits. "We can picnic and talk," she said. "Oh, Father, I am so excited. Thank you so very much."

*

June 11, 1831

Dear Diary, of all the lovely and wonderful turns of events, I could not imagine one so splendid. A holiday. Edward will be there–and Fini will go too. I know it will be a wonderful journey filled with lots of good talk and deep thinking. I am overjoyed at the prospect for it surely will drive all thoughts of the horrible Reverend Finney from my mind. My outlook has been so bleak and sad, so I am happy beyond belief to imagine awaking each morning with a bright perspective on the day. We leave as soon as the carriage can be made ready.

23

June 1831

Conversation bounced back and forth among the four people in the carriage as it rumbled through the countryside.

Elizabeth opened the *Constitution of Man* text on her lap. "Oh, my goodness gracious. It says here employers can demand a phrenology examination to see if a job applicant is honest and trustworthy." She traced the lines with a lace-gloved finger. "Do you think that's possible, Edward?"

"It is a new scientific development. Who knows yet if it is correct or not?"

"I can tell you, I do not want anyone feeling around on my head so I can get work," Elizabeth said.

"What woman would want a strange man's hands poking around beneath her bonnet?" Tryphena asked.

"You do not have to work, Lib," her father said.

He appeared to be dozing with his eyes closed, but she knew he didn't miss anything. His assertion that she should be content with her life oddly disturbed her. Perhaps she would like to work. After the encounters with Finney, she'd begun to doubt many things. Ignoring her father, she continued reading, turning the pages in quick succession. "Oh, listen to this. The practitioners claim to match up couples better than if they fell in love the natural way. Now that's just plain silly."

Edward laughed.

"Close the book," her father said. "Let us talk about something else for awhile. In fact, I think it is time for one of those sandwiches Mrs. Brewster packed for us." The judge tapped the top of his walking cane against the carriage roof signaling Peter to pull the horses to a stop.

When their picnic baskets were open on a blanket spread in the shade of a Flowering Crabapple tree beside the road, Elizabeth lay on one elbow, her skirts in disarray, absently picking at crumbs of cake from her meal. Choosing to ignore her sister's frown of displeasure, she let her thoughts drift. Why had she fallen so completely under Finney's spell? His vivid rhetoric? No one described the perils of rejecting salvation greater than he did. Compared to the sermons of her stoic Calvinistic upbringing, Reverend Finney evoked colorful and passionate beliefs. Neither religious approach seemed convincing now. The result was healthy skepticism. She smiled, letting her thoughts wander and envisioned fingers massaging her scalp to determine which beau would suit her best. Her gaze lingered on Edward's profile. He sat leaning against the tree trunk, eyes closed. *He was so handsome. If only I could meet someone like him.* She sighed then stood to begin gathering the lunch things and pack them back in the basket.

"Edward dear," Tryphena said waking her husband. "It is time to go. Father is anxious to get moving again." Judge Cady stood by Peter and the horses were moving about with impatience.

With their lunch basket safely stowed, the group's conversation once again turned to the religious revival movement sweeping the country. Edward described what Elizabeth encountered as a delusion of sorts, born aloft on the shoulders of churches that permit such excitements. Elizabeth asked, "Even though Reverend Finney's words are most convincing, they are nothing more than colorful suggestions? Superstitions?"

"Ah! You have understood me perfectly," Edward said, seeming thoroughly amused. With that, the mood of the travelers, especially Elizabeth, seemed lighter.

"Let's take turns reading *Emma* as we travel," Edward said. "We need to divert our thoughts to more fascinating adventures." He opened the small leather-bound trunk at his feet and pulled out a book with its cover barely worn.

"*Chapter One: Emma Woodhouse, handsome, clever and rich, with a comfortable home and happy disposition, seemed to unite some of the best blessing of existence; and had lived nearly twenty-one years in the world with very little to distress or vex her.*" Edward began in his deep voice. "*She was the youngest of the two daughters of a most affectionate, indulgent father; and had, in consequence of her sister's marriage, been mistress of his house from a very early period. Her mother had died too long ago for her to have more than an indistinct remembrance of her caresses; and her place had been supplied by an excellent woman as governess, who had fallen little short of a mother in affection.*" As he continued reading, and as the sound of his voice grew fainter, Elizabeth fell deeply asleep despite her love for this book, lulled by the rhythm of the horses' gait.

She awoke when the carriage jolted to a stop in front of an inn at Little Falls. They had traveled all day covering nearly 35 miles. Despite the innkeeper's kindness and hot bowls of barley soup filled with chunks of carrot and pork, Elizabeth wished for nothing more than to wash her face and to crawl into bed.

The next morning, once the picnic baskets were replenished, Elizabeth sat quietly beside her father as the horses gained speed and began to trot.

The rigorous conversations of the day before had left her subdued, and as they hurried along she dreamily rested her head against a window of the carriage thoroughly absorbed in the passing landscape. Now and then a coal black Angus calf and its mother would keep an eye on their carriage as it passed. Along wide fields of newly planted corn, farmers wiped their brows in the shade of leafing out Sugar Maples. The lift of a hat acknowledged Elizabeth's handkerchief wave from the carriage window. Once the wagon drew near Oneida with its Shaker residents, she frowned.

"What is that expression all about?" asked Tryphena.

"It is religious."

"What is?" Tryphena asked.

"Oneida. I'm not looking forward to stopping there. Those people follow Reverend Finney."

"Nonsense, Father would never allow his influence to put us in jeopardy," her sister assured her. "The journey is over two hundred miles. It will take us six days to reach the Falls. Rest assured Father has planned this trip well."

"Your sister speaks the truth," their father said. "I chose lodging for us that professed no religious bent whatsoever. All types of travelers stop at the Oneida inn regardless of their beliefs or not having any at all," he continued. "This particular inn is recommended by Cousin Gerrit."

Night had fallen by the time the carriage stopped in front of the plain clapboard building housing the Farmer's Stop Inn. Peter drove the horses around to the back to unharness and feed them for the night. Judge Cady ushered Elizabeth and Tryphena into the inn's low-ceilinged great room while Edward carried their valises. Two men sat hunkered over tankards of ale in front of the fireplace. The younger man jumped up knocking over his chair as the door swung open to reveal Judge Cady.

"Gibbs." Her father said. He seemed stunned.

The older man reached to shake the judge's hand.

"Dr. Hiram Corliss," the older man said, rising and nodding.

"This is a colleague, Leonard Gibbs," Elizabeth's father said after introducing his family. "I have faced him in court, not always happily I might add. These men are acquainted with Cousin Gerrit."

The younger man's face seemed familiar to Elizabeth. When he spoke she remembered where she'd heard his voice. Even though she heard it from her hiding place in the basement of the courthouse, his distinct deep bass rumble stayed with her. She recalled the excitement of his expression when he'd related the terrible plight of the Negroes and why abolishing slavery must occur soon.

"You are on holiday?" Gibbs asked.

"Of a sort, yes," Judge Cady said. "And, you?"

Gibbs and Corliss exchanged looks.

"You might say we are making traveling arrangements."

At that, Judge Cady signaled the innkeeper hovering nearby and requested a meal. When the family was directed to a long table in an adjacent room, the judge joined Gibbs and Corliss briefly, returning with a troubled look on his face.

Something was happening. Father seemed friendly with these two men, but reserved as well. Elizabeth recalled Cousin Gerrit, the Negro boy spirited away in the night, and the muffled conversation in her father's office when Vice President Calhoun had pleaded for help in fighting efforts to free the Negroes.

"You've not finished your meal," Tryphena said to Elizabeth, interrupting her thoughts.

She looked down at her plate and the fat congealing around the untouched beef loin. She picked up a chunk of bread and began picking at it, placing bits into her mouth.

"I'm not hungry, I suppose," she said, laying the bread beside her plate. "Just tired." She left the table, kissed her father's brow then climbed the stairs to bed hoping this strange encounter did not result in a nightmare.

*

June 15, 1831

Dear Diary, we made good time today. Having Edward's handsome self in such close proximity is strange; I must be careful near him. I know now how foolish I am to allow him to capture my imagination so. It will not happen again. We reached another inn where Father knew two of the men. They seemed uneasy in each other's company. The topics of slavery and abolition came to mind. I haven't thought about those words in a long time. I do not know why.

24

June 1831

The journey from Johnstown to the Falls of Niagara resumed, passing through the unfurling spring landscape. Elizabeth chose on some days to sit beside Peter on the carriage driver's seat. She questioned him about the birds and wildlife along the way, and occasionally in the easy flow of their conversation she asked about his childhood. One such fair day, he'd helped her up onto the leather-upholstered seat and had made sure a blanket wrapped around her legs protected her against the early morning chill.

"I am going to miss you, Peter," Elizabeth said.

"Where you going, Miss Elizabeth?"

"Back to school. I have not finished, you know."

"I thought you done. What else you got to know?"

"I wish I did not have to return, but it is a fine chance to learn more about things only teachers can tell me. Like history. Did you know just now the White House is getting two wings put on it?" she asked. "I guess the government thinks they need a bigger house. We are getting ready for a presidential election. It is Mr. Clay against Mr. Jackson."

Peter glanced sidelong at Elizabeth, drawing his brows into a frown. She could barely see his eyes beneath the wide brim of his leather hat.

"I don't know much about such things. Which man does your pap think is best?"

"Mr. Jackson is trying for his second election. Father does not think Mr. Clay has much of a chance."

"Well, no one is asking me."

"Me neither, Peter. You and I cannot vote for such things."

"But Miss Elizabeth, you educated."

"Women cannot vote."

"Seems unfair to me," Peter said, slapping his hand with a fist startling the horses.

"It is unfair you cannot vote either."

The curious encounter with Mr. Gibbs and Dr. Corliss that first night in Oneida troubled Elizabeth. She knew it had something to do with her father's passion about the wrongness of slavery. Was slavery similar to the way women were treated? Why didn't all Americans have the right to vote if they all lived here? It shouldn't matter if an American was white or Negro or a woman.

"Peter, do you remember being a slave?" she asked.

"Not much, Miss Elizabeth. When your pap took us in, I just minded my business. I heard stories though."

"I am sorry about your mother." She looked up at his kind face. "Abraham told me hard work killed her when you were still a boy."

"That's all right. She in God's hands now. Sometimes I think about her..." his voice trailed off, and beneath his coarse woolen jacket his shoulders seemed to grow smaller.

Elizabeth reached to pat his hand.

Peter flicked the reins and clicked to the horses as they began to climb a small densely forested hill and pull the carriage around a bend. Ahead, too close, a throng of people walked toward them in the road. Hundreds it seemed. Peter yanked back on the reins pulling the horses up short. Few carriages and wagons on the road had passed them since they left the inn at Oneida, mostly people headed in the same direction. This caravan of horse-drawn carts and people walking alongside came as a surprise. After a bit, Elizabeth stopped counting. Men, women, children and old people too, were piled into the carts along with bits and pieces of furniture. The people's faces were drawn and tired looking. Some of the children appeared ill, held in a mother's arms or lying on pallets.

"What do you suppose is happening?" Elizabeth asked.

Controlling the horses took Peter's attention away from her question. He could only shake is head. Once he pulled the horses off the road and quieted them, he jumped down to talk to Judge Cady who'd poked his head out of the window when the carriage came to a stop.

The two men spoke briefly, their expressions becoming grave, and then Elizabeth's father told them Peter would drive alongside the road, staying clear of the walkers and their wagons until he found a break where they could travel unimpeded.

After the wagon began to move again the forest gave way to wide fields stretching to the banks of a river swollen by spring runoff. Still the people kept coming. Peter pulled the carriage off the road whenever there appeared to be a gap, but often he could only stop the team to let the walkers pass by. From her perch on the driver's seat Elizabeth looked down into the faces of young women like herself, their skirts streaked with mud, bonnets askew. Sometime her wave elicited a wan smile, often just a blank haunted stare.

The family reached a crossroad leading to the Falls of Niagara and the road once again became empty. Elizabeth craned her neck to watch the stream of people until she could no longer see them.

"Peter, has something bad happened?"

"You best ask your pap about that, Miss Elizabeth."

They continued on in silence, now returning to the forest and heading toward water, but Elizabeth's mind churned with questions. Soon the landscape became lush and dark. Ferns grew in the shade of the trees, and in the rare patches of sunlight she spotted wild Columbines growing.

"Oh, that is so splendid," she said, grateful for the change of scenery. "We must stop here for our dinner." She rose to her feet, but sat down hard as the carriage swayed.

"Miss Elizabeth, you must not do that," Peter said, reaching for her arm to settle her back onto the seat.

"Draw the horse to a standstill off there," she pointed.

At the sudden change in pace, Edward poked his head out of the carriage window. "What is going on?" he asked.

Elizabeth leaned down to look into his face.

"It is time for our dinner meal," she said, and as the carriage rolled to a stop, she jumped down, ignoring her skirts flying about her. This would be the perfect time to ask her father about the crowd of people walking on the road away from New York.

"Well, I would like to have been consulted," Judge Cady said, feigning anger. He stepped down from the open carriage door and stretched. He turned to help Tryphena, while Edward climbed up on the back of the carriage to lift down the picnic basket strapped to the top.

Peter fetched buckets of water for the horses and now sat cross-legged beside them on the riverbank. He'd eaten in a hurry and had saved his apple cores for the horses.

Judge Cady and Edward walked over to talk to Peter, their conversation drifting toward Elizabeth.

"Can we reach the Falls of Niagara by the end of the day?" Judge Cady asked.

"Yes, sir, if I push the horses. A groom at that last place told me the road is much improved from here to Youngstown."

"I see. Well, I would like to get there if we can. I wrote ahead to reserve a cottage and a place in the stables. It is supposed to be ready by nightfall," the judge told Peter.

Elizabeth jumped up to join the conversation, brushing bits of leaves and crumbs from her apron.

"Father, why were there so many people on the road back there? Hundreds and hundreds. They appeared dreadfully tired. Some were ill, too."

"The newspapers say there is a terrible disease sickening many in New York City. I suspect those people are fleeing for that reason."

"We did not expect to encounter so many people on the roads. Your father and I spoke of turning back, but it would mean further association with those who may be ill," Edward said. "Peter also does not believe the horses can make it without rest."

"We're near our destination so we will continue," Judge Cady said.

The thought of such a serious issue proved sobering. At once, the reasons for their own journey seemed trivial.

"Father, let us do drive quickly. I am anxious to get there, are you not?" She forced herself to think happier thoughts.

Judge Cady wrapped his arm around his daughter's shoulders and drew her with him back to the carriage.

"I will be happy to see the Falls of Niagara roaring waters again, Lib, and for you to see them for the first time." Despite his attempt at a lighthearted response, his expression remained grim.

When the carriage rolled into the drive of the inn moonlight bathed the area. Their cottage lay situated a short walk from the entrance to the falls. A lantern glimmered in the inn's window. The loud roar of the falls was unmistakable.

Peter unloaded their valises while Edward went inside to announce their arrival. Moments later a tall man with broad shoulders emerged with Edward behind him carrying a cloth-covered basket. The man held a candle aloft, a key hung from his wrist.

"Evening folks, I am Caleb Marshall, the innkeeper. My stable master will show your driver where he can get those tired horses fed."

Judge Cady nodded.

"Come along this way," the man said. "You arrived too late for the evening meal, but Mrs. Marshall packed some fresh bread and a meat pie. There is a beaker of milk for the young ladies and a bottle of ale for the men, too. We drew water for you ahead of time. It is in the cottage kitchen."

The family trudged up the path behind Mr. Marshall. The exotic scent of night-blooming jasmine surrounded them as they approached the house. Two, slat-back rockers flanked a deacon's bench on the front porch beneath the deep overhanging eaves of the Dutch Colonial structure. When Mr. Marshall threw the door open and stepped back, Elizabeth gasped.

A bright Persian carpet lay on the shining waxed wood floor of the keeping room where guests would most likely relax and read. To the right through a short hallway, a cast iron stove dominated the idle fireplace. In front of it, a metal pitcher filled with wildflowers sat in the middle of a long sawbuck table surrounded by Windsor chairs.

"Fini, this is no modest cottage at all," Elizabeth said. "It is as grand as our own home."

Judge Cady laughed. "Your mother made me promise to settle you and your sister in comfort."

"The bedrooms are upstairs," the innkeeper said. "There are three as you requested, Sir."

Elizabeth raced up the wooden stairs to peek into the rooms. "Oh, I see mine," she called back to the others. "The walls have paintings of birds and butterflies on them. There's a featherbed just like home, and a window out of which I can see stars." She pushed the casement open to the night air breathing deeply of the jasmine perfume.

"Mr. Marshall, a word please?" Judge Cady said, nodding toward the porch outside.

Elizabeth heard the front door open and close then the voice of the innkeeper.

"Yes, Sir?" Mr. Marshall said.

"Has the disease in New York affected anyone staying here?" her father asked.

"No, it has not to my knowledge. At least none of the folks staying in our cabins has become ill. Can't say for sure about the ones who just come for the day to see the falls."

"Thank you Mr. Marshall. You will keep me informed?"

"Certainly will do that. Goodnight, Sir," the innkeeper said.

Elizabeth sat on the edge of her bed and began to unbutton her shoes. Should she be happy she was safe here when so many others were becoming sick? Was her holiday spoiled? What an ugly thought.

The next morning after washing up and dressing, Elizabeth sought the rest of her family downstairs. A fire in the keeping room blazed and the table, now covered in a linen cloth, bore the work of the innkeeper's kitchen helpers. A bowl of strawberries and platters of beaten biscuits, eggs and rashers of bacon lay diminished, by her father and Edward most likely. The men were nowhere in sight.

She frowned. "This looks lovely, but I thought we would be preparing our own meals," she said.

Tryphena sat across from her at the table and sipped her tea before she spoke. "This is my holiday too. We have arranged for all our meals to be taken in the inn or brought to us here."

Elizabeth blushed. "I am sorry for being so thoughtless Fini," she said. Then she brightened. "Without kitchen chores to manage, we shall have much more fun."

Her sister took up her embroidery and bent to the task of knotting pink cotton into rosebuds. Elizabeth ate without comment, and looked up when the front door opened admitting her father and Edward. Their shoulders were wet. Droplets clung to Edward's hair and dripped from the brim of her father's beaver-pelt top hat.

"It is not raining, is it?" she asked rushing to the front windows of the cottage to look out.

Her father stamped his boots on the braided rug inside the front door. His cheeks were red but he smiled as he answered her question.

"Not at all. We woke early while you two were still snug in bed and decided to take a walk. We have been to the falls. You have no protection from the damp, daughters, so take your umbrellas when you go," he said.

Judge Cady removed his hat and shook it over the carpet, then hung it from a peg on the wall. He poured a cup of coffee and settled into an overstuffed chair by the fire. Soon

Elizabeth heard the sound of his regular breathing and soft snores.

"Will you be reading this morning or joining your sister in her embroidery?" Edward asked Elizabeth.

She pushed her plate back and stood up.

"Fini and I are going to explore, are we not?"

"Certainly," Tryphena said. "You cannot go alone and I do want to see what the falls are all about too."

"Take Peter with you," Edward said. "I will tell him of your journey," he continued, starting for the stable where the man bunked with the horses.

A few minutes later, Peter appeared on the cottage porch wearing his broad hat.

Elizabeth and Tryphena headed down the path toward the falls, taking note of the directional signs. Peter followed behind carrying the umbrellas.

The two girls chatted about their adventures thus far, the comfort of the cottage, and the pleasant nature of their visit. Soon the growing roar of the Niagara River reaching its precipice became too loud for conversation. Elizabeth ran ahead, excited by the noise and the billowing clouds of mist. The sound, like hundreds of horses at full gallop, stunned her.

"Hurry," she called over her shoulder. Peter rushed to unfurl one of the umbrellas and press it into her hand.

"Miss Elizabeth, keep yourself dry now, hear? The Judge, he be angry with me if you come back soaked to your skin."

When Elizabeth and her sister reached the end of the path they walked out on a wooden viewing platform confined by a sturdy fence rail. The boards beneath their feet were slick. For all her exuberance Elizabeth slowed to pull her skirts up, ignoring the water damage to her boots and continued to make her way to the edge alone. Beyond the people crowded on the platform, the expanse and volume of the immense waterfall robbed her of words. When Tryphena joined her, Elizabeth reached for her hand.

"Is it not splendid?" she said raising her voice to be heard.

"It is enormous."

Tryphena didn't seem to hear her so she shouted. "It seems to extend forever. I have never seen so much water." She could feel the fresh spray on her face.

Tryphena squeezed her sister's hand then pointed. "Look, a rainbow."

Elizabeth's eyes widened, unable to look away. "The cascading water takes on the colors of the sky."

Shouting voices behind them interrupted their appreciation of the waterfall's splendor.

Elizabeth turned to see what caused the commotion and heard Peter's voice, loud and pleading. Four men surrounded him.

"You have no business here, nigger," an older red-faced man yelled, punching his finger into Peter's chest then drawing his arm back to take a swing. Peter stepped back and threw up his hands to protect his face from the man and stumbled to his knees on the wet ground, dropping his umbrella.

"Stop that this instant," Elizabeth shouted and ran to Peter's side to help him. Her sister rushed to her aid.

"This man is our employee," Tryphena said. "He is a freed man."

"He has as much right to see the falls as anyone," Elizabeth said, glaring at the men. A crowd of tourists pressed closer to the group, expressions of curiosity on their faces.

When the crowd dispersed with the four men muttering, Peter gingerly got to his feet and began to wipe the mud from his breeches with his handkerchief.

"Are you all right?" Elizabeth asked.

"Yes, Miss." He hung his head then whispered, "I am sorry for all that, Miz Tryphena, Miss Elizabeth."

"It is too bad Father or Edward are not here. They would put those men to rights straightaway," Elizabeth said.

"I think it is best we return to the cottage," Tryphena said. "We will come back again with Father and Edward this afternoon to catch the sunset. I am sure it will be glorious."

Tryphena's words barely registered with Elizabeth. Her thoughts were on the incident that occurred because Peter was a Negro. On the route they traveled from Johnstown, she had seen Negro people walking alongside the road or piled into modest wagons headed the same direction. Their clothes appeared patched and ragged, not clean and well made like Peter, Abraham and Jacob's. None of the Negroes turned onto the road to the Falls of Niagara either.

"Elizabeth," Tryphena said. "Are you listening to me?"

"I must have been daydreaming, what did you say?"

"I suggested we have some lunch and a rest, especially after that unsettling confrontation. I am quite damp and want to dry out, too. Do you not as well?"

"Yes. And I want to tell Father about the incident with Peter."

"Let us wait on that, Elizabeth," Tryphena said.

"No."

*

June 16, 1831

Dear Diary, a confrontation between our dear Peter and a group of rude, uncouth men spoiled my first view of the Falls. One man called Peter a vulgar name. I hope the crowds of Negroes along our route heading toward New York are safe from fearful acts like we encountered. Tryphena seems to want to forget it. I do not. We may not speak of it, but I hope our views about the plight of Negroes are the same.

25

June 1831

Despite the serious incident at the falls Elizabeth and Tryphena did postpone telling their father. Instead Elizabeth and Edward argued throughout lunch. Edward teased and she responded, growing more adamant as the conversation continued. Instead of resting as Tryphena requested, they began to discuss Elizabeth's interest in Jane Austen's books, *Northanger Abbey* and *Persuasion*. Now the sounds of their voices gained volume.

"Jane Austen braved ridicule to write stories about her life in England," Elizabeth said. "Like Tryphena and Mother, women there were only supposed to manage the house and keep their opinions to themselves."

"It is different now," Edward said. "You have a college for women. That did not exist in Austen's time."

"A college that teaches dancing and music but offers no occupational guidance," Elizabeth said, her voice rising. "If

Emma were a real person she would have seen better choices for women. Perhaps valuable work."

"Most women choose to have a home and family, Lib," Edward said. "It is not so different now than then."

"Mother and Fini did not have choices because they were expected to marry and run households. Servants could do much of what takes up their time."

"Please change the subject to a more pleasant topic. Perhaps one that you both agree upon," Tryphena said. "Your bickering is harsh."

Edward ignored his wife. "Elizabeth, please do not reduce your sister's importance in our household to that degree, it is not polite."

"I can defend myself, thank you," Tryphena said.

"What you contribute is important," Elizabeth said. "But Fini, every time I hear you and Edward discuss something, his views are the ones accepted. It cannot always be that way."

"Do you challenge your father, too?" Edward asked.

"I do sometimes, depending on the topic. But he is a man, and just because I am a woman, he sees little value in what I have to say or think," Elizabeth responded.

"What is this all about?" Judge Cady stood in the doorway wakened from his nap.

"It is true, Father," Elizabeth said. "You wish I were a boy. If I were, only then would I gain importance to you."

Judge Cady walked over to where Elizabeth sat and stood beside her. "Daughter, you are important to me." He reached out to touch the top of her head. Elizabeth pulled away from him.

"Father, I love and respect you, but please do not pet me like a dog. It is inconsiderate of my feelings."

The expression on her father's face turned from compassion to shock. He seemed at a loss for words.

A knock at the door interrupted them. Mr. Marshall stood on the porch with a folded piece of paper in his hand.

"Begging your pardon. Delivering a letter to Miss Cady," he said.

"Oh my," Elizabeth said after scanning the letter. "My dear school friends Mavis and Camille Van Wyck are here." She explained who the twins were and how she knew them. "They say they were in the crowd this morning and saw what happened to us."

"What is that?" Judge Cady asked, alarmed.

"I should have told you right away, Father," Tryphena said. "But my goal to rush Lib and Peter back to the cottage concerned me more."

"A terrible incident occurred," Elizabeth said. "Some men accosted Peter for no reason." She recalled the ugly expressions on the men's faces and their hurtful language. "I feared for him."

"They did have a reason, Sister," Tryphena said. "Not a pleasant one though. For as long as we are here I think either Edward or Father should accompany us on our explorations."

"They thought him a slave and one man called him a nasty name and tried to hurt him. You would have defended him as we did if you were there," Elizabeth added, directing her remark to her father.

Judge Cady frowned. "I did not expect that type of behavior this far North. But tourists come very far to see this place, even from the Deep South."

"We were frightened, but…" Elizabeth said. "We rushed up and defended him and chased the men away. Is that not right, Fini?"

"Why yes, I suppose it is, but nevertheless, I will feel safer with Father, or Edward with us."

Elizabeth smiled. She'd made her point. She could not only think like a man, but when required she could act like one too. Stepping up to defend Peter felt powerful. She recognized the improvement in her outlook.

Turning her attention back to the letter from the twins she read, "Camille and Mavis have been in New York City and stopped here for a week." She caught her breath–could they have been exposed to the disease? "They have invited us to dinner tomorrow, Tryphena. Just you and me. Will that not be fun?"

"It is a grand idea, Lib, and for you too, my darling wife," Edward said. "The company of Elizabeth's young friends will be a respite for you."

"So it is settled then?" Elizabeth asked, turning to her father.

He nodded.

"I have to choose what I will wear tomorrow," she explained heading toward the stairs, dismissing any thoughts of her friends being ill. "It is an ever so difficult task, since I brought so few clothes."

Although she loved her family dearly, and especially loved debating with Edward, she looked forward to the excitement of Camille and Mavis. Surely they would have read all of Jane Austen's books. Other than these two girls, her schoolmates rarely discussed topics outside their courses, except for which boy favored which girl and visa versa. The plight of women, or the Negroes enslaved to work on farms, seemed of interest to her closest friends only. Though lately, talking about romance and courting gained in interest for her. Maybe the influence of the Austen books stirred something? Perhaps one or both of the twins were betrothed? She promised herself to ask.

Most of the next morning gave way to tossing dresses one after the other into a pile on her bed. Finally she chose one of blue lawn embroidered with a pattern of dark blue pansies caught under the bodice with a blue ribbon that tied in the back.

There, that is perfect. Oh, I wish I had brought more gowns, she thought. *And at least more than two bonnets.* She picked up a white bonnet trimmed in blue braid and frowned. Its brim had become creased in the hatbox. "This will have to do," she murmured with dissatisfaction.

When Tryphena tapped on her bedroom door, Elizabeth opened it with a flourish. "I am ready," she said.

"You look lovely," her sister said as she smoothed the skirt of the grey Redingote afternoon coat that covered her striped dress from head to toe. She held her bonnet trimmed with grey and white roses by its ribbons.

"As you do," Elizabeth said.

"Come along ladies or you will be late," Edward called up the stairs.

Judge Cady looked up from his newspaper as his two daughters came downstairs. His face lit up.

"Have a lovely time with your friends, Lib, I am delighted they are here to host you both for an amusing afternoon."

"Careful of the damp stones," Edward said as he walked up the path to the Van Wyck cottage just out of sight of their own rental home.

Madge and Camille were waiting on the porch and waved with excitement when they saw their friend.

"Oh, my dear Lizzy," Camille said running to meet her.

Elizabeth embraced her and then gathered both girls in her arms.

"This is my sister Tryphena," she said drawing her into their circle. "And Edward Bayard, her husband," she added.

The twins' mother, Mrs. Van Wyck, stepped forward to grasp the hands of Elizabeth and Tryphena.

"It is so lovely to meet you all," she said. "Mr. Bayard, would you like to join us?"

"Thank you, no," Edward said. "Judge Cady and I thought we would venture out into the village. We will call for my wife and Elizabeth at two o'clock. Will that be all right?"

"It will indeed," Mrs. Van Wyck said.

After Edward left, the twins and their mother ushered Elizabeth and Tryphena into their dining room. Set with a heavy linen cloth and fine china the table bore an arrangement of tiny sandwiches, a bowl of strawberries, a pitcher of cream, and a silver teapot on a stand.

Elizabeth's eyes widened. "Such a grand meal for a holiday visit," she whispered into her sister's ear. "Do you suppose they brought the teapot from home?"

After finishing their dinner, the twins took Elizabeth outside onto the porch where they continued to chat and giggle.

"I have a secret, Lizzy," Camille said.

"Ooh, you are not supposed to tell," Mavis said.

"I shall tell, nevertheless. Lizzy, I have a beau."

"Oh good gracious, who is it?"

"Mr. Guilden, from Saranac. He graduated Rensselaer last term. He is twenty-one and going into his father's law firm."

"I am so very envious, as I have no one," Mavis said, feigning sorrow.

"Oh, pish posh. You will be at all the parties and balls just as we will," said Camille. She dismissed her sister with a wave.

"And you, Lizzy? Anyone special? Mr. Bayard is quite handsome," Mavis said. Her eyes glittered with mischief.

Elizabeth blushed and stammered, "He is my sister's husband." She felt uncomfortable and sought to change the subject.

"Are other girls from school here?" she asked.

"There are other girls," Mavis said, "But I doubt you know them. First year."

"We plan to remedy that," Camille said. "We are having a party with dancing. Everyone we know here is invited."

"We have a lovely meal planned, too, with oysters we brought from New York. The fishmonger gave Mother a huge piece of ice to keep them fresh," Mavis said.

By the time Edward returned to chaperone Elizabeth and Tryphena back to their cottage, the girls were exhausted. First they had debated the latest fashions and manners published in *Godey's Ladies Book*, longing to learn popular English dances from the sheet music in the magazine. That discussion fizzled when no two of the girls could agree. Lastly, the trend of wearing one's gloves when the weather proved too hot made them laugh. Elizabeth spotted a story that made her furious. "This writer says men should buy this magazine to make their wives and mothers better homemakers," she said. "Nonsense. Looking at the latest fashions is one thing, but following the edicts of an editor who cloaks information with lovely prose to show men how to control women is horrid."

*

June 17, 1831

Dear Diary, so much is happening so quickly I felt I must write about events before I forget. Edward goads me and I cannot hold my tongue. I grew angry and when Father intervened I lost my temper. I am not sorry for it either. I cannot abide patronizing behavior from anyone and do not know what stronger sentiments I might have uttered. Even a fine afternoon with my friends didn't change my mind. Oh, dear, I forgot. The bad dreams have vanished.

26

June 1831

Two days later, the innkeeper delivered another note from Mavis and Camille inviting all of Elizabeth's family to the party. Eager for excitement she opened it.

"The Misses Van Wyck, request the pleasure of your company at a country party..." she began reading. "Oh, it is Saturday at 6 o'clock. We can go, can we not, Father?"

"Since we are all invited, of course," he said.

"This will be such fun," she said, clapping her hands. "Such fun." She looked at her sister with the expression of a young woman who has suddenly realized she has but one other suitable gown to wear. The others she judged too plain for a party. "Fini, what shall we do about our dresses?"

"It is two days hence, so we have plenty of time to amend our wardrobes," Tryphena said.

Impatient, Elizabeth ran up the stairs to sort through her clothing. "I am planning now," she said over her shoulder.

By Saturday afternoon, both Elizabeth and her sister rearranged their meager assortment of clothing and accessories to their satisfaction. While Tryphena's appearance took on a more festive style than usual for a married woman, Elizabeth looked more sedate. "If only we had brought our fans," she said.

"Hush, Lib, the weather is fine and the windows will be open wide to the soft evening air. We shall not need fans."

At six o'clock precisely, the Cady entourage walked onto the porch of the Van Wyck cottage. The sounds of a piano being played and cheerful laughter greeted them when Mrs. Van Wyck opened the door.

Camille ran to greet Elizabeth. "Mavis will be down in a moment or two. She is changing her attire."

Elizabeth noticed Camille's discomfort. She kept glancing at the stairs. When Mavis appeared, Camille took her hand to draw her into the room. "Here is my dear sister," she said, smiling broadly.

Elizabeth pulled Camille aside. "Neither of you seem to be yourselves, is something wrong?" she asked.

Camille leaned in to whisper. "Mavis became ill and soiled her undergarments, that is all. She is very embarrassed."

The formal introductions took seconds, as the Van Wyck twins were eager to present Elizabeth to the other young guests. All the while Camille kept her eye on her sister as Mavis went from person to person, greeting each with a kiss on the cheek. When Mavis' lips brushed Elizabeth's skin they felt dry and papery.

Soon Elizabeth found herself involved in conversation with girls from Emma Willard whom she never met and young men who recently graduated from Rensselaer. They were also vacationing at the Falls of Niagara. Morgan Thurgood, a distant cousin of the twins, had invited his friend, Ezekiel Thomason. They were traveling together before they took up positions with an engineering firm in New York City. The two men had heard of the ruckus involving Peter.

"Mr. Thurgood, what do you think of Negroes being allowed to view sites such as these falls?" Elizabeth asked.

He laughed then replied, "Unless the Negro is blind, I have no care at all."

"That is hateful, Cousin," Mavis said, her voice uncharacteristically loud. "Shame on you."

"So you would have defended us?" Elizabeth asked.

"I suppose. Of course if the other chaps were bigger than me, I might have thought differently."

"They were not, merely ignorant louts," Elizabeth said.

"Miss Cady, if I accompanied you and your sister, there would have been no commotion at all. Do you not agree?" The twin's cousin crossed his arms against his chest and leaned back to look down his nose at Elizabeth.

"Mr. Thurgood, considering your attitude I would rather be chaperoned by my long time Negro friend, Peter, than by you." She glared at Morgan Thurgood.

"No more arguing, please," Mavis said, her voice rising. "This is a party to enjoy each other's company, not to set about feuding. I will not have it." Mavis' cheeks glowed and beads of sweat ringed her brow. Elizabeth looked at her in alarm.

"Are you feeling faint, dear friend?" Elizabeth asked, alarmed by her friend's sunken glassy eyes.

"I am very tired," Mavis said. "That is all," she added, then clutched her stomach and abruptly collapsed onto a nearby chair.

At once Camille appeared at her side. "She has been unwell since morning, not keeping down her breakfast meal," she said.

"Please might someone get me some water"? Mavis asked. "I am so very thirsty."

Morgan Thurgood touched Mavis' brow with his fingertips.

"She is very warm," he said. "Someone call her parents to the room. She needs attention immediately."

Mr. Van Wyck rushed into the parlor where the young people hovered around Mavis, gathered her up in his arms and took her upstairs to her bedroom. Moments later he emerged, his face ashen.

"She is barely breathing," he said. "Please attend to her," he said to his wife, "while I fetch a local doctor."

"Whatever could have happened to her?" Elizabeth asked.

"She has not been able to keep down any food since the lovely fresh oysters she ate two days ago," Camille said. "We dined in a restaurant in New York City that claimed to have fresh seafood. Only she ate the oysters."

The party guests mingled in the parlor speaking in hushed voices, stunned by the unfolding events. It seemed like hours, but it was merely minutes before the front door burst open admitting Mr. Van Wyck followed by a man carrying a physician's valise. The two men rushed upstairs and almost at once a terrible cry of anguish echoed down the stairwell.

Judge Cady, Edward and Tryphena had joined Elizabeth during the wait. At the sound of the cry, Elizabeth's father put his arm around her shoulders and pulled her close.

The doctor appeared at the head of the stairs.

"She is dead," he said. "It is the cholera."

Elizabeth wrenched away from her father to seek Camille. When she spotted her being comforted by her cousin, she rushed over.

"Oh, I am so sorry..." she started, only to be waved away.

"Go! Please go," Camille said. "Do not risk yourself."

Edward opened the door and hurried his wife, Judge Cady and Elizabeth down the path toward their cottage.

"I did not think the disease would reach this far," Judge Cady said, his voice taking on a worried tone. "I have read the accounts of its terrible effect, but never expected it to touch us. We must leave at once for home." He paused, "Did any of you eat the oysters?"

"I did not," replied Elizabeth.

Edward and Tryphena shook their heads.

"Why do you ask?" Elizabeth asked.

"The newspaper accounts say physicians now believe the cholera disease is carried in water, and especially in shellfish," Judge Cady said. "Regardless, I do not believe we should stay here."

When they arrived back at their cottage, Edward told Peter of the change in plans. By dawn, Elizabeth sat beside her sister in the carriage, looking back one last time at the Falls of Niagara recalling the terrible events of the visit.

The night before they departed the falls Elizabeth's father and Edward discussed at length the possibilities of the disease following them to Johnstown and into their home.

"Choose one traveling garment from those not worn thus far, and place the remainder into your trunk," Judge Cady told them. "When we arrive home the clothing in the trunk and the trunk itself will be burned."

"My bonnets too?" Elizabeth asked. "They are so lovely and cost a great deal."

"All of our clothing can be replaced," Tryphena said.

"Do not argue."

"The return journey will not be pleasant, but if we take haste and rid ourselves of any object that might carry the cholera, we might prevent illness among ourselves," Edward said.

Traveling home proved more arduous and tiring than expected. Stays at the same inns were marked by sadness and the worry that they were exposed to cholera. Making it worse, their garments began to show traces of being soiled, creating a rank odor in the carriage. Once home Elizabeth lost all interest in keeping her traveling clothing, regardless of their former beauty or cost. She gladly threw them into the bonfire that Abraham built.

To her mother's initial dismay, her father ordered all the bedclothes, the linens, their undergarments, the curtains and the rugs washed in boiling water and lye soap. The house servants worked into the night scrubbing the floor and walls. Every surface the family and servants touched felt soap and the heat of water almost too hot to touch. Even the interior and exterior of the carriage experienced the onslaught of their brushes and rags. Edward and Judge Cady poured through the daily newspapers seeking new reasons for spread of the disease, but only the speculative results of it being waterborne or of living in squalor were reported.

The trip to the Falls of Niagara did succeed in driving out all Elizabeth's remaining thoughts of Reverend Finney's dreadful religious world-view. Yet, the loss of her friend preyed on her mind. Eventually she decided to focus on her happy memories of Mavis and on the concept of life's fragile purpose. Resolved to discover exactly what that meant for her she decided to concentrate on her courses when she returned to Emma Willard. Would her purpose be found there, or did it exist somehow in her growing concern for the plight of women? The dreadful treatment of slaves? For all the trivial pursuits she considered, her thoughts always returned to these sobering realities.

With Tryphena still at the helm of the household responsibilities, as her mother's health improved, Elizabeth spent the remainder of the summer with her sisters, her father and mother, and tried not to focus on Mavis' death.

*

June 18, 1831

Dear Diary, I am devastated. When cholera took my sweet friend, I worried first about myself. Have I been exposed? Will I get it too? I am wicked. Such shameful thoughts when my dear friend has died. Oh, Camille, how you must be suffering the loss of your sister. I am desolate. What if I get sick?

27

September 1831

In a few days she would return to school for her final year. She dreaded seeing her schoolmates who would by then know about Mavis. Letters from Camille reinforced Elizabeth's sense that life was fleeting and should not be taken for granted. The day before she left for Emma Willard, she sat at her desk to write Camille a letter, for she knew Mavis' dear sister would not return.

September 10, 1831,

My dear Camille, I will miss you so in our courses, but particularly during those hours we spent chatting and gossiping about trifles. Please know that I will always be your friend, and you will be in my heart, as will your dear sister. I will never forget her or you and will remember the joyous times we spent together. Please come for a visit when you can and are able. I hold you in my thoughts,

Yours, Elizabeth Cady.

She folded the letter and dropped sealing wax on the flap to close it. "There," she said, pressing the warm wax with her initial stamp. "That is done." She placed the letter by the front door, knowing it would be taken to the post office the next day, then paused by the front window to gaze at the street beyond. The first cold days painted the leaf tips of the poplar trees bright yellow. The trees were beautiful, but she grimaced, recalling a childhood memory of the nasty worms that dropped from them onto people's heads in summer.

Female passersby now wore wool gloves and heavier Redingote coats covered their dresses completely. Bursts of frosty mist marked the words of men hurrying along in conversation. Jacob and Abraham were raking up trimmings from the bushes, piling them into a wooden cart to drag to the back. Their ordinary preoccupation with attending to the seasons comforted her. Lost in reverie, she didn't hear her mother approach until she spoke.

"Elizabeth?"

"Why, Mother, you came downstairs. Are you joining us this evening?" she asked.

Behind her mother stood Madge and Kate, no longer victims of matching dresses. At fifteen and thirteen, her sisters now chose their own clothing and each delighted in exhibiting her own distinctive style. Madge preferred more sedate dresses, while Kate's gowns were beribboned. Her sisters each held one of their mother's hands.

"We have come to gather you up for supper in the dining room," Madge said. "It is to be a grand meal since tomorrow you leave us."

Even though Mrs. Brewster prepared chicken cutlets and artichokes with butter that Elizabeth adored, she pushed her food around on her plate.

"Dearest Lib," her mother said, "We have apple tart for dessert. Please do eat something."

Elizabeth glanced at her mother not wishing to distress her.

"Yes Ma'am," she said, picking up her knife and fork to cut a small bit of chicken. Of late, preparations for her return to school evoked sad memories and the events surrounding Mavis' death obsessed her. Did the cholera come from food she ate too? Why didn't she get it? Or Camille? Or Fini? Edward? Her father?

"Excuse me please," she said then jumped up and rushed from the room.

When her mother came to check on her much later, Elizabeth sat in the window well of her bedchamber looking down on the street below. Gas lamps glowed on the cobbles and reflected off the tops of carriages going by. The stream of people walking alongside the road from New York, and their makeshift camps that they passed on their journey to the falls, gained new meaning. She now knew they must have been fleeing the cholera. She shuddered when she recalled the sight of men spading fresh earth beside a wagon pulled off to the side of the road and what that must have meant. Elizabeth devoured stories about the epidemic. After her father and Edward cast aside the daily papers, she gathered them up and took them into the library to read. Early reports claimed nearly 100,000 people perished, yet fewer incidents now occurred. Some people were exposed to the same environment, but did not get sick.

"What has so possessed you of late?" her mother asked. "You have had your nose in that stack of newspapers there for days." She pointed to the floor beside Elizabeth's chair where she had placed a heavy book on top of the papers to hold them in place.

"It is the cholera disease," Elizabeth responded. "I am trying to figure out how Mavis came into contact with it. The disease started in England, the *New York Tribune* reports, and then came to New York aboard a ship in June. Maybe with an ill sailor. Many of the men who work aboard the ships live in that deplorable Five Points area near the docks."

"Surely Mavis and her family would not come into contact with men of that class," Elizabeth's mother said.

"I think not also. Yet when seafood comes ashore at the docks it is set aside onto streets that teem with garbage and filth and water flowing through it. If a sailor handling it were ill..." her voice trailed off. "Mother, the reports say pigs walk among the people there. You know how dirty a pig can be. And people empty their chamber pots in the street too. The Sanatory Committee of the Board of Health claims fumes from rotting food and such carry the disease."

"I recall Tryphena said Mavis did eat oysters."

"It could also mean that a kitchen helper lived in one of the squalid cellar rooms there too," Elizabeth said. "If he were ill with the disease, his spittle or worse could have been on his hands. It is so dreadful." Tears filled her eyes as she thought about Mavis' last moments.

"Dearest Lib, you must not worry about this," her mother said. "We are healthy and, with all the precautions your father insisted upon, it is not likely anyone in our family will fall victim to the disease. Please do not vex yourself so."

"Mother, I love Mavis and Camille like sisters. We were true comrades and Mavis, in particular, offered such help to me after those awful Reverend Finney encounters."

"And so Camille needs your friendship now. Even more than before," her mother replied. "It will do you good to return to the Troy Seminary and you must encourage Camille to accompany you. Even if she does not choose to do so, it will help her to know you are a good friend willing to support her."

Elizabeth took a deep breath, continuing to stare through the window during the conversation. "Mother, do you see how the carriages are black. Not a gay color at all? Perhaps they are hearses, not carriages, and drive by filled with friends we will no longer visit."

Her mother came to Elizabeth's side and sat down behind her. "My brightest and most passionate daughter, I cannot stand to see you so sad and morose. Please consider some happier thoughts, for tomorrow you leave and I must believe you are strong enough to finish your schooling." She reached out to touch her daughter's shoulder, but Elizabeth turned to fling her arms around her mother's neck.

"I love you, Mother," she said, "and I am glad you are in good health again. I missed you so much." She didn't know if she wept for her mother, or for Mavis, or for them all.

The next morning, Madge and Kate came into her room just as she finished washing her face. Her traveling suit lay on the bed and with her trunk already downstairs she needed but to dress and go down for breakfast.

"You will write?" Kate asked.

"Of course she will," Madge explained.

Kate rolled her eyes.

*

September 10, 1831

Dear Diary, I am back at school now, but I am not myself. I still cannot shake off the sadness of Mavis' death. The cholera took many people we knew but none so close as my friend. I am glad I did not get sick. If that is selfish, so be it. Camille did not return. She sent me a mourning pin that I wear every day. I miss her. For the remainder of summer I did not enjoy much of anything and lost my appetite for food. One of father's students said I looked gaunt. My petticoats are still so loose I had to wrap a ribbon around them so they would not slip to the ground. I do not care. Mother's strength and belief in me helped mend this break in my heart. I love her and do not tell her enough. Classes start tomorrow. I know I must eat. How will I survive?

By early evening, her diary lying open on her bed, forgotten, Elizabeth sat glumly in her room, the same one that housed her first two years. Her trunk stood pushed against the wall still locked. A knock at the open door broke her reverie.

"Mrs. Willard," Elizabeth said. "Please come in. I am glad to see you again."

"Miss Cady, you did not take tea with us. You must be hungry." She placed a tray on Elizabeth's small desk.

"Just a bit of cold meat and cheese, some bread, an apple and hot tea."

"Thank you for your kindness."

"I know about Camille's poor sister. You must miss your friend. In time, though her memory will last, your sorrow will fade. You must eat to keep up your strength, dear."

Mrs. Willard's gesture warmed Elizabeth's heart. Perhaps memories of the woman's everlasting support of her students or her sweet mothering instincts appealed to Elizabeth or merely the aroma of the food ignited her hunger. "I do appreciate your thoughtfulness," she said, "and I will eat. And sleep, I think."

"Good," Mrs. Willard said, patting Elizabeth's hand. "By tomorrow you will be revived and ready for your first class. It is French, I believe. I am looking to you to help the first year students. Your French is quite good."

Too tired to unpack her clothes that night, after consuming everything on the tray and licking her fingers she climbed into bed resolved to be cheerful in the morning.

Three months passed and Christmas drew near. Her correspondence with Camille flew back and forth; each missive became happier and less about Mavis than the first.

Constant letters from her sisters talked of parties, their lessons, and Mother's return to strict behavior requirements for which they were not pleased. Just before Elizabeth left for Christmas with her family, Camille wrote that she would return to school in January. Her family's period of mourning would soon end, Camille said, soon enough for her to finish her education. Elizabeth's elation knew no bounds.

Snow flurries already blanketed the ground and there was the prospect of frozen roads, so Elizabeth wrote her father asking to be allowed to return home for Christmas on the train. Train service had just begun between Troy and Johnston with the Troy station near Emma Willard. Although her father wrote that at first he did not approve, he said Edward convinced him to allow her to embark on the adventure. Edward had assured Judge Cady and her mother that he would accompany her. Although Tryphena had intended to travel along with him, she begged off, pleading that she had Christmas preparations to attend to. Edward sent a note telling Elizabeth he would call for her alone. Could she trust herself with him?

*

December 15, 1831

Dear Diary, it is snowing hard and piling on the ground in great heaps. In two days I leave for home. Edward has not seen me for a while so I must wear my most becoming dress. It will be lovely to spend the time with him without Fini.

*Just the two of us. I think of him too much. I know
I should not. Oh my. This will be exciting.*

Elizabeth stood waiting inside the main Seminary entrance, having decided on a midnight blue wool traveling suit with a fur collar that would keep her warm. Her matching bonnet lined in blue silk matched her eyes, or what one could see of them from the depths of the bonnet's deep brim.

"Edward," Elizabeth exclaimed when he opened the door and stood stamping his feet on the wooden mat inside. "Thank you for fetching me. I know you must have spoken with great skill to convince Father."

Edward's broad smile widened as she spoke. She thought he had never been so handsome. The cold had flushed color into his cheeks and the tip of his nose that made her smile.

"Are you ready? We have but moments to get to the train. I have a sleigh at the curb. A fellow offered them for lease at the station," he said, loading her trunk, then grabbing her valise.

The train belched gusts of steam and mist as it stood at the station waiting for passengers. They drove up and Edward handed the reins and a fistful of bills to a porter. A nervous conductor shouting "All aboard!" walked through the crowds of people, some corralling children, others loading baggage.

Edward helped Elizabeth up the train steps and found a bench midway down the car. He brushed off the wooden surface with his handkerchief then hurried to stow her valise with the porter. When he returned to tumble into his place as the train lurched, the aroma of his cologne and the wool scent of his coat engulfed her and did much to dispel the reeking bodily odors of some of the passengers. Still, she held a perfumed handkerchief to her nose.

"A bit unsteady on my feet," he said and laughed.

"Better you than me walking about this rocking train," Elizabeth said, grateful she did not have to manage bulky petticoats along the narrow aisle for any distance.

By noon his questions about school and her animated responses waned.

"I am going to find us something to eat, and perhaps hot tea," he said. He stood to investigate the train's meal possibilities just as a young woman wearing a striped gown, a clean apron, and a starched bonnet began making her way down the aisle of their car. She carried a large basket covered with a white cloth.

"Lunch for all," she cried. "Meat pies. Cakes. Hot tea." When she turned their way, Edward beckoned her over.

He looked down at Elizabeth. "Well?"

"One of each," she said. "I am starving."

Edward braced himself in the narrow aisle as the woman came abreast of them. He made a selection from the basket, paid the young woman and with shaky hands handed Elizabeth a small teapot and two china cups. When the saleswoman eased by him to serve other travelers, Edward sunk down on the bench, his hands full, looking puzzled.

"I am not sure how we might consume these without a proper table." He smiled at the absurd situation and shrugged his shoulders.

Elizabeth rummaged in her reticule handbag for another handkerchief. "Here," she said, spreading it across her lap. "This will manage nicely for me. You have a similar handkerchief to protect your trousers as well." She drew her skirts to her side to allow room between them for the cups and teapot then reached for the paper-wrapped pie in Edward's hand. "Place the cakes here," she said, gesturing to a narrow space beside the teapot.

Edward appeared to be uncomfortable with the cramped dining restriction, but she chose to ignore him and began devouring the food. Eating helped distract her from thinking about his closeness and how much she liked it.

For ten or so minutes the clanking of the train on the tracks, and its mournful wail as it rushed through a tiny village, combined with murmurs of polite chewing. The tea cooled by the time Elizabeth braved the sway of the railroad car to dare pour it into a cup. It revived her, nevertheless. In time the young saleswoman made her way back through the train to gather the debris from their luncheon. By then, Elizabeth's curiosity about the remainder of their trip grew once again. Edward brought a book with him and opened it to its ribbon bookmark.

She glanced at the title: *The Conquest of Granada* by John Dryden.

"You have not recommended this author for me, Edward. Is it a good book? One that I would like?" she asked.

"It is a play written long ago in poetic stanzas–a tragic story of love and jealousy," he replied, clearing his throat. "I rather like the words Dryden chooses," Edward continued almost in a whisper. "You might like it too. When we arrive home, take the book. Read it."

Elizabeth turned her attention to the landscape sliding by their window. Her face burned and she felt unsettled. What could he mean recommending a book with such a sensitive plot? Was there more to this than might be on the surface? With Edward here so close, she could steal glances at his profile without his knowing and then abruptly look away. Perhaps he was sending her a message. *It's nice having him here, warm and smelling of good cologne, leather and wool.* She pressed her nose against the glass, recoiling at its sharp tingle. Best think of something else, she reckoned, pushing her careless thoughts of Edward deep down inside.

*

December 16, 1831

Dear Diary, the railroad train trip home turned out to be noisy and dirty. The best part? Edward. Having the dear man beside me and all to myself. He seemed a bit ill at ease, which surprised me, as we have been friends for so long. Having his handsome self so near was wonderful, though. I know envy is a sin, yet I envy my sister for her marriage to him. I will never be an angel for my thoughts are too wicked.

28

December 1831

Peter waited for them, bundled to his ears in a gray wool coat, hunched down on the driver's seat of their trap at the train station. A red muffler wrapped tight around his neck covered everything except his brown eyes. He stood out against the snowy landscape as the horse stamped its hooves and snorted huge bursts of frosty breath to stay warm. Elizabeth waved through the window to catch his attention. Peter jumped down from the carriage and hurried to the doorway of their car, ready to grab her trunk and valise. Travelers poured out of the railcar doors and began to mingle with families and friends on the platform. The brittle cold air, now full of shouts of *Merry Christmas* and laughter, heightened Elizabeth's excitement to be home.

Once she and Edward were tucked into the carriage under a pile of blankets and a bearskin rug, Peter slapped the reins and the carriage wheels began to rumble and rattle up the frozen cobbled street. Even with the precautions Peter took to make sure they were warm, Elizabeth wished she'd worn woolen stockings. Vanity made her choose the thin blue cotton pair that matched her dress, likely now the same color as her frozen toes.

Peter drove the trap right up to the front door because of the heavy snow, stopping the horse in an unfamiliar location. The confused animal danced about, refusing to stop, jerking the trap to and fro. The front door to the Cady home flew open to reveal Elizabeth's sisters and her father and mother.

"Whatever is happening out here?" Judge Cady asked.

"Elizabeth!" "Sister!" Madge and Kate shrieked in the background and then ran into the snow to grab Elizabeth as Edward helped her down. Peter wrestled the horse into submission and stood by the animal's head, speaking to it in soothing tones.

Elizabeth's mother stood inside the door, clutching a shawl to her throat. She held her husband's arm. "My dears, what an exciting arrival," she said. "Hurry, it is frightfully cold."

Elizabeth finally made it inside followed by Edward carrying her valise and Peter hefting her small trunk into the vestibule.

"Peter, you get inside and get yourself some hot coffee in the kitchen after you take care of the horse and carriage. We have no more need of your services today. Have a pleasant evening," Judge Cady said.

"Mother, the house is so beautifully festooned. I am sorry I did not get to help," Elizabeth said, breathing in the resin scent of fresh-cut fir branches tied to the staircase banisters with red ribbons.

"I stood in for you," said Tryphena emerging from the kitchen wiping her hands on a floury apron.

Elizabeth ran to embrace her sister ignoring protests that baking remains would soil her traveling coat. "You are assisting Mrs. Brewster, I see," Elizabeth said. Her eyes twinkled. "Let me change and put my things away, then I shall help, too."

"Father and Mother said you would take us into town," Kate said. "I want to do that now, and not bother with the baking."

"Stop complaining," Madge said to her youngest sister.

"Nothing has changed, I see. It is good to be home," Elizabeth said. "I have missed you all."

That night at supper, Elizabeth and Edward told the family about their train journey. Throughout the conversation, Elizabeth listened for comments Edward might make about the personal nature of the trip. None were evident that she could recognize. Did she imagine their closeness?

"The smell is dreadfully bad," Elizabeth said. "Farmers and working men whose clothes reek of manure and perspiration were the worst. Some of the men spit their chewing tobacco onto the floor. I feared the hem of my skirt would be despoiled."

Her sisters gasped. "Were there no spittoons?" Madge asked.

Elizabeth shook her head. "Not that I saw."

"She kept her handkerchief to her nose, save for when we ate our meal," Edward said.

"Did you choose a safe car, my dear?" Tryphena asked her husband.

"Yes, but the train is a public conveyance, making no discrimination about its passengers," he said.

"I can only imagine what it must be like in warm weather. The cold keeps odors at a minimum," Mrs. Cady said.

"True, but even so, having my perfumed handkerchief became a blessing."

Judge Cady cleared his throat. "Enough talk about aromas and train trips. Let us concentrate on the pleasantries of celebrating Christmas," he said.

"Quite right, Mr. Cady," Elizabeth's mother said. "Tomorrow we women, and that includes you, Tryphena dear, will go into town for a leisurely day of shopping and a stop for tea and cakes."

"That is lovely, Mother, thank you so much," Kate said. She clasped her hands beneath her chin. "I have a new fur muff to wear that keeps my hands warm. It will snow on us, I am certain."

After Elizabeth went to bed, Madge and Kate rapped on her door then opened it a crack to peer inside. "Can we come in?" Madge whispered, then without waiting for an answer they slipped in and crawled into bed with her.

Just like when they were children, the three girls chatted and giggled about everything until Elizabeth asked about their mother's health.

"At first her illness kept her in bed," Madge said.

"Yes, I knew that, even at school."

"She pined so much for the baby. When you left, Mother seemed to fall apart. No one could console her," Kate said.

"God bless Fini. I do not think it is her choice, but what could she do?" Madge asked.

"Having our sister in charge of everything has been fun, though. She makes us study, but allows us time for our painting and needlework, too. Mother's rules did not permit so much leisure time," Kate said.

"You two are doing well at the Academy?" Elizabeth asked.

"Because of you, we have to do well," Madge said. "Father could not say no to us attending after you convinced him. And stop teasing. You know I go to Troy Seminary next year. I will be quite finished with the Academy in June."

"And I will be home to help Kate with her studies," Elizabeth said. "That is, if I do not marry."

"What? You have a beau? Do our parents know about this?" Kate asked.

Elizabeth giggled and pulled her sister close to whisper in her ear, "No, and no. But I shall have one and when I do I will tell you first. Then Mother and Father."

"Good," Kate said.

"Mother is feeling stronger, do you not think?" Elizabeth asked.

"She and Fini have had words—you remember how they argue—so yes, I believe she has improved," Madge said. Her eyes twinkled.

"And, she has the maids polishing the silver, too. Tryphena did not do that," Kate said.

After a long silence broken only by the wind breaking icicles from the eaves, Elizabeth yawned.

"I love Christmas, do you not as well?" she asked.

"Oh yes, truly," Kate said.

"Tomorrow's outing will be lovely," Madge said. "I am so glad you are home, Lib. We missed you dreadfully."

"And I you, my dears." Elizabeth yawned again. "Now let us all get some sleep so tomorrow we have energy enough to pull Mother and Fini through all the shops," she said.

"Good night, Lib," Madge said, kissing her sister on the cheek and then joining Kate to slip out of bed and close Elizabeth's bedroom door behind them.

The house bustled with activity the next morning when Elizabeth came down the stairs for breakfast. Four of her father's law students sat at the table along with her sisters and mother. Each of the young men seemed to be talking at the same time, interrupting to punctuate their comments with a piece of toasted bread or a raised fork.

"Gentlemen, please," her mother said just as Elizabeth entered the room and a bit of bread flew into the air.

"Oh, I am so sorry Mrs. Cady," the youngest of the men said, rising to his feet to retrieve the crust from the floor. His cheeks reddened. He ducked his head in embarrassment when he looked up to see Elizabeth standing in the doorway.

"My daughter, Elizabeth," her mother said.

"Mrs. Cady. Miss Cady. Excuse my poor manners," the man said then rushed from the room.

Kate giggled behind her napkin.

Elizabeth filled her plate from the sideboard, adding poached eggs, a rasher of bacon and a cup of coffee. She chose a chair directly across from the law students.

"Whatever issue caused that display of flying toast?" she asked, her gaze fixed on Robert Geyer, the shortest of the men, whose collar bit into his neck.

"The issue of abolition, Miss Cady," he replied. "We have been studying the possibility of changes to the law with your father and arrived at differing opinions."

Elizabeth took her time adding milk and sugar to her coffee before she responded.

"So you know his opinion on the subject?"

"I do. He wishes to abolish the practice of owning slaves and I am not sure he is correct."

"How so? He is your teacher and you are a pupil. Do you not consider that his views might be correct?"

"Well, yes I do, but historically–"

"And history is merely a change in the ways things are done," Elizabeth interrupted. "So, perhaps abolishing slavery, which is dreadful and a demeaning condition, is history in the making."

"Pardon, Miss, but you do not know the implications of abolition. The country's economy would slip behind. Farmers would lose money. We would all suffer if the price of goods gained as a result of losing the slave labor force."

"Why do you presume I would not know that line of discourse?" Elizabeth asked.

Geyer stuttered, his expression that of surprise. "It is a topic for men, Miss," he said. "Not for the delicate ears of women."

Edward Bayard entered the room and stopped to listen.

"Sir, our Constitution says 'all men are created equal.' It does not say 'all but Negro men.'" Elizabeth continued. "When the ink on the Constitution was still wet, the abolitionist Thomas Jay claimed it a hypocrisy to be an American patriot and, as he said, 'brandish a whip over his affrighted slaves.'" Elizabeth pressed her point. "Argument for its sake alone is futile, but to shed light on an old tired law when the future looms bright and promising is to argue that change is good."

Elizabeth's sisters looked on in silence, stunned. However, the remaining law students dispatched their meal with haste and excused themselves, along with Robert Geyer, to return to Judge Cady's law office.

"Your powers of argument have grown, Lib," Edward said.

"It is your coaching, my husband," said Tryphena.

"No, it is her education," Edward said.

"You made Mr. Geyer spit on his waistcoat, Lib," said Kate.

"I think he might be quite sick," Madge said, "having lost an argument to a girl. When I go to Emma Willard I shall learn to speak up just like you do."

Elizabeth looked up from her plate where she buttered the last bit of toast and added strawberry jam. "Girls have every right to speak up," she said.

Her mother sighed. "Daughters, do not vex me so," she said.

*

December 16, 1831
Dear Diary, Mother is up, having recovered from losing the baby. Now, two brothers I might have loved. However, we are thoroughly involved in Christmas preparations that brighten everyone. Father's law students are about the house as usual, dining with us and speaking their opinions when asked, and when not asked as well. I have found one whose comments are more displeasing than informed. People with closed minds infuriate me.

29

December 1831

After two days of Christmas shopping, one spent merely gazing into shop windows and planning, Elizabeth's small gifts were beribboned and ready. For Kate, she'd chosen two new cedar pencils sharpened by Peter. Madge would receive a lace-trimmed handkerchief embroidered with pansies. A tortoiseshell hairpin suited Tryphena, and for Edward she'd wrapped six peppermint twists she knew he liked. Mother would open a small packet of notepaper and for her father she wrote a poem about the love of family.

Even with the onslaught of winter keeping most people inside, Judge Cady's law students arrived for study as usual on Christmas morning for study. Elizabeth and her sisters rose early, including Tryphena, who supervised preparations of the special recipes for Christmas breakfast. They were underfoot in the kitchen dodging Mrs. Brewster and her helpers when the young men arrived.

Judge Cady appeared at the kitchen door. "Elizabeth, one of my students would like to speak to you," he said.

She looked up from the mound of cookie dough she'd begun to role out for cutting shapes. "Now?" she asked. "Or might I come in a few minutes?"

Her father cleared his throat. "If I am to have his attention for the rest of the day, now would be better."

Elizabeth cleaned her hands of the sticky cookie dough, removed her apron and followed her father into the hallway.

Robert Geyer stood there reeking of bay rum cologne. His starched shirt glowed white in the dim light of the hall. Judge Cady waited nearby.

Elizabeth cocked her head. "Yes?"

"Miss Cady, I would like to apologize for my outburst and say that I have never experienced such a lively conversation with a young woman before. In fact, never with a woman who would not stop talking."

"Mr. Geyer that does not sound like an apology but an incitement to debate again," Elizabeth said. "That you think I cannot stop talking is insulting," she added, taking a breath to continue.

Robert interrupted. "Miss Cady, if you will cease speaking for a moment, I have a proposition for you."

Elizabeth pressed her lips tightly and crossed her arms.

"If you will do me the honor, I would like you to accompany me on a short ride tomorrow to take a deposition in Gloversville. I will be speaking to a young woman and believe your presence will ease her discomfort. Your father has approved."

When her father nodded she said, "I accept your invitation, and if you think my talking would interfere, I pledge to be quiet."

Robert smiled. "Thank you Miss Cady, I will call for you at ten o'clock in the morning," he said, then turned on his heel and walked with haste into her father's office.

Elizabeth clapped her hands over her mouth.

"Lib, please do not do anything mischievous," her father warned. "This young man means well and he is becoming a fine lawyer."

"Yes, Father," she said dropping her hands to her sides before she hurried away, laughing.

The following morning Elizabeth greeted Robert when he came to the breakfast table. "Father has asked Peter to drive us. Since the weather is cold, I prefer to ride inside the carriage, but you will need to sit with Peter to direct him," she said.

"As you wish, Miss Cady. I am indebted to your father for his kindness. I will gather my books and documents. Thirty minutes then?" he asked.

As Elizabeth nodded she said, "The journey will be quieter too. I can read and you will not have to listen to my chatter." She smiled the sweetest way as she could. "I will get my shawl and bonnet and be in the carriage when you are ready to go," she said.

When Robert left the table, Elizabeth rushed into the depths of the house to find her youngest sister. The two girls hurried to the stable and with Kate's help, Elizabeth removed her dress and donned another, then began to stuff the clothes she'd worn at breakfast with straw.

"Pack it in tight," she said, pushing hands full into the balloon-like sleeves.

Kate giggled. "What shall we do for the head?" she asked.

"Oh, dear. Let me think," she paused then said, "Grab the end of the shawl and pull it through the back of the dress. We'll just fill it."

Once the straw dummy looked almost like a person, Elizabeth tied her bonnet onto it.

"Lib. It is marvelous. You are so clever. He will never notice," Kate said.

The two girls dragged the dummy to the carriage then pulled and pushed it into the seat inside. Elizabeth tied the ends of her shawl together in the front of the dummy concealing the straw poking out of the sleeves.

"It does look like you, Lib. Like you are reading," Kate said, clasping her hands in delight.

The door to the stable opened wide to reveal Peter striding in to saddle the carriage horses.

"Miss Elizabeth. Miss Catherine. What are you young ladies doing in here?" he asked.

"It is a secret, Peter," Kate said. "Sister is playing a joke on Robert Geyer. It is all in fun."

"Miss Elizabeth?"

"It is all right. You just drive around to the front door and tell Mr. Geyer that I am waiting in the carriage. Everything is arranged, he will not ask any questions."

Peter shook his head and muttered something under his breath that Elizabeth thought sounded like, "You be in trouble, Miss."

As soon as Peter drove the carriage into the drive, Elizabeth and Kate ducked into the house and ran to the front window to peek out behind the draperies.

Robert Geyer walked out of the judge's office, glanced at the carriage door window and then climbed up on top to sit beside Peter.

Inside the house, Elizabeth and Kate laughed so loudly Madge came to investigate.

"Oh my side hurts." Elizabeth grasped her waist as she tried to tell Madge what happened.

Tears ran down Kate's face, and she ran for a glass of water to stop the fit of hiccupping that overcame her.

"This is such a clever prank," Madge said. "Serves Robert right for thinking he is so superior to us because we are girls. Father will have something to say about this once he finds out, though."

"He encourages us to argue with his students, so I think he will understand," Elizabeth said. "Well, perhaps."

"He will not. Just like when we were younger, we shall be in trouble."

"I do not care," Elizabeth said. She did care though, and steeled herself for the inevitable confrontation with her father.

Later that day, she put aside her copy of *Ladies Magazine* when she heard the rumble of the carriage return.

Immediately she ran to her window to look below and saw Robert jump down, holding his leather documents and books case, and stride into her father's office.

Moments later, the office door opened and she heard her father calling her name.

She walked to the upstairs railing. "Yes, Father?" she said.

"Come down, Daughter. Now."

She found Judge Cady leaning against the corner of his desk when she entered his office. "You embarrassed young Geyer," he said.

"He no more needed me there than a muzzled dog. Saying the deposition would be easier is pretext. Nothing more. He seeks favor, Father, that is all."

Her father shook his head, his expression that of a person who wonders what he has wrought.

"Did he get the deposition?" Elizabeth asked.

Her father nodded.

"See?"

"Lib, you argue better than most of my students. If you had been a boy, I believe you would have been a fine lawyer. Placate me though. Do not do this again. And, if you can contain yourself, do not bait the other young men either."

*

December 18, 1831

Dear Diary, Robert Geyer, got just what he deserved. I probably should not have involved Madge and Kate but the result was priceless. Father acknowledged that I am as good as any boy. Not for the prank, but because I can argue as well as his students. Of course he admonished me, too, and I promised never to play another such trick. My fingers were crossed though.

The family stayed late by the fire Christmas Eve decorating their spruce tree with garlands of popcorn and strings of cranberries. Adding fifty or so white candles to the branches, a job that had always been Eleazar's while he lived, now fell to Elizabeth's father. The change in the tradition always evoked a somber hush when the time came to light the candles. As the tree grew warm from the candle flames its resinous scent filled the room, evoking a melancholy emotion in Elizabeth. Later, her mood lightened when exchanging gifts developed into an exciting event with much laughter and teasing. When her father opened and read the poem she'd written for him, he wiped his eyes then reached for her hand to squeeze it. One final tradition remained. Eleazar always read aloud the Reverend Clement Clarke Moore's poem, *A Visit from St. Nicholas* that had appeared in the Troy newspaper in 1823. Once everyone held a cup of mulled apple cider, Tryphena took his place.

"*Twas the night before Christmas and all through the house, not a creature was stirring...*" She began.

The sound of Tryphena's voice grew softer as she read the beloved words. Usually her spare conversations, explicit and easily interpreted, were directed to the servants or to Edward, so her taking over the tradition was an unexpected treat. Elizabeth sat in a corner of the sofa and gazed into the fire, listening with a hand on her chin. Abraham came in bearing an armload of wood accompanied by a draft of freezing air, and Elizabeth pulled her shawl closer to her shoulders and up around her neck

"Is all well with you and the men?" Her father asked Abraham.

"Yes, Sir. We's fine and snug in our cottage. I thank you Sir for the goose and the sweet potatoes. Peter is mighty pleased with the woolen shirts too. Merry Christmas to you all," he said.

Elizabeth looked around at the faces of her family, glowing and relaxed in the warmth of the room. This special time would end soon. Her last semester at Emma Willard began in a week.

Christmas morning dawned with ice splinters glazing the windows. Elizabeth dreaded stepping onto the wood floor but if she didn't appear soon, her mother would come looking for her. Their holiday breakfast would be laid out by now. She hurried to pull on her petticoats and the blue velvet dress she'd chosen for the day. Robert Geyer, along with the rest of her father's students, would be there to dine. It would be the first time she saw him since the day he learned just how quiet she could be. He certainly would have a comment or two. Elizabeth paused to stare in her looking glass. She fastened the sapphire earrings her father gave her on her birthday and pinched her cheeks. After she arranged the curls across her brow in a becoming fringe she smiled at her reflection.

The students who clustered around her father at the end of the table were shoveling food into their mouths in silence.

Sarah Bates

Except for Robert Geyer, deep in conversation with her brother-in-law. Immediately, Elizabeth went to her mother seated at the other end of the table.

"Happy Christmas, Mother," she said, bending to kiss her mother's cheek and noticing some improved color in her skin. Her eyes sparkled, too.

"And to you, Daughter," her mother said. "Your father has suggested a sleigh ride after breakfast. Does that appeal to you?"

"It does. For all of us?"

"Edward and Tryphena will stay here, but the rest of the family will go. Uncle John is staying nearby, taking a holiday from his real estate interests in New York. We are to visit him."

"Oh, that is lovely. I wonder if he still carries sweets in his pockets for me?" Elizabeth asked.

"If not for you, Lib, perhaps for Kate."

Elizabeth filled her plate and sat down between Kate and Madge. Her sisters' eyes were glowing. Madge kept glancing at the handsome students now talking to their father between bites of smoked ham and beaten biscuits.

Kate looked sidelong at Elizabeth and said, "Robert Geyer has asked for you." Her soft giggle gave away her lie though, and Elizabeth shook her finger at her.

When she rose to seek another pastry from a tray, she encountered Robert at the buffet table.

"Miss Cady," he said, nodding.

"Mr. Geyer."

"Your small joke embarrassed me," he said. "I see that you do not take me seriously."

"I meant it in fun," Elizabeth said.

"I did not think it funny," he said, turning away from her to return to his place with his colleagues.

Foolish man.

"What did he say?" Kate asked when Elizabeth returned to her place beside her sister.

"Nothing really. I detest people with no sense of humor." Could she be the only one with merriment in her mind along with more sober thoughts? Too much somberness with those men. There is a time to be serious-minded, but it is dreary to behave like that all the time.

Tucked into the sleigh, wrapped in blankets and a fur coverlet, and flanked by Kate and Madge, Elizabeth looked across at her mother and father. Facing them, she could watch their expressions as they talked. The pain of her mother's loss of the baby seemed to have passed and she noticed her nuzzle her father's cheek.

"Are you girls warm enough?" her mother asked, reaching to push a corner of a blanket under her own legs.

The tip of Elizabeth's nose felt cold, and she knew it must glow red, but she nodded all the same.

Sliding through the fresh powder blanketing the road became dream-like and Elizabeth reveled in the pristine beauty of the landscape.

She pondered the relationship Robert Geyer tried to establish. Why didn't she like the man? He had certainly seemed interested in her before her practical joke fell flat. His face was pleasant enough. His fawning demeanor with her father? That was it, she decided. And, he didn't respect her mind. That was worse. Only Edward saw her as an equal. Her cheeks flamed and to cover her discomfort she pulled her wool muffler up over her nose.

By the time the family reached the inn where her Uncle John had booked rooms, her cheerful attitude had returned. Most important, Robert Geyer and all his nonsense had been dismissed.

*

December 25, 1831

Dear Diary, this Christmas has been filled with new and unusual events. My sharp tongue and eagerness to prove I am an equal hurt the feelings of a young law student. I must be terrible because when he confronted me with his plaintive remarks about the prank I played, I could not find it in myself to apologize. I am not sorry. I recognize this as a terrible character trait that emerges when I least expect it. I will never find a beau (if I were looking for one) let alone a husband, if I measure all who claim interest in me by Edward. He is perfect, but taken.

30

January 1832

Returning to school for the remaining few months of her last year perplexed Elizabeth. She knew it would be different: new classes, new students, and diverse experiences. She had changed too. What of the happy routine with friends she trusted, now destroyed by a dreadful disease? Would seeing Camille without her twin be painful?

A knock on the door interrupted her pensive mood.

"Camille! I am so happy to see you at last," she said. She threw her arms around her friend whose grasp threatened to throw her off her feet.

Both girls were in tears, sniffling and blowing into handkerchiefs as they tried to talk.

"It will not be the same," Elizabeth finally ventured.

"Yes, but Mavis would want us to make new memories. I know that," Camille said.

"And so we will," Elizabeth agreed. "Let us find out who is new. Perhaps it will be someone we can bedevil." She laughed out loud and grabbed Camille's hand to pull her into the hallway.

When the two girls went down for supper Mrs. Willard called them aside. "Young ladies, I know you were friends with Amy Lee Mathews. I am delighted to tell you she married at Christmas time and will not be returning for her last year with us."

The girls exchanged glances.

"Who did she marry? Someone we know?" Camille asked.

"Someone from Rensselaer?" Elizabeth asked.

"Her mother wrote that Amy Lee's new husband is a Berkeley, descended from George Berkeley, the famous philosopher. He did attend Rensselaer."

"Sounds awfully dull to me," Camille said. "An engineer."

"Their conversations must be so varied," Elizabeth said. "Clothes and dancing was all that interested Amy Lee. Whatever can they talk about?"

"That is not important, is it?" Mrs. Willard said. "You two please make the new girls feel welcome. Can I count on you?"

Elizabeth nodded. "Yes Ma'am."

That evening the two girls set about introducing themselves to the new students. The chatter in the dining hall sounded familiar and reassuring, and as Elizabeth and Camille walked from table to table, Elizabeth's spirits rose.

"You were here when the Reverend Finney conducted his revival meetings. Am I correct?" asked a girl whose complexion verged on the color of chalk. Her eyes gleamed.

Elizabeth glanced at Camille before she answered. At her friend's subtle nod she replied. "I was," she said, "and I became quite taken with his sermons. I have returned to my home church now though."

"Why?" The girl asked. "He is such a passionate speaker."

"The religion I learned as I was raised suits me better," Elizabeth said, and then moved away from the girl whose zealous expression troubled her.

A short girl with long red hair stood up, her hand outstretched. "My name is Julie. I believe we have something in common."

"And what is that? Elizabeth asked, grasping the girl's warm hand in both of hers.

"Two things really. First, I love the law, and second, I love music almost as much." The girl beamed, her rosy cheeks seeming to glow.

"My father is a lawyer," Elizabeth said, "And much of what I know I heard from him. Perhaps yours is as well?"

"Yes, Miss Cady," the girl replied. "However, my father is much older and has left the law to younger men. One day might we have a conversation?"

"Perhaps we will have a course together this year," Elizabeth replied. "Afterward we could share a meal. Camille could along too. Would you like that?" she asked turning to her friend.

Camille leaned forward to signal her agreement.

The redheaded girl nodded so vigorously she set the combs flying from her hair. "Oh, dear," she said as she scampered off to retrieve them, her blush displaying her embarrassment.

A few days later Elizabeth and Camille were studying in the school library when Camille pushed her book away from her and sighed.

Elizabeth looked up from the notes she was writing. "What is it?" she asked. Until now, her friend's attitude had become sunnier each day. She thought Camille was growing stronger.

"I miss her terribly," Camille said.

"As do I," Elizabeth said, reaching for her friend's hand. "I know it is different," she continued, "but I loved her as I love you."

"These new girls," Camille said, "did not even know my sweet sister."

"They know you though, and through you they will become acquainted with her. Soon the new girls will not be new–just friends."

Once Elizabeth became engrossed in her courses, however, making new friends lost its luster. Perhaps she backed away from the closeness of a new friend because she knew the pain of losing one?

As the weeks unfolded, Elizabeth found that Julie almost outdid Amy Lee in her chatty behavior and the girl obsessed by religious fervor left Emma Willard under mysterious circumstances. The gossip about her departure lasted a little over a week and then the girl was forgotten.

With two of her merry friends gone, Elizabeth finally acknowledged that life would be different, but for the remainder of the term, she and Camille were inseparable.

By the time the last week of school arrived, they had vowed to stay in touch forever. Camille's impending marriage to Mr. Guilden dominated their conversations, allowing for little study or music practice.

Camille asked Elizabeth to be a bridesmaid and talk of their gowns continued for days. When Camille decided Elizabeth should be the Maid of Honor, for whom she chose a sapphire blue dress, Elizabeth beamed.

"It is my favorite color," she said. It would flatter her complexion and highlight her eyes. Secretly, she envied Camille for having found her soul mate. So far no one measured up to her ideal man. Except Edward of course.

*

April 21, 1832

Dear Diary, Although I will miss Camille once she is married, I will travel to New York where her wedding will take place and Father is seeking appropriate lodging for me there. What a wonderful way to spend the spring. Still no man has expressed interest in me. At least no one that I would consider. Is it my fault?

The wedding, planned for the first week in June in New York, posed another problem. Elizabeth would go, of course, but who would chaperone her? The answer to that question presented itself in the hiring of a young governess from Scotland, charged with educating Kate.

Margaret Christie had joined the family in Elizabeth's absence as governess to Kate. She taught French, music and dancing and, when at home, Elizabeth joined the activities with enthusiasm. Nurses no longer assisted the young sisters, so learning to manage their own upkeep gained importance. When Elizabeth returned home that May, her mother sat the girls together with Miss Christie to spell out their responsibilities.

"You all shall be minding the cleanliness of your rooms. Should your clothing need mending, you shall do that too," Mrs. Cady stated.

Elizabeth and Madge glanced at each other as Kate rolled her eyes.

"I saw that, Catherine," their mother said. "And tend to your ironing, too," she added.

"Miss Christie is here to teach you, not to take care of your personal needs. When you learn these skills," she said, "You will be able to instruct your own children or the people you hire to help in your homes. Am I clear?"

Elizabeth and Madge nodded.

"Yes Mother," Kate said.

As the days grew warmer with the approach of June approaching, Elizabeth discovered that managing her wardrobe took less work than she expected. Miss Christie showed her and her sisters how to fold their undergarments and sit on them during their reading lesson, eliminating the need to iron them. Their mother still insisted that they iron their dresses, collars, cuffs, and handkerchiefs. Elizabeth left hers to accumulate in a pile until she had nothing left to wear, and then spent the cool mornings with a hot flat iron in her hand.

It was decided that Miss Christie would accompany Elizabeth to New York to attend Camille's wedding, so she thought carefully about her behavior to make sure her mother's wishes were obeyed perfectly. She would be eighteen in November, but with no marriage prospects in sight, she still remained a little girl to her parents. As such, they believed she needed looking after. Miss Christie seemed kind so as Elizabeth planned her trip to New York she tried to make sure everything would transpire perfectly for both of them. To shorten the trip, they did not have to travel by carriage all the way. Peter would drive them to Albany and they would cover the rest of the distance by steamboat on the Erie Canal. The novelty of transport by water had gained popularity with crowds of people seeking passage to New York City. It fast became a sought-after choice. When Elizabeth insisted she travel that way, her father first had concerns but as usual she wore him down. He arranged for her and Miss Christie to stay with the Newbold family with whom he did business in New York City. Elizabeth knew nothing about them. Still, their home near the site of Camille's wedding would be agreeable and her father knew they would be safe there.

She felt a pang of sorrow as she waved goodbye to her sisters and Peter at the wharf where they boarded the steamboat *Paragon*. Once underway, crowds of passengers pushed against the rails fighting for space. A number of the people on board did not appear to have the funds for passage and Elizabeth wondered if she had made the proper decision to travel in this way. But as the engine clanked and heaved picking up speed, she felt the fresh breeze in her face and her mood brightened.

At tea that evening, she and Miss Christie squeezed into a group of women and children seated at a long table. The women looked up and pulled children onto their laps then scooted together more closely to allow Elizabeth and her companion to sit comfortably. The other tables in the galley were crowded with noisy men, all talking at the top of their voices. Judging from the growing laughter and the array of metal buckets and stone crocks on the tables, more beer than food was being consumed. The *Paragon* served no meals to passengers, so Mrs. Brewster had packed an ample basket of foods. Miss Christie handed Elizabeth a cloth napkin, took one herself that she placed on her lap, then spread another on the table in front of them. When she pulled out butter and jam sandwiches, sliced cheese wrapped in paper, four boiled eggs, and two red apples, Elizabeth noticed a few of the women eyeing their meal.

"This is like a picnic," she said loudly. "Some of this must be set aside for our breakfast, though." The two women ate in silence, for conversation was impossible because of the chattering of the other table occupants and the boisterous behavior of the men.

"A cup of hot tea would be nice," Miss Christie said.

"Impossible, I suspect," Elizabeth replied. The odors of food, perspiration and spilled beer filling the closed galley space were beginning to make her nauseous. "I think I would like to go up on deck for air," she said. "Would you?" When Miss Christie nodded, Elizabeth quickly repacked the remnants of their meal.

In a few minutes the two women stood watching the darkened landscape slide by with its pinpoints of lights indicating small villages and single homes along the canal. Elizabeth filled her lungs with fresh air and began to feel a little more like herself. The excitement had worn off and she longed for her bed and soft pillows. Instead she and Miss Christie had to settle for a narrow berth hidden behind a curtain.

The next day, after a noisy and uncomfortable night of trying to sleep, the transportation choice proved to be a mistake. Tired and cranky, Elizabeth and her companion were grateful for the small but enthusiastic greeting party at the New York City Wharf.

Camille ran to embrace her.

"Oh, my dear friend, you are here at last. We have so much to do, and little time before the wedding. I am glad to see you for I know you will bring calm to this chaos."

Elizabeth hugged her and then introduced Miss Christie. Caught up in Camille's giddy excitement, she forgot her weariness.

"You are welcome too," Camille said extending her hand. "Elizabeth has told me about you. We would all have been great friends at school," she said, and winked.

Once Camille's driver loaded their luggage into the chaise, the man wove through the New York streets dodging the hectic tangle of horsemen, wagons and a variety of horse-drawn vehicles unfamiliar to her. Soon they approached the iron gates of a long drive lined with sugar maple trees.

"I am taking you straightway to the Newbold's where you can settle in and get rested for tomorrow. A huge party is planned and you will meet my betrothed. Mr. Guilden is quite handsome as you shall see and his family is lovely. I know they will find you irresistible." Camille leaned forward to grasp Miss Christie's hand. "And you must come as well. Members of my family came from Scotland too, and I think you will find that you have much in common."

Just as Elizabeth lifted her hand to knock at the elaborately carved front door of the Newbold home, it flew open to reveal a ruddy-faced young man with a shock of blond hair standing out at all angles.

"Hallo! You must be the famous Miss Cady," he said, reaching to shake Elizabeth's hand in an iron grip.

"Famous?" she managed to say taken aback by his energetic greeting. "And this is–"

"I know, your traveling companion. Miss What's-er-name?"

"Christie."

"Oh, yes." He ducked his head in a brief nod, then ran his hands through his hair in a futile attempt to flatten it. "You caught me at my calisthenics. Standing on my head. Do come in," he said with a sweeping gesture that rocked him back on his heels. "Sorry." A red flush began to creep up his neck.

"Albert," a woman's voice called from the recesses of the house.

"Mother, our guests have arrived," Albert Newbold said.

A slender woman dressed in gray approached, shaking her finger at her son. She smiled at Elizabeth. "Please forgive my son's bad manners. Albert is impulsive and forgets himself around young ladies. I am Patience Newbold," she said. "You and your companion are welcome in our home for the duration of your stay. Your father and my husband were great friends as boys. We have a soft spot in our hearts for him. We do not see him often enough."

"Want to see my birds?" Albert asked. "Come along," he added, grasping Elizabeth's hand. She looked back at Miss Christie with an expression of dismay.

"Go ahead," Mrs. Nebold said. "I will show your friend to the rooms set aside for you."

Albert strode down the long hallway from the entry door with Elizabeth scrambling behind him. Inside a sunlit domed glass room ornate wire birdcages hid among hundreds of Palm trees and exotic plants. Large purple orchids, tall sprays of white ginger, and the delicate blossoms of fragrant plumeria branched like trees dripped with moisture. The squawking and screeching calls of the birds reverberated off the walls, creating a terrible din. She clapped her hands against her ears and stared in wonder at the rainbow plumage of the creatures hopping from perch to perch.

Albert threw his arms wide. "Is it not magnificent?" He said, grinning.

"Are they always so noisy?" Elizabeth shouted. She dared not drop her hands to her sides. Underfoot the crunch of discarded seeds, shells and smears of fruit created a hazardous path.

"Just now as they have eaten their meal. In the morning too." He sped between the cages, pointing and identifying the inhabitants. "The parrots. An African Grey, a Crimson-winged Lory. Red-spectacled Amazon. Orange-bellied Parrot. Hyacinth Macaw, that's the largest one." The birds skittered back and forth on their perches as he passed. "Scarlet Macaw, Blue and Gold Macaw, White Umbrella Cockatoos. Sulphur-Crested Cockatoos." They passed a huge spindly wooden cage filled with tiny birds that fluttered up and flew madly about their enclosure. "Four different types of finches, not the ordinary ones," Albert said waving his hand at the structure that resembled a pagoda. His cheeks grew redder as he explained. Elizabeth scurried to keep up.

"Mr. Nebold," she finally said, out of breath from attempting to keep up with him. "I am quite impressed, but please, may I stop for a moment?"

"Oh surely, let us do that," Albert said. "The garden is just this way." He opened a door in the domed room to the outside leaving the chaos of the noisy birds behind.

"Sit," he said gesturing to a stone bench beneath a gnarled tree thick with honeysuckle vines.

Elizabeth collapsed on its cool surface.

"Miss Cady, you are a remarkably handsome young woman," Albert said. He'd paced up and down in front of her as she recovered from the tour.

"Handsome?"

"Well, yes. Bright blue eyes like my Hyacinth Macaw. The bearing of the Umbrella Cockatoo. Yes, quite handsome, I'd say."

"I suppose that is a good thing?"

"Oh, yes, indeed," Albert replied, sinking down on the bench beside her to gaze into her eyes.

His straightforward appraisal surprised her as quite attractive. She felt a bit uncomfortable, but in a good way.

"Oh, there you are," Miss Christie said, heading toward them from the entry hall.

Albert jumped to his feet. "Sorry to keep Miss Cady occupied for so long," he said. "But she did seem to enjoy looking at the birds."

Elizabeth rose to join her companion.

"Thank you for the exciting introduction to your home, Mr. Nebold. If you will excuse me, though, I do need to freshen up and rest a bit," Elizabeth said.

"Of course. Of course," he said. "And please call me Albert. Mr. Nebold is too formal for friends and I do think we will be friends," he said grabbing her hand to shake it.

Once the two women began ascending the staircase, Elizabeth laughed. "He is a most spirited young man," she said.

"Your equal," Miss Christie said.

"Oh my, I think not."

"The Nebolds have invited me to join you for supper, Elizabeth, and I accepted. I hope that is all right with you. I believe your father would approve. Camille has sent you a message stating your dress fitting is at ten o'clock tomorrow morning, so we must retire early. She is sending a carriage to fetch us."

The next morning, Albert stood on the front drive, waving goodbye to Elizabeth and Miss Christie as their driver flicked the reins over the carriage horse.

"What do you think of that young man, Margaret?"

"He is quite charming and sociable. A wee bit roguish too, I would say."

"Yes he is." Elizabeth recalled the piercing stare of his brown eyes in the garden. "Handsome also."

*

June 6, 1832

Dear Diary, I write these notes as quickly as possible for I am exhausted from the trip and from the sights and scenes of New York. Sleeping on the steamboat–disastrous. Loud conversations all night long, snoring men flopped on the floor from too much drink; I have never been so uncomfortable. I have no one to blame except myself for insisting on traveling by boat. Sometimes I am stubborn to a fault. Tomorrow I will send a letter asking for Peter to fetch us after the wedding. I do not know how Father knows the

Nebold family, but their son Albert is an amazing man. Full of life and energy and certainly not dull like the men in Johnstown. Miss Christie and I are getting on quite nicely. She is a perfect traveling companion.

31

June 1832

The anteroom of the seamstresses hired to construct dresses for Camille's wedding bustled with chattering young women when Elizabeth arrived.

"Here is my Maid of Honor," Camille said, rushing to hug her. Miss Christie settled into a chair near the door.

Camille introduced the bridesmaids, none of whom Elizabeth knew, and then hurried her to one of the seamstresses.

The woman brought out a sapphire blue taffeta dress and displayed it over the back of a chair. She looked to Elizabeth for comment.

"It is so beautiful it takes my breath away," she said.

The seamstress guided Elizabeth into a small room where she asked her to disrobe then held the dress for her to step into. Its wide neckline draped her shoulders and fell into puffed sleeves caught at the arms by beribboned rosettes.

Another bow caught the middle of a great swath of fabric across the bodice.

"This gown fits your tiny-waist figure perfectly," the woman said. "Miss Camille chose the pattern and the fabric for you."

Elizabeth inspected her image in the large looking glass propped against the wall in the room. She turned left and then right, looking over her shoulder at the back of the dress, then at its voluminous skirt.

"I especially like the ruffled overskirt split that drapes over the underskirt," she said. "The bows that keep the overskirt in place add weight, too. I love this dress." She whirled around in a whispering swish of fabric.

"Would you please fetch the lady in the gray dress seated by the door?" Elizabeth asked the seamstress.

When Miss Christie entered the small room she gasped. "This gown suits you perfectly," she said. "It is lovely."

"Now I know why Camille asked me to bring the matched sapphires for my ears," Elizabeth said.

"Lizzy! Can I come in?" Camille called from outside the closed door.

Miss Christie opened the door wide to admit Elizabeth's rosy-cheeked friend.

"I've just received a response from the Nebold family accepting my invitation to the ball following our wedding ceremony," she said. She waved an ivory colored folded note above her head.

"You barely know them," Elizabeth said. "Oh dear, you did this for me."

"But you have made a new friend. And a man at that," Camille said. "Now you will surely have a dancing partner."

"I appreciate your thoughtfulness and kindness, dear friend, but I have never lacked for partners," Elizabeth teased.

Even though the bride and groom protested that they could not stay at the ball another moment, stay they did until a midnight supper announced by Camille's father drew the guests to the dining room.

For the duration of the dancing, Albert Nebold monopolized Elizabeth. Early on he sought her out, plucked the dance card from her hand, and scratched out all the names of other young gentlemen to whom she promised a dance.

"There now, that is settled," he said, and with a flourish, handed the card back to her. Albert's practiced and elegant dance steps thrilled Elizabeth. Her experience thus far with boys from Rensselaer never reached this level of skill. That he excelled surprised her.

By mid-evening he'd whispered something in the ear of the violinist, who had then convened his musicians in hurried conversation.

While the wedding guests gathered on the sidelines of the ballroom recovering from a reckless quadrille, the violinist tucked his instrument under his chin and began to play the romantic strains of a waltz.

At that, Camille and her new husband glided onto the floor and, quite alone in their own world began to circle the floor in swooping graceful turns.

When Albert returned to Elizabeth's side and bowed, he said, "May I have this dance, Miss Cady?"

"I do not know how to waltz."

"I will show you. Just rest your hand on my shoulder and step as I do while I guide you with my other hand," Albert said.

The orchestra played only one waltz, but Elizabeth thought it the most beautiful dance of the night. She fairly skimmed the floor in Albert's grasp. She knew her curls were coming undone as he whirled her around the floor, but she didn't care. This dance felt delicious and Albert's strong arms and skill were perfection. By the time supper awaited the wedding party's hungry guests, Elizabeth gratefully took her seat, not surprised that Albert's place card adjoined hers.

As they ate, she felt his gaze fall on her more than once, even though Camille's pretty cousin who sat on his other side flirted in exaggerated gestures.

"Miss Cady, I should like to call on you," Albert said. "Would that please you?" he asked, his expression open and eager.

"Mr. Nebold, you barely know me," she said, but with his shock of blond hair, now pomaded in a sheen curled around his ears so sweetly, how could she resist?

"Indeed you do not know our Lizzy, Mr. Nebold," Camille said. "She is a tyrant as an debater. Do not let her beauty misguide you," she added, leaning forward to catch his attention.

"Oh? On what subject, Miss Cady?"

"Several."

"Such as? Perhaps we have similar leanings."

"Two topics at present concern me. Abolition and the role of women." Elizabeth took a sip of water and then forked a piece of roasted lamb into her mouth.

Albert Nebold choked and, to her surprise, seemed at a loss for words. She chewed and waited for his response.

"Abolition is a topic for men to discuss and for our Congress and President to handle," Albert said.

"No it isn't," Elizabeth said. "This is precisely my point. Both men and women have vested interests in the outcome of abolition and how it will affect our country."

"But the role of the fairer sex is defined by motherhood. Women need not bother themselves with anything outside the home."

Down the table, Elizabeth heard Camille laugh and from the corner of her eye she saw her friend's new husband reach for his wife's hand and draw it to his lips.

"The 'role of the fairer sex?' Which is what? Bearing children only? Sweeping floors? Scrabbling for a dowry to please a husband who is penniless and wants nothing more than money?" Elizabeth asked.

All conversation at the table stopped with the only sound the clinking of silver as servants offered the next course. Elizabeth felt her face redden and her appetite dwindle. She rose, pushing back her chair.

"Camille dear, thank you for including me in this memorable event. I fear I may spoil it should I stay longer so will retire now," she said.

As she rushed from the room, followed by Miss Christie, Albert rose from his chair, sputtering, with an expression of bewilderment.

During the drive back to the Nebold home, Elizabeth pondered her outburst and Albert's response. Had she baited him? Had she merely bristled when confronted with illogical arguments counter to her intelligence? *Would Edward and Father be the only men I shall meet who believe as I do?*

The next morning when Elizabeth and Miss Christie came down for breakfast to dine alone, a folded note lay beside Elizabeth's place at the table. She took a sip of coffee and began to read.

Dear Miss Cady, please forgive me for insulting you last evening. I did not know that your beliefs in suffrage so strongly define you. As such I fear our paths are different. Regretfully, Albert Nebold.

She crushed the note and thrust it into her pocket.

Later when Peter arrived with the chaise, prepared for the long trip home, Elizabeth's spirits were as low as they had been high the day before. She packed with haste, stuffing the sapphire taffeta dress inside her trunk without care. She bounced on the closed trunk to secure its lid, and was so out of sorts she spoke with anger to Miss Christie. That was unfair, she realized immediately, and apologized for her rude behavior. Miss Christie put her arm around Elizabeth's shoulders to comfort her.

"You have strong beliefs. Do not let anyone dissuade you from them," she said with kindness. "Your family loves you and that is all important. One day a young man will come your way who looks forward as you do, and you will know he will never look back."

*

June 10, 1832

Dear Diary, the enchantment of Camille's wedding will be with me forever. On the other hand, the man whom I thought so charming, Albert Nebold, revealed his true self to me while trying his best to impress me. For all his New York lifestyle, exciting adventures, and his passion for birding, he is an old stick in the mud believing, as do men twice his age. Not only did he rebuke me for speaking my mind, his is so closed it rusted for lack of new thinking. Why it is that men are so afraid of a woman learning something? Good gracious. I embarrassed myself by leaving the dinner party, I was so angry. Father will surely hear about that.

32

June 1832

When Elizabeth and Miss Christie arrived home, Elizabeth's concerns over her comportment at the Nebold home had either been dismissed by her father or had never reached him. In her absence he had become very busy. Regardless, she would be ready to defend herself if it came to light.

Judge Cady's office bustled with a new crop of students. By now they were cautioned to confine themselves to their assignments and the law library. The perils of practical jokes and wicked debates they would confront with the Cady sisters were well known, yet despite her father's warning, soon one or two would be distracted and the hook would be set. Now nineteen and confident, and as usual the leader, Elizabeth set the stage for Madge and Kate to provoke the excited young men as she did. While Elizabeth's motives were usually intellectually challenging, the schemes of her high-spirited sisters often resulted in laughter and flirtation.

Even though Edward practiced law with their father, he served in a limited role with the students. So, Elizabeth continued to seek him out. No one disputed her theories as he did. Their conversations were lively and she began to sharpen her ability to thrust and parry in rhetoric as a lawyer might. He became her confidante the day he consoled her in the garden when she won the Greek prize. As the years passed, she realized her depth of feelings for him had developed to a level greater than those of a mere friend. Perhaps she measured all the young men she met against Edward. She believed he favored her, didn't he? Why else would he seek her out to inquire about her life? What books interested her? Who called on her? He fostered her love of debating and argument and she basked in the attention. Perhaps there could be more? She allowed herself to daydream about the touch of his hand on her skin, the tenderness of his kiss. Such thoughts excited her but made her uneasy as well. Did she betray Tryphena with this type of fantasy? Worse, did this obsession with him cause the infernal comparison with other men?

Something seemed to distract Edward since Elizabeth returned from Camille's wedding. He didn't seek her out for conversation, which worried her. Even Tryphena appeared busier than ever. With her mother now resuming some of her duties, it seemed odd to Elizabeth that such extraordinary turmoil in their household should still exist.

Two months after she returned home, Judge Cady called the family into the parlor.

"Edward and Tryphena have made a change in their life that affects us all," her father said.

Edward stepped forward and looked around at the assembled group, pausing for a moment to meet Elizabeth's gaze.

He cleared his throat. "I am leaving the law to study the practice of homeopathic medicine. Its curative methods so clearly healed me of the disease that affected my heart I feel I must discover ways to help others. To do that, we will travel to Seneca Falls. Tryphena and I have found lodging there for the duration."

Elizabeth gasped. "When were you ill?" she asked.

"While you were at Troy Seminary. The first year," Edward said.

"We did not tell you, Lib, for we believed you would worry and neglect your courses," her mother said.

"Edward and I made the decision," Tryphena said.

"So with Mother needing care and Edward ill, you all spared me?" She looked at her sisters. "You knew too?"

They nodded.

Her heart sank. She worried so about herself she had not noticed anything amiss at home. How could she be so selfish?

"Will you return?" she finally asked, immediately feeling a sense of unbalance. Edward was part of her life. What would she do without his support?

"It is not likely. I intend to open a medical office there after my training."

Tryphena linked her arm through her husband's. "The household is running well now," she said. "With Mother feeling like her old self, I am no longer needed to fill her shoes. It is time to establish our own home." She smiled at her mother and sisters.

"But who will teach us philosophy? Whom can we argue with?" Kate asked. "Mother and Father do not allow it."

"Elizabeth has learned a lot," Edward said with an amused expression. "I have taught her everything I know."

He has not. There is more, I know it.

"When will you leave?" Madge asked.

"September," Tryphena said. "Everything is in order in Seneca Falls and Edward's classes begin the second week."

"Your mother and I regret Edward will no longer be part of my law practice, and I am not certain that this new type of medical treatment has merit. But it is not my decision. I wish them both well."

Though her father's words seemed optimistic, Elizabeth recognized from the tight lines around his mouth that his comment was merely polite.

Late that afternoon she took a book of Lord Byron's poems with her to the garden where lush foliage created a bower over the bench she favored.

She was lost in the stanzas of the poet's lovely sad words and didn't notice Edward approaching until he sat beside her.

"Ah, Byron," he said taking the book from her hand.

"In secret we met—
In silence I grieve
That thy heart could forget,
Thy spirit deceive.
If I should meet thee
After long years,

How should I greet thee?" Edward stopped reading.

"With silence and tears." Elizabeth said, ending the poem.

"I felt I needed to explain," he started.

"You must follow your inclination," she said.

"We have become close, and I do not want you to think I am abandoning you," Edward said.

"It will be different here without your laughter and keen ear for discourse."

"There will be others who will challenge you."

"I suppose," Elizabeth said.

"I'll miss you," Edward said taking her hand.

"And I you," said Elizabeth. She felt her throat close.

Edward drew her hand to his lips.

"No!" She jumped up. "I will take my book back, please."

When Edward handed her the volume, she saw the glimmer of tears in his eyes.

"Oh, here you are," Tryphena said emerging from the depths of the garden along the path. "Dinner will be ready soon. Mother sent me to fetch Lib."

Elizabeth brushed past her. "I will be right there."

That night, conversation about Edward and Tryphena's impending departure flew around the dinner table with most of the questions coming from Madge and Kate. While Tryphena responded often, Edward's answers were perfunctory. Elizabeth contributed very little.

Early the next morning, her younger sisters rushed into her room attired for riding.

"Edward is taking us for a ride up through the Mohawk Valley after breakfast, Lib. Please come too," Madge said.

"Please?" Kate begged.

Elizabeth sat up and stretched, surveying her sisters as they plopped on her bed and began tugging at her hands.

"Oh my. I suppose I have to," she said. "Go ahead to the table, I will be right down."

Jacob saddled all the horses and stood chatting with Edward when Elizabeth and her sisters approached the stable.

"I have been trying to convince Jacob to ride with us," Edward said. "What do you think, Elizabeth?"

"That would be lovely."

"Pardon, Miss Elizabeth, I reckon it would be unseemly," Jacob said.

"Nonsense, you've known us forever, and everyone hereabouts knows you, too," she said.

"No thank you just the same, Miss, I'll stay here and do my jobs as usual," Jacob said, tipping his hat.

After he helped the girls settle onto the mares they rode, he handed Edward the reins to Zeus, the chestnut stallion that would travel to Seneca Falls.

"Let us investigate, Zeus," Edward said, flicking the reins on the back of the big horse and trotting up the road at the back of the Cady property. "Come on, young ladies," he said.

Within minutes they left the outskirts of Johnstown behind them. Elizabeth drew up to Edward's horse, her hair undone and flying about where her bonnet had slipped from her face.

"Let us race," she said glancing in his direction then digging her heels into her mare's flanks. Not waiting for a reply she cantered ahead with Kate and Madge right behind.

Moments later the sisters were riding at full gallop up the meadow until Edward pulled ahead and disappeared from sight.

When the sisters' horses reached the level Cayadutta plateau, they saw Edward silhouetted against the wooded slopes of Klip Hill. Elizabeth waved and the girls cantered to meet him at the highest ground, where to the east the Adirondack foothills revealed a forest of changing color. A breeze cooled their faces, predicting an early autumn. Even now splotches of gold glimmered in the forest along the silver ribbon of the Mohawk River below.

Edward drew his horse alongside Elizabeth. "You ride so well now. I had forgotten." He turned with a sweep of his hand to admire the view from the plateau. "I have always been partial to this area with its changing colors. Even when it is snowing it is beautiful. Do you remember when I first brought you here? You were twelve."

She nodded. "I had just learned to ride Junie. I had a red scarf and you wrapped it around my head and tied the ends at my neck." She smiled at the recollection.

"You were freezing," Edward said, "because you refused to wear your wool jacket even after your mother insisted."

"Mother chastised you for allowing that, too," Elizabeth said.

"You were always strong willed. You still are."

"And I will always be that way," Elizabeth said.

"I hoped we might have a chance to talk."

"We are talking."

"I mean about my leaving," Edward said.

"I believe I should have been told sooner." Elizabeth raised her chin to watch a hawk circle overhead then dive.

"Ah. I agree," Edward said.

She saw the hawk rise from a patch of dry grass near the forest, with a small rodent in its clutches. Poor thing. A fleeting moment of great sadness engulfed her.

"Also I am furious that no one told me you were ill," Elizabeth said, facing him. "You are my dear friend. I respect you, just as I do my parents. That all of you believed my feelings needed sparing is ridiculous and insulting."

Edward's stricken expression failed to move her. "I know it is for the best, but I am truly sorry that we are leaving," he said.

She refused to look at him. Instead she feigned interest in watching her sisters dismount and lead their horses to the shade of a nearby tree. The girls bent to the ground and began picking up the last of the black walnuts, stuffing them into their pockets.

"Elizabeth."

"I heard you."

Long blue shadows had begun to fall across the plateau and a hint of wood smoke lay on the breeze. Elizabeth shivered and pulled her coat closer to button it. She pushed her hair under her bonnet and tied the ribbons.

"Madge," she called. "Time to return home." Her sisters laughed, pulled their horses around and remounted.

"So soon?" Kate asked riding up alongside Elizabeth.

"Mother expects us for dinner."

Edward hung back from the girls as they spurred their horses to a canter back down the trail leading to the plateau and the meadow.

Her attraction to Edward wasn't over, Elizabeth knew. But with him and Tryphena out of the house the influence of his presence would grow fainter. Since Seneca Falls was 150 miles away, the journey took too long to make often. Still, she had to convince herself that she would not miss him.

*

August 27, 1832

Dear Diary, whatever am I going to do? Edward is leaving. His behavior with me is confusing too. He has been part of my life for so long I cannot imagine living without him. It's his flame that keeps my quest for knowledge fueled and burning. No one understands me as he does. From the very beginning he told me which books to read, kept after me to perfect my mathematics, and made sure my elocution withstood the dizzy pace of my mind. I could not have become the quick-witted person I am without him, nor adept at catching the law students off guard with my arguments. I will not have his handsome self to admire, or hear his warm and lovely voice, or see him standing so tall and elegant in his suit as he walks down our halls. Does he not know how much I need him? I am mad for having these feelings and Fini must never know. What shall I do?

33

September 1832

Elizabeth stood on the front steps of her home with the rest of the family, waving goodbye to Edward and Tryphena. Of them all, only her eyes remained dry. She usually eagerly anticipated autumn's pleasant routines: the vibrant color changing of the trees, their household's storing of food for the winter, the last repairs to their home and outbuildings with the noise of hammering and the smell of fresh cut wood. Her world would forever be different now. What would she do without the familiarity and comfort of Edward and Fini in the house? Madge and Kate in school. The legal demands on her father. Would the company of her mother be enough?

Madge left for Emma Willard within a week. With her closest ally in mischief gone to begin her formal schooling, Elizabeth faced the uneasy freedom to do as she pleased. At first she roamed the house, its empty rooms mocking her. She expected to encounter Edward around every corner. Then she tutored Kate a bit, but grew frustrated with her sister's tendency to fritter her time away rather than study. Each morning after her father had finished with the newspapers, Elizabeth gathered them up to read front to back. Her mind filled with information she desperately wanted to discuss with someone. But that person–Edward–was gone. Her father had warned her about interfering with his law students, too. Once it had been an engaging pastime that he tolerated, but his campaign to create Fulton County and name it after his wife's cousin was underway, so his schedule left little time to train the young men. Hence, she had been told to find something else to do.

"Make some new friends," her mother said.

"It is not easy, Mother," she replied. "I have no patience for constant gossip, or talking of babies and needlework."

"Do attend some of the parties to which you have received invitations. I do not like you moping around the house, pining for a life you do not have. Perhaps you will meet a nice young man with whom you can share ideas."

"Yes Mother," she murmured, resigned to do just that.

When the next stack of invitations arrived, she began to flip them into two piles. One, for yes, a second one, for no. Over time she grew rather fond of the events outdoors; the rollicking hayrack rides, sleigh rides in winter that concluded with gallons of hot cocoa, picnics in the summer. In the years that followed, however, the sameness of her activities began to annoy her with its predictable nature. She saw the same familiar people and grew bored with their unremarkable topics of discussion. To escape the monotony, she began to accept so many invitations to parties and get-togethers, some of which were from people she barely knew, that her mother finally warned her of fatigue or worse.

"It is unseemly, Elizabeth, for a young woman to have such a busy schedule," her mother said. "I should not like to hear about your escapades from sources who trade in gossip for its unsettling reaction."

"First you insist I stay busy by accepting invitations, then you tell me not to do this," Elizabeth teased. "How shall I find a husband, as you suggest I must, if I but stay here and embroider?"

Margaret Cady looked at her daughter, her expression stern but not displeased. "Goodness, Lib dear, twenty-two is not the age of a spinster. I cannot decipher if you are serious or not."

"Staying in surely means accepting a solitary life, and that is not my choice. Visiting the same people of my age whom I see at each event I attend is not stimulating," Elizabeth explained. "I know I must be selective, Mother, it is just that at every party I attend I may meet someone new with whom I could have a conversation about topics other than tatting or pudding recipes."

"Scrutinize your invitations for their suitability, Daughter," her mother said. "If you accept for tea, do not reply you will also attend a ball the same night. That's all I ask."

"Thank you for your kind advice, Mother. I will behave as you request." What Elizabeth really meant was that she would try to behave, but could not promise to do so.

Her conversations with each new crop of law students interning with her father presented yet another predicament. Even though she had been instructed not to do speak with them, she could not resist.

"You will never interest a prospective husband," her mother said, "if you continue to display your intellect and controversial opinions."

"I respect your advice Mother, but I am me and I think more like Eleazar would have if he were here," she said. "That I do speak up is true to myself." When she saw the influence of her remarks in her mother's expression, she regretted her hasty comment and apologized immediately. However, she continued to embrace opportunities for debate.

Inevitably, at least one student whose demeanor hinted at future courtroom drama would challenge the eldest Cady daughter. Her father never warned the students that they would find a formidable adversary. Perhaps their discourses trained the student to never expect to be bested by a woman.

Elizabeth's favorite gambit involved slipping quietly into the back of the room while her father conducted a discussion about a point of law. Some days the rustle of her petticoats gave her away, but usually the arguing of the law students drowned out all but their own voices.

One afternoon, returning from a ladies luncheon that her mother insisted would help her find new friends and possibly a suitable husband, Elizabeth heard loud voices when she stopped in the vestibule. The open door to her father's office revealed a group of students huddled around a newspaper having a loud discussion. At the center, her father first pointed at a story and then shook his finger.

What is this? Elizabeth slipped into a chair against the back wall in the room and leaned forward to listen.

"I say we Americans have more rights than those savages in Georgia," said James William Andrews, one of the students. "President Jackson is right. They should be moved if they will not go on their own. The law is on our side," he added in a loud passionate voice. "It is shameful."

"Gentlemen, please," Judge Cady said holding up his hand to get their attention. He looked down at an open book on his desk and began to read. "*The Nonintercourse Act passed in 1790 prohibits purchase of Indian lands without approval of the federal government.* It stipulates, according to President Washington, '*No State nor person can purchase your lands.*' Here he refers to the Indians, '*unless at some public treaty held under the authority of the United States. The general government will never consent to your being defrauded. But it will protect you in all your just rights.*' That law has been amended four times and is before Congress again."

"The original law did say that, but the revision before Congress now says it must conform to the Constitution, does it not?" Andrews asked.

"It does, Mr. Andrews," Elizabeth's father said. "But the intent of the law is in the word 'defraud.' President Washington's original intent to protect the lands on which the Indians live is being changed. Do you see how language affects the outcome?"

Oh, yes, let's see what they say about that.

"The law is a living thing, you said, Sir. If it changes, why then, it should change, right?"

"Yes, Andrews, but much study and care has to occur before a law changes in such a dramatic way."

"In this case it would mean amending the Constitution?"

"It would, and history proves that is no easy task," her father said.

"What do you think of emancipation of slavery, Sir?" another young man asked.

"The British Empire did away with it last year," a second voice added.

Yes, do let us have your opinion on that, too.

"With Garrison publishing stories about colonizing in that newspaper of his–the *Liberator*," said a tall man whose ill-fitting jacket draped his narrow shoulders, "who knows how many people follow his ideas on that. Maybe sending the Negroes to someplace on the coast of Africa is not a bad idea."

"It is impractical Mr. Alter," Judge Cady said. "Besides, states have already begun to make their own laws governing slavery. In 1808 Congress passed a law prohibiting the import of slaves. There will be no more."

"Except for those born here," Mr. Alter argued. "What about them? Maybe they all should go back where they came from."

"There is great unrest in the southern states because of the Negro slaves. Just three years have passed since the Turner rebellion sacrificed white Americans," another student said.

"Even better that they all go back. Emancipation means they would be living right next to us. You want that? Negroes?" Alter looked around at his fellows, his expression incredulous.

Is this man blind? He lives cheek by jowl with Negroes now.

Judge Cady said, "What about the freedmen? Where would they go? They're just as American as I am."

Elizabeth turned in her chair to watch her father, knowing full well the young law trainee had worked his way into a corner.

"I have three freedmen in my employ," her father said. "They have lived with us most of their adult lives. I suspect they greatly appreciate their homes here and would have nothing to do with Africa."

"Excuse me, Sir, I did not mean to speak out against your choices." Mr. Alter's face reddened with embarrassment.

"You know there is a school for Negro girls in Connecticut," Andrews said. "Been open awhile."

"Probably those two Quaker sisters, the Grimkes, supported it," another student remarked. "They are speaking out for giving women voting say-so. That is, every place they go that they are not thrown out." The speaker, round-faced and plump, raised his eyebrows in an exaggerated gesture. The law students laughed.

Elizabeth began to squirm in her chair, fearing any noise she made would give her away and her father would banish her.

"Perhaps, but Prudence Crandall is the name I heard," Andrews said.

"Mr. Vanderhoff," Judge Cady said, directing his comment to the plump-faced student, "you are referring to the Canterbury Female Boarding School."

"No Negroes there. That is a finishing school for wealthy families. I cannot imagine any of them wanting a Negro in the classroom," Vanderhoff said.

"You are wrong, it is a school for Negro girls. Last month an angry mob broke all the school windows and smashed furniture. It does not sound like it will be around much longer though," Andrews said.

"And what is your opinion of that, Vanderhoff, setting aside the violence and destruction of property? Legally, that is?" Judge Cady asked.

"Doomed to fail. Educating women, and Negro women at that? Giving them a vote on laws? Just not needed," Vanderhoff said throwing up his hands as if to conclude the conversation.

Elizabeth jumped to her feet. The students turned at the sound of a chair crashing to the floor, followed by the rustle of petticoats.

"Which is more odious to you gentlemen? Respecting the Indians' lands, abolishing slavery, or giving women rights? Such as the vote?" she asked.

"Lib, please," her father said. He moved to face the cluster of students standing with their mouths gaping. "Gentlemen, please make the acquaintance of my daughter, Elizabeth. You have not met her yet."

A murmur rose from the young men.

"Miss Cady, I am sorry if I offended you," Mr. Alter said.

"I am not offended. Just wondering if you truly believe laws will change as you so eloquently claim. Perhaps it is men who think like you who stand in their way."

"Well, some...might," he said. Then, "Will change."

"It appears Congress is more concerned about taking lands from the Indians that are rightfully theirs," Elizabeth said, "than the importance to the country of their own mothers, sisters and daughters, never mind their color."

"But it has always been this way," Vanderhoff stated.

"Even if it's morally wrong? Then it's all right to uphold a law simply because 'it has always been'?" Her voice grew loud.

"And what if, Mr. Vanderhoff, women are allowed to vote for or against laws in this country? Could it change things all that much? Would a woman's vote be more compassionate? More fair? More equal?" Elizabeth asked.

Mr. Vanderhoff's face had turned a frightening shade of purple and he had begun to sweat. "Miss Cady, I did not intend..."

"Intend to what? Infer women were not as good as men?"

"Lawyers can only apply the laws on the books, not make new ones," Judge Cady said, his expression and conciliatory tone of voice an attempt to placate her.

"Father," she said with emphasis. "You have always taught me to respect the law, and you yourself said the only way to change it is to work to do just that." Elizabeth's eyes glittered with anger. "I have been listening the whole time to the discourse in this room. What motive do you men have to be so closed minded that changing the law for you is unthinkable?" At this she directed her remarks to James William Andrews. "Do you not consider the future of this country and what as lawyers you can do to make life better for people? Surely you recognize the plight of people enslaved as untenable?"

Her father's expression grew wary. "Elizabeth, if you–"

"It seems to me, Mr. Vanderhoff," she said, ignoring her father, "that you are discussing not so much the law but power. Over the slaves treated like animals, over the Indians, and your own mothers, sisters and wives. Power–not a sense of fairness. Or compassion. Or upholding treaties signed by honorable men before you," Elizabeth said. The room had grown quiet with only her voice reverberating off the walls.

"You are right." Her father threw up his hands. "I surrender to your argument." He laughed, breaking the uneasy tension in the room.

"You see before you, gentlemen," he said to the students, "a lady whose remarks will not be suppressed. I am responsible for raising an educated woman who is not afraid of standing up for what she believes. She is not a man, but thinks like one," he said.

Elizabeth flung her arms around her father's neck. "Thank you," she whispered into his ear.

The doors to the office flew open to reveal Kate.

"Father, I have been pounding on the door forever," she said. "Mother sent me to call you all in for dinner."

She ran to Elizabeth's side and linked her arm with her sister's. "I heard you," she said.

Elizabeth looked into Kate's expressive eyes.

"Good," she said.

*

October 2, 1836

Dear Diary, I am still trapped in the pursuits of women and have grown so weary of ladies luncheons, desultory shopping trips and non-stop embroidery work. Mother insists that I cannot accept only the dancing and party invitations where good conversation with men would exist, that those where only women attend must be on my social calendar. The prattle of these women bores me to tears. They remind me of how little women are expected to know of the world and how living subservient to men is supposed to be perfectly fine. I do so wish Father would allow me to join his students in their study of the law, for it is the conversations I have with them on occasion that shakes me out of ennui. I believe I would make a good lawyer. What good is it though? Only men can become lawyers. For now. Father warns that if I continue to bait the students with distaff arguments, I will never find a suitable husband, an issue high on his list for me. But what is suitable to Father and Mother, I believe, is for a man to have money enough to care for me. Bah.

When all I want is a challenging mate who believes in equality. A partner. A helpmate with whom I can share ideas. I am frustrated here at home. Johnstown has so little to recommend it for enlightened conversations. I miss Edward.

34

November 1836

After supper one evening, Judge Cady asked Elizabeth to join him in his office. When she did, she found her mother seated beside him on the small sofa reserved for clients.

"Is something wrong?" she asked, puzzled by their grave expressions.

"No," her mother said reaching to grasp her husband's hand. "We have received an invitation to Peterboro to visit Cousin Gerrit just after Christmas."

"Oh, that is wonderful. When do we leave?"

"That is just it, Lib. It is you who has been invited, not the entire family. You will travel alone if you choose to go."

"Father? You look uncertain." Elizabeth said.

"The invitation is fine, Lib, it is just that it might appear unseemly for you to travel without a chaperone."

"I am a mature woman. My birthday is in a few days. I will be twenty-three, so I do indeed choose to go. A chance to meet the interesting people who come to his home," Elizabeth said, "and the opportunity to spend time with Gerrit and Ann and little Lizzy is too sublime to refuse." *Besides the house was so very empty with Edward gone.* "But why are we not all going?" she asked.

"Your sisters must return to school and your father's schedule will not permit it," her mother said. "It is settled then. I will write to Gerrit and tell him to expect you just after New Years. I thought perhaps Miss Christie could accompany you, but Peter will drive you, so there is no need for a chaperone."

The day dawned cool and clear for November 12– Elizabeth's birthday, a date typically plagued with snowfall. Elizabeth and Kate stood near the barn waiting for Jacob to saddle their horses.

"Mother told me of your plans to visit Peterboro," Kate said. "I wish I could go too, but she says I must study with Miss Christie until I have my sums perfect."

"A thorough knowledge of mathematics is important for keeping ledgers," Elizabeth said. "Mother and Miss Christie plan for you to be as accomplished as Fini."

"I will go to Emma Willard next year. I do not know why I cannot just learn it then."

"There are many distractions, Kate. Boys at Rensselaer, for instance, who will annoy you with flattery."

"I rather think I will like that."

"Father and Mother prepared all of us for the courses there, and you should do well. But I became homesick. I hope you avoid that." Elizabeth pulled on her leather gloves and tied her bonnet ribbons tight.

Jacob came from the barn holding the reins of the horses the girls had decided to ride that day. Junie's foal Augusta had grown into a glossy bay, fifteen hands high, whose frisky nature pleased Elizabeth. For Kate, Jacob saddled Matilde, a smaller horse with a gentle disposition that still loved to gallop alongside Augusta.

"Here are the two baskets you asked for, Miss Elizabeth," Jacob said holding them up after she eased into her saddle. "What you planning to do with them?" he asked.

"There are walnuts on the ground at the back of that abandoned orchard three miles east. We are going to bring them home."

"Hmmph. You young ladies be careful up that way, and mind you don't bring home no wormy ones. Miz Brewster be after you for that."

"We will pay attention," Elizabeth said, then digging her heels into Augusta's side, she rode off with Kate right behind.

When the girls reached the two-mile mark up the road toward the derelict grove of walnut trees, they spied young Mr. Andrews walking along the trail toward them eating an apple and leading his horse.

"Hello, Mr. Andrews," Kate called when they were within shouting distance.

The law student looked up, appearing surprised to see the two girls.

"Good morning, Misses Cady," he said removing his hat. The sun glinted off his curly brown hair and Elizabeth thought it looked to be the color of Augusta's coat. She laughed.

"Something funny, Miss?" he asked.

"No, not at all. I am just pleased to see you, that's all." Elizabeth said, embarrassed by her thoughts.

"And I you, Miss."

"What is your given name, Mr. Andrews?" Kate asked.

"James, but my friends call me Jimmer. You may call me that too, Miss Cady." His horse wandered up onto the bank of the trail and stood munching grass, tugging at its reins. Andrews glanced at Elizabeth, as he tried to drag the animal back. She tried very hard not to smile at his discomfort. Then seeing he didn't know what to do, she slipped to the ground, grabbed the horse's lead and with an expert hand turned it back onto the trail.

"You must feed your horse, Mr. Andrews," she said. "Or find one that does not favor field grass."

"That grass makes the horse break wind," Kate said.

"I asked the stableman at the edge of town for a gentle mount, not a disobedient one," Jimmer said. "I know little about horses."

"I can teach you," Kate said, favoring the young lawyer with a wide smile.

My, oh my. Little sister is quite taken with this man. Perhaps that is why she has been lingering outside Father's office door.

"When you reach our home, ask Jacob to stable your mount and instruct you on its proper care and feeding," Elizabeth said. She looked down at the horse's right front hoof. "This animal has lost a shoe. It needs to be re-shod. The blacksmith just inside town can help with that."

"I could teach you all about horses," Kate said. "You could ride with me when Elizabeth is away."

Jimmer turned to regard Kate before he replied. "That would be fine, Miss Kate," he said. "When your father does not have me studying, which is not often, I shall ask for permission to learn about horses from you."

Elizabeth took note of her sister's big smile.

"And, from you, Miss Elizabeth, I should like to learn the art of potent argument."

"Oh, you must only pay attention to my father to learn that," she said. "He is as sharp as they come, make no mistake about that."

"Thank you for the advice," the young man said doffing his hat and touching the brim.

"Come along, Kate," Elizabeth said, feeling a maternal twinge as she snapped the reins over Augusta's ears and the horse cantered off. She had not expected to be involved in her sister's flirtation. Why was Jimmer Andrews not interested in her instead of Kate? She was too outspoken, she reckoned. Once again, speaking her mind had caused an unwelcomed impression.

By the time the girls reached the edge of the orchard and dismounted to fill their baskets with walnuts, the sun was throwing long shadows across the grass. Deep in thought about the effort of choosing perfect nuts, Elizabeth didn't notice the waning light until Kate spoke.

"Mr. Andrews favors you."

"I doubt it. If anything at all he is likely angry about my comments in Father's office yesterday."

"He is quite handsome."

"I suppose, but his opinions about things I care for are so dissimilar that I do not see him as attractive."

"Father says his family has wealth. He would be a good husband," Kate said.

"For you perhaps. I will marry who I choose and it will be someone with whom I share my beliefs and dreams."

"Not Mr. Andrews?"

"No, Sister, he cannot be that person. Besides, I think he favors you."

Kate picked a walnut from her basket and threw it at Elizabeth. Within moments the two girls were pelting each other with the nuts and laughing so hard their horses whinnied in alarm.

A cold breeze lifted the hem of Elizabeth's shawl against her face and she looked up to see purple shadows against the Adirondacks behind them.

"Kate, we've been here too long. Mother will have supper on the table and surely will be worrying about us. We must leave at once."

The girls tied the baskets onto the pommels of their saddles and retraced their path at a gallop. By the time they rode onto the road at the back of the house, all the lamps blazed in the house and both Jacob and Abraham were pacing in front of the barn.

"Oh my, Miss Elizabeth, your mama is sure worrying about you," Jacob said, grabbing Augusta's lead from her as she swung to the ground. "You and Miss Kate better hurry on in afore she takes it out on me and Abraham for letting you go by yourselves."

The two girls ran into the back door of the kitchen to find their mother standing with Mrs. Brewster. The older women glared at the sisters for the cook had prepared a celebratory meal.

"Elizabeth, you know better," Margaret Cady said.

"I do, Mother, and I am sorry. The fine day captivated me and I lost track of time." She handed the baskets to Mrs. Brewster. "For your work in preparing this supper for me, I am particularly embarrassed for being late. I know these walnuts will not make amends, but please take them with my gratitude," she said.

"You girls freshen up immediately and come right back down," her mother said. "Your father has invited some of the law students to dine with us tonight in honor of your birthday."

"Mr. Andrews?" Kate asked.

Elizabeth pinched her sister's arm.

"I do not know if he is among the guests," Margaret Cady said. "Hurry girls. The beef roast is resting which means we will be serving in fifteen minutes."

When Elizabeth came down the stairs she heard peals of laughter coming from the dining room. Kate's animated retelling of the nut war seemed to amuse everyone except her mother.

She hurried to her place beside her father and Miss Christie who looked up to catch Elizabeth's attention and pulled her mouth down into a mock frown.

"Lib, Mr. Andrews tells me he encountered you earlier today," her father said, leaning close to ensure his words reached only her.

She took a sip of water and used the gesture to surreptitiously glance around the table. Sure enough, Jimmer Andrews, seated beside Kate, looked away from her beaming face to catch Elizabeth's eye. He nodded, and she looked away.

As the meal progressed, Kate flirted with Jimmer, touching his arm to make a point and apparently laughing or smiling at every word he said. Elizabeth considered the scene, knowing full well who favored whom. If Andrews had once considered Elizabeth, Kate had changed his mind.

All for the better.

Soon servants cleared the table and Mrs. Brewster brought in a large cake covered with a white shell made of sugar. Bright yellow and orange flowers plucked from the garden adorned it.

"This is almost too beautiful to eat," Elizabeth exclaimed. "You have done yourself proud, Mrs. Brewster."

While the cook's sharp knife divided the cake into serving pieces, Kate placed a small pile of wrapped gifts on the table beside Elizabeth.

In between bites of cake, she examined the tags on the gifts.

"Open mine first," Kate said, pushing a small package toward her sister.

Elizabeth untied the satin ribbon, taking great pains to smooth each crease with her fingers.

"You are dawdling on purpose," Kate said with an expression of mock anger.

Elizabeth laughed then ripped off the pink-sprigged paper to reveal a handkerchief with her initials embroidered on the corner.

"It is lovely," she said, leaning to kiss Kate on the cheek. "Your handiwork is much finer than mine. I will cherish this and dab it with perfume to carry with me in my sleeve."

Judge Cady placed a brown paper wrapped box tied with string beside her. "This is for your own fine handiwork, Lib. Use it to ferret out details for your oratory." The box contained a delicate magnifying glass with a carved handle made from horn.

"Thank you, Father," she said rising to hug him. "I promise to use it as you intend and for much more."

When she held it up to show the gathering, laughter and groans erupted from a few of Judge Cady's law students.

"Mr. Andrews, did I hear your voice?" Elizabeth said, holding up the magnifying glass to peer at him down the table.

"No, indeed you did not," he said, glancing at Kate. "I am fully aware of your attentiveness to details."

The remaining parcel wrapped in sapphire colored paper had creases at its corners. Elizabeth picked it up and looked at her mother, with a questioning expression.

"It came by the post."

With all eyes on her, Elizabeth removed the paper to reveal a slim volume of Lord Byron poetry. She looked at her family then down the table to the students seeking the giver's recognition. When no one acknowledged the gift, she opened the book.

"Oh, dear. Excuse me," she said, leaving the table with such haste her chair fell over backward.

*

November 12, 1836

Dear Diary, I have not written for a while because my life has contained nothing of interest. Parties and balls with the same people over and over again became so tedious I dared not comment for fear of ugliness. Today on my birthday however, a wonderful event occurred–a gift from Edward, a volume of Byron. He knows I love this poet. How fine he is to remember me, with his life now full of medical terms and treating patients. Fini has little interest in poetry. My thoughts of Edward lessen, but today with this tender gift, his face, his voice and his affect on me are renewed in all their brilliance.

35

November 1836

With the book under her arm, Elizabeth grabbed a wool shawl from her room and hurried to the garden. She sank down on the cold bench, unmindful of the damp autumn leaves scattered on its surface and at her feet.

With trembling hands she re-opened the book and read the inscription inside.

My dearest Elizabeth, I miss you so. Since I cannot regard your sweet face with my own eyes, please allow the words of this great poet to express my feelings for you. –Edward.

A green satin ribbon marked a divide in the book. Elizabeth turned to that page revealing the poem *She Walks in Beauty.*

By the time she read through the poem, tears blurred the words. For a moment she recalled Edward's bright smile and his handsome profile and could almost hear his voice. She pulled Kate's gift of the embroidered handkerchief from her sleeve and dabbed at her eyes.

Murky early evening light now filled the garden and she pulled her shawl close against the growing chill.

"Lib? Are you out there?" Kate called.

"Here," she said, rising to her feet and starting in Kate's direction.

"Mother's worried," Kate said. "Come inside. We are playing games and need you there." She grabbed her sister's hand.

"You have been crying," Kate said, alarmed.

"Yes, for a moment, but I am fine now," Elizabeth assured her. "Let us do play a game and we will sing too. It is a fine way to celebrate my birthday. I apologize for running out as I did."

"The book is from Edward, is it not?" Kate asked.

"It is, my intuitive little sister. I became overcome with emotion when I tore off the paper and saw who sent it. He has meant so much to me–to all of us. I think it surprised me," she said.

Whatever could he mean about his feelings? Perhaps I have been wrong all along? Does he regard me as I do him? What do I make of this? Oh.

At the back door to their home Kate reached for the knob.

"Wait," Elizabeth said. "Please do not tell mother and father of our conversation. They will not be pleased," she asked.

Kate turned to hug her sister. "No worry," she said. "I love you, and especially love that you confide in me."

Boisterous laughter greeted the girls as they rejoined the party celebration.

It seemed the young men's attempts to draw Judge Cady into a humorous conversation about a point of law succeeded, for he laughed as loudly as the others.

Her mother appeared a bit disproving when Elizabeth and Kate walked into the room, but when she saw them, her behavior changed.

"Gentlemen, my daughters have returned," she said in a tone of voice that left no misunderstanding.

Judge Cady swiped a handkerchief across his face and coughed. "Yes, indeed, Mrs. Cady, it is time for a quieter celebration."

"Mother, let us play *Hot and Cold* as we did when we were little," Kate said.

"Oh my, that is a game for children. Are you sure, dear?"

"I would like that too," Elizabeth said. "It is such a charming reminder of our lives as little girls. I will bet that Father's students played it too," she said.

A few of the young men nodded.

"Girls against the boys, and Mother you must join our meager team," Elizabeth said.

"I will, if we contain the game to this room alone. I am not sure I could run up and down the stairs or outside if needed."

"All right with you, men?" Judge Cady asked. "There are more of us, but these women are sly and tricky."

Jimmer Andrews stepped forward. "As spokesman for the students," he said in a sonorous voice, "we agree."

Kate held out a slender painted fan. "We shall be hiding this," she said, "and for the person who finds it, there is a prize."

"And what would that be Miss Cady?" Vanderhoff asked. He winked.

"Never you mind just now," Kate said.

"Out into the hall with you then," Elizabeth said, shooing them through the open doorway. "Close the door and no peeking through the keyhole."

Andrews took his time closing the door as slowly as possible, while his friends goaded him on and laughed.

When Elizabeth heard the click of the door, she rushed to lock it. Then in whispers and gestures the three women chose their hiding place. The fan was too long to fit into her father's tobacco humidor and it would be obvious perched on a bookshelf. Elizabeth searched the room for a location the students might not dare look. When she spotted her father's worn leather easy chair that no one in the family was allowed to sit in, she pointed. "There," she whispered.

Her mother's face lit up and Kate grinned then tiptoed to the chair and pushed the fan down behind the seat cushion.

"We are ready," Elizabeth said as she opened the door.

Soon the house once again rang with laughter and shouts of "Hot", and then "Cold", as the game proceeded.

Her father found the fan, for none of the students would go near his chair. The game continued with the Cady sisters knowing the best hiding places and the students' rowdy attempts to vainly find them.

Finally, interest waned and the exhausted players fell onto the sofa and into chairs scattered around the room.

"Elizabeth, would you and Kate favor us with a song," their father asked. He settled into his chair, facing their piano, using the fan to cool his face.

When Elizabeth began playing the chords of *I Know a Bank Where the Wild Thyme Grows* her parents smiled in approval and listened with pleased expressions. Kate's clear soprano and Elizabeth's alto filled the room with music. Even the young men standing in the back of the room appeared captivated. As the notes of the last line concluded the song and Elizabeth lifted her hands from the keys, Jimmer Andrews broke into loud applause.

"You are splendid musicians," he exclaimed. "Miss Kate, I hope you will sing for me again," he said, rushing to her side and lifting her hand to his lips.

She beamed. "Of course, I would like that."

"You did not award the prize," he said. "What was it?"

"Your kiss upon my hand," she said.

The evening drew to a close and Judge Cady bid his young law students goodbye with a reminder to be on time the following morning.

Kate trailed behind them chatting and giggling with Jimmer Andrews.

When the door closed behind the entourage, Kate stood at the window waving.

"Thank you all for a splendid birthday celebration," Elizabeth said to her mother and father, and Kate. "I am very tired and seek my bed." She yawned, clapping a hand over her mouth. "Good night."

"I will go up with you," Kate said.

Elizabeth climbed the stairs anticipating the comfort of her featherbed with Edward's book of poems in her hand.

"Lib, do not be angry that I find Mr. Andrews so charming," Kate said.

"Oh, dear Sister, I am not at all angry. He is a fine young man, and very much taken with you. I can see that. Our views may differ on many things, his and mine, but you and I are different, too." She kissed her sister's cheek and told her goodnight.

Once in her room, Elizabeth lit the lamp by her bedside, changed into her nightdress then relaxed against the soft pillows and opened the book.

Soon she fell into a deep sleep thinking about Edward and what might have been if he had chosen her instead of Tryphena.

The next morning when she came down for breakfast, everything seemed the same. She had turned twenty-three, but nothing seemed different. Still no proper suitors and no interest in embroidery or cross-stitching. Except for the promised trip to Cousin Gerrit in January, her days ran on without much change.

She bit into a piece of toast and chewed.

"Mail for you, Lib," her mother said, dropping a stack of folded notes beside her plate.

Elizabeth brightened. "Oh, how lovely," she said.

She tore into the notes with interest. Invitations to two balls, for which she would surely need new gowns, and an appeal to attend a Lyceum organizing event featuring Horace Greely as its speaker.

"Mother, I have so many offers and plan to respond 'yes' to all," Elizabeth said and gave her mother the details.

When she opened the last letter she yelped.

"Amy Lee is coming to Johnstown," she said, scanning her friend's delicate handwriting for particulars. "She and her husband are passing through town in a week and she has something to discuss with me."

"Where will you meet your school friend?" Margaret Cady asked.

"Mrs. Henry's Boarding House." She looked back at the note from Amy Lee. "They are staying the night there only, before traveling on to New York."

"Well, that will be a lovely tea then. Mrs. Henry's cook is accomplished. Perhaps they will offer you a private room in which to dine to avoid the other boarders."

"Oh, listen to this. She is with child," Elizabeth said looking up from the letter. "Traveling must be so tiresome for her." Somehow this bit of news saddened Elizabeth. She never thought of her merry little school chum as a mother. Now, being twenty-three seemed old.

"That bit of news changes things. I think it best she and her husband stay here," her mother said. "Please write to her at once and extend the offer. Tell her I insist. Mrs. Henry's home is comfortable, but we can provide a more suitable accommodation for someone expecting a child soon."

"I will do it today. That is a fine idea and Amy Lee and I can spend more time together too, no matter what it is she wants to talk about."

"The invitations to the balls?" her mother asked, changing the subject. "Can you wear the same gown to each or should we plan on two different ones?"

"The same people attend them all. I really do not care one way or the other, but I should have two to numb the tongues of the gossips," Elizabeth said. "Since it is the Christmas season, perhaps dark blue velvet and a bright green?"

The two women spent the next half hour discussing fabrics and looking at drawings of new fashions in the *Ladies' Fashionable Repository* magazine sent to their seamstress from England. Confidant in their choices, they agreed orders must be made immediately for the tailoring of the gowns.

Finally, Elizabeth's mother asked about the Lyceum. She'd heard nothing about this, she said.

"It is because your tasks running the house so wonderfully do not allow you to linger over the daily newspapers as I do," Elizabeth said. Her mother's interests did not go beyond their doorstep, so Elizabeth hoped her choice of words were tactful.

"I see. And, does your father know of this Mr. Greely?"

"I believe so. The gentleman is a journalist and is said to be a fine writer. He is planning on starting a newspaper."

"Another one?" Her mother asked.

"Yes, but different than those we read now. He claims they are biased in their outlooks and because of that people do not get all the information they should have."

Her mother nodded, but Elizabeth didn't know if she understood the difference.

"I have heard Mr. Greely is an exciting speaker and I so look forward to attending his address," Elizabeth said. What she didn't tell her mother was that Greely was an outspoken supporter of abolition, a topic that interested her but one that her father would not discuss with her.

*

December 4, 1836

Dear Diary, not only am I preparing to visit Cousin Gerrit in January, my holiday calendar of social events abounds with commitments. Mother and I are rushing around to make sure the gowns we ordered are fashionable. I care more about the comfort, but for Mother I feign interest. The seamstresses are dreadfully busy. I choose my gowns to please myself. There certainly are no men whose heads I try to turn. Still I see them looking at me. Or is it Father's money that is attractive? Likely the money. The wealthy men unspoken for are either very old or very ugly, or a bit of both. Rich or poor, it makes no difference to me if our souls undertake to seek each other out in love and harmony of thought. Not ugly though.

36

December 1836

Elizabeth rose at dawn to prepare for Amy Lee's arrival. When her friend's fine mahogany and leather carriage stopped in front of their home she rushed onto the front porch. A husky young man with a florid complexion opened the door and jumped out, reaching inside to lift down a step stool. Amy Lee's bonnet barely cleared the doorway when she placed her foot on the stool and looked up to see Elizabeth rushing toward her.

"My dear friend, I am overjoyed to see you," Elizabeth said, throwing her arms around Amy Lee, whose considerable girth made the gesture almost impossible.

"What a journey," Amy Lee said. She appeared exhausted. "I am so pleased to finally be here. The carriage rocked back and forth on the roads, and passersby often frightened the horses. I feared we would never get here."

"Come inside straight away," Elizabeth said. "I will have tea and some small sandwiches brought for us and you can warm yourself by the fire. Mother is waiting to meet you, too."

"This is my husband, Mr. Berkeley," Amy Lee said pulling the young man to her side.

"Miss Cady, Davison Berkeley at your service," he said, looking her up and down, then bowing slightly.

"Davison, please do not be so formal. I have told you all about Lizzy and our escapades at Emma, so do be cordial," Amy Lee said. "I must sit down soon or this baby will drop right here on the cobbles."

With everyone relaxed in the parlor and Amy Lee's swollen feet on a hassock, Elizabeth's mother began to serve the tea. Mrs. Brewster brought a platter of cakes with the sandwiches and Amy Lee ate as if starved. "It is the baby," she said between mouthfuls. "It wants to eat, so I help it."

Margaret Cady said, "With each of my children the experience varied, but I always craved food." She held out the platter of cakes, from which Amy Lee took two and put them on her plate. When Elizabeth's mother smiled in a knowing way, the young woman took another cake.

Judge Cady joined the group from his office across the vestibule and offered Mr. Berkeley a sherry that he drank immediately, then gestured toward the bottle and asked for a refill. Elizabeth's father ignored the discourtesy but after refilling the man's glass he capped the bottle.

"Mr. Berkeley, what is your occupation?" Elizabeth asked.

"Finance."

Amy Lee rolled her eyes. "Bank of the United States," she said adding, "His father got him the job, but it is a good one. Finance indeed, Davison."

The young man blushed, making his skin almost purple.

"That is a fine occupation, Mr. Berkeley," Judge Cady said. "Next to the law, that is," he added in a perfunctory way.

An uneasy silence followed his remark.

"Father," Elizabeth said. "Not everyone can be a lawyer."

"Sorry. My attempt at humor is not successful," Judge Cady said and then apologized to Mr. Berkley.

"Perfectly fine. If I did not have a career in finance it could easily have been the law, or engineering. I attended Rensselaer and quite enjoyed building things."

"The boys at Rensselaer courted many of Emma Willard's girls," Elizabeth said.

"Like me," Amy Lee said. "And look where it got me."

She glanced at her husband, her expression cheerless.

Mr. Berkeley choked on his drink and began to cough. His face grew redder.

Judge Cady jumped up to pound the young man on the back.

"You all right?" he asked. "Mother, ring for a glass of water."

By the time Mr. Berkeley recovered, the tension caused by his wife's remark had eased.

"Come, let us get you settled into your rooms," Elizabeth said in a hearty way, hoping to change the atmosphere.

Amy Lee's husband pulled his wife to her feet and with a valise under each arm he followed her and Elizabeth up the stairs.

That evening, with Kate at the supper table adding her youthful exuberance, the conversation flew. It changed from topic to topic with energy and excitement, Mr. Berkeley's remarks growing more boisterous with each glass of wine. Finally, with a knowing look at his wife, Judge Cady motioned to a servant to remove the wine bottles.

Much later after everyone retired, Elizabeth answered a knock at her bedroom door. Amy Lee stood outside with her silk dressing gown pulled tight across her belly.

"Are you unwell?" Elizabeth asked, fearing the doctor might be needed if the baby's birth proved imminent.

"Oh, no. I cannot sleep. This child is kicking me so. I thought perhaps we might finally talk a bit. May we?" Amy Lee asked. Tears filled her eyes.

Elizabeth opened the door wide and then grabbed her friend's hand to guide her to a sofa in front of the small blaze in her fireplace. She handed Amy Lee a clean handkerchief from her pocket.

"Whatever is wrong?" Elizabeth asked. Her expression softened. She reached to hold Amy Lee's hands in her own.

"I should not have married Mr. Berkeley. Now I have this." She tore her hands from Elizabeth's grasp and placed them on her belly.

"But you told me that being married with babies would fulfill your fondest dreams. At school you were the most sure of all of us."

"I thought marriage would be everything I ever wanted," Amy Lee said. "It is not and now I am trapped."

"Your husband seems like such a good sort, smart and charming," Elizabeth said. "Is he not perfect?"

"It is a charade," Amy Lee responded. "Here, with your family and especially your father, he is motivated to be on his best behavior. With just me, and the servants, he is unkind and demanding."

"Surely you must have suspected this? Did you not court for months?"

"We did, but I was blind to his true self. He wooed me in a most earnest manner with flowers, lovely gifts. His behavior with my mother was impeccable too."

"When did he reveal his real personality?" Elizabeth asked.

"At first he merely grew distant," Amy Lee said. "Pleading he needed time alone. So I agreed. But when I realized I was with child his attitude turned dark and hateful."

"I am so sorry."

"He beat our Negro groom when the poor man failed to bring his horse to the gate at the precise time he asked. The groom explained the blacksmith had needed to finish shoeing the horse, but Davison's tirade and abuse did not stop. That is just one of many incidents."

"My dear friend, I am so sorry for your dilemma. How can I help you?"

"I will not raise a child with this man. Would you ask your father if he would preside over my divorce from Mr. Berkeley?"

To gather her thoughts, Elizabeth glanced out the window at the flickering gas lamps on the snowy street. *Amy Lee has no idea what her life will be like. Her dowry will be gone. Her husband could take the child. Divorce is so perilous and fraught with unexpected hardships for women.* These were serious issues her father would discuss, but Elizabeth knew he would help if he could. Finally, she said, "If this is truly your wish, then I shall ask him."

With relief Amy Lee's expression of sorrow changed to joy.

"You leave tomorrow so you must speak to my father in the morning. I will talk to him before breakfast to prepare him, for you should discuss this before you depart."

Amy Lee embraced Elizabeth.

"Thank you so much. I will be ready."

"And Mr. Berkeley? What of him?" Elizabeth asked.

"I doubt he will be surprised. He might even be grateful. He has plenty of money, so he does not need me for anything really. I believe he married me to please his father because of my family connections."

"And what will you do?"

"Return to my parents' home. My mother is so very pleased there is to be a grandchild that I know she will welcome me. I have no other place to go and he will take the house and all our furnishings as his own. What little personal money I have, the law says it is his. There is not much."

"I know of these unfair laws. My father often represents women who share your predicament. There is very little he can do to preserve the things you brought to the marriage, but I know him. He will do what he can."

"I will be ready to present my problem to your father in the morning. Thank you for helping me. Perhaps you can visit once the baby is born," Amy Lee said, rising with difficulty to embrace Elizabeth again. She paused at the door to say, "You are a good and compassionate friend, Lizzy."

When Amy Lee and her husband stood on the front steps waiting to board their carriage, Elizabeth knew the conversation with her father had taken place judging by Mr. Berkeley's grim expression.

She took Amy Lee aside. "Will you be all right during the trip home?" she asked. "Mr. Berkeley seems to be in a foul state."

"He will not do anything to me now," her friend replied. "He has too much to lose if my family believes I am in any danger. He likely wants to be rid of me quickly. That way he can resume the life of leisure he imagined for himself before we married."

Elizabeth hugged her. "Be safe, my dear friend. I shall write to you, and please do invite me for a visit. Babies are not in my future yet, but I do love them."

When the carriage rumbled out of sight, Judge Cady told Elizabeth she need not worry about her friend. "The divorce will go through smoothly," he predicted. "Because the aspect of money does not cloud the settlement, Mr. Berkeley has agreed to a speedy resolution."

"Will she lose her jewelry as well as her home?"

"If it is of great value, she might," her father said. "It depends on him. He can take nothing or everything."

"I know," Elizabeth said. Once again this demoralizing behavior touched her life. She recalled that childish moment when she believed she could change these laws with a pair of scissors. That her friend should suffer from them pierced her heart.

*

December 10, 1836

Dear Diary, I am heartsick. While I selfishly worry about nothing more than dresses and parties, dear Amy Lee is experiencing a terrible rift. I am so embarrassed in the face of her sadness that I hurt from it. I should not have feelings of joy at all when she is suffering. Who knows what will become of her? I looked into her eyes seeking the sparkle of the carefree girl I remembered and saw only dull confusion. Why must divorce be so distressing to women? In fifteen years those abominable laws have not changed. It should not be like this. Regardless of my parents' pressure, I will not marry just to avoid spinsterhood.

37

December 1836

When the letter arrived from Amy Lee, Elizabeth broke the sealing wax to open it and ran to find her mother.

"The baby is born, Mother," she exclaimed, her eyes racing down the page. "It is a boy named Daniel Alexander, after my father, and her favorite uncle. She is calling her son Alex. She says her divorce decree arrived two days before the baby and she is happy beyond belief. This is lovely news."

"It is indeed. Your father used his influence to hasten the dissolution of the marriage. How honored he will be to know the child bears his name." Margaret Cady looked up from her cross-stitching to smile at her daughter's pleasure.

Elizabeth read on aloud, "*My mother barely lets me hold the baby for fear I will drop it. She is nearly insufferable. But I prefer this to a loveless marriage. I thank God every day for your father's good will, counsel and help.*"

"She sounds happy," Mrs. Cady said. "Take note of this. A good and proper husband who provides both financially and emotionally is the choice you should make and you should not consider otherwise."

"Like your marriage to Father. It is 'good and proper'. I am pleased to have your example to follow," Elizabeth said kissing her mother's cheek.

"I see you have other letters in your hand," Margaret Cady said.

"Oh, yes." She forgot them completely in her excitement. "Another invitation to a ball. Oh, this is tiresome. It is from someone I barely know so I believe I will decline this one."

"Someone our family knows? One of your father's clients perhaps?"

"No, I think not." She handed the invitation to her mother.

"Elizabeth, this invitation is from your Uncle John," her mother exclaimed. "He will be hosting President Van Buren at his new hotel."

"Why did I not recognize it as that?"

"It is on Astor House stationery and sent by his assistant whose name you have not heard, Mr. Rupert Watkins."

"So we will be traveling to New York City for a ball? Even Madge? Because she will be home for Christmas."

"All of us," her mother answered. "Oh dear, this means more ball gowns and formal dress for your father. How he hates that. It is for December 31st, too." She sighed with pleasure. "New Year's Eve. What a grand affair it will be."

Christmas Day came and went with its usual chaos in the Cady family home. Added to it were the preparations for the trip to New York City. Elizabeth's father decided the family would travel by carriage the entire way so as to have Peter's help, and Jacob would accompany them as well.

Even Miss Christie would go, squeezed into the carriage and making the journey warmer inside, but doing nothing for the two men who must sit atop on the driver's seat.

As the group neared the outskirts of the city, Elizabeth nudged Kate who had fallen asleep on her shoulder. "You are missing so much. Wake up at once," she said.

Miss Christie peered out the window alongside Elizabeth's mother for Peter had driven into the city straight up Broadway, the grandest thoroughfare.

"Yes, young ladies, there is much to see," Elizabeth's father said. "That impressive building is City Hall." He indicated a three-story structure topped by a cupola. "That one," he said, turning to point out the opposite side of the carriage, "is Saint Paul's Episcopal Cathedral. Is it not the grandest church you have ever seen?"

Kate nodded, but Elizabeth tapped her mother on the shoulder to direct her gaze to the beautifully dressed women strolling on the sidewalks arm in arm with men in handsome and colorful clothing.

"I have never seen day clothing so artfully designed or of such captivating fabric," Elizabeth said. Would her gowns and dresses from Johnstown be dowdy, she wondered?

"Their costumes rival ours I dare say," her mother commented as if reading Elizabeth's mind. She leaned forward to make her point. "Never mind what others wear, my dears, and that includes you, Miss Christie," she said. "We are as grand a family as any in New York City."

Elizabeth did admit she felt like a country mouse taking in the bustle and excitement. Compared to Johnstown, with its quiet pace, New York City buzzed with energy. When Peter drove the horses into New York City proper and onto Broadway at the corner of Vesey Street, he reined them in, pulling the team to a walk. Elizabeth and Kate poked their heads out a window of the carriage again to gawk at the massive five-story blue stone Astor House building.

"Uncle John's hotel is splendid," Kate said. "There are so many fashionable people walking in and out, and arriving just as we are in fancy carriages and hansoms. Oh look, Lib, see the men dressed in uniform opening the doors and helping with trunks?" she said with excitement.

Peter halted the carriage at the grand front entrance. Before he could alight to assist the family, one of the uniformed men grasped the carriage door, flung it open and with a gloved hand reached inside to help Elizabeth's mother to the walkway.

Judge Cady set about finding their rooms while their trunks and valises were carried inside. Peter and Jacob drove the horses to the Astor House stable buildings where accommodations for them and other drivers were arranged.

Inside the lofty reception area with its marble columns Elizabeth and Kate barely kept their enthusiasm in check.

"I have never seen a blue and white marble floor like this," Kate said bending to peer down more closely. "Look, it is made of tiny bits."

"It is called mosaic," Elizabeth said. "I read about it in one of our fashion books."

Margaret Cady ran her hand over the gleaming wood of a black walnut table adorned with a large silver vase filled with cedar and holly.

"It is so beautiful, is it not?" Elizabeth asked.

Once registered, the family settled into their rooms, though they were not one of the top floor rooms that would have had a better viewpoint of the city. They nevertheless exclaimed over the modern innovations–the gaslights, the hot and cold running water and toilets on each floor. Just as Elizabeth finished hanging her dresses it was time for Peter to leave for the train station to fetch Madge. The family had not seen her since she entered Emma Willard in September. A modest Christmas dinner would celebrate the family reunion. When Peter pulled the horses onto the street, Elizabeth bounded down the stairs and through the lobby to yank the carriage door open and jump in.

"I am going too," she shouted, pulling the door closed behind her.

They waited alongside the tracks with other carriages and wagons pulled up to watch the train chug into the station and stop in a cloud of steam. It seemed hundreds of passengers poured through the car doors, flooding the platform in a commotion of scurrying people bundled in overcoats, furs and mufflers.

Elizabeth spotted Madge hurrying through the crowd holding onto a red hat pinned to the top of her head. In the other hand she struggled with a valise and an enormous bag out of which poked boxes wrapped in Christmas tissue.

"There she is," Elizabeth said, pointing in the direction of her sister's path. "Wave to catch her attention."

Peter pulled off his brimmed hat and held it aloft brandishing it like a flag.

"Madge," Elizabeth shouted. "Over here."

Her sister looked around bewildered, and then she grinned when she saw them and headed in their direction.

Elizabeth ran to Madge and took the bag from her hand, hugged her and kissed her cheek. Peter grabbed the valise.

"Miss Margaret, I am happy to see you again," Peter said.

"Thank you Peter, it is good to be home or here or..." she stopped.

"Everyone is waiting at the hotel. We have not dressed for dinner–at least I have not," Elizabeth said.

With the sisters tucked into the carriage, Peter started off for the hotel. The two girls gossiped and laughed during the entire return trip. Madge began to relate her adventures at Emma Willard, while Elizabeth interrupted over and over asking for details.

"And do you like the new French teacher, Madame Fleur?"

"Despite her lovely name, she is a tyrant. An ugly one at that," Madge said. "She has a big hairy wart on her lip that wiggles when she speaks. We all think it is funny, but dare not laugh for fear of reprisal."

Elizabeth smiled, remembering the woman who taught her French as being so timid and soft-spoken few girls but the ones in the front row could hear her voice. Now whenever she heard the words *excusez-moi*? Elizabeth thought of that teacher who must have answered that question a hundred times.

"And you, Lib? What do you do all day? With me gone, you are probably becoming an expert seamstress," Madge said, poking her sister in the side.

This time both sisters laughed, Madge dabbing at tears in her eyes. She sniffed and poked her handkerchief back into her reticule.

"I do miss you, Madge. We have such fun together. Now all I do is read and go to parties with the same dreary people. With Edward gone, and Fini, there is no one to talk to. Father is in Washington more than he is home now and he has stopped training lawyers, and Mother is busy running the house and the acreage. Without the steady stream of law students to tease and make fun of, I am just plain bored."

"No beaus?" Madge asked.

"They are all afraid of me. Men do not know what to make of a woman who speaks her mind or says anything controversial for that matter."

"There must be someone."

Elizabeth shook her head. "I do go to Peterboro come January. Cousin Gerrit invited me to stay for a few weeks. There are always such interesting visitors there. Perhaps I will meet someone with whom I can have a decent conversation without embarrassing Father or Mother. But truly Madge I am not seeking a husband."

When the family members were dressed for dinner and seated in the dining room, waiters placing their soup course on the table were startled when a boisterous voice rang out. "My lovely Cady family has arrived." John Jacob Astor strode to their table with a bevy of wait staff behind him who hovered nearby when he stopped.

Elizabeth's father stood to embrace Astor in a warm hug. "It is good to see you," he said. "Thank you for inviting us to this magnificent hotel. It does you proud."

Astor smiled broadly. "Nieces? A greeting for your old uncle please?"

Elizabeth, Madge and Kate ran into his arms, engulfed by a cloud of bay rum cologne.

Uncle John moved to the side of the girls' mother and reached for her hand. "Margaret," he said, bowing slightly then releasing her fingers.

A young man with a lustrous butter-colored moustache stood slightly behind Astor, listening with concentration.

"My assistant, Rupert here, will take care of your every need," he said, waving a hand at the young man. "I will see you all tomorrow night for the grand event. Daniel, I shall be busy with many people, but please do make some time to talk. I have need of your help," Astor said. And with a grand bow that made the sisters giggle, he hurried off.

A string quartet seated on a platform in the middle of the room began to play while the family exchanged gifts with Madge, one voice exclaiming over the other as the rattle of crumpled tissue paper added to the growing noise in the dining room. When dessert arrived, a cake glossy with swirls of chocolate sprinkled with sugared violets, Elizabeth decided she could not remember a night so magical. Scented with hothouse roses and French colognes, the room glittered with facetted crystal and candlelight while through the high windows she could see snow begin to fall. She looked down the massive dining room at the vibrantly colored gowns of the women and the men in their velvet suits and starched white shirtfronts. Edward would look so handsome attired like these men. She touched the back of her neck and found it hot. Did the sudden thought of Edward provoke this? Or did she have a wistful longing for romance after all?

Margaret Cady leaned toward her. "Dear, are you feeling unwell?"

Elizabeth shook her head. "I am fine, Mother."

Just before dawn the family woke to the sounds of running footsteps and men's voices shouting in the corridor outside their rooms. Judge Cady pulled on his dressing gown and stuck his head out of the door. The sisters and Miss Christie also opened their doors to peer out at the commotion.

"What is happening?" Judge Cady asked of a policemen hurrying by.

"Some fool blew out the flame on his gas light instead of turning off the jet. Happens all the time. These folks think those lights are candles. They know so much, a person cannot tell them a thing," the policeman said. "No offense, Sir," he added, touching the bill of his cap.

At the breakfast table the next morning rumors circulated that the man taken to hospital in the early hours had fallen victim to drinking heavily and nearly died from asphyxiation.

Regardless, the hotel sent a note to each room with instructions for the operation of the gaslights.

The President's Ball that night kept Elizabeth and her sisters busy all day preparing their clothing. Since Miss Christie had accepted an invitation to attend but did not have a suitable dress to wear, a seamstress had remade one of Elizabeth's gowns to fit her. Green taffeta trimmed in matching flowers around the neckline and hem suited Miss Christie's creamy skin. The teacher's red hair arranged into thick ropes and curls piled on top of her head appeared quite glamorous.

"See how lovely you are with your hair done," Elizabeth said, holding a looking glass up to the back of Miss Christie's head.

"I hardly recognize myself," she said, her color high. "Thank you for helping me and for giving me this splendid ball gown. I never expected such generosity. You are truly kind."

The Cady family caused heads to turn as they swept down the staircase and up to the entrance to the ballroom. A liveried attendant looked down at a list, and then as they entered the room announced: "Judge Daniel E. and Mrs. Cady, the Misses Elizabeth, Margaret and Catherine Cady, and Miss Margaret Christie."

An enormous orchestra situated at one end of the vast ballroom played a lyrical waltz as dancers whirled on the floor. Elizabeth gasped at the ballroom's beauty.

"I did not know the dancing came first," Kate said to Elizabeth. "I am so hungry. I thought food would be served."

"It is a midnight supper," Elizabeth said. "You should have eaten the bread and milk Mother ordered for all of us."

"I drank the milk and put the bread in my reticule," her sister said. "Do you suppose it will anger her if I nibble it?"

"Behind your fan so she does not see and make sure you turn away from Father, too."

The sisters stood off to the side with Miss Christie behind their parents, engrossed in the buzz of conversation and the swirl of elaborately gowned women and men in white tie and tails.

Miss Christie leaned forward to whisper in Elizabeth's ear. "I have never seen anything so grand. Thank you so much for allowing me to accompany you."

Elizabeth smiled and squeezed her friend's hand. "I have never witnessed such a spectacle either," she said. "It is lovely that you can experience it with us."

"Oh look, Uncle John's assistant is coming this way," Kate said with a subtle gesture of her fan in his direction.

He is quite handsome, Elizabeth thought, welcoming him with a demure smile.

"Misses Cady," he said, bowing slightly. He then turned toward Miss Christie. "May I have this dance, Miss?" he asked.

Kate's hands flew to cover her mouth. "Oh my," she said.

Miss Christie looked stunned.

"Of course she would love to dance, would you not Margaret?" Elizabeth said, gently pushing her friend forward.

The three sisters watched as Rupert led Miss Christie onto the dance floor.

Within moments both Kate and Madge had joined the dancers with partners whose skills matched theirs, leaving Elizabeth with her mother and father.

A loud commotion at the door caused her to turn in time to see three young men enter to a round of applause.

"Who are those people?" her mother asked.

Elizabeth strained to get a look, rising on her tiptoes to see above the heads of the crowd surging toward the new guests. "The tall man, with the silk top hat in his hand is James Fennimore Cooper," she said. "I have seen a drawing of him in the newspaper. The other two are Ralph Waldo Emerson and Nathaniel Hawthorne. Their portraits appear regularly in the newspapers too." She felt a thrill of excitement that three of America's popular authors were in the same room as she.

"How do you know this, Lib?"

"I read the newspapers daily. Emerson's essay *Nature* expressing his philosophy of Transcendentalism has just been published. There are always drawings of these men because they are so famous. That is likely why they are here."

The men headed for a corner. They appeared enmeshed in a heated conversation. Elizabeth left her parents to push through the crowd hoping to hear what the men were talking about.

"But my dear Hawthorne, the only idealistic explanation of Transcendentalism is its application to religion and nature. And to life," Emerson said. He paused to emphasize his remark with a gesture.

"I agree it is a new manner of thinking, like mesmerism and phrenology or homeopathy," Cooper said. "It is new thinking that attacks established scientific beliefs. Like Graham's doctrine and others who think vegetarianism is the road to good health. Their followers also believe they also gain greater spirituality." He seemed about to raise his voice.

Elizabeth stepped forward and placed her hand on the speaker's arm, stopping the man mid-sentence.

"Excuse me, Mr. Cooper, what you're saying is of great interest to me. I have studied phrenology and agree with you."

The author turned to her with a quizzical expression.

"Have we met, Miss?"

"I am Elizabeth Cady, Mr. Astor's niece."

"You are a follower of new thinking?"

"I am. My brother-in-law Edward Bayard assisted in my early education. He presented all types of books to study, including Mr. Gall's. And others to read for pleasure, of course. Such as yours," she said, directing her last remarks to Nathanial Hawthorne who joined his colleagues to listen.

"And have your read my writing as well, Miss?" asked Emerson.

"Yes I have, Sir. My father, Judge Daniel Cady, purchased a copy of *Nature* at its first printing. He too has always encouraged my sisters and me to read everything we can. I particularly like: *The eye reads omens where it goes, And speaks all languages the rose,*" she recited.

"Is your interest in nature, Miss Cady, or affairs of the heart?" Mr. Emerson asked. "I find young ladies often quote those lines as memorable and meaningful in a romantic context."

Elizabeth thought of Edward and she blushed.

"They are meaningful to me in a variety of ways," she responded, reaching for composure. "Your superb writing inspires many emotions and thoughtful contemplation. I imagine both women and men reach their own conclusions."

"Bravo, Miss Cady," Hawthorne said. "I believe she has you there, my friend," he added, turning to clap Emerson on his back.

"Gentlemen, I say we go meet Van Buren. Give him our regards," Cooper said. "I am hungry and my throat is parched," he added. "Best get the pleasantries out of the way before we share a brandy and dance with the ladies."

He threw his arms about the shoulders of his colleagues to pull them away, but Hawthorne turned back.

"Are all your dances spoken for, Miss Cady?" he asked.

Elizabeth scanned the pages of her program.

"Do you favor a Quadrille or a Galop?" she answered with a smile, catching her bottom lip in her teeth as she waited.

"Surely a Galop suits a young lady with such an energetic mind. Add my name to that one. I shall be back to fetch you," Hawthorne said. And with that he disappeared into the crowd.

When Hawthorne returned to claim his dance, Elizabeth's cheeks were red from dancing the Polka with a gentleman from New York in the employ of her uncle. He had talked about the details of his job endlessly over the sound of the music, barely catching his breath and making the dance more athletic than enjoyable.

Now she gazed into Hawthorne's wicked brown eyes as he took her hand in his warm grasp. *How like Edward he appears.*

"Miss Cady, I asked 'are you well'?"

She touched her cheek. "Why of course," she replied, shaking off the memory. "I am indeed fine and pleased to be your partner."

Out of breath once again, Elizabeth clung to Mr. Hawthorne's arm as he led her off the floor to a nearby chair. She pulled her fan from a pocket of her gown and waved it to cool her cheeks.

"Oh dear, I am fairly dripping."

"No Miss Cady, you are glowing with health," Hawthorne said then bowed. "Thank you for the dance. I regret I return to Boston in the morning. If I were not betrothed, I should like to call on you. Instead I will send you a copy of the magazine I edit. Watch the post for the *American Magazine of Useful and Entertaining Knowledge.* I hope you will find its contents amusing and provocative."

When he bowed again to make his way across the room, Elizabeth could still smell the cologne he wore and watched his retreating back with mixed feelings. So few young men like Mr. Hawthorne and his fellow writers existed in her life. She missed Edward so.

*

January 1, 1837

Dear Diary, I write almost breathless with excitement. Uncle John's grand party for the new President of the United States–he hasn't been sworn in yet–buzzed with luminaries of all stripe. My head turned so many times, I believe my neck will be sore tomorrow. Men asked to dance when they discovered who father is. I saw right through that device. Not interested in me at all, or engaging in conversation about matters serious to our country. Tomorrow we return to Johnstown and its dull, repetitive pursuits. I look forward to Peterborough with gusto however. I am restless for anything that challenges my mind.

38

January 1837

On the trip home Elizabeth contributed little to the conversations that captivated her family.

It seems that Rupert declared great interest in Miss Christie and planned to visit her soon. Elizabeth's sisters speculated on the seriousness of his interest, especially when Miss Christie blushed when she told them.

Madge and Kate claimed the adventure to be the most exciting of their lives. They continued to laugh and gossip about the people they met and the sweating hands of the men with whom they danced.

"Are they not supposed to wear gloves?" Kate asked.

"If they have them," Madge replied. "I think most of the men I danced with merely wanted a chance to touch the skin on my hands. But they could not. My gloves were damp and soiled by the time I retired."

Elizabeth's father and mother dozed against the seat of the carriage, her mother's chin dropping to her chest with a jerk, continually waking her.

"Lib, which of the men did you like best?" Kate asked.

Her sister Madge leaned forward to hear her reply.

None of Elizabeth's dance partners impressed her at all, she told them, save Nathanial Hawthorne. His likeness resembled Edward's, but did she dare mention it? No, she decided.

She gazed at the passing landscape through the window of the carriage for a moment, and then continued. "They all seemed so banal as if nothing but porridge existed in their skulls. My goodness, with the President-elect honored that night, I expected these young men to have comments about the election; it was fraught with dissention as it turned out, yet not a word. No one spoke of abolition or the lyceums," Elizabeth exclaimed. "A vigorous conversation about Alexis de Tocqueville's *Democracy in America* or word of the battle in Texas would have been interesting."

Judge Cady's eyes flew open.

"There were such conversations. You did not hear them for the simple reason that such topics are those discussed by men, not women."

"Father," Madge declared. "There are no topics women cannot discuss."

Elizabeth looked at her younger sister and shook her head. "You will learn that it is not that we cannot think or even talk about topics as men do. Simply that they do not believe we have the intelligence to do so."

"Is this true, Father?" Kate asked.

"If you three were young men instead of young women, no matter what your education, you would be on equal footing with all men," he replied.

Father! Have we not crossed that hurdle? You believe I think like a man—when I choose to do so—hence, why this repetitive comment?

"I detest their stuffy condescending attitudes," Elizabeth said. "I leave for Peterboro and Cousin Gerrit's collection of interesting guests next week. I will find both men and women in their home who do not have closed minds on every topic. Everyone is treated equally in their midst."

"And if I were not going back to school, I would go with you," Madge said.

"And, I too," said Kate.

Margaret Cady reached for her husband's hand, a gesture not lost on Elizabeth.

When Peter pulled the horses to a halt in front of their home Elizabeth spotted a familiar buggy parked beside the stable. She caught her breath and felt her heartbeat grow faster.

"Tryphena and Edward are here," she exclaimed. She opened the carriage door to step out and Kate and Madge nearly pushed her to the ground in their enthusiasm. Within minutes her older sister and Edward were on the steps, their arms open wide to embrace the family, everyone talking at the same time.

"It is so good to see you," Elizabeth said, grasping Tryphena's arm in hers to walk into the house.

"Your color is so high," Tryphena said. "Are you feverish, dear?"

"Good gracious no," she said in an attempt to explain her reaction to seeing Edward again. "Just weary from the journey and the excitement of New York." Elizabeth touched her hair. "I cannot imagine I look like anything but a frazzled wraith." Over her sister's shoulder she noticed Edward staring at her. She looked away.

"When did you arrive?" Margaret Cady asked.

"Yesterday," Tryphena said. "We thought we would surprise you and have Mrs. Brewster prepare an evening meal to welcome you home."

"That is a lovely gesture. I so appreciate the thoughtfulness. Girls, let us get settled before we come to table. Do join us," she said to Miss Christie who entered the vestibule with a valise under each arm.

"Edward, would you like a brandy?" Judge Cady asked, nodding his head toward his office. "We will join the ladies later."

A heavy snow had fallen during the night before they arrived and Elizabeth expected her room to be cold and gloomy. Instead flames blazed in the fireplace spreading warmth across the floor. She unbuttoned her damp shoes and tossed them onto the rug near the hearth to dry. She turned toward her bed, considering a short nap, and noticed a folded square of ivory colored paper on her pillow.

The wax seal splintered when she broke it to read the note.

Elizabeth, please come for a ride with me alone tomorrow morning after breakfast. I have something imperative to discuss with you privately.

–Edward

What could this mean? Did she trust herself with him? *Of course, do not be silly.* Still, what could be private that he could not talk about with the family?

That evening they gathered around the dining room table for the welcome home meal Tryphena arranged. Edward sat at the table beside her father. When Elizabeth caught Edward's eye she nodded her acceptance. During the evening's conversation he mentioned that Jacob said Elizabeth's horse needed exercise and since she would be leaving for Peterboro directly after Christmas that he had agreed to take her for a ride in the morning.

"The horses shall have a bit of a run, too," he said.

"That is a fine idea," Tryphena said. "Kate and Madge and I will be engrossed with Mother in last minute Christmas plans. There's much to do." She smiled at her husband.

The next morning dawned clear with the sun so bright it hurt Elizabeth's eyes when she opened the draperies to her room. She dressed quickly, pulling on long woolen socks and a worsted wool dress in her favorite shade of blue. The voices of the family echoed up from the dining room below where they attacked a spread of fresh biscuits and gravy, plates of ham and eggs, a pot of coffee and hot milk.

Edward sat reading a newspaper in her father's chair at the table. Judge Cady's adherence for promptness gathered his law students early, well before this late start to the morning.

"Good morning all," Elizabeth said. She began filling her plate refusing to look at Edward whose gaze she seemed to feel directed her way. When she finally turned to confront him, she'd composed herself.

"I am ravenous, Edward. Just let me eat a bit, and we will be on our way. I look forward to galloping Augusta. Perhaps we can ride east toward the walnut groves."

"Of course. Fine idea," he said from behind the paper.

It seemed to Elizabeth, that for all the mysterious hints in his message, Edward was nonchalant. In fact, when he helped her into her saddle, his actions seemed brusque. Perhaps she'd misread his note?

With the streets of Johnstown behind them, Elizabeth pulled Augusta into line behind Edward's horse as they made their way up a single-track path toward the thicket of now-bare walnut trees. The horses trotted with ease, but Elizabeth wanted to give Augusta her head and let the pretty horse take off. The sun began to melt what snow remained in the field alongside the track, and Elizabeth knew the terrain well.

"Come on, Edward," she called out, "Let us work the horses as we planned." And with that, she flicked the reins on Augusta's neck and sped past her brother-in-law, galloping far ahead, her skirts billowing behind her.

Soon a full-on race kept the two riders side by side until finally, Elizabeth reached the groves and reined in her horse to catch her breath.

"Like everything you do, you ride with authority and excitement," Edward said, drawing his horse alongside hers.

Elizabeth laughed. "Everything *is* exciting to me. You have taught me to be curious and I have learned to seek out activities that prompt excitement."

"You are so unlike your sister," he said, suddenly grave. "That is what I want to talk to you about."

"If this is something that cannot be shared with the family, tell me now. I insist," Elizabeth said. "We have been friends for a very long time and whatever it is I can help."

"This is not about friendship."

"Is something wrong with Fini? Is she ill?"

"No."

Edward leaned forward to grasp Augusta's halter, his expression stricken.

"It is I, Elizabeth dear. I am wrong," he said.

"Whatever do you mean?"

Edward looked away for a moment, as if rehearsing his response.

"I never should have married Tryphena. She is a good woman, but I am in love with you." His expression softened with the relief of confession.

Elizabeth caught her breath. "No, Edward, this cannot be."

He pulled their horses closer and leaned in to her, his mouth close. When she felt the warmth of his lips on hers she yielded for a moment reveling in the scent of his body and the insistence of his kiss.

"You must not love me," she said, pulling away.

"But I do. I have known for a long time. You and I are soul mates, dearest girl, and I could do nothing about it."

"What am I to do with this information?" she asked.

"And what of you, how do you feel about me?" He rushed ahead ignoring her question and her troubled expression.

"I have always loved you, first as a friend then...well," she sighed, "something more." The confession gave weight to her emotions.

"I will divorce Tryphena. We can marry," he said, his voice eager and persuasive. "I will explain it to your father, he will understand."

"Oh no, Edward, that would be a mistake. Please do not think about that at all."

"But would you marry me if I did?"

She turned away from his pleading eyes to gather her thoughts.

"No, I would not. I honor and hold you in high esteem and will always keep your kindness and care for me close to my heart. But I cannot betray my sister who loves you in many more ways than I can." She could not tell him how her youthful infatuation excited her. How profoundly handsome she thought him to be. How his leaving snuffed a flame for her that she longed to be rekindled.

Edward released his hand from her horse's bridle and turned away from her, his shoulders slumped. Elizabeth reached out to him then thought better of it. The wind had picked up blowing sleet onto the frozen track of the trail. The sting of it hitting her face brought tears to her eyes.

"It is growing colder," he said indifferently.

"Yes." Elizabeth looked back toward Johnstown and flicked the reins against Augusta's neck. "The family will wonder what is keeping us," she said.

Snow began to fall again on the ride back. Elizabeth shivered and pulled her wool cape closer. Edward's confession both thrilled and worried her. She contemplated its impact on her family and her relationship with him and her sister. Her life changed in those few minutes. It would never be the same again, that she knew. She could no longer hold him at a distance and romanticize about him. All of this confirmed her notion that subconsciously she compared every man she met to him.

Edward and Tryphena cut their visit short, surprising Margaret Cady and the Judge, but not Elizabeth. The comings and goings around their Christmas celebration continued as it always did–the opening of gifts, the Christmas meal, and if her sisters were aware of changes, they didn't acknowledge it. Only she knew why her relationship with Edward grew strained. She barely stayed abreast of her responsibilities and she compensated by involving herself in Tryphena's activities for the remainder of their stay. She joined the family on the front drive to wave goodbye when her sister and Edward left, but looked away when Edward turned to gaze at her just as he pulled the carriage door closed.

*

January 3, 1837
Dear Diary, the unthinkable has happened. I cannot talk about this to anyone but you. For all

my romantic notions about Edward, it seems his affection for me grew as well. I do love him. I will never know if I fell in love with him, or with what he represents. Is it merely that he respects me as an equal? He is devoted to my sister and she to him. He must love her too. He says he does not, but their destiny is set and it does not include any disruption by romantic nonsense that I might cause. I know Edward believes he loves me too, but I cannot be the one who shreds the fabric of Tryphena's life. She would never forgive me, nor would I forgive myself. Perhaps Mother knows what happened. I will not ask her though.

39

October 1839
Over a year later

As it turned out, Elizabeth's trip to Peterboro did not occur as anticipated. A brief note from Cousin Gerrit arrived the day before she planned to leave, explaining that he must attend to his contracts with the fur trade in the Pacific Northwest. He would not return for months.

A dejected Elizabeth began to fill her calendar with parties and teas again. She watched her friends announce engagements, attended their weddings, and grew more jaded and frustrated by the day.

Her mother's letters from Tryphena were full of the news of their lives. Edward's homeopathy practice thrived and he added patients every day. Tryphena managed the books for him, scrimping and saving as best she could. Their needs were few, she wrote. He did miss the Cady family, especially the laughter of the girls, and said to tell them so.

"Edward says he doesn't miss the law at all," Elizabeth's mother said, looking up from the most recent letter she held in her hand. "You would think for all the time he spent with your father, it would have meant something."

"He is busy with his new life and it takes all of his time," Elizabeth said. Edward did not mention her at all. But why would he? She spurned his advances because it was the right thing to do. As the months went by she thought about him less and less. It was almost as if a shade had lifted letting in the sunshine of possibilities.

"I have written to Tryphena and Edward that you are still seeking a beau," her mother said.

"Why would you do that? It embarrasses me and appears that I am unworthy."

"Dear Lib, it is only idle chatter. I am sorry if my remarks to your sister bother you."

"Goodness gracious Mother," Elizabeth said with a shake of her head.

She barely contained herself when the invitation to visit Cousin Gerrit was extended once again. Upon his return he had planned a grand soiree for his many friends and hoped with great enthusiasm that Elizabeth would grace his home with her presence.

"Mother, I insist," Elizabeth said. She and her mother sat in the parlor in front of a blazing fire, their needlework forgotten in their laps. A dense October winter storm enveloped the Cady home in a blanket of snow and sleet, and

Margaret Cady suggested Elizabeth post-pone her trip to Peterboro again.

"No. I have readied my trunks and Cousin Gerrit's family is expecting me. You have read the letters he sent explaining who will be there during my visit. I cannot miss this chance to meet these people."

Mrs. Cady sighed. "Elizabeth, it is not a safe journey."

"I will be fine," Elizabeth insisted. "Peter will drive me in the sleigh and he assures me the trip will be an easy one."

Her mother threw up her hands in defeat.

"Thank you," Elizabeth said, rising to kiss her mother on the forehead.

"I promise to be careful and you know Peter will never let anything happen to me," she said.

The next morning, bundled up in wool blankets and a bearskin rug tucked under her chin, Elizabeth struggled under the weight to lift her arm to wave farewell. Kate ran out to the sleigh at the last minute to thrust a basket into her sister's lap.

"Cakes for the journey and two jars of berry jam for Cousin Gerrit," she said and then hurried back to the front porch, shivering as she waved goodbye.

"Ready, Miss Elizabeth?" Peter called from his perch on the sleigh's driver seat.

"I am. Peter, please let us hurry before we freeze."

As the sleigh began to move, its rails sliding on the ice, Elizabeth looked back at her mother standing on the front step and Kate, still waving.

The trip would take but a few hours, time Elizabeth needed to consider the grand possibilities that might be ahead.

She contemplated the last letter she received from Gerrit, noting that Horace Greely and Henry Ward Beecher might be there as well as members of the Oneida Tribe. His home also temporarily housed escaping slaves on their way to Canada, a fact he had not written about, but that she suspected from casual conversations with her father.

When Peter pulled the sleigh up to the Smith mansion in Peterboro, and began to unload her luggage, Cousin Gerrit, his wife Ann Carole Fitzhugh whom he called Nancy, and their daughter Lizzy were on the front steps to welcome her.

As usual Gerrit Smith's enthusiastic greeting nearly overwhelmed her.

"Cousin Elizabeth, welcome," he said folding her into his arms with a sincere crush of affection

"I have been so eagerly waiting for your arrival," Lizzy said, linking her arm in Elizabeth's to draw her inside. "Father and Mother made so many plans for you I barely got a say in having you all to myself for even a minute."

"I am sure we will have many hours to visit," Elizabeth said. "For I intend to stay here until you make me take my leave."

"Miss Elizabeth, I will be going on home now," Peter called after her.

"What? No such thing," Gerrit said. "You shall stay the night here and have a grand meal and a warm bed. I will not be sending you home this late. It looks like snow again. It would be a dangerous trip at night."

Peter tipped his hat. "Why thank you, Sir, I am obliged."

"Put your team in the stables, and once they are fed and watered, come on in. The kitchen door is closest. We will expect you inside."

Peter nodded and his expression of surprise became a smile.

Inside the house, Elizabeth looked for a familiar face among Cousin Gerrit's guests, but found none. A tall dark-skinned man made even more striking by his elaborate headdress of feathers, two upright and one drooping down his back, stood in a corner. He spoke quietly to a small group of men. She learned the man was Oneida Chief Daniel Bread, a long time friend and ally of her cousin. He had stopped by on his way home to Wisconsin. Weary from attempts to negotiate long-standing land treaties that involved her Uncle John Astor, the chief and his family found promised solace under Gerrit Smith's roof. Bread's tailored grey suit appeared in stark contrast to the intricate beaded necklace dominated by a large medallion that hung from his neck. Fresh from arguing for The Treaty of Buffalo Creek that once again affected the land on which the Oneida tribe lived, his conversation flowed in elevated and passionate language.

She edged closer to the group to listen.

"Has Congress not complied with the treaties?" asked a lovely woman with her shining brown hair pulled back into a chignon.

"Why do you ask, Madam? Is it of concern to your husband?" one of the men asked.

"It is not of interest to a husband I do not have, but to me," the woman replied.

"Miss Beecher, I did not know you had arrived," Gerrit Smith said, breaking into the conversation with a big smile and hearty handshake for the young woman. After introducing her to the others around Chief Bread, Elizabeth's uncle caught her eye and waved her closer.

"My cousin Elizabeth Cady," he said to the woman and then turned to Elizabeth. "This is Harriet Beecher. Miss Beecher is a writer, Lib. She is about to publish a children's book about…geography?" He looked at the woman for confirmation. She nodded. "The two of you must talk, for I believe you have much in common," he added.

"Indeed, I have heard about your efforts working among the less fortunate, Miss Beecher. Please sit with me so we can compare opinions," Elizabeth said, grabbing the woman's hand. She gestured to a settee in front of the fireplace in the parlor nearby. "Cousin Gerrit draws such interesting and controversial people to him. When I visit I never know who I might meet," Elizabeth said.

"And, you, Miss Cady? You know me, but you have me at a disadvantage."

"I believe it is to our mutual interest in abolition that my cousin referred."

"Your views?" Miss Beecher asked.

"I firmly believe everyone should be equal. Not just the Negroes but growing more important to me, women. Do you agree?"

"I do," Miss Beecher said, "but the path to this equality is cratered with pitfalls and strewn with barriers. Make no mistake, equality for women will take a mighty effort to succeed."

"You believe change is possible?" Elizabeth asked.

"Yes, of course, but regardless of how much we want that change to come, it will take a long time."

"As long as men make the rules."

"As long as men with *closed minds* make the rules," Miss Beecher said. "That is the difference. Men like your cousin Gerrit are rare. But he is a powerful leader. Many people respect him and can be persuaded by his comments and opinions."

"He draws people of influence to him," Elizabeth said. "Like you."

Harriet Beecher laughed. "I am not an influential person," she said, "just a writer with more ideas than I can possibly write about."

"Perhaps that is why you intrigue my cousin," Elizabeth said. "He also has many ideas about countless topics, and advice, which he doles out in bountiful measure."

"I have written advice books on homemaking and child rearing, but what interests me most–and I always have opinions about this–is social injustice. That is most likely the reason your cousin invites me to his home."

Without thinking, Elizabeth yawned. "Oh, please excuse me," she said. "I arrived today and am afraid I am more fatigued than I thought." She looked around with surprise to see that few people remained. "It seems most of the guests have retired. I am sorry I have kept you from other conversations."

"I too am tired, so perhaps we can continue this discussion tomorrow?" Miss Beecher said.

"I would like that," Elizabeth said.

She fell into bed exhausted from the brief but jarring trip over the rutted frozen roads to Peterboro.

Her thoughts drifted to her conversation with Miss Beecher, and to eavesdropping on the group of men crowding around Daniel Bread. Tomorrow she would seek out this man and learn why he was here.

By morning, though, loud voices outside her door woke her and she quite forgot her objective. She poked her head out to investigate.

Down the hall ran one of her cousin's maids with an armful of sheets and a down comforter trailing behind her.

"What is happening?" Elizabeth asked.

"Mr. Douglas has arrived, Miss. No one expected him. We are rushing to get his room ready. He has two children with him and Mr. Smith says they all should be together."

"Mr. Frederick Douglas?" Elizabeth asked.

"Yes, Miss, I believe that is his name. Excuse me, Miss, I do have to hurry," the woman said and rushed away, skirts flying.

Elizabeth walked across the hallway to the railing and peered down into the foyer. A tall, greying Negro in a fine black worsted suit stood holding the hands of a very young boy and a girl who appeared to be about twelve. The children looked around the foyer and up to the landing where Elizabeth stood, their eyes wide.

Elizabeth waved and the children crowded closer to the man, trying to hide behind him.

While Elizabeth prepared for the day and dressed her hair, she grew more excited about the days ahead and regretted every moment lost in her morning toilet. Later at breakfast she looked for Mr. Douglass and the children, but they were not to be found.

"Cousin Gerrit," she said, spying him piling a plate full of eggs and biscuits. "Where are the honored guests?"

"All of my houseguests are honored, dear cousin; to which ones do you refer?"

"Frederick Douglass, I saw him arrive this morning."

"He is resting. Nancy has taken the children into the garden to play in the snow with the dogs. They were too excited to sleep," he said. "Have something to eat then join her and Lizzy. You will react very little with the remainder of the guests until dinner time."

They chatted awhile with Elizabeth asking questions about the guests, and Gerrit Smith providing answers when he could. When he finally excused himself, saying he had business to conduct, she hurried through breakfast and made her way to the garden. Fir trees and holly bushes laden with red berries lined a path cleared through the snow to the field beyond the garden, where a small group had gathered to throw sticks for the hunting dogs. The dogs' breath billowed as they bayed and ran back and forth on the frozen ground, excited from the exercise.

A tall young man with long, brown curly hair and pink cheeks stood out from the group, his red muffler wrapped almost to the brim of his hat. He hoisted a young Negro boy onto his broad shoulders then crouched to let the boy pick up a stick. When the two of them made their way to the edge of the crowd, the man's boisterous laugh boomed.

"Throw the stick far," he said. "Use all your strength."

Elizabeth watched the scene unfold and wondered about the young man's identity. Seeing Lizzy in the crowd, she approached the group and tapped her on the shoulder.

"Elizabeth. Good morning to you," Lizzy said, turning to hug her.

"Who is that man with the child on his shoulders?" Elizabeth asked.

Lizzy smiled. "He's handsome, isn't he?" she replied. "That's Henry Stanton, the abolitionist. He is one of father's great friends. I think he is speaking somewhere nearby."

Elizabeth watched the young man as he ran up and down before the group, making sure the boy's toss of the stick caught the attention of the dogs. When Mr. Stanton finally stopped running, clearly out of breath and heaving for air, he lowered the boy to the ground.

"You've worn me out, you scamp. Go find your sister and let me rest a bit," he said, giving the child a playful tap on the back of his breeches.

"That's my cue, Cousin Lib. Come with me while I collect the two children and take them back to the house," Lizzy said.

Elizabeth trailed behind as her cousin gathered the boy and girl to her and began walking back to the warmth of the kitchen. Just as Elizabeth left the path, she turned to look over her shoulder and saw Mr. Stanton watching her. When their eyes met she smiled.

*

October 10, 1839

Dear Diary, wonder of wonders, Frederick Douglas is here. A woman about my age is also staying. A writer. Her views are the same as mine on matters of antislavery and the rights of women. It's as if we are sisters–in thinking, certainly. I have not met someone whose ideas are so in line with my own. A very energetic and handsome man, an abolitionist friend of Cousin Gerrit, is staying in the house too. I haven't met him yet.

40

October 1839

By teatime the next day, the entire mansion practically shook with activity. Each of the many bedrooms situated on the upper floor was occupied, some merely relatives, others well known or celebrated people, all friends of her cousin. Within the walls of the Smith family, there existed an atmosphere of friendliness Elizabeth had not experienced elsewhere. One of the more frequent visitors, Charles Dudley Miller of Utica courted Lizzy. He lived next door and often arrived with a college friend or two in tow. They worked hard to persuade Lizzy and Elizabeth, along with some of the younger guests to participate in a midnight sleigh ride. Using a combination of teasing and laughter, they finally convinced everyone to go.

At teatime, while the guests milled about the vast dining room, selecting tea or coffee and a selection of savory and sweet pastries, Elizabeth looked for Mr. Stanton.

Lizzy caught her eye across the room and joined her at the tea table. "He is not here, Cousin, but with his fiancé I imagine," Lizzy said.

Flustered, Elizabeth felt the heat of a red blush creep up her throat. She laughed with embarrassment.

That night three sleighs draped in bells were driven to the front gate of the Smith mansion. As luck would have it, Elizabeth found herself wedged into a seat with another cousin, Mary Fitzhugh, and her friend Lily Van Schaack. With their layers of woolen coats and Miss Fitzhugh's fondness for sweets that added her own layer against the cold, Elizabeth could barely move. Her head began to ache and she regretted accepting the invitation. Across from the three women, two of Mr. Miller's college friends sat tipping a flask, hiding it beneath their blanket. As the sleigh bumped along the frozen road, the voices of the young men became louder.

"Cousin Charley," one of the men called out as he attempted to stand and fell back laughing.

"That you, Cheever?" Charles Miller responded from the sleigh in front of theirs. "For heaven sake, man, stay seated lest we lose you over the side."

"Got my temperance pamphlet right here," William Cheever said. "Nothing in here about spirits being consumed in a sleigh." Again the man tried to get to his feet.

"Sit down," Elizabeth said, grabbing the sleeve of his coat and yanking on it. "You turn us out into the snow and I will have you in jail," she added, perhaps a little more strongly than intended.

"What? You?" Cheever asked, waving a hand in front of her face.

"Not me, my father Judge Daniel Cady. So stop. You're spoiling the outing and putting us in danger." The man's annoyance was worrying. By now Elizabeth's head pounded and she wished for a packet of powdered willow bark to ease the pain. Instead she closed her eyes and tried to shut out the noise of the drunken conversation. This experience was not what she came here for. As much as she believed in free-thinking and behavior, perhaps the temperance movement merited consideration after all.

"You always so outspoken, Miss Cady?" Cheever asked, his words slurred.

"When I need to be," Elizabeth said.

By the time the sleighs returned to the Smith mansion, Cheever snored loudly beneath the blanket covering him and his companion.

Elizabeth climbed the stairs to her room, more exhausted than the day she arrived. Once inside, she tore off her clothing, dropping it piece by piece until clad in her undergarments, she climbed into bed and yanked the down-filled comforter to her chin with a sigh.

Sunlight streamed into the room when gentle tapping at her door woke her the next day.

"Miss? May I come in please?"

Elizabeth jumped out of bed to open the door, admitting the chambermaid.

"What time of day is it?"

"Fairly near mid-day, Miss," the chambermaid said. "May I tidy up then?"

"Yes of course. Please excuse my late sleeping. I did not intend to be so lazy." She splashed cold water on her face and hurried to dress, taking care to pin up her hair neatly.

The house appeared vacant of guests when she entered the parlor, except for Cousin Gerrit who was deep in conversation with the handsome man she'd seen with the boy on his shoulders in the snow.

Gerrit waved her over when he spotted her standing at the parlor door. "Come in, my dear, you must meet my friend and colleague, Henry Stanton. This is my cousin, Elizabeth Cady," he said.

Stanton jumped to his feet with a brief bow.

"Pleased to make your acquaintance, Miss Cady."

"Thank you, Mr. Stanton," Elizabeth said. "Are you in the land business, too, or do you side with my cousin's political and moral viewpoints?"

Mr. Stanton appeared amused. "It depends on the moment, I suppose, Miss Cady."

"Ah, that is the response of a politician," Elizabeth said.

The man's expression changed. "I have given you the wrong impression. I am a lecturer and no politician at all."

"Often they are one and the same," Elizabeth said.

Gerrit broke in. "Mr. Stanton is on the executive committee of the American Anti-Slavery Society of New York."

"So your colleague shares your views on abolition, Cousin, am I right?"

"Indeed," Gerrit said.

"And you, Miss Cady, do you have an opinion on the subject?" asked Stanton.

"Henry, my friend, do not get her started. She rivals you in oratory, and I fear, should you disagree, a heated debate may ensue on this very spot if you persist."

Henry Stanton threw up his hands in concession. "Miss Cady, I did not intend to provoke you."

Elizabeth smiled. "Perhaps we can discuss your views on abolition at some later date," she said. "Right now I am in need of a meal and since it is so very late in the day, I will seek out the kitchen and find something to eat."

Gerrit spoke up. "Cook will have bread, cheese and some sliced meat there. And hot tea as well. Go, Cousin."

After eating, she did feel better. All remnants of the headache were gone and she felt revived. When she returned to the parlor she found Mary Fitzhugh and Lily Van Schaack seated by the fire, their hands busy with needlework.

"You missed breakfast," Mary said. "And the most divine pineapple cake so scrumptious I ate two pieces."

"Three," Lily said, pursing her lips and giving her friend a sidelong glance. She reached for a pair of small scissors to cut a dangling thread.

"I will ignore that sly rude comment," said Mary.

Elizabeth laughed. "You two are so very amusing," she said. "You tease each other as sisters would."

"We have an invitation to early tea at Deacon Huntington's home," Mary said. "Just we three."

"And Nancy says we must attend," Lily said, grimacing.

A loud noise outside drew Elizabeth to the windows.

"What is that awful racket?" She asked, pulling the draperies aside to peer outdoors.

"Workmen are laying a plank walkway at Charles Miller's house," Lily said. "They've been hammering and sawing all day." She looked up at Elizabeth still standing at the window. "That is why we closed the draperies. It helps with the noise."

Later when the three women returned from their dreary tea with the deacon, having listened with earnest concentration to his opinions on religion and temperance, Mary and Lily excused themselves for a nap.

"We want to be rested for tonight," Lily said. "Because of the special guests, you know."

An invitation accepted by Mr. Emerson and Mr. Hawthorne at Van Buren's soirée at the Hotel Astor had caused a stir among the young guests, especially the ladies. Emerson had sent a note to Cousin Gerrit that his great friend Henry Thoreau was visiting and would accompany him. Elizabeth looked forward to renewing her acquaintance with the two men and meeting Thoreau, whose writing she admired.

When the hour grew late, and Mary and Lily were still missing, Elizabeth and Lizzy plotted to wake them. The two cousins did not work out their plan in detail, but the giddy nature of the prank kept them moving forward.

"Come with me," Lizzy said, pulling Elizabeth by the hand. Down the back stairs they went, making their way into the garden shed.

"It is too cold," Elizabeth said shivering. "Why are we here?"

Lizzy ignored her cousin's complaint and rummaged amongst the garden tools until she found two watering cans. She grabbed one and thrust the other into Elizabeth's hand then ran back up the path with Elizabeth right behind.

In the kitchen, Lizzy filled the watering cans, again handing one to Elizabeth.

"Hurry," she said, "Let us wake those sleepyheads in a proper fashion."

The cousins tiptoed up the stairs and down the hall where Elizabeth turned the handle on the door to Mary and Lily's bedroom and gently pushed it open. A board squeaked as they reached Mary's bed, waking her. When she sat up Elizabeth drenched her in a rush of cold water, pouring the entire contents of the can. Mary shrieked, waking Lily who tried to shield herself by ducking under the blankets. Lizzy and Elizabeth laughed so hard they scarcely noticed when the watering cans were empty. *Lizzy is as full of fun as Kate and Madge.* When had she last felt so giddy? She could not remember.

"More water," Lizzy shouted. Behind them Elizabeth heard the bedroom door slam shut. Those few moments proved to be their undoing. When they returned, the door suddenly flew open to reveal Lily and Mary holding the syringes used by the gardeners for bugs, pumping water at Elizabeth and Lizzy as fast as they could.

Elizabeth tried to turn away, but took the full force of a syringe spray in the face and, with her hair in disarray, drenched and clinging to her neck, she ran down the stairs, pulling Lizzy into a closet with her at the bottom. Out of breath and giggling, the two girls used all their strength to hold the door closed. Had she lost her senses? Surely she was too old for these pranks. Just as she had thought she was too old for them at Emma Willard. She smiled.

"What?" Lizzy mimed.

"Be quiet," Elizabeth whispered.

Lizzy gulped for air and glanced down at her soaked dress. "I think they have gone," she said after a few moments.

"It is very quiet. Perhaps they gave up," Elizabeth said, shivering. She had forgotten how cold it was. "I'll peep out," she said, but as she did, Mary jerked the door open and showered them once again. Screaming, Mary and Lily fled down the hall and ran into an open pantry where the kitchen help had placed milk in buckets. They slammed the door shut behind them, leaving Lizzy and Elizabeth banging on the wood.

"What is all this ruckus?" Charles Miller said, coming in through the kitchen. "I can hear you next door." He began to laugh at their disheveled appearance.

When the cousins explained the situation, he locked the pantry door with a flourish and returned to his workmen. However, just as he passed beneath the pantry window, Mary and Lily lifted a bucket of milk and dumped it on his head. Seeing tubs of laundry soaking nearby, Charles began to throw dripping shirts and trousers through the open window pelting Mary and Lily.

"Oh look," Elizabeth cried pulling Lizzy into the doorway to see the man's onslaught.

"Stop," Lily yelled, her voice loud and desperate.

"Please let us out. We are freezing in here."

"Shall we call a truce?" Elizabeth shouted through the door. Snow had begun to fall and they, too, were cold.

"Yes. Yes," Mary called out. "Please let's stop."

Lizzy nodded. But when Elizabeth unlocked the door, believing the silliness was finished, Lily and Mary rushed out throwing milk directly in their faces and then ran up the stairs to their rooms.

Elizabeth instinctively closed her eyes and turned away while Lizzy ran after them trailing milk in her wake. "You are not fair," she called out, pounding up the stairs, "I will get even with you, mark my words."

Left behind with milk dripping down her face and into her eyes Elizabeth fumbled vainly in her pocket for a handkerchief when she heard a heavy-booted stride on the stairs.

"Miss Cady, may I be of assistance?" A familiar voice asked.

She squinted as best she could to see Henry Stanton holding out a white handkerchief. She took it and wiped at her eyes.

"Thank you Mr. Stanton. You must think me terribly childish..." she began, and then noticed his amused expression and his obvious attempt to suppress a laugh. She was acting immature and knew it. What an embarrassing predicament for a smart young woman.

"Not childish at all. Coping with revenge as you have is commendable," he said. "I have been talking to Charles Miller who told me about your escapade."

"He talks too much," Elizabeth said, keeping her eyes down to dab at the milk on her dress front.

"He is very kind and says for you to get involved like this is a rare thing indeed. You strike him as having a more sober outlook."

"Not always. Most of the time I do," she said, raising her gaze to look Henry Stanton directly in the eyes. She knew her bedraggled appearance caused his amusement and handed back the damp handkerchief.

"Thank you for coming to my aid," she said as she pushed past him down the hall to her room. Did she hear his deep laugh as she walked away? Most likely. Still, she believed his face showed an expression of real concern. She glanced into the looking glass on the wall of her room as she entered and stopped, her mouth gaping. The sticky milk clung to her curls, plastering them against her skull and congealing on her collar.

No wonder he laughed. She shrugged and called the upstairs maid to ask that a bath be prepared.

*

October 11, 1839

Dear Diary, just as I thought I had gained stature with Cousin Gerrit's guests with my beliefs and opinions, I let one of my silly pranks define me. I hope Miss Beecher has not found out.

And, oh my, if Father and Mother hear about this, they will surely send word that I must come home. Why did I let my behavior fall so far from control? The worst thing that occurred is that Mr. Stanton caught me in frightful dishabille looking forlorn and dreadfully unkempt. Now he will think of me as a fool. I am a fool. A frightfully messy prank may have been my undoing.

41

October 1839

A few hours later, now gowned properly with her hair freshly shampooed and curled, Elizabeth peered into her looking glass to fasten the sapphire earrings that matched the necklace she wore. She dabbed rose water behind her ears and preened one direction, then the other, to ensure the completion of her toilet. She pulled on white leather gloves, grabbed her reticule with a lace handkerchief inside and joined her cousin's houseguests in the parlor.

The crowd seemed larger than the night before. Lizzy ran up to grab her hand and draw her to the side of the room.

"Mary Fitzhugh and Lily Van Schaack are in a turmoil over our escapades. We must settle them down for they are naming us as the masterminds," she said.

Elizabeth cocked her head. "We were. And is that so bad?" she asked and winked at Lizzy.

"Oh. I suppose not. But Mr. Miller will think me a fool," Lizzy said, her pretty face pulled into a frown.

"I doubt he thinks of you as anything but a lovely young woman. If he did not, he would never get involved in our mischief and you know he always does."

"I am so very taken with him; I merely did not want anything to change his mind about me."

Elizabeth laughed and hugged her.

A blast of cold air accompanied by the front door slamming caught their attention. Cousin Gerrit's booming voice welcoming a newcomer drew the interest of the other guests to the visitor.

"Who is that?" Lizzy asked.

"It's Mr. Hawthorne," Elizabeth said with excitement. "We met at President Van Buren's party at Uncle John's hotel."

"He is so very handsome," Lizzy said. She stood on her tiptoes to get a better look.

"He is betrothed. Lucky is the lady who stole his heart."

Lizzy pulled Elizabeth closer to whisper in her ear.

"Father confirmed that Mr. Stanton is betrothed, too."

"Why do you remind me of this?"

"Because I have seen him staring at you, and perhaps you took notice."

"Most likely he is wondering if my hair reeks of sour milk," Elizabeth said. "Come, I will introduce you to the famous writer."

When the two cousins got close enough to catch his eye, Nathaniel Hawthorne stepped forward to grasp Elizabeth's hand and press it to his lips.

"Miss Cady, we meet again. How delighted I am to see you once more. We shall have time this evening for a long conversation. Directly after supper, if you are not already engaged, I shall come find you," he said, his eyes reflecting genuine enthusiasm. "And who is this?" he asked turning his gaze to Lizzy.

"This is my daughter," Gerrit Smith said, joining the conversation. "She is much too young for your attention, my friend," And with that he swept the man off to meet Chief Bread and the members of his entourage.

The evening continued, a whirl of serious conversation lightened with laughter and flirtation. Cigar smoke and brandy-laden breath combined with aromas of roses from the Smith's hothouse. Fans stirred the air over low-cut gowns and added scents of chic Parisian jasmine and lily-of-the-valley Houbigant perfumes. Invigorated and excited, Elizabeth flitted from group to group, learning here, adding her comments there. Later that evening, still waiting for a chance to talk to Mr. Hawthorne, she seated herself at the piano to accompany Lizzy, Mary and Lily as the girls had decided to sing. They were bent over the sheet music choosing their song when Cousin Gerrit interrupted to call them together into the hallway.

"Young ladies, I have someone here I want you to meet," he said, being somewhat mysterious. "Come with me."

He led them upstairs to the third story of the house, an area unfamiliar to Elizabeth. When he put his hand on a doorknob he turned to them, his finger to his lips.

"This is an important secret which you must keep for twenty-four hours. Do you agree to do that?" he asked.

The girls nodded.

He opened the door to reveal a beautiful Negro girl, about eighteen, in Quaker dress, seated on a chair. Despite the freshness of her clothing and starched white bonnet, she appeared tired and nervous.

"This is Harriet," Cousin Gerrit said. "She has escaped from the man who owns her. He is visiting in Syracuse and does not know she is gone. Tonight she will travel to Oswego and from there into Canada where freedom awaits her."

He turned to the girl. "My dear, please tell these young ladies about your life and what you have suffered. I want them to be good abolitionists. Your story will enforce their belief that slavery is wrong."

Harriet's soft voice did not reduce the sting of her words as she began to speak. "My pap tried to hide me, for he said I be too pretty for field work. He reckoned a white man would spot me and take me into the house where he slept. But that old master he didn't do that. He too old. Instead he took me in a cart to New Orleans and sold me. At fourteen."

Elizabeth gasped and memories of her own life of privilege at that same age crowded her mind. Hearing the indignities suffered by another girl shocked her. It is one thing to hear these stories second hand, but from the lips of a girl not much younger than her struck her heart with pain.

Harriet continued her story, telling about the beatings and the humiliation of being dragged into the new Master's bedroom at his whim. "That man, who bought me, he in the prime of life, with a nice wife and all, why he need me I do not know. Soon as I see my chance I ran."

The girls sat wide eyed as she spoke, finally breaking into tears when she loosened her dress to expose her back covered with raised scars, some still red and healing.

Elizabeth spoke up. "Why did you not leave before?"

"Cause of this," Harriet said. She folded down the top of her boot to reveal a wide scar around her ankle. "He chained me up everywhere we went. Showing me off I suppose. I looked real pretty sitting beside him. One day I notice a small crack in the chain link. Soon as I could I smashed it with a rock and you know the rest. Mr. Gerrit, he cut the metal piece from my leg there."

"Did you have any babies?" Lizzy asked, her voice a squeak.

"No, and I thank the good Lord for that. If I did, that Missus there would have sold the child right out of my arms I believe."

As Harriet continued her story with her audience of rapt young women asking polite questions, Elizabeth experienced a fierce stirring of emotion. *To live like Harriet has, and like so many other Negro women and men have done, is just wrong. God created all of us equal and in His image. What right do men have to challenge God? To make their own rules?* What could she do to help? She pledged to find out.

Two hours passed before Gerrit returned. "It is time to leave, Harriet," he said. "And girls, you will recall your promise?"

When they nodded he added, "And do you all feel stronger about abolition now?" They nodded again.

Contrasting their silly prank, Harriet's story had a sobering affect too disheartening to shake off. The experience further confirmed Elizabeth's resolve to embrace abolition of slavery and to work toward giving women the right to choose their own destiny. When she rejoined the party, all thoughts of singing were forgotten as the impact proved difficult to ignore.

Coffee and liqueurs were served in the parlor in their absence and Elizabeth spied Mr. Hawthorne in lively conversation with Mr. Stanton. She made her way through the gathering to where Mr. Thoreau and Mr. Emerson stood by, appearing unsuccessful at breaking into the discussion.

"Mr. Thoreau, you were at Harvard?" Elizabeth asked trying to shake off the wretched story she'd just heard. She touched the man on his sleeve to get his attention.

"I was, Miss Cady."

"It is a fine school and although women are not yet allowed to attend," she said with emphasis, "I suspect any education one might receive there is extraordinary."

Thoreau appeared uneasy when he responded, "My parents wished it, and my brother paid for my stay, but my desires are elsewhere."

She would have relished attending such an institution of higher learning, regardless what she was taught. Emma Willard paled in contrast to the courses that must be taught at Harvard. Why was it so?

"Elsewhere?" she asked. "What occupation would you desire?"

"I am not cut out for business or the law. Instead I seek to understand the ways of nature."

"How do you find the company and the writing of your philosopher friends?" Elizabeth said, puzzled by the man's response.

"We find topics of agreement, and discourse that provokes healthy controversy. To me their views are stimulating. We argue then hold our ground when we reach an impasse."

"Our politician friends believe any Harvard graduate can be molded to serve their ends," Elizabeth said.

"Not if he's disinclined. I am a man who prefers the company of trees, wild creatures and splendid changing seasons," Thoreau said.

"And what of abolition?" Elizabeth asked. "What is your view on that subject?"

Thoreau leaned in to whisper. "Slavery is an abomination."

Mr. Emerson overheard and laughed.

"Abolition of slavery, Mr. Emerson, is not a humorous subject," Elizabeth said recalling the dreadful scars she'd seen on the former slave. She ignored Emerson's reaction to look Thoreau in the eye. "Surely, enslavement is against the laws of nature," she said. "If seeking to rid the country of such an abominable practice is a good thing, why whisper about it?"

"I wish to rise above all that." Mr. Thoreau appeared uncomfortable with Mr. Emerson's response, and tried to turn away.

What did he take her for? You cannot cloak man's evil practices in nature's laws. Just when she thought she would gain insight about the great writer's true beliefs, she found shallowness.

"Sir, this one issue affects us all," Elizabeth said. She grabbed his sleeve.

Thoreau pulled away.

"My man, do not flinch when you are challenged," Emerson said.

"Certainly not," Mr. Stanton said, breaking in. He'd been watching with a bemused expression as the conversation flew back and forth like a badminton shuttle. "Especially when the challenger is a lady."

"Thank you, Mr. Stanton, but I believe I can speak for myself," Elizabeth said, looking directly into Henry Stanton's brown eyes.

When his disarming smile softened the impact of his remarks, Elizabeth felt the blood rush to her face.

"Perhaps in Mr. Stanton you have met your match, Miss Cady," Thoreau said. "Oratory that goes unchallenged is a haze of words that dissipates as does the fog before a sunny day."

"Your poetic interpretation, while subtle, makes the point, my friend," Emerson said. "Be watchful of this young lady, Stanton," he said turning to Henry. "She uses words to force the sun to shine before it is dawn."

"Gentlemen, please can we not divert the subject?" Elizabeth said. Their focus on her made her uncomfortable.

"Indeed. Stanton, we leave you to forge your own way here. I'm dragging Thoreau to that far corner there to find a brandy, good cigars we can smoke, and to chat up my friend here about trivial subjects," Emerson said.

Silenced bloomed between Elizabeth and Henry Stanton when the two talkative men left their intimate circle.

Elizabeth dabbed at her upper lip with the handkerchief she kept in her reticule. She felt vulnerable in his presence and the strangeness of it discomforted her.

"May I fetch you a glass of lemonade, Miss Cady?" Henry said. "Or would you prefer a bit of fresh air, perhaps on the veranda? I could bring your wrap for you," he added.

"I believe I would like both, Mr. Stanton. Thank you for offering."

She watched Henry's broad back as he pushed his way to the long table where the Smiths offered wines and lemonade. He moved with such lithe grace.

Her hand trembled when she took the crystal glass from his fingers when he returned with her black wool shawl looped over his arm.

Fresh snow glowed in the light of the moon. Voices lifted in argument and laughter ebbed and flowed, muted by the thick walls of Cousin Gerrit's house.

Elizabeth sipped her drink then set the glass on a porch rail to pull her shawl close. She felt Henry's body heat by her side and instinctively moved closer.

"Are you warm enough?" he asked. "We could return to the party once you're refreshed."

"I am fine, thank you. The crisp air is exhilarating especially after all the heady conversations."

Henry stood quiet for a moment as if he were choosing his words carefully and then asked, "I am speaking at a convention in Wheelerville tomorrow and would greatly appreciate your presence there," he said. "Would you come?"

Elizabeth looked up into his face and saw the serious nature of his expression.

"Of course I will. I look forward to hearing your arguments for abolition."

A wide grin of delight spread across Henry's face. "I believe you agree with me," he said, pounding his fist into his palm.

Startled by the gesture, she stepped back.

"Anti-slavery is a topic which greatly interests me," she said, "because I believe abolition will lead to stronger roles for women. For that I am greatly committed."

"The immorality of enslaving people cannot be denied, but its political influence? Particularly in the states that depend on this labor? It is complicated," Henry said.

"I suspect you are right." She shivered. The cold had penetrated her shawl and she knew she must go inside, but lingered to prolong the conversation. Finally she asked, "Mr. Stanton, at risk of being forward, may I ask if your fiancé, Miss Stewart, will be there as well?"

Henry looked bewildered. "I have no fiancé," he said. "In fact, Miss Stewart is now Mrs. Luther Marsh, a marriage recently culminated in Utica," Henry said.

"I beg your pardon, for the gossip surely became muddled in its retelling," she said, wishing she could take back her words.

The door behind them opened with a draft of warm air.

"There you are," Cousin Gerrit said. "Your writer friends are in their cups, my dear, and asking for you. Come back inside." He threw an arm around Elizabeth's shoulders and drew her in. "Stanton, one of the judges desires a conversation with you about the legality of slavery. I am sure you want to discuss it with him," Gerrit said with a laugh. "Do set him to rights."

"Tomorrow then?" Henry Stanton leaned in to whisper in Elizabeth's ear.

She nodded, smiled, and touched his arm as Cousin Gerrit placed his hand at her waist to direct her into the roomful of noisy guests.

*

October 11, 1839

Dear Diary, I met a slave girl whose dreadful story nearly broke my heart. My dear cousin is helping her escape and I cannot tell a soul save for you. Should he be discovered, he would certainly pay a terrible price. It is against the law to help slaves escape their masters. Mr. Stanton is not being married, I learned. Gossip is so exciting, but can be false. He captivates me. He has a lovely way of speaking. At once so robust and dogmatic, and then tenuous and flexible. It is a most attractive trait.

42

October 1839

By the time Elizabeth came down for breakfast the next day only one of the two carriages taking guests to hear Henry Stanton speak stood in the driveway in front of the house. She realized she had missed the first group of people headed for Wheelerville so she gulped down an egg, took a sip of coffee and rushed outside, a piece of toasted bread gripped in her hand.

Lizzy leaned out of the carriage window waving frantically. "Hurry, we almost left without you. I told the driver to wait for I knew you wanted desperately to go today," she said opening the door for Elizabeth to climb in.

"I am so sorry to be late. My head is still spinning from the wonderful conversations and merriment last evening," Elizabeth said. She leaned back against the soft leather cushions and snuggled into the wool blankets around her.

"Mr. Stanton is in the first carriage," Lizzy said. "He paced up and down the driveway, all the while glancing back at the front entrance," she said. "I have no idea why."

"Nor do I," Elizabeth said.

"Finally, he took out his pocket watch and looked at it. Then he shook his head, boarded, and told the driver to leave."

Elizabeth changed the subject and for the remainder of their journey, having discovered that Lizzy brought with her a copy of *Godey's Lady's Book,* the talk turned to a discussion of the latest fashions. Since they were the only two passengers, their raucous laughter continued for the entire trip. Foregoing weighty subjects in exchange for topics favored by women lightened her spirit.

Soon the snow-clad roofs of the village of Wheelerville came into view. Plumes of smoke curled from the chimneys. The Episcopal church in the center of the village where the convention would be held could only hold a limited number of people, so Elizabeth didn't expect there to be carriages and traps of all sizes lined up on the street in front. To her dismay, crowds pushed to get into the church just like they had at Finney's evangelical meetings. A deacon posted on the steps, watching for the last of Gerrit Smith's carriages, hurried to escort Elizabeth and Lizzy inside, saying the speaker had set aside two seats for them up front. Inside the room the air reeked of wet wool, men's cologne and talcum powder. Thawing mud flecked with horse manure lay on the floor. Elizabeth pulled a handkerchief from her pocket and clapped it over her nose.

The deacon led the two women to a wood bench set up in front of the first row of pews then tipped his hat and walked to the back.

Elizabeth threw off her wool cloak and tucked its long hem up under her skirts as best she could.

"It is dreadfully hot in here," she said using her handkerchief to stir the air around her face. For all the freezing weather outside, the crush of people in the tightly packed room pushed the temperatures upwards. With the windows closed tight, the accumulating odors added to the uncomfortable atmosphere. "The doors have been closed too," she said, turning to look behind her at the entrance. Along the back wall an unkempt cluster of men passed around a liquor bottle.

Lizzy nodded. She'd already removed her cape and, though she carried a muff, its warmth caused her hands to perspire. She showed her palms to Elizabeth in disgust.

Just as the din of voices rising from the audience threatened to overcome any close conversation, the crowd hushed and began to applaud.

Henry Stanton walked to the pulpit, raising his outstretched arms in a gesture of welcome. He scanned the crowd then turned his solemn gaze to the front where Elizabeth sat with Lizzy. When he saw them he smiled.

"Go get 'em, Henry," a man's loud voice called drunkenly from the back of the room.

"Amen," another man shouted to which the crowd added their approval.

Henry Stanton seemed to grow taller with the praise and endorsement. Color rose in his cheeks as he began to speak, pacing up and down behind the pulpit, clenching his hands into fists to make points in defense of freeing slaves. Elizabeth couldn't take her eyes off him.

"Is it a matter of conscience that we in the North no longer tolerate slavery?" Henry asked.

The crowd roared, "Yes!"

"Do we not wear clothing spun from cotton picked by slaves in the South whose hands bleed from the task as the cat o' nine tails flicks over their heads? Does that bother our conscience?"

Quiet reigned, yet an uneasy emotional movement in the crowd gave them away as they shifted in their chairs.

"Why is it Northern states chose to free the Negroes they owned," Henry said, "giving them a choice as freedmen to stay or journey on to a new life? It is because in the North, we believe in the good of man, in equality, that each, white or black, may choose his own destiny." He paused to sweep the crowd with his gaze. "Southern states would have you believe abolishing slavery has created mobs of embittered criminals roving the land," he continued. "It is not true! For in every state where slavery has been abolished, people live in harmony and peace. No sooner did the last British scallywags. leave our soil, than the spread of abolitionist laws began. New York," he said, after which the crowd roared again. "Maine, New Hampshire, Vermont, Massachusetts, Rhode Island, Connecticut, New Jersey, Pennsylvania, Ohio, Indiana and Illinois are free states. The Southern states, where the cotton from which our clothes are made, believe owning humans is perfectly fine. They do not have to pay a living wage for a free man to work their fields, because slaves have no say-so. To that end, leaders of those states want to extend slavery into the new territories in the West. We cannot allow that to happen. Why do they do this?" he asked. "To keep a balance of power in Congress, that is why." The crowd roared once again, louder. "It is greed, pure greed. Bags of gold picked from the cotton plant, money earned by the backbreaking labor of poor Negroes. My work, if it is ever done," he said, his voice rising, "is to ensure slavery is abolished in all the states. I will not stop until that objective is reached." Henry's shoulders slumped as he bowed his head to catch his breath and then pulled a handkerchief from his pocket to mop his face.

Why, he is like Reverend Finney, speaking so eloquently that everyone in the room becomes a believer. The timbre of his voice awakened emotions in her, a tingling she could feel in her hands. She thought back to those revival meetings when the Reverend's seductive reasoning swept her up in girlhood passion and then plunged her into fear with its terrible aftermath of nightmares. She shuddered. She no longer was victimized by rhetoric without basis. Instead, her own skills at reasoning the difference between truth and lies now served her well.

As Henry took a deep breath to continue, Elizabeth began to consider their thinking as being incredibly like-minded. She thought back to their brief meetings. He was like Edward but focused on what is possible, rather than on an esoteric puzzle. Though letters from Tryphena to the family carried news of Edward, Elizabeth hadn't thought about him much lately. She tried to summon his image, but Henry Stanton's commanding presence stood in the way.

Elizabeth all but jumped to her feet when Henry's speech reached its midpoint. "First, I advocate freedom for all Negroes and second, assimilation into the fabric of America. This is in direct opposition to William Lloyd Garrison's suggestion that Negroes be relocated to Liberia," he said. Finally, when he launched into his conclusion he quoted the Declaration of Independence: "...that all men are created equal, that they are endowed by their Creator with certain unalienable Rights, that among these are Life, Liberty and the pursuit of Happiness." The crowd stood, as she did, stamping their feet, clapping and shouting.

Would that the founding fathers had included women as being "created equal." Elizabeth recalled that as a child she had recognized the ethos of women as different than men. Her father had told her to change the laws to apply to women and men equally. Change the Declaration of Independence? Could that be done? The Constitution? The Bill of Rights? In many ways slaves were the same as women. She knew what she must do.

Henry became lost in the people surging onto the stage to shake his hand and congratulate him on his eloquence.

Elizabeth stood transfixed in the moment, unaware of her cousin's pleas to leave. When at last she felt Lizzy tugging at her sleeve, the room began to empty. She pulled on her cloak and tied it beneath her chin, still reluctant to leave, when Henry appeared before her.

"Did you enjoy my speech?"

She blushed. "Ever so much," she replied, annoyed that she felt so flustered. "I learned we have more in common than I believed." Seeing the opportunity to chide him, she said, "While I know the Declaration of Independence is signed, I do take umbrage with the word *men* used in its text. Should it not be *persons*?"

Henry seemed rattled for a moment before he answered. "All things in due time," he said and smiled.

"The carriages are waiting," Lizzy said, tugging at her cousin's sleeve.

"Would you both consider riding back with me?" Henry asked.

"Certainly, if there is room," Elizabeth said looking to Lizzy for approval.

Once the guests from Gerrit Smith's home were redistributed with much jostling around and complaining about their new seating places, Henry helped Elizabeth and Lizzy into one of the carriages for the trip home.

Still exhilarated from the speech, Elizabeth could not stop talking and asking questions. "So I should not wear cotton clothing? I prefer silk spun by worms," she said.

"It is your choice. If I have made you think about that choice, then I have done my job well."

"Not all the Northern states are free, am I right?"

"Michigan is considered the North and their legislature is expected to be next. However, Maryland, Delaware and the District of Columbia are holding out."

"Why is that?" Elizabeth asked. "It would seem they are in the North."

"Rightly so, but their leaders hold allegiance to the South."

"I have read that. The Mason-Dixon Line, correct?"

"You are indeed," Henry said.

He continued to answer her questions with fervor and commitment until her curiosity exhausted her and at last the carriage enclosure grew quiet. Lizzy dozed with her head against the muff she'd pulled off to cushion her cheek against the window, but Elizabeth remained restless. She felt the warmth of Henry's body next to her and smelled the faint scent of cedar pomade he used on his hair.

Lights blazed in the Smith home when the carriages pulled into the driveway, but only a few servants were moving about.

Henry Stanton held the door for the two cousins, grabbing Elizabeth's arm as she passed him.

"Wait a moment," he said.

"Are you coming, Elizabeth?" Lizzy asked without looking back, already climbing the stairs.

"In a minute," Elizabeth replied. Conscious of Henry standing so close, she busied herself removing her cloak then handed it to a maid waiting nearby.

"Excuse me Miss. Sir," the woman said looking from Elizabeth to Henry. "Mrs. Smith told me to tell you that should you be hungry, there are some victuals in your rooms."

"Thank you," Elizabeth said as the maid nodded and scurried off to the closet to hang up her cloak. Elizabeth turned back to Henry.

"Miss Cady, I have enjoyed your company greatly during my visit here and I am pleased you attended the convention today," he said.

She paused to think about her response. When she looked up into Henry's eyes she felt an emotion like a key fitting perfectly into a lock. The effect unsettled her.

"I am glad we will have days ahead to get to know each other better, Mr. Stanton." She clapped a hand over her mouth in embarrassment to stifle a yawn, and then laughed. "But you see I am too tired to continue our conversations further today. Goodnight."

Elizabeth started up the stairs then on impulse turned back to see him watching her.

"Mr. Stanton. You are a most agreeable man."

For the remainder of the month, Elizabeth trailed Henry Stanton from convention to convention as part of his entourage. Soon she realized their commitments to change and to moral values was in perfect harmony. Not only did they believe passionately in anti-slavery, but temperance as well. The principle of equality for women however, wasn't far from her mind.

At dinner a few nights later, Henry announced he would be leaving for New England in a day or two. Another schedule of speeches arranged for him meant travel for months or longer.

The next morning, the sky cleared over Peterboro revealing a blazing sun that threatened to melt the snow. Elizabeth walked out onto the broad piazza adjoining the Smith garden to gaze at the snow-laden trees now hanging with glistening icicles. Lost in thought, she did not hear Henry approaching.

"Good morning," he said.

She whirled around. "Oh, you startled me. It *is* a good morning," she said, "Just look at that cardinal there flitting amongst the branches." She pointed with one gloved hand at the red bird. "It is so beautiful against the snow and the black limbs of the tree."

"Ah. Yes, it is," he said and moved closer to her. "Since this is my last day and I have no schedule until tomorrow, I wonder if you would join me for a ride on horseback this morning?"

"What a splendid suggestion. I will change into my habit and ask the stableman to bring two horses for us," she said. "Fifteen minutes out in the front drive?"

"I will meet you there," Henry said.

When they were free of the rutted Peterboro roadways and off into the woods on marked trails, Henry led the way, holding heavy branches back to let Elizabeth pass. Though they rode at a leisurely pace, soon the shoulders of her blue habit and Henry's jacket sported a sprinkling of water drops.

"Where is that coming from?" she said aloud, looking up. "It is not raining." She wiped her forehead with the back of her hand.

"The snow on the tree branches is melting," Henry said.

Elizabeth laughed and dug her heels into her mount's side, urging the horse faster as she tried to dodge the huge clumps of snow falling from the upper tree branches. Henry followed at such a pace Elizabeth scarcely kept a length ahead until finally she reined in her horse, breathing hard from the effort. She pulled the animal off the road onto a patch of new grass where the sun had melted the snow. Henry rode up beside her and slid from his saddle to the ground, his chest heaving.

He stared up into her face, then turned on his heel and walked a few yards away as if to inspect the mountains beyond. When he returned with a grave expression, the sobriety of his demeanor alarmed her.

"What is it?" Elizabeth asked. She dismounted and put her hand on his sleeve.

"I did not expect this." Henry turned away again seeming caught in a dilemma.

"Expect what, Mr. Stanton? Surely you are not referring to this glorious day or splendid ride."

"No, Miss Cady. Oh, blast it. Dearest Elizabeth," he said, "It is you I did not expect." Henry took both her hands in his.

Her breath caught in her throat and her heart began to flutter. She thought of nothing else than the sweet longing in his eyes and for once she could not find words.

"Perhaps I have always sought a woman like you. I didn't realize it though," Henry said. "You are my intellectual match, and your spirit of adventure and curiosity pulls me into a higher plane where all things seem possible. More important, dearest one is your incredible passion for what is right and what is wrong. It captivates me."

She did not want the moment to end. Yet Henry's next words could not be restrained.

"I ask for your hand, Elizabeth Cady. Will you marry me and be a part of my life forever?"

She started to speak, but could only nod, mute in the glow of his confession. When he folded her into his arms and gently placed his lips on hers she felt like she had come to the end of a very long journey.

As they rode back to Cousin Gerrit's home, Elizabeth and Henry talked about nothing else save their impending marriage and began making plans, stopping often to kiss again as if they would never have another chance.

That night at dinner, once the guests were seated, Henry rose to tap his wine glass for attention.

Elizabeth looked at the faces of Cousin Gerrit's friends and colleagues as Henry made his announcement.

"Here, here, my friend," Mr. Emerson said clapping his hands. He nodded at Elizabeth, then smiled and winked. She basked in the gestures of congratulations that went around the table until she saw Cousin Gerrit's unsmiling face.

At that moment servants began to place bowls of soup in front of the diners. Elizabeth turned her attention to her food, knowing that soon after dinner, she must seek out Gerrit to find out why his displeasure seemed so ominous.

*

November 15, 1839

Dear Diary, Mr. Stanton asked me to marry him and I will. I have been too busy following him from speech to speech to write much here, and many days have passed, but now believe I must. This is such a momentous change in my life. I am so sure of my feelings. It is as if all paths I walked led to this man and all the others who sought my attention were mere paper cutouts with no substance or suitability. My emotions are in a whirl.

43

November 1839

"Your father will not consent to this marriage," Cousin Gerrit said. "He disapproves of slavery, but cannot risk having an avowed abolitionist in his family. Think of the implications to his career."

Gerrit had ushered Elizabeth into his land office in the building across from the main house. Flames crackled in the fireplace warming the small room. He settled her into a strait-back chair facing his desk then sat facing her, his expression grim.

"But why, Cousin? I know his leanings are toward abolishing slavery, why would he not approve of Henry?" Elizabeth asked. She crossed her arms, protective of her emotion and felt her heartbeat quicken and her mouth grow dry.

"I respect Henry Stanton's good intentions and his passionate commitment to this cause, but your father will not be of the same mind."

"I do not understand. Henry is a principled man with strong beliefs in making the right choices. He believes the country can be better if people no longer enslave others. Slavery is wrong, you know it and I know it." Elizabeth leaned forward her hands outstretched beseechingly.

Gerrit stood to place more logs on the fire, taking a moment to stir the embers. He wiped his hands on his breeches before he turned to face her.

"Your father's place in New York politics puts him in a precarious situation, Elizabeth. You know he's working on establishing a new county in which your home resides, and perhaps even more importantly, he's being considered for the New York Supreme Court," he went on, pacing up and down the room.

"But I am no longer beholden to my father," she said. "Besides, New York is a free state. I would think he has many allies."

"Beholden? Of course you are," Gerrit said. "What you do will reflect on your entire family."

"Well, it should not."

"It will. No matter what you think or believe. As for allies, there are many people in power in New York who did not approve of freeing slaves. They are waiting for someone to discredit." He sat down again, his voice taking on a softer, more intimate tone. When he spoke, Elizabeth recognized he'd changed his strategy. "Oh, my dear, have you considered there is more to marriage than blossoming love?" he asked. "It will not always be this way. This giddiness I observe in you will pass."

"Of course I have considered that. Henry and I have discussed this. Cousin, I have two exceptional marriages to pattern my life after: my own parents' and yours with Nancy. I am not a child and regardless of what you might think, I have considered my decision thoroughly."

She continued to argue her point of view in an attempt to dissuade her cousin, until finally he threw up his hands in surrender. "If you will not listen to reason, I free myself from any responsibility for your actions. I regret this event took place under my roof, for I feel somewhat responsible for it," Gerrit said, rising from his chair to embrace Elizabeth. "My dear, lest you believe I am being too harsh, your happiness and that of my good friend Henry Stanton are close to my heart. God speed," he said. Then as an afterthought, added, "I think you will need it, too."

The next day, Henry and Elizabeth stood on the front drive beside the carriage that would take Henry on the remainder of his yearlong speaking tour. Their whispered words of love and assurances and gentle caresses reinforced her decision to marry him. But as the carriage rolled away with Henry hanging out the window to shout his last goodbyes, Elizabeth knew she faced a battle with her father that would surpass any that her beloved would encounter.

"When will you return home?" Lizzy asked a week after Henry's departure.

The two cousins discussed everything about Elizabeth's romance she cared to divulge, keeping Lizzy in a prolonged state of romantic excitement. Since her cousin had little experience with love or exposure to serious courting,

Elizabeth chose to share few intimate details. With Henry gone, and most of Gerrit Smith's guests departing as well, Elizabeth should have said her goodbyes. But there was no urgency. Being in the location where she fell in love with Henry kept her tied to the Smith home.

"February, I suppose. It's as if Henry were still here," she answered. "I suspect I linger to keep that feeling fresh."

"But school starts again soon, and I must leave," Lizzy said. "I will miss you if you are still here. If you go home then I could make arrangements to visit you. Papa would like that."

"Your father might think I am a bad influence on you now."

"No, he will not. He knows your persistence is strong and that I would be fine with you regardless of where we are," Lizzy assured her.

"I must face my parents. Your father suggested I write a letter to my father explaining that I planned to marry Henry, but by the time it reaches him, he will surely have the news from some gossip. I have to talk to him in person to defend myself." She sighed. "I suppose I will leave for Johnstown on Monday of next week. The weather seems to be growing warmer so the travel will be easy."

The following week, as planned, Cousin Gerrit's servants loaded her trunks and valise into his carriage and she bade farewell to the remaining guests at breakfast.

"Be strong, my girl," Cousin Gerrit whispered, pulling her tight against his broad chest. "If this is meant to be it will work out."

With tears in her eyes she embraced Lizzy and Nancy, then kissed them all and climbed into the carriage and tucked a blanket around her legs.

She waved from the open door as the carriage pulled away from the house and down the drive to the open road, fighting the urge to jump out and return to the home where she felt welcomed and where Henry's presence still seemed close to her.

As the carriage wheels churned through the muddy road track she attempted to rehearse what she would tell her father. Arguing with a master of rhetorical skill, especially one she loved and whose approval she always sought, would be difficult. *I love him, Father.* That was not enough. *He can take care of me financially.* Maybe not? She did not know. *We share the same passions about abolishing slavery and women's rights.* She must be very careful with that comment. She composed the argument over and over, writing notes to herself on a scrap of paper tucked in her diary. But each time she looked down at the words she saw Henry's face smiling at her. He did love her. She did love him. That was all that truly mattered.

Night fell by the time she arrived. Her father opened the front door when the carriage rumbled up the front drive. Behind him stood her mother who rushed to embrace her and pull her into the warm house.

"Welcome home Lib, I have missed you so," her mother said, her expressive face lighting up.

She kissed her mother's cheek then turned to her father, her arms outstretched. Judge Cady turned on his heel. "Come into my office, Elizabeth," he said.

She glanced at her mother whose expression of delight vanished. "We have had news from your cousin," she said. *So Cousin Gerrit sent word ahead to inform Father. Or to soften him?*

"I will take care your trunks are delivered to your room and come up to see you later," her mother said, permitting a weak smile.

Elizabeth expected reproach from her father but not a cold reception. She sat in the wooden chair beside his desk and began to pull off her gloves. Her father's scowl worried her. "Father, please let me explain..." she began.

"I cannot allow this, Lib. You do not know your mind," Judge Cady said, jumping to his feet. "I blame Gerrit for this. He never should have encouraged your relationship with this Stanton person."

"Father, Cousin Gerrit told me you would not approve of me marrying an abolitionist, but your own sympathies lie in that same moral stance," Elizabeth said.

"It is more than that. This man makes little money and you have lived in a condition of luxury that few young women experience. Did you think of that?"

"He has money enough. And I am willing to live on what he can provide."

"Not like you have here," her father said. "Does he have a home to take you to? Where will you live? On the road with him? While he travels from town to town speaking? Can he afford your clothing? Your food? The servants you presently depend on?"

"I will be fine, Father." She sensed that the points her father made were possibly true. Had she been blind to all of this?

"Besides, have you considered what this marriage would do to our family?" he said. "The political investment that I have made in Johnstown, and in New York State in general for that matter, will be in jeopardy if I welcome an abolitionist into the family." Her father paused to look her in the eyes. "Even my own assistance in that regard will be open to scrutiny." He paced the room, stopping now and then to glare at her. "I cannot allow the marriage," he finally said.

Her chest tightened and she felt tears welling. "Why do you berate me so?" she said. "You are so important to me, I would think you wished me well, not this." All logic deserted her and she buried her face in her hands.

Her father came around the desk to offer his handkerchief. She took it and wiped at her eyes.

"Thank you."

For now, she knew the argument must end. Having eaten her breakfast meal hours earlier, one of the black headaches that afflicted her thudded against her eyelids. When she rose to leave the room, her father reached out for her, "It will be all right, Lib," he said, but she closed the office door between them and fled up the stairs.

That night, unable to sleep for the controversy filling her thoughts, she replayed the conversations with her father and Cousin Gerrit and realized they made sense. For them, not for her. Why did she care what impact her marriage to Henry would have? She loved her father. Could she go against his wishes? No matter what she did, it would never be enough to gain his full support and understanding. Even though he grudgingly accepted her intelligence as he would that of a man, she would never replace Eleazar no matter how hard she tried. And this? Finally wanting to marry someone whom she respected as she did her father? Why did he view this as another failure? Never once did he tell her what he thought she should do, only that what she did do, didn't measure up. Her sisters obediently followed in her mother's footsteps, but she did not. Perhaps that was the problem. She was too much like her father, she concluded. Not willing to compromise her beliefs, standing up for what she believes is right. Still, did she accept Henry's offer of marriage with too much haste? Did she really love him? The more she thought about the decision she must make, the more difficult it became.

Elizabeth and her father avoided each other as much as possible in the following weeks. If she postponed calling off the engagement, she believed, she could continue to hold her love close. Staying clear of her father kept her resolve strong.

Well-meaning friends continued to call and suggest suitable young men for her when they learned Judge Cady had forbidden her marriage to Henry Stanton. Elizabeth entertained the hopeful beaus with courtesy, but very little enthusiasm and none gained her favor as Henry had. She wrestled with the idea of breaking off her engagement when her female friends presented arguments that seemed logical. But just when she thought she had summoned the courage to make the break, a sweet letter from Henry would arrive filled with loving thoughts about their future together.

Finally, her father confronted her. The family had finished their evening meal and Judge Cady motioned for Elizabeth to stay behind at the table.

"Have you sent Mr. Stanton a letter declining his offer of marriage?" her father asked.

"Not yet." Elizabeth toyed with the silver napkin ring on the table, her fingers caressing the engraving.

"I thought we had settled this," her father said. "I have noticed several young men calling on you, some asking my permission to do so."

"And I have received them. None were suitable. Besides, I have found the perfect husband, but he is not to your liking. Not that you would be married to him," Elizabeth said.

"Do not be impudent. You know I have your best interests at heart."

"Father, it is your best interests you have at heart," she said, "not mine."

With that remark she saw her father's face cloud with fury. He stood, pushing back his chair with a force she did not expect.

"Break the engagement, or I will do it for you," he shouted.

Elizabeth fled to her bedroom, choking back tears.

She slept little that night and woke early to pen a brief note to Henry.

"Dearest,

I cannot marry you for it would displease my father and have a distressing effect on his reputation as a judge and lawyer. My entire family would suffer and I cannot abide that. Although I love you, it is not to be.

Elizabeth"

She folded the paper, wrote Henry's address on the letter then pressed her lips against it. When she took it to the front door where a servant would take it to the post office her eyes filled with tears.

*

March 1, 1840

Dear Diary, I have never felt sadder than I do today. I know I love Henry and believe our lives were meant to entwine forever, but it cannot be. I know Father and Mother wish me to find a husband, but their requirements are not mine and I dare not go against them for all they have done for me. Father believes I must have a life of indulgence, but I have seen lives ruined by money and care not for that. I know what poverty is. I have witnessed it among the poor who pass through my life. Henry will not put our lives in jeopardy. Not for money, at least. For principles are riches that cannot be spent except for good. My outlook is as bleak as it once glowed bright.

44

March 1840

"I have done it, Father," she said, walking into her father's law offices where he sat pouring over a sheaf of papers between two stacks of law books. He looked small and frail.

"Done what?"

She could barely speak the words. "I have broken off my engagement to Henry."

"Good. I think that decision is wise." He rose from his chair to embrace her. "You will not regret this, for supporting your family is brave and courageous."

She pulled away. "I do not feel brave or courageous. Please let us not talk about this anymore."

Judge Cady stepped back. "As you wish."

She left his office, closing the door behind her. The quiet of the house appealed to her sense of loss. Through a window she saw her mother in the garden scattering birdseed onto the melting patches of snow. Two blue jays fought for the food.

This simple nurturing gesture by her mother made her smile. Margaret Cady turned and waved when Elizabeth tapped on the window to get her attention. With Madge and Kate off at school her mother's tasks were fewer so maybe it was best that she keep her mother company. She picked up the cross-stitch sampler she'd tried to finish so many times and immediately pricked her finger. She threw the sampler across the room and stuck her finger into her mouth to stop the bleeding.

"I am a self-indulgent woman who cannot stand up to her family. I do not deserve love from a man like Henry," she said aloud. How pitiful she was, feeling sorry for herself.

"What is that?" Her mother said, coming into the parlor. She pointed at the hoop containing the needlework project hanging precariously from a lamp.

Startled, Elizabeth hurried to retrieve her needlework, apologizing to her mother in the process.

"If you must talk about subjects that bother you Lib, talk to me. Perhaps I can help," her mother said.

"Henry will be aghast when he receives my letter," Elizabeth said. "And I still love him. I do not understand why my choices cannot be considered when they interfere with Father's." At once she felt the sting of her remark reflect in her mother's expression. "Forgive me Mother, my peevish words were thoughtless."

Margaret Cady rang for a pot of tea. "I think perhaps we might talk this out," she said.

"It will do no good. Father's mind cannot be changed."

"He is a stubborn man of that I am certain. But he does have your interests at heart," her mother said.

"So he says."

"It is because he expects so much from you he does not want your future impeded. You alone, dearest daughter, resemble Eleazar for whom he planned so much."

"If I have never pleased Father in the past, how can you say that?"

"Do you not realize he has never forbidden you anything? Even when he believed in his daughters serving the customary role of a woman, you were given opportunities unlike any other of your sisters."

"And now they follow in my footsteps," Elizabeth said.

"Yes, and this branch bends slowly," her mother replied. "Your father only wants the best for you."

"He forbids me marrying Henry."

"It is because he believes in you."

"Believes in me? He has never once said so. I argued vehemently for every chance to prove my worth to him. When I got my way I never considered it an achievement, but rather, wearing Father down."

"And is that your tactic now?"

Elizabeth shook her head.

"My loving Henry–who he is and what he stands for–is too great a cost for Father. Henry will receive my letter in a few weeks or months, depending on where he is, and that will be that."

A great sadness engulfed her that she could not shake. She attempted to read a new issue of *Godey's,* but the styles failed to catch her eye. Later, Jacob saddled a horse for her and Peter rode with her over the familiar country thawing from winter. Even the exhilaration of galloping amidst the greening forest did nothing to brighten her outlook.

Two months later a messenger pounded on the front door. Elizabeth, her mother and father were seated at the breakfast table.

"Miss Elizabeth, you have a letter," a maid said handing it to her.

She recognized the handwriting immediately and clapped a hand over her heart. Margaret Cady looked up.

"Everything all right?"

"Excuse me please," Elizabeth said ignoring her mother's question to hurry into the parlor and tear open the letter.

As she read her mood lifted.

"My sweet girl, I cannot accept that your affections can be so diverted. My warm esteem for you will not abate, no matter how you rationalize the reasons we should not marry. You have my heart in your hands, and your visage controls my every waking moment. Even my dreams. Change your decision, my dearest, for I will take care of you the rest of your life and make your father proud that I am your husband. Please reconsider. I implore you.

—Henry"

Elizabeth re-read the letter over and over, each time imagining his face before her. Seeing the honesty in his eyes. Hearing the sincerity of his expressive words.

She did not realize how her momentous decision affected her until she began to weep, losing all control.

"From Henry?" Her mother stood in front of her, a handkerchief in her outstretched fingers.

Elizabeth could only nod. She grabbed the handkerchief. "Oh, Mother, what have I done?"

"He truly loves you, Lib. You have spurned him to gain favor with your father. Perhaps you should reconsider."

Incredulous that her mother would suggest this, she said, "You know how Father is. He loves me too, and how can I go against him?"

"It takes a strong woman to make wise choices," her mother said. She sat on a hassock in front of Elizabeth's chair and took her hands in hers.

"What are you telling me?"

Margaret Cady leaned forward to soften her voice.

"Your father courted me because of your grandfather's political leanings. He believed since we thought alike, we would be a good match. And I knew it to be true. Yet Grandfather Livingston did not approve of my choice of husband," she said. "He is too conservative. He is not ambitious. My father regaled me with ridiculous arguments. Even so far as to say 'His stature is too short'"

Elizabeth sniffed and laughed.

"Yes, even that," her mother said. "But between your father and me there occurred a sweet understanding that our lives would be incomplete without the other. We persisted and your grandfather finally gave us his blessing even as his stubborn reluctance became almost too odious for him. Not that it would have mattered to us."

"Thank you for telling me this, Mother. I shall think upon your words. I believe Henry and I have a 'sweet understanding' too," she said, "And Father will recognize it once I suggest it."

For the first time since she wrote the fateful letter, she felt better, as if a door opened to let in light where before only darkness existed.

No sooner did she pull out the chair at her desk to take pen to compose a response to Henry, than the maid dropped another letter from him on her writing paper. Its postmark bore the name of the next town on his lecture tour.

"He is very sincere, Miss," the maid said, turning to leave.

"Alberta, do you have a beau?" Elizabeth asked.

"Yes, Miss, Woodley Robinson who works on one of Mr. Smith's farms."

"My Cousin Gerrit's farm?"

"Yes, Miss. We met when I accompanied you to Mr. Smith's home on one of your earlier trips."

"Are you happy? Do you very much love him?"

"We are betrothed."

Elizabeth shook her head. "Everyone but me," she said.

"Excuse my boldness, Miss Elizabeth, but it would seem to me that if your happiness resides with this man who writes to you while he travels, then perhaps it is in your power to lift the sadness that engulfs you."

Elizabeth threw her arms around the maid, startling the young woman whose face grew red.

THE LOST DIARIES OF ELIZABETH CADY STANTON

"Thank you Alberta. You have shown me a great truth. It *is* my destiny with this man I face, not a life with my father."

With great excitement, Elizabeth opened the letter from Henry, read through it then dipped her pen in the inkwell and began to write, the words scratching across the paper with flying speed.

*

March 15, 1840

Dear Diary, It seems my hasty rejection of Henry is for naught. I am still torn but believe once we are reunited Father will see how useless his protests are. I must be strong and rely on how much I love Henry, and his affection for me. If he persists, and I hope he does, I can see nothing but happiness ahead. If only time would not move so slowly. I miss him.

One week later, Camille and her husband called unexpectedly to pay their respects. Elizabeth rushed down the stairs when she heard the familiar voice of her Emma Willard friend.

Camille and a tall man wearing a beaver hat stood in the hallway with two small children.

"Oh, my, what a marvelous surprise. I wondered when I would see you again," Elizabeth said flinging herself into her friend's embrace. Tears ran down her face.

Camille stepped back to hold Elizabeth at arm's length. "What is this?" she asked. "I expected delight, not weeping."

"Dear friend, you have come at an unsettled point in my life, and I am so very glad to see you," Elizabeth said.

The man's expression of confusion matched that of the children who gazed at their mother with fear.

Camille pulled away. "You remember my husband, Mr. Harvey Guilden, and these are our twins, Ava and Devin," she said.

Elizabeth shook the man's outstretched hand and looked into the solemn brown eyes of the children.

"I knew your mother at school," she managed to say. "We were best of friends. The three of us." Realizing what she just said, she reached for Camille's hand and squeezed it. "I have such fond memories of our chats and gossips with Mavis. I miss her, too." Remembering her manners, she brightened and invited the guests into the parlor. Alberta hovered in the background awaiting instructions.

"Let us have some lemonade, and perhaps tea?" she said addressing her guests. "Alberta, please ask Mrs. Brewster to prepare a tray. Some fruit and tea cakes too, for the children. Thank you."

Once everyone had settled in and the twins had received a top to spin on the waxed wood floor, Elizabeth ventured a question about their visit.

"We are taking rooms in Johnstown for a month or so. Mr. Guilden is trying a case here," Camille said. "He is affiliated with the firm of Willard and Hall and represents several of the large landowners in this area." She looked at her husband for assurance. He nodded.

"Who do you represent, Mr. Guilden?"

"The Wadsworths of Genesee County," Camille's husband replied.

Elizabeth laughed. "Why, you are doing battle against my father and his legal assistants."

Harvey Guilden smiled. "Yes, I know that," he said.

"I hope there is no ill will, Miss Cady. I look forward to confronting your father. He is famous."

Elizabeth threw up her hands. "God speed, Sir," she said. Turning to Camille she asked, "Have you taken rooms in town yet?"

"Yes, at the Rose Arbor Cottage," she said.

"Elizabeth frowned. "Dreadful place, in spite of its name. You shall stay here with us. Mother will be delighted to have small children underfoot for a while, and you and I can catch up on every little thing that has happened since we left school. Oh, and I shall tell you all about Henry," she exclaimed.

"Did I hear voices?" Margaret Cady asked coming into the room followed by Elizabeth's father.

"Mother, do look at who is here," Elizabeth said with excitement.

"Guilden," Judge Cady said, shaking Camille's husband's hand. "So you are the one Seward sent up here to defend Wadsworth."

"I am honored to meet you Sir, and am looking forward to arguing against you in court."

Elizabeth took her mother aside to tell her of the invitation she offered and smiled when her mother nodded her approval.

"Two of our daughters are away at school and we have many unoccupied rooms upstairs, including a nursery still full of toys." She looked at the wide-eyed twins. "We welcome you and are very happy to have you stay with us."

That evening at dusk another letter from Henry arrived and Elizabeth tucked it into the bosom of her dress near her heart. *I'll read this when all the excitement is over.*

Once she climbed into bed that night and opened Henry's letter, she drew the candlestick close to the paper and gasped.

45

March 1840

A week later, Elizabeth rapped gently on the door to her mother's bedchamber. "Mother, may I come in please?" she asked.

Margaret Cady lay in bed propped against pillows, sipping her first cup of tea for the day. Early morning light illuminated the room, golden with the rising sun. The house was quiet as Camille and her family had decided to rent a small home in Johnstown where they could hire a governess to teach the children for the duration of the trial.

Elizabeth sat on the edge of her mother's bed and unfolded the letter.

"He's coming here," she said. "To talk to Father."

"Oh my. That should be a lively conversation," Margaret Cady said. "When?"

"He's working his way back on his speaking tour by horse and expects to arrive before May."

"Tell your father."

Elizabeth held up her hand. "There's more. In June he's planning to go as a delegate to the World's Anti-Slavery Convention in London."

"Yes?"

"He wants me to go with him."

Margaret Cady smiled and reached to embrace her daughter. "It appears you have a decision to make, dearest. A rather important one."

"I must think on this," Elizabeth said, folding the letter and slipping it into the pocket of her dressing gown. "I am feeling happy though, and not just a little bit giddy," she said. "I'll be down for breakfast after I dress. I will tell Father then."

Elizabeth stared at her reflection in her looking glass as she pinned up her hair. The exciting current that flew through her when she neared Henry Stanton was thrilling, and she imagined the power forming a circle drawing them together. Regardless of her father's objection or even his approval, when Henry arrived she would run into his arms and pledge her troth to him forever. Nothing as large as an ocean would separate them, for who knew what might happen if it did? The days would pass easier before Henry arrived if she said nothing to Judge Cady so she vowed to stay out of his way for fear that he ask. For now, her decision would be a secret that she shared with her mother only.

Late March another letter from Henry arrived.

"Dearest Elizabeth,

No matter your father's objections, I know your heart and you love me as I love you. I hope to be with you soon. I realize, dearest girl, that waiting for each other is dreadful, but my love for you grows even as we are apart. We will have a wonderful life and our union will be blessed with profound passions. We will have grand conversations about great books and, as we are intellectually matched so well, I envision our talks weighing topics both heavy and light. Oh, my dear Elizabeth, my heart stops a beat when I think of your lovely face and how the flames of your fiery nature color your cheeks. I must close and lay down my head, as I am exhausted from the speeches and the travel. Excuse my moment of weakness, for the crowds who fill the rooms where I appear are full of eagerness for a new country where no man is different from the other. Listen for my weary 'Haloo' near May the 1st, for I will be traveling the last leg by boat up the North River.

My heart is forever yours,
Henry"

The first of April came without another letter from Henry. Elizabeth paced the floor, brushing off all attempts by her mother to mollify her.

"He may have tried to post a letter but could not find someplace to do it," her mother said.

Elizabeth refused to be comforted. "Every town, even the small ones, have a post office now," she said. "What if he changed his mind?"

"From what you have told me of him, I doubt that he would do that. Do not worry so, Daughter, he will be here," her mother said.

Madge and Kate were home from Emma Willard, but Elizabeth felt so wretched she ignored them as they giggled and chatted over their needlework. What if something happened to Henry? His horse could bolt. An angry anti-abolitionist with a weapon could attack him. She tried to throw herself into preparations for a wedding. A voyage. Every time she became engrossed, she envisioned him lying prostrate in the woods covered in blood.

Finally, her mother took control.

"You must eat Lib, you are growing too thin. Your clothes will not be attractive hanging from a bony frame," she warned.

Elizabeth nodded, then looked up from her bowl of soup, now cold.

"Good thing your father is still engaged in that land sale litigation, for if he were not, he would notice your frail appearance."

"I wish Camille were still here," Elizabeth said. "She and the twins would take my mind off this worrying."

On May 2 another letter from Henry was delivered. Elizabeth grabbed it and ran to her room, almost too fearful to open it. The brief message startled her.

*"My dearest, I will reach you by May 5.
Please be ready for I shall marry you the instant I
arrive, with or without your father's blessing.*
Yours faithfully,
Henry"

She tore down the hallway shouting for her sisters and mother. "He is coming, he is coming! In three days. Oh my."

Madge and Kate rushed into the hallway followed by their mother, filling the space with laughter and each talking over the other.

"You are not ready," Madge said. "Your clothes are in disarray."

"Why did we not have the dressmaker craft a new traveling suit?" Margaret Cady asked. "I should have thought of that."

"Never mind Mother, my clothes are quite perfect. I do not need new ones." She embraced her mother to comfort her.

"A wedding dress," Kate exclaimed. "What about that?"

"There is no time to sew a new dress, so I shall be married in that very simple white evening gown in my closet," Elizabeth said.

"This is so very exciting," Kate said clapping her hands. "Can I be in the wedding?" she asked.

"Yes, both of you can. We shall make bouquets from whichever flowers may be in the garden and I will ask Reverend Hugh Maire to preside over the ceremony."

Elizabeth's mother looked startled. "Dear, you know how he goes on and on, are you sure you want that?"

"Yes, Mother, I rather like his Scotch brogue and his mannerisms suit me, and Henry will like him too, I believe."

What Elizabeth did not tell her mother is that she intended to change her wedding vows and hoped the reverend would not object too strenuously.

"I will converse with Mrs. Brewster about the menu for the wedding. Shall we have a late breakfast or an early dinner, Elizabeth?"

"Late breakfast with loads of meats and cheeses, for we will be leaving straightaway for New York after the ceremony," Elizabeth replied, pretending to ignore her mother's chagrined expression. She turned to grasp her hands. "I know this is all very sudden Mother, but if I am to make the break, I must do it on my terms."

Margaret Cady nodded, a gentle smile playing on her lips. "Yes, you are right." She brightened as if a new thought occurred. "There will be family and friends at the wedding to fawn over you two, so that will be a lovely time for all of us. I will be satisfied with that."

Elizabeth hugged her mother again and for all her resolve, she too would feel the separation and did not consider it in the excitement.

She quickly turned to Madge and Kate whose eager faces begged for their assignments. "Sort out which flowers will still be blooming," she said. "Make a list of how many you will need for my bouquet and yours and for Mother, too, and come see me. All right?"

Everyone flew off in different directions; Elizabeth to her bedchamber to organize her clothing for the ceremony and voyage to England. As she climbed the stairs she hoped the conversation between Henry and her father would not be too fraught with anger and pain for she had not told her father Henry was coming for her after all.

That afternoon, she called on Reverent Maire to discuss the vows.

"My dear Miss Cady, do come in and sit yourself by the wee fire, there," the reverend said. The jovial fellow bustled about, arranging a pot of tea and a plate of cakes that his cook delivered to the room. Now he stood in front of the fireplace his thumbs stuck in the pockets of his waistcoat. "You've come no doubt to arrange the final details, then?" he asked.

"Yes, Reverend Maire. I am grateful that on such short notice you would find time to do me this honor."

"Then it would be a Christian service, keeping to the favored vows?"

"For the most part yes, but I do wish for one change."

The reverend frowned. "And, what would that be?"

"The word *obey* must be struck from the pledge."

"What? But that is unconventional. It is not done." The reverend's face grew red and he began to pace and mutter to himself.

Elizabeth watched the little cleric struggle with his emotions until finally she broke in with an explanation.

"Dear Reverend Maire, my husband-to-be and I are on equal footing in all things. We have agreed to that type of life together. The marriage vows are important to us and they must suit the objective of our life."

"Very, very unusual," the reverend said. He stopped his pacing to stand in front of Elizabeth staring down into her face. "You are determined?"

She nodded. "Very determined, Sir."

Reverend Maire sighed and flopped into an easy chair facing the fire. "Hmmph. Very unusual," he said.

"You will perform the ceremony, will you not? I so want you do to it. For your eloquence is well-respected."

He pushed himself up with difficulty to stand in front of her. "Yes, lass, I will do it. Reservations aside. I do wish you a happy life full of love and bairns who will observe the will of God."

That evening, having kept all of the arrangements secret from her father, Elizabeth barely slept for worrying. Tomorrow Henry would arrive and her life would change forever.

*

May 5, 1840

Dear Diary, I tried not to think about him being in danger, but failed. I cannot sleep. My meals go untouched. I know Mother is worried, and Father surely sees my stress but says nothing. Have I made a fool of myself? Oh, dear God, I hope not. Has he lied about coming here? Is he dead somewhere along the way? A victim of a highwayman or a storm that dashed his boat onto rocks? I am delirious with anxiety and so confused.

46

May 1840

But Henry did not arrive.

"Come away from the window, Lib, it will do no good to keep drawing the curtains aside to peek out," Elizabeth's mother said. "The neighbors will think there is something awry."

"Oh, pish posh on the neighbors," Elizabeth said. "Where can he be?"

Madge came into the room and plopped on the chair opposite Elizabeth, her head bowed over her needlework.

"I should think he is merely delayed in some way," she said. "Perhaps his horse threw a shoe," Madge suggested.

Her practical suggestion irritated Elizabeth. "He is coming by boat," she said, her concern giving way to bad temper. A dark thought struck. "Oh, what if the boat has sunk?"

Madge looked up. "Well, I am sure we will hear about that soon enough. Friday's newspaper will be here early in the morning."

"You are no help," Elizabeth said. "Oh dear, I must tell Reverend Maire that we are postponing. What shall I tell him?" She looked at her mother for guidance.

"I will send Peter to him with a note explaining that the ceremony has been moved to Friday," Margaret Cady said. "He will not be happy for he claims to do his shopping on that day, but for us I know he will make the effort. If it need be postponed again, why, we shall deal with that."

Elizabeth's mother disappeared down the hallway leaving Madge to comfort her.

Kate ran into the parlor holding a bunch of lily of the valley stems and an apple blossom cutting.

"These smell divine, Lib, will they work?"

Elizabeth looked at her youngest sister, distracted for a moment from her worry. She bent her head to take in the fragrance of the spring blooms then lifted her eyes to Kate. "Yes, they will be splendid."

"Sister, you are crying. What ever is wrong?" Kate asked, sinking down on the sofa beside Elizabeth, the flowers slipping to the floor.

"Lib is distressed because Mr. Stanton has not yet arrived. Please pick up the flowers and take them to the kitchen and ask that they be placed in a vase," Madge said.

Another hour passed and with the creak of each passing carriage or the clip clop of horse's hooves, Elizabeth's pulse quickened and she rose to look outside.

At noon her mother called the girls to the dining room table for dinner. With one end of the room once again crowded with her father's noisy law students clustered around him, if Judge Cady noticed the unusual quiet among his female family members, he didn't acknowledge it.

Elizabeth barely touched her food. She pushed a spoonful of eggs back and forth across her plate and then stopped to crumble a biscuit onto a congealed dab of gravy. Her mother had told Mrs. Brewster what happened and asked that a simple meal be served in lieu of the celebration spread expected.

Judge Cady had just ushered the students back to his office and closed the doors when a loud pounding on the entrance door startled the women still at the table.

Elizabeth ran to fling open the door. Her face crumpled when instead of Henry, Reverend Maire stood there, his arm raised for another knocking onslaught. Peter stood behind him looking very distressed.

"He insisted I bring him here directly," Peter said. "I am so sorry Miss Elizabeth."

She touched his arm, "You did the right thing, Peter."

"Miss Cady, you cannot be married on a Friday. It is bad luck," Reverend Maire said." He barged into the front hall and handed his hat and coat to the maid who appeared to see what caused the commotion.

The Cady women quickly surrounded the cleric to herd him into the parlor.

"Reverend, would you like a cup of tea?" Margaret Cady asked.

"If you have a bit of top milk that would be fine," he replied. "And five sugars, if you please."

Elizabeth's mother fetched the tea and brought with her a small plate of biscuits spread with butter and jam. She set the tray on a table in front of the cleric and they all watched as he busied himself clinking and stirring and then stuffing a biscuit into his mouth and chewing vigorously. Finally he wiped his lips to protest again.

"Reverend Maire," Elizabeth's mother began, cutting him off, "It is imperative that the wedding take place Friday because the couple must arrange to depart for Europe as quickly as possible."

The cleric frowned. "Then I shall take no responsibility for whatever happens with this marriage," he said, shaking his finger. "Bad or good luck, it will all be in God's hands."

Elizabeth smiled. "Thank you very much, Reverend. It will be our honor to have you officiate and I will never forget your kindness."

The cleric nodded, appearing appeased, then asked, "And where is the husband to be? I would like to make his acquaintance before this rushed marriage."

Elizabeth glanced at her mother. "He has not arrived yet," Margaret Cady said.

"What? But surely he understands the importance of this step. He should be here, having this discussion with me," the man said, his face growing red again.

"He will be here in time for the ceremony, Sir," Elizabeth's mother assured him. "Now, can I have Peter deliver you back to the parish?" she asked, rising.

Reverend Maire looked around at the women then stood. "That would be quite fine. I do thank you," he said.

In the face of the reverend's protestations Elizabeth gamely kept her thoughts positive, but as the sun began to slip behind the Adirondacks her concern for Henry's absence began to gnaw at her again.

At supper that evening, Elizabeth responded to her father's conversational questions with brief replies, drawing a curious look in her direction. Margaret Cady chattered about nearly nothing to keep the mood light. Madge and Kate teased each other until their parents both stepped in with admonishments. Again, Elizabeth ate little and finally excused herself, pleading fatigue.

She fell into bed half dressed, and pulled the comforter folded at the foot of her bed over her head. Hot tears rolled down her cheeks as she sobbed into her pillow. She must have slept because the light tapping on her bedroom door woke her, leaving her confused and disoriented.

"Miss Elizabeth?" Alberta's muffled voice said. "Your father would like you to come downstairs. Miss Elizabeth, are you awake?"

"Yes. What's the matter?" Elizabeth blinked her way out of the fog of sleep. "Never mind, I will be right there."

She slid out of bed, pushed her feet into slippers and opened the door to reveal the maid standing just outside in the hallway.

"Miss, let me tidy your hair first," Alberta said, pulling Elizabeth back inside. She began to re-pin Elizabeth's curls, and then tugged her wrinkled dress straight.

Elizabeth glanced into her looking glass. "What a fright."

"You look presentable," Alberta said.

"What time is it?" Elizabeth asked.

"Nearly two in the morning. Best get downstairs now. Your father is waiting with a visitor."

All of the gaslights in the parlor were turned to their brightest revealing Elizabeth's father who stood just inside the vestibule and was in deep conversation with a tall man in a greatcoat holding a top hat, rotating it nervously with his long fingers.

At Elizabeth's gasp, the two men turned toward her. "Henry," she cried out, running into his arms. Laughing and weeping at the same time, she buried her face in his shoulder unable to tear away from his embrace. Finally, he gently pushed her back. She looked into his eyes and saw nothing but love and adoration. "I worried so," she said, ignoring her father's expression of mild surprise.

"I should have known," Judge Cady said, glancing up to see his wife in her dressing gown behind his daughter. "Preoccupied as I was with a troublesome case, I noticed the family's infernal scurrying about, but dismissed it. You should have warned me, dear."

Elizabeth saw the look that her parents exchanged.

"Father, please do not be angry with Mother. She hoped Henry would arrive in time to talk to you days ago and has been supportive of me while we waited. It has been a very stressful time for her."

"Well, we have talked now, Lib, and Henry has asked for your hand. He is a very convincing man, I might add," Judge

Cady said. "I have taught you to be independent and do not know why I am surprised that you are." He shook his head. "Now let us all get some sleep because I think your mother has a wedding planned."

Elizabeth threw her arms around her father and hugged him. "Thank you, Father. I love you and always will. And you will learn to love and respect Henry as I do. I promise you that," she said.

*

May 7, 1840

Dear Diary, at long last my beloved has arrived and our marriage is imminent. In two days we shall be one. His gaze of love so enthralled me I forgot the wait and long delays. Any reservations about loving Henry or marrying him vanished when I looked into his eyes. God sends people their soul mates making the search difficult, so the result is magnificent when it occurs. I have never been happier.

47

May 1840

The newlyweds stood on the deck of the *Montreal* watching the New York skyline grow smaller. Henry's arm felt warm and reassuring around Elizabeth's shoulders. She recalled the excitement of the hurried wedding preparations, Reverend Maire's hour-long sermon before the vows–especially his stumble over the omission of *obedience*–and the gasp from the small group of family and friends who attended the ceremony.

With eighteen days at sea ahead before they reached England and the convention that would monopolize Henry's time, Elizabeth looked forward to having her new husband all to herself.

Henry looked down at her, pulling her even closer.

"Are you happy, my beloved?" he asked.

"Do you need to ask?" she said, feigning anger. Then she stood on tiptoe and kissed him.

"I love you, Elizabeth Cady Stanton. God willed me to wait for you. And I am glad I did. We have a promising future ahead of us and with you at my side I feel a strength I only hoped for before."

A bell announcing supper tolled just as a spray of seawater nearly engulfed them. Elizabeth laughed, backing away.

"Come to the cabin before we dine?" she asked, tugging Henry's hand playfully.

He scooped her up into his arms. "Why yes, that's a fine idea," he said.

48

Massillon, Ohio
February 1875

Elizabeth falls silent. The memories feel so fresh they bring tears to her eyes. She rummages in her pocket for a handkerchief. The remainder of the wood in the stove lays covered in ash and a biting chill begins to seep into the room.

The quiet is palpable.

Amelia sits hunched over, folded into herself as if trying to become smaller.

"What is it?" Elizabeth asks, alarmed that the vivacious girl so attentive earlier now looks weak and defeated.

"You are no better than any of us," Amelia whispers. "You are self-centered and vain. No wiser, no kinder."

"Surprised that I am not the paragon of virtue you expect? How dare you. I am human."

"Even so, if other people know what I do now, your followers will turn away from you in disgust," Amelia says, her voice stronger.

"My work for women's rights knows no boundaries," Elizabeth says. "It makes no difference how I got here." Instinctively, she reaches to finger one of her sapphire earrings. Her touchstone. A father's gift from long ago.

"It does," Amelia says. The girl stands over Elizabeth shaking her finger. "Women idolize you, like I do–*did*." She shouts this last word and begins to pace the room.

"That is nonsense," Elizabeth says, but an unfamiliar apprehension begins to grow. Will these moments shared with an admirer be her undoing? She vowed to make a difference on that disgraceful day in London when she and other women delegates were forced to sit by themselves. The men were in a dither that female delegates were allowed in at all. The notion that women had opinions on the subject of abolition astonished them. She married Henry believing he agreed that the role of a woman could be the same as a man's. At the convention she discovered he grew vexed when she spoke up. In private he assured her they were equals, but in public? His stand on abolition dominated his behavior, relegating her beliefs as secondary.

So much is different now. Her efforts to abolish slavery and grant women equal rights must not be jeopardized. She has worked too hard. Elizabeth laughs at the memory of her young imposing husband trying to tactfully ask her to defer to him in public.

"I do not find this amusing," Amelia says.

How can this girl, with the revealing diaries fresh in her mind, know how difficult this is for Elizabeth? The diaries are damning evidence revealing the shortcomings of a young woman who became a dedicated suffragette. If others learn of the traits that stamped her personality, how can she go on? Who will trust her? Who will believe her fight is for nothing more than freeing women from the bonds of male servitude? Her heart begins to hammer. "Leave me," she cries, pointing at the door.

A teacup clatters to the floor when Amelia shrinks from Elizabeth's fury. The girl bends to pick up the pieces and Elizabeth shouts at her again.

"I said, 'leave'. Now."

The door slams and its impact rocks Elizabeth. To steady herself she reaches for the arm of the chair then sinks back into its well-worn cushion. Her breath is labored and she fumbles to loosen the buttons at her neck.

What have I done? Will succumbing to this girl's flattery be my undoing? Have I learned nothing in all these years? Who will believe me? Few people if any, Elizabeth reckons. But if the evidence is gone? She looks down at the floor where her diaries lay open in disarray.

Frantically she begins to leaf through them again, stopping to rip out a page–she knows which ones are most damning–and tosses it into the stove. Within seconds an ember ignites the fragile paper. She works steadily, adjusting her glasses over and over to scan the pages carefully. Tears welling, she stops now and then to hold one of the diaries to her bosom. The flames in the stove warm her face and perspiration glazes her brow. With each page she destroys, she believes her legacy becomes more secure. Panting now from the effort and exhilaration, she suddenly thinks of the hour and reaches for the watch hanging as a pendant from her neck. Five minutes before her speech.

She thrusts the last of the ruined diaries into the trunk just as a timid rapping at her door breaks the silence. Elizabeth gathers up her notes and pulls her shawl tight.

"Mrs. Cady?" a muffled female voice cries, "I must take you to the auditorium right now."

Elizabeth flings the door open. "Amelia…" she begins, her hand on the doorknob, and then steps back when she sees a tall girl of about thirteen years standing there.

"I am supposed to fetch you," the girl says.

"What is your name, child?"

"It is Sara." The girl smiles, her brown eyes wide. "This is an honor for me," she says. "We drew lots to see who would guide you to the stage."

"Thank you Sara. It is an honor for me, too," Elizabeth says and steps into the hallway behind the girl. With each stride the familiar rumble of conversation from the crowd awaiting her becomes a roar. Her step lightens and a ripple of exhilaration quickens her breathing. Sara holds Elizabeth's elbow as she helps her up the stairs to the stage and across to the podium.

When Elizabeth raises her arms to acknowledge the women seated there, they stand, cheering.

"Women's rights now," the crowd yells.

"Equality for women!"

"Elizabeth, Elizabeth, Elizabeth," a few women begin to call out, and soon all of them take up the chant. Except for one person. In the front row, her mouth set in a scowl, arms crossed against her chest, Amelia stares up at her.

"Thank you. Thank you," Elizabeth finally says. "Thank you for coming out on this miserable cold night. Your commitment gives me strength. It is for you I serve this cause. I am but one woman, like you, who is imperfect."

Her gaze sweeps the crowd then she pauses to look down at Amelia. "If I can speak for you, to help raise you up, so be it. If it is not I you wish to follow, that is fine too. Forge your own path and gain strength from your accomplishments. Most of you are young and will carry on in my stead when I am too old to stand before you to urge you forward."

She looks down at her notes, not because she needs them but to catch her breath. She begins to speak again. "We are in the midst of a social revolution, greater than any political or religious revolution that the world has ever seen because it goes deep down to the very foundations of society. A question of great magnitude presses on our consideration, whether man and woman are equal, joint heirs to all the richness and joy of earth and Heaven, or whether they were eternally ordained, one to be sovereign, and other slave..."

Elizabeth pauses to let her gaze linger on Amelia. To her surprise the young woman's expression has softened and tears run down her cheeks.

Afterward

Elizabeth Cady Stanton's fight for women's rights resulted in the 19th Amendment to the Constitution of the United States that gave women voting rights. She died before seeing it passed into law. Read more about her in *Eighty Years and More,* her own memoir and in her official biography, *In Her Own Right,* by Elisabeth Griffith. To write this novel, these two books became primary reference, as I blended fact with fiction to craft scenes around her life. In that context, Henry Stanton's speech in Gloversville is in part borrowed from his remarks to the Massachusetts House of Representatives on February 23 and 24, 1837. Further, in the last chapter of the novel, Elizabeth's speech to the women of Massillon, Ohio is an excerpt from "Home Life" an address she often delivered during 1875.

The *Lost Dairies* may have really existed in some form because according to Griffith, Mrs. Stanton did not like the way her first memoir portrayed her life so she destroyed it and replaced it with *Eighty Years and More.*

Regardless of fact or fiction, the intent of this novel is to honor Elizabeth Cady Stanton and reveal how the efforts of one woman changed history through the way she lived: not a mythical heroine, but a real live girl.